Penguin Books
The Wort Papers

Peter Mathers was born in England in 1931 and
travelled to Sydney as an infant emigrant with his
parents, who were re-emigrating to Australia. He
attended state school in Sydney and Sydney Technical
College, where he studied Agriculture. He has 'farmed,
clerked, woolled, gardened, landscaped, chemicalled,
taught and done other things.' He now writes.

In 1961 he married and went to Europe where for
some months he lived in a cork forest in France. His
two daughters were born in London. He took up a
writing fellowship at an American university in 1967
and returned to Australia a year later. He now lives in
Melbourne. His first novel, *Trap,* won the Miles
Franklin Award in 1967, and he has written numerous
stories, radio pieces, articles and reviews. *The Wort
Papers* is his second novel.

The author wishes to acknowledge the
assistance given to him by the
Commonwealth Literary Fund

Peter Mathers

The Wort Papers

Penguin Books

Penguin Books Ltd, Harmondsworth,
Middlesex, England
Penguin Books Australia Ltd, Ringwood,
Victoria, Australia

First published by Cassell Australia Ltd 1972
Published in Penguin Books 1973

Made and printed in Australia at
The Dominion Press, North Blackburn, Victoria

Thomas opened the letter from Uncle Fred . . .

I saw your mother and father last week and he is very feeble what with the tough life and she is looking drawn through the effort. They feel you've forgotten them since you took your family to see them three years ago. He is talking of getting a sulky and driving down to see you, though it would take months. I don't think you'd like to be forgotten by me the way you've forgotten your own mum and dad. Are you ashamed of them?

He angrily screwed up the letter.

Thursday was one of Roma's work days so she had little patience with him, and though he drove off ten minutes before her she passed him on the freeway. As he waited in the second jam he remembered his unspeakable Uncle Fred. Roma was going to answer the letter. Thomas wondered if he should treat his parents to a holiday at Surfers Paradise. By rights they should sell the farm and invest in holiday flats. If only the farm was an hour instead of thirty from the city. He chain-smoked as the traffic edged on. Somewhere a driver or passenger screamed. Red lights, haze, bird splat on the wind-screen, water and wipers. Was I once an exploiter of farmers? Brake.

Forty minutes later a single lane was opened past the three

burnt-out cars and as he passed them he wished, again, he had been closer and had a chance to rescue people. He'd have pulled with tow-rope, bulldozed, foamed with extinguisher and first-aided with kit. Heroism was so rare nowadays. More heroism was needed in the new Mediums' series tracing a young man's rise from rural obscurity to city fame.

Within sight of the freeway exit a rough car bumped into the back of him. He shuddered with anguish and got out. The young driver smiled apologetically. Thomas scowled at a scratch in the duco. Horns jarred. Go on, called the driver, Act out your cliché. Thomas stared at him then turned away. For the rest of the journey he listed clichés: The car, ulcers, company feuds, investments, Roma, smoking, cancer, take-overs, the dog, skiing, infamy of war, time for a Labor government, cities falling apart, conscription needing leaven, cars ruining things, time to get out of the Bohemian Club, bamboo rampant, his wine not good enough, parents an embarrassment, the children too mature for their age.

At work Thomas was known to his associates as a deter-mined implementor of innovations. In this hurly moment of time, he once declaimed, We must be burly. Our seconds into minutes and all becomes hours. His colleagues knew him as an implement of progress and wished to share in the future he envisaged, some from fear, others for want of alternatives.

He spoke at a luncheon:

I am a director of Mediums Limited which, as everybody knows, is a not unimportant company in the media. Eight newspapers, twenty-seven theatres, twenty-eight radio stations, a significant country television network, an interest in this city's Channel Five, a printery, processing labs and so on. More than mere gestures of communication. We even publish books and our manuals, textbooks and works of imagination do anything but detract from our lustre. Fiction we publish as a gesture to the cultural heritage, though there is little money in it unless a novel is translatable into the wider media of film and television.

Here he was interrupted and handed a telegram. He smiled. I'd like to correct an error, he proclaimed, We do not own eight papers and twenty-eight radio stations—from this morning we have nine papers and thirty-five radio stations. (Applause.)

He went on to discuss the ethics of media and touched upon ownership, responsibilities, peaks, ratings and rates. A second telegram arrived. A few members of the audience displayed irritation. He read the telegram, gaped, recovered, reread, and produced a smile.

Good news followed by better news is indeed more than enough to turn a fine luncheon into a banquet. Mediums Limited is to become an associate of Mountain&Molesworth Ltd, the brightest star in the mining firmament. He paused for a moment, then continued with his speech, hurrying here, galloping there. At its conclusion he shook hands hurriedly and departed. He did not watch himself amongst the evening news but Roma told him he was wonderful. Days later a misaddressed telegram reached him:

I SAW YOU I SAW YOU ON THE NEWS WELL WELL STOP MARVEL-
LOUS TO RENEW OUR ACQUAINTANCESHIP THOMAS STOP I HAVE
MINED YOUR FAMILY ARCHIVES STOP
SIGNED NONAME

To hell with mining! he cried, Nowadays everything's to do with mining. I don't want to be owned by a mine. Miners leave holes.

Not nowadays, darling, replied Roma. They daren't. You're going to move up—so be content with what you've got.

What she had said was, of course, quite correct. Mountain &Molesworth Ltd was a very big company indeed, with the creed of executive exchange within the family companies.

One of Thomas's occasional functions with Mediums

3

Limited was the acquisition of material, so he took advantage of his position to travel westwards to meet Mister Mountain, the eighty-year-old founder of Bedends Limited, at his mansion-workshop, to impress him with his ideals of progress, public concern and tradition. Mister Mountain told him he was being squeezed out of M&M. He wanted a greater say in affairs. He insisted that M&M commemorate the contribution Bedends had made to the might of the holding company. It was not enough that every M&M executive have a Mountain watercolour in his office. Bedends signified regeneration and generation.

Why not, offered Thomas, use bed ends as fences for your new mining town?

I'll buy that one, screamed Mister Mountain.

Back at the Mediums office Thomas found that his particulars, together with those of the others, had been dealt with by the M&M computer. He was sent to Afghanistan for three days, and on return underwent a three-hour ordeal at the hands of customs and quarantine men. He was despatched to Patagonia, spent the flight learning Portuguese and on arrival found himself regarded as an authority on eucalypts. From Patagonia he flew to Lincolnshire, England, where he fell into an ill-humour, crossed into Cambridgeshire, befriended Manhattan naturalist Edith Window in Ely Cathedral, spent two days with her in fen and ditch, was suddenly recalled to London and returned to Australia weakened by leeches. Roma took but three days to restore him to a semblance of normality.

He went on a tour of the M&M mines in the west.

See? said the pilot.

He is going to tilt the aircraft, muttered Thomas, and I don't want him to.

The pilot was very proud of everything, and recited tonnages, values, manhours, details of the terrain, the bounties of nature, changing the face of nature, the terrors of nature, unnatural demands, tides, monsoons and prospects. He reminds me of my father, thought Thomas. It's not the accent, manner or dress—o yes—he wears sandles and sox.

See? said the pilot.

He is tilting the plane, Thomas groaned. I hate tilting. Reminds me of mechanical games. In fun parlours, tilt to score, do not tilt. We are more than tilting, we are going right over. I did not come all the way up here for aerobatics. Worse than octopus and dipper at Luna Park. I know there is an inch or so of tough transparent plastic between me and the terrible below and I know the plastic is of the best quality, has been tested to destruction in prototype and under battle conditions; has simmered in radioactive iodine, boiled in vinegar, stewed in pressurized blood; has orbited as a satellite and gone to the bottom of the Mindanao Deep. It is imperishable. However it has been known to fall off. Weakest at its fastenings. A plastic bubble fell off an aircraft just last week, was impaled on a chimney. We are returning to a normal plane . . . ah, he is tilting again. We go round and round as though caught in the vortex of the object he insists on showing me. In a moment he will describe the scene. As though I am blind with vomit. He is very keen. He loves M&M which loves him. We are in a capsule of corporate love. It is his duty to make me feel the same way. As M&M thinks highly of me so must he for I would not be loved without proper reason. Somewhere inside the computer a horrible mistake was made.

Down there, said the pilot. Red riches into her steel belly, the biggest ore-carrier on the run, off to Yokohama at 2 a.m., 2,000 tons an hour lower her into the pellucid tide. (pause)

The tide may be pellucid, muttered Thomas, But the water round the ship is stained red as though the ship be wounded.

Scratch the wrinkled skin of this sunburnt land, said the pilot, And you'll find riches; we are indeed a fortunate people. Yes, fortunate, a fortunate people, indeed we are, and far too many people do not appreciate our fortunate position.

Round and round we go and his mind's stuck in the groove.

Scratching the wrinkled skin's all very well but I fear infection under the fingernail. The mountains of iron-ore thirty miles away are red like carbuncles. The chairman is a man of action, he is pleased with his large red hands. His directors have smooth hands. The rough hands have shaken the hands of all the important prime ministers and presidents. I have been told all this. I have not met him. My guide on the ground is director of p.r., he is my inquisitor, he pries, he pries. The computer programmer must have put one hole too many in my card. Perforation in the wrong place. A perforation in this plastic globe would rip it off, unfasten the harness clasps and send me into the horrible below. The plastic is said to be invulnerable but in the Asian wars guerillas often pierce similar plastic and contents fall like fish from a broken bowl towards scattering groundsmen. I know all this because I know what it is like to be an aerial hunter. Ever so low we flew, peering for the fugitive. And saw him, but were too late.

The next morning Thomas was introduced to General Wu, who was to preside over the opening of the new loading jetty. The general's lack of inscrutability surprised him. He was a stout, middle-aged, smoothly-suited man with lots of twitches and a cordon of bodyguards whose smooth suits bulged and peaked with weapons. They closed in on their leader and expelled Thomas who asked the omnipresent p.r. why did he not stay with the general whose worth and needs were greater than his.

Why are you my public relation—aren't you sick of it?

I find our association fascinating.

Go and p.r. the general, Thomas snapped.

There's no room for me with all those guards round him. A misanthrope has pointed the bone at him. I don't want to be too close.

Pointing the bone only works among Aboriginals—you've got to be kin for it to work.

The general, replied p.r., Believes in steelworks, body-

6

guards, international alliances, co-operation, the Queen, the Holy Ghost, Lee Harvey Oswald and that a witch doctor holds him responsible for the imminent removal of a small sacred mountain which happens to be seventy per cent iron ore.

I guess I know how he feels, sighed Thomas, Having had a computer card pointed at me.

Everybody boarded the electric train and set off to the end of the jetty. The general was to consecrate it and after lunch, when the ore carrier arrived, press the button to begin loading.

A dinghy with an outboard engine rounded the rocks to the south. Bodyguards, utility escorts and others surveilled it. Thomas, being on that side of the train, and eager for diversion, waved to the man and woman. She stood up and gave him the two-finger greeting. P.r. elbowed Thomas. Stupid, he hissed, It's the Chloros come to disrupt us. Their trespassing won't be forgiven. Ignore them. The train rumbled on. The dinghy tied up to a ladder. Thomas glanced at M&M's chairman, Patrick Emperor. This normally jovial, dynamic, warmhearted, blood-and-thunder industrial colossus gazed at the wake of the dinghy. He is such a colossus, thought Thomas, He could zap the dinghy with a spit. The train stopped and everybody got off. The Chloros stepped onto the jetty.

I'm going to stop them once and for all, snapped p.r., and set off. Thomas followed. The Chloros wore jungle-greens. Tall and red-haired, she was the most beautiful woman Thomas had ever seen. The man, tall, fair-haired, the sternest man he had ever seen, took a movie camera from his haversack and began filming. P.r. ordered Thomas to wait. The Chloros argued with p.r. He tried to push the woman towards the ladder. The man laid a hand on p.r.'s shoulder while he in turn passed a hand across the woman's breasts.

Go—leave this place immediately, cried p.r. pointing to the water.

And they left. P.r. strode back, took Thomas's arm and led him to the party.   A pair of nuts, he explained, waving at the

7

dinghy as it sped away. It was about three hundred yards out when it exploded. He shuddered, squeezed Thomas and gasped, Too much.

Thomas broke free, dashed to the edge, tore off his shoes and prepared to dive. He was seized.

Friend, intoned p.r., They're gone—to the sea they so deeply—and misguidedly—loved.

They died for ecology, sobbed Thomas.

Ecology? No. It was because they weren't invited to the opening but were determined to come. They were minor shareholders too big for their boots. M&M has forty thousand shareholders, we simply couldn't cope.

A launch put out from the jetty and probed the litter of the Chloros. P.r. led Thomas into the official party. General Wu was enthralled by what had happened. His bodyguard was almost, but not quite, inscrutable. Patrick Emperor's translator was unable to communicate with the general. Patrick Emperor was irritated. Crisis, crisis, crisis, muttered p.r., digging his fingers deep into Thomas's flesh. My hip, thought Thomas, he's got hold of my hip.

Sucking in his cheeks. Gazing at the blue illimitable heavens into which all traces of smoke had vanished. I must remember all this, he thought, it is history.

General Wu and Patrick Emperor chattered through the medium of their interpreter who sometimes uttered words of English which froze the chairman with horror, and now and then offered words of Thai which made the general guffaw, or on one occasion quiver with fear and seem about to slither from the jetty.

The water is pellucid, thought Thomas, the tide is slack and nothing bleeds. Spotless sky, harsh sun, ore-works, dust, clunk-thump-clunk, jellyfish, twenty-foot tides. This isolate orescape, ancient, stubborn and once-timeless now rapidly ground by hours. He reached for his notebook and pen to be able to record these interesting sentiments. Hello . . . he saw a frogman in the water. So did a bodyguard. The frogman held up a red and yellow company pass. The bodyguard lowered his magnum-horwitz ·44. P.r. explained that it was the frogman's job to save anyone who might happen to fall in.

He looks black, said Thomas.

He is wearing a black suit and mask, explained p.r.

His skin, I mean.

He's Blue Ore, said p.r., He used to live in a gunyah hereabouts.

Then he's not the bone-pointer.

Blue? P.r. waved and Blue flourished his speargun. Hi, Blue.

If it's his job to haul people out, said Thomas, Why is he armed?

The ceremony concluded with the release of forty-seven white and blue Thai doves, the survivors of which fled to a gantry to avoid the hawks. The skindiver gave an impromptu display of aquabatics which concluded with a long sad tune played on a seaweed. General Wu threw a handful of gold Thais into the limpid, cyanotic water. The water is sort of cyanotic, said Thomas. What? demanded p.r. It's a kind of blue, explained Thomas. I'd be careful, said p.r., about using deadly-sounding words like that.

The skindiver did not dive for the coins. General Wu stared down at him icily. The skindiver climbed the ladder, speargun over shoulder. What an interesting barb, thought Thomas. The black skindiver reached the top and bowed to the General. The barb, thought Thomas, is a piece of bone set with shark's teeth. The skindiver flip-flopped towards the general. Complimentary remarks were uttered. Thomas, on the other side of the general thought: He is going to shoot the general, how bloody fantastic. He dived on the general and dragged him down. Bodyguards wheeled, shooting with deadly effect. Screams, rattles, groans and ouches of surprise. Asiomen, bodyguards, flunkeys, directors and a mixed sprawl of celebrities bled down the gutter. The general fired a bullet through Thomas's shoulder blade and into the face of an ore-foreman attending his first company commissioning.

Thomas was acclaimed as the saviour of General Wu who presented him with the Order of the Peacock and the Centipede. Much was made of the attempted assassination. People everywhere deplored the passing of old Aboriginal ways. Anthropologists spoke of the ominous union of bone-pointing mysticism with modern technology. The skindiver was outlawed but not apprehended. It was said he had been hidden by General Motors, M&M, Angus & Robertson, the Australian Mutual Provident Society, radical students, the Church Missionary Society, the Melbourne & Metropolitan Tramways Board, the Church of Jesus Christ of Latter Day Saints, the Transcendental Worm and others.

Thomas was the subject of many radio, television and press interviews. As relaxation he took up pruning, grafting, dune claret, bathing with his wife, the local council, stroking the backs of strangers' hands, the problems of accountability, the ethics of pollution and the morality of media.

His heroism and ability sent him back to his old, but by now considerably enhanced, position with Mediums Ltd.

His secretary gave him the manuscript of a novel, FISH. From an unknown, racked writer, Matters. Who had enclosed a note.

Dear T, Have heard all about you. I hope you are well and now able to shoulder what I offer. Haven't seen you in years. Good health. Matters.

Matters—or is it Mutters?

Dear Mr Matters, We thank you for . . . we do not see our way . . . what about . . . your interesting ms. . . . interested in seeing your . . .

Something familiar about the name. Familiar. Am not keen to revive the near-forgotten.

10

Matters telephoned Thomas at home. From a long way away. Matters immediately took command with the explanation that he had only a small heap of coins and would therefore have to be brief. He: thanked Thomas for reading the ms; had found the comments interesting; applauded (clap-clap-clap) Mediums Ltd for interest shown; cursed the situation and those concerned; applauded the take-over of Mediums by Mountain&Molesworth; described M&M as a hatful of sphincters, an inexplicable symbol but one which nevertheless should be described viz—an embrace of arms of indescribable hue embracing something heart-shaped and heart-coloured with severed arteries leading nowhere; there are no gushes, not even a drip; the arms bear freckles which could be cancers or scars; there is pulsation. Matters rang off.

A week later Matters sent a telegram requesting work as a reader of manuscripts. Thomas tested him with a couple of novels. Matters reviled the one Mediums had accepted and recommended the other. The next day another telegram:

I ONCE READ FIRST DRAFT OF A SHORT NOVEL STOP WHAT I COULD FOLLOW WAS VERY GOOD BUT AUTHORS DEROGATORY MARGIN NOTES BETTER STOP I AFTERWARDS DECIDED HE HAD WRITTEN A NOVEL WITH DEROG MARGIN NOTES AND WHY NOT STOP PAGES STREAKED WITH BLACK LINES AND ERASURES WITH FANTASTIC PALIMPSEST AND LEGIBLE UNDERLYING WORDS STOP WOULD YOU LIKE TO SEE SOMETHING SIMILAR RECENTLY UNEARTHED NEAR VILLAGE OF UPPERSASS STOP REGARDS MATTERS

Thomas told his secretary he had to see a gangster about his memoirs and left the office. He sat in a thicket in the park and gloomed. A cur squirmed along the ground and bit his hand. A gardener turned on the sprinklers and wet him. Back at the office he was handed another telegram from Matters.

HAVE ESTABLISHED MYSELF AS A LITAGENT HAVING PLACED HITHERTO UNKNOWN MANUSCRIPT WITH ENGLIT GENT WHO

HOPES PLACEMENT OF MANUSCRIPT IN BOTTOM DRAWER WILL
ENCOURAGE SILVERFISH TO EAT OUT OBVIOUS INCONSISTENCIES
FOR HIM AND CREATE A PASSABLE MASTERPIECE STOP

Thomas went home and picked up the children from school.
His secretary phoned and read him a telegram from Matters:
In my capacity as agent I submit three plot precis stop first a
young nun falls in love with outside world climbs a dangerous
part of nunnery wall bracket mother superior cannot afford
repairs bracket changes her mind attempts to regain sanctuary
has vision and falls onto methodist social worker stop second
in which a young married milkman with three children is
seduced by a rich bored housewife with milk allergy stop
three a young idealist joins a voluntary aid scheme in Vietnam
and is fondled by communist ecologist in airport lounge then
kills her with plastic palm stop.

Thomas thanked Susan for the message. He consulted the
pink pages. He realized he did not know how to go about hiring
a private detective. I want you to put a tail on a guy. Would
not this instruction be open to misinterpretation? Susan rang
again. Apologetic, because she had an idea the pest Matters
was getting at them. She had had another telegram: The three
precis of previous telegram coalesce into single splendid plot
stop a mendicant nun disillusioned by affair with protestant
milkman meets a bored housewife with lesbian tendencies on
the ruined wall of convent falling through lack of ecumeni-
calism stop they go to Cambodia where they meet a ruined
baptist at a Whither Defoliation symposium stop they retire
to abandoned rubber plantation for chaste discourse but only
the nun survives the ensuing confrontation with Cambodian
warlord stop.

He told Susan not to acquaint him with any further telegrams.

He dreamt he sat at his great red-cedar desk interviewing a
huddle of yokels who spoke of paspalum, lanteena, kikuyu,
tits, terbacca bush, potholes, and tick fever. A motorbike

ridden by a man with a blank face roared in. Cocks crowed, his mother winked from a doorway, his father headed a band of wanderers, his sister, with wormy hair, rode a bicycle along a beach, and in a mirror he saw himself wearing an astrakan suit and a fox as a hat. Lesser and greater visions occupied the remainder of the night.

At the office he sat at his great red-cedar desk. Ten a.m. Ten am—if only I could become the old I Am. I am not leaving my mind. I will never leave my mind. I must stop others entering it. I must evict the nine squatters.

Susan crept in and handed him an unopened telegram.

AM SENDING YOU PERCY WORT PAPERS STOP YOU REMEMBER PERCY OF COURSE STOP THE WORTERIANA COMMA OF CELLULOSE COTTON GRAPHITE AND INK COMMA MAY AT FIRST SIGHT COMMA TOUCH AND SNIFF COMMA APPEAR INEDIBLE STOP EXAMINE CLOSELY HOWEVER AND NOTE ONCE APPETISING SPOTS OF HONEY MARMITE SARDINE STOP PAPERS COULD BE CONSIDERED OBJECTIONABLE SO I ADVISE THAT IF YOU ARE APPREHENDED EAT PAPERS STOP WEATHER HERE IS EXCELLENT AND AM LOOKING FORWARD TO EXCELLENT STORMS FOLLOWED BY EXCELLENT SUNSHINE AND WINDS STOP

Thomas went home. He did not want to see Matters' Worteriana. But it would come, as inevitably as night followed day, and as fearsome. Dusk was worse. Dusk to follow the final incandescence of the sun. The sounds of chaos a telegram boy's bicycle bell, if addressee not in place then message card placed under appropriate meteorite.

He watched the telegram boy bounce his bike over the kerb, wobble to the front gate, lean over, open it, cycle up the path, leap up onto the porch; he heard him hammer on the door; the boy rode away pausing once to pollen his hand on the giant sunflower. Thomas had only to walk from the room to see the telegram under the door. There was no saying it was from Matters. It could be from Sir Thomas Loane, M&M,

the Council, the Prime Minister, the President, the General, the Pope.

He heeled the envelope. It made the usual sound. He kicked it to the wall, behind the green carboy. He set himself to watch a Mediums panel game but could not manage more than five minutes of it. The carboy distorted and magnified the envelope. He switched from channel to channel. Beauty queen, dog food, varicose veins, American gunships, impending strike, Betty Grable, physics for schools, Tony Henry, Bob baby, Suzie, Helen and the reverend Tony Mortar, cat food, wondabra, paper towels. The envelope wobbled behind the carboy. Tony got fifty thousand a year. Tony was charm and ice. Thomas's ambitions had been frozen by Tony. At noon he walked to the pub.

When he got home he found a small packet among the letters the postman had left. It contained a small, old-fashioned ink bottle with little air bubbles in it, stoppered with a pared wine cork. The accompanying note read: A Precis from Matters. He gingerly removed the cork and tapped some of the contents onto a sheet of paper. It was either dry earth or ash.

He thought he may as well return to the office but as he walked to the car a post office van delivered an express delivery letter. So he slouched back to the house. He pulled the telegram from behind the carboy and read it.

I ADMIT TO MALICE IN MY COMMUNICATIONS STOP THERE IS HOWEVER AN END TO ITS ACID STOP IT IS NECESSARY THAT YOU BE ETCHED TOO FOR YOUR OWN RECOGNITION STOP MATTERS

He then sat down to read the letter . . .

Dear Thomas,

These are not Percy Wort's pp.; you're not getting out of it so easily. Percy disappeared on a new leaf/life, fifteen years ago.

Well I've got what he left behind—to be exact, what he

left BELOW—it's a box of story. Have read it. Here and there you'll find my comments. It's sure to be a goer and they're mad if they refuse it. You know them so butter them up. If they're crazy and you don't feel like bringing it out yourself get onto one of these yank cruise ships and flog it to some millionaire collector for the JFK Cornking Library. Ms is in a butterbox, a bit musty but the smellier the cheese the keener the epicure. Epicureanism increases with wealth so grab the richest Yank. Help him keep the research mills rolling. Got to admit you're not the first I've offered it to. Roderick Dessimle the dealer was the first but he wouldn't touch, let alone read it. Thank God I didn't hop into that pool of dealers now a trough where grunts, snorts and fine-toned talk swirl. Do I sound envious? Am not. We are not (tho sometimes wife grizzles and kids want that, that & that). I just want a few things on shelves, the garden, the seventeen acres with economic beasts, ridiculous menagerie, all of us just five minutes from the water and the boat.

From his dealer fastness Dessimle has offered me a dozen books, first eds. Gee, eh? Provided I buy *vintage* farm machinery on adjoining farm. Great, eh? One only Fordson kero tractor with faulty diff (meaning I'd not even be able to drive it off to a scrap depot), and one Crump spreader with lime attachment. Conditional on all goods purchased being removed by tomorrow by order of Mid-Sludge Historical Society per their agent Roderick Dessimle, the ubiquitous medium (what the media lost when he went into junk). He's in the air, everywhere. Soon all things will have to go to Dess, the great porous membrane, anything taken in & only the worthless allowed passage. I don't want his Fordson, even as an anchor. I don't want his first eds. The machinery is on Raddle Park which is about to become a National Heritage. Raddlers also want us off *our* place. We're a blight, ruin etc. on the landscape. (I didn't mean to go on about Dess but when you're heated you've got to dissipate, right?) The way Dess went on about the machin-

15

ery you'd think he had the first tractor landed in the
country, that the Crump came with the First Fleet. I mean
the stuff wasn't old enough for the historical society for a
start. And you wouldn't catch him laying a finger on it.
Nowadays he'll touch only Aston Martin, first folios and
Louis cans. Gloves and tongs he needs for second-hand
books. Earwigs, bugs and invisibles he fears. He's ever so
fond of crystal, cutlery & shares. Percy's papers gave him a
rash.

If the tractor and broadcaster were together I could go
out at night, dig a hole and bury them in the Raddle acres.
Or shove them into a nearby dam. Or burn them in situ
and let burnt scrub camouflage. Undetectable in the black
until onset of rust; then red in black and green. Then sued
by society who want to restore the farm to what they feel to
be the 1870 condition. Slab walls, bark roof, rammed floor,
with undressed yards of undressed poles watched over by
suitably garbed caretaker and wife, wandering over acres in
1870 clogs or on horse watching over 1870 sheep, Vermont
strain if possible, with 1870 blowflies—70s hens, 70s cows
yielding cupfuls of 70s milk well germed with TB and
undulant fever for period pallor of curating couple who,
for an extra five or ten dollars, will make it on 70s bag bed
either fully or on belly or into eucalypted muslin. But no,
they'd not practise prevention, they'd want the seed to swim
home to tunes of Sudan, they'd want babies for the farm,
to spread wide the family name for Queen and Empire, and
they would need many names for in 70 was beginning
Populate or Perish, and there were many wars to come.

Two hours to go before lunch. Sunny with a stiff Nor'
Easter. Should be down working on the boat, slapping on
red lead. Or writing red words on bare hull. Must finish
soon and off to sea and earn a dollar. Or mount rotary
clothes-hoist merrygoround on ute and take zacs from holidaying kids (the country's real poxes and lesions are decimal
—how could we let them jettison trays, zacs, bobs, quids,

16

deenas in favour of one-, two-, five-, etc. cent pieces? How long before dime and nickel—bucks are in already). Words on the boat; haven't decided on a name. Maybe SEA or just C. I fancy something special and plain like BOAT. BOAT it is. Big block letters. A fine word.

My room's lined with words, filled with them. In books, bundles and folders. On the light bulb, on pen, pencils, typewriter, enamel mug, collar, insteps. Do they move around at night? I should get the ladder and see if the right ones got back onto the light bulb or whether it reads Vote Incandescent, or Smoke 100 Watt 240 Volt. Light bulbs made in the one factory. Bright Mondays, Lumes Tuesdays, Flares Wednesdays; the unforgivable error is to send out Bright in a Flare wrapper.

In lines, thousands of them, black marks with white between ever flowing. Everything from: the shaving cut he stopped with lint from her navel, to: the rent lobe I staunched with eight hours sleep. Black marks on an orange as with so and so's citrus co-op. Groin's Trusses white on blue as though alphabet of heaven is falling. And all coming to an end they say. Farewell, Gutenberg, Caxton. Print interred. But not in a real one, no, not a real one, and do you know why it's not in a real turd? Because the communicating beast was com(m)a'd. I read yesterday that communication, through print, is finished. Words no longer *convey*. Film IS. Every frame tells a story. Twenty-odd of them a second. Grave wherein the words do sleep. Plastic grave clothes, coffin and marker, lens-decorated. However there's no keeping out graverobbers.

Peace,

MATTERS.

(2nds out of the ring)

The butterbox was delivered to the office at two-fifty, two afternoons later. The man put it on a chair. Thomas stared at it. Susan watched with a fixed bright smile. She offered to

17

open it. He said he would handle it alone. He was surprised Matters had not sent it freight to pay. On the reverse of the address label was written: Literally a Disinterment. He undid it. Musty. Crumbs of soil. Butterbox crammed with stinking paper and rag. Suppose I should be grateful it doesn't weigh as much as previous contents, 56 pounds. Bound to be papers stuck together with butter. Manilla, bond, rag and rice-paper sandwiches. If the writing's of the forbidden sort and agents make a raid I will eat it. Just a rice-paper sandwich, officer. Most of it's typewritten, double or triple spaced so should be a quick read. Don't want to. Yet terrible compulsion. Am reminded of recent book made up of hodge-podge of diaries, papers, recollections, an anthology of rubbish and this'll be no improvement, no development. Get rid of it quickly, waste no time. Return it to Matters before silverfish devour. Is fit for a midden scratcher but nobody else. Perhaps it *is* the work of Matters. The whole business. Percy couldn't have done all this.

Beginnings; My Life on Trains; Farm Life; City Life. My God—A Short History of the Cow; Tales for Children; Memoirs of a Bike Rider . . .

Ants silverfish, cockroaches and mice have munched, mated and nested in it. Little words have been ingested and voided as points and commas.

I will not read this infamography. At least not more than a quick glance. *I* cld. do a lot betr. Wht. a tale *I*'d tell. My own story.

Later Thomas read bits of it to Susan. She cried: Has he no shame, no feeling for history and environment? Hasn't he heard of our list, our documentaries—*Magic of Mining*; *Wattle Heritage*; *Population Implosion or Explosion*? How dare he send us his pollutions.

Thomas stroked her wrists, forearms, elbows and calmed her.

He thought: Matters is bad enough, but really he's only a mild-mannered acolyte to demon Percy.

18

WORT'S WORDS

I have decided to put it all down. Makes me sound somewhat imperial/imperious/a queller/putter-down of subjects; or a bookkeeper registering debts; or an herculean creature getting from under and depositing his burden—but with a crash or with infinite gentleness? Imperiously quelling querellous debits like Hercules the one minute, then beaten bald Samson, then sorry, sir, for the broken plates but I tripped in the shit. Anyhow enough of this scribbling.

I intend putting it down in words. On paper I hope though I have only a limited quantity. Therefore no margins. Also I must keep my spare shirt clean. I wish it had a boiled collar and stiff cuffs so I could embroider with words, alfresco, the way Beethoven, Liszt and Brahms did clefs etc. at a restaurant, halfway through the soup or lobster. But I'll make do with what I've got, battler that I am (ho ho), between baked beans and biscuits. Life on a shirt. Mellifluous passages for under-arms and tail, heroic utterances for chest, long perorations for arms, asides for pockets, hollow promises round buttonholes. All scripted in finest pencil and ballpoint. Marking ink not allowed (and certainly not available where I am).

This is the story of Percy Wort. And of William Wort. And

19

of Thomas Wort. The Wort Story. Rise of the Wort episodes. Instalments of the Wort Plan. Instruction in the use of world wortery. The worthiness of wortsworth. Wheatswort. Snapperwort. Saltwort. Ironworts. Indentedwort. And crowwort. Corvuswort, the bird of allover, the blue-black-with-touches-of-white bird, the talking splendid-beaked bird, eater of insects and a little grain, intelligent, humorous, very strong in the big-toe, blamed by oafs and yokels for all sorts of rural crises so that said oafs and yokels may connive with quasi-men of quasi-science in exercises in extermination in which intestines of murdered crows are exposed, examined and pickled. Oh what a tough time has the crow.

A leading wort problem is how do you pronounce it, Wort. Wert? Wart? Amongst the Worts there is no agreement. My family generally says Wort but my father, on the rare occasions nowadays when he wishes to declare his Englishness, says Wert. His brother, Fred, likewise. English people generally say Wert. Natives say Wort. As with St John's Wort. Which, although it does not grow in this district, is known to most. It favours cooler, more elevated regions. Its leaves do not have scaly protuberances or warts; they do however, possess oil glands or oil warts within. It will grow up to about three feet high and display bright yellow flowers and reproduce itself by seeds or underground stems. (I am a devil for dropping in botanical bricabrac.) Now for a little animal physiology: ingestion of the plant produces photosynthesization in unpigmented skin and sunlight causes irritation of said skin which is rubbed, bitten and scratched to great detriment and often dementia. I.e. they go mad with wort. Ah, the worts . . . St John's Wort is indigenous to Asia and Europe. In Australia it is probably a garden escape.

IN FLIGHT

I am writing this part of the story in a temporary wortarium. I wanted to sneeze twice but dared not for fear of demolishing the wortarium. Thank God there is no wind. I look down a small valley which is returning to bush. The Boers left here thirty years ago. I believe they simply walked off and when the rates went unpaid for many years the Shire tendered it and some Smith who has never been here, took over.

The Wortarium is not even a humpy or ruin of humpy. It was probably the stye of wretched sows, the hopeful light in the eye of their desperate owner. Who must have lived in a tent for there are no house ruins here. Coddle the livestock and bury the family; great husbandry.

Perhaps termites took the house. I tried listening for them earlier, just to set my mind at rest, to hear the white beasts gnawing, but there was nothing I could positively identify; though to be sure what I heard was no pandemonium; what I heard was the stretching, contracting, pullulating earth. But never a termite. For some reason the termite has abandoned the site too.

I arrived here at dawn and almost froze. I made a fire but it had to be small so as not to give me away. Life on the run, is fun, only if, you're skipping down the rainbow, to the pot of gold. I do not recommend living on the run, even if you've a fatness likely to prove fatal unexercised. I am ill-equipped for this sort of life having only the clothes I wear, a few changes, an army disposals webbing haversack, six tins of baked beans, two port fritz, an army one-day ration, one tin melon and lemon jam and two packets of hard biscuits and the Remington. Such insufficiency appals me. Where are the vitamins and minerals going to come from? I suppose I'll have to graze and chew stones.

So, on with Wortiana before beri beri, scurvy, rickets or other malnutritions sap me.

THE UPPERSASS COMMUNITY HALL
One Day, Another d, & Another, Yet Another . . .

One day I decided to do something about the Community

Hall. It is half a mile down the road from the homestead. (Known as Fisons, once owned by the Fisons of Newcastle, that smoking wen one hundred to one hundred and fifty miles to the south. Distance depends upon route. By plane it would be about a hundred. I cannot check it. I have no map within reach. It is four hours away by fast car. A few drivers claim three. I have done it in less than three on the Norton. I have done it in three with Doris pillion. My family farm Fisons, William Wort is the mortgagee, Mary Wort assists him, I give a hand whenever I'm here, and bro gives advice from town.)

As befits a person with a somewhat scientific slant of mind I am going to write this memoir in a plain, straightforward manner.

William, my father, has been on many farms. As farmhand, cowman, labourer, partner, assistant, sharefarmer and farmer. For years he was a sharefarmer. The Wandering Sharefarmer. If the post-office keeps files of changes of address his would be among the thickest. Before we came to the north coast we were on the south coast and inland; city addresses are another thing.

Our district is known as Uppersass. We have a post-office store and lots of ruins. We are in the hills, above Peeny, between the Pacific and the Great Dividing Range.

Uppersass got going as a community more than fifty years ago. Earlier, the region belonged to Grabling Station. Then R. V. Russell arrived, bought a few thousand acres and set about turning his ideas into reality. Russell built the Hall, a weatherboard place on the side of the hill, the front a few steps above ground level, the rear on six-foot stumps with boards across to stop empties rolling down the hill. The Hall appears to rest on a mound of bottles. From some angles the glass looks like igneous rock exuding from the earth, as though this is active volcano country. Fifty feet away on flattened ground is the official bottle heap ordained by several Hall Committees. There were several attempts to market the bottles, particularly in the Depression. One truckload went through a bridge and another went off the road on a hairpin, sank into a soft shoulder and tipped. The two loads were flushed into creeks and the river by twenty inches of rain in three days and began bobbing past the town of Peeny. In fact they went through Peeny, for the river rose and put ten feet of water through Main Street and its tributaries, and after the rain the sun shone and people could not see for the glare on flood and glint on bottle, and reporters, photographers and cameramen came in and recorded for city people the bobbing bottles and convinced them Peeny was the booze town of the world. A Salvation Army relief team had to be forced to stay but got its revenge by claiming that the deluge was God's punishment for drunkenness. And Peeny never forgave Uppersass. They even blamed Uppersass for the eddy responsible for bottling them (quite true in one sense: the waters swept down because so much hill country has been cleared; shaved, even, with gullies and potholes running sores and sunken pimples). A couple of infuriated ratepayers took to their chimneys and sniped bottles. Other marksmen, in joy, took up the challenge. Three people were wounded by ricochets, and later, in the mud, there were many gashed feet and boots, and a week later when cleansing rain fell dozens of houses leaked. Where the river joins the ocean the vast spread of alluvium in the ocean was bottle-markered.

The bottle marketers were not people of Uppersass. Uppersassians are proud of their bottles. Every now and then there is a proposal to commemorate them. As though they need commemoration when they are in themselves a memorial. Old Osstich wanted to build a community atom bomb shelter with bottle walls. The Tanks wished to build a house with two rooms, one green the other amber. O'Riordan wanted a herd of bottle cows coming up the hill and Oflake proposed an amber statue of the last tribal leader. Mrs Oflake wanted to sell them for the CWA, the Jones for a starvation fund, but as that meant disposal, they never did anything.

All I needed to do for *my* scheme was sell a load of bottles for funds for the Hall. Nobody wanted to spend a penny on the Hall itself. They were prepared to see it collapse for want of attention. Now and then I would do a bit of patching. I was unwilling to spend my own money on it. The Hall owed me at least a load of bottles. I could not see much logic in my stand, but then I could not see much logic anywhere.

In the past the bottles had been saved by the economics of transport and price per dozen (and condition of roads, availability of trucks, hands, and petrol, fires, flu, anthrax, ticks and wild dogs).

Recently the price rose and it was possible to sell. I discussed it with my brother. He checked my figures and was agreeable; also, he insisted on a half share. Cash. He ridiculed my notion of using all the money on the Hall. I told him that half a load—my share—would not yield enough for me. He told me that we should therefore take two loads. I could not agree to this, nor could I tell him that two loads would leave insufficient bottles for my scheme. He did not understand what I was trying to do.

The weatherboards are flooded gum, floorboards tallow-wood, windows and doorways rosewood, and the doors, until recently, when they were stolen, red cedar. Here and there patches of white paint adhere, but thankfully only a little. What the timber needs is a proper oiling. My father would like to see the Hall so deteriorated as to be written off by the committee and sold to himself. He would then unstump it, place onto slides and shove it down the hill. He has never specified this treatment but I have juggled with his hints, jokes, jibes and curses. Not much remains of my father's Englishness; there was a lot a few years ago; lately it has diminished greatly; what remains he would like to see fixed; he would fix it, he thinks, by shoving the Hall into the gully, about two hundred and fifty feet of gentle then steep, paspalum'd slope. He would take his knapsack spray and linseed oil the grass. He would announce beforehand his intention. One day the Hall would be in its usual position, the next day, not. He feels the Hall is overpowering him. However; I feel that if he does destroy it he will fix himself forever in our locality. I.e. his Englishness is not worth a fart, that he's here whether he likes it or not, that his few years in Uppersass have fixed him in the ways of Uppersass, that Uppersass is the culmination of his years in this country; in the city, the southern tablelands, South coast, North coast, the Kimberleys.

WILLIAM WORT, FRAGMENTS OF BEGINNINGS

The suppliers, accepting references and credentials, guarantor, medical report, the soundness of life assurance and bank deposit, and convinced he was a man of merit well able to sell in ever increasing numbers what they had to supply, agreed to allow William Wort to purchase the business. He made arrangements to move into the place where for months he had been working mornings and Saturdays to get the hang of things.

William and Mary and their children Tom, Percy and Edna, moved into residence behind and above the shop. A side passage a little wider than a bicycle led to a small concrete yard which opened on to a lane. Theirs was one of a row of twelve shops facing an iceworks and more shops. On one side stood a toy shop and on the other a haberdashery. Over the road the land, crowded with houses, rose steeply to a narrow plateau which ended in steep cliff overlooking the ocean. A mile or so in the other direction was the harbour. Estate agents called the suburb comfortable and respectable. Aspidistra, asparagus fern, staghorn, elkhorn, hibiscus and oleander were popular. A hardy variety of box capable of surviving severe pruning grew on many streets.

Several times a day bundles thudded to the footpath in front of the shop; the first at four in the morning, the last at five-thirty in the evening, though if anything momentous had happened anywhere the final delivery could be as late as seven. Generally, William was dressed and waiting and drinking tea when the first truck arrived. His joke was that the thud of delivery to a shop a mile away worked as an alarm and woke him. He carried the bundles of newspapers inside, opened then counted them, loaded up his Morris and set off on his round. Saturday and Sunday mornings Tom and Percy helped him. At six o'clock on the fifty-fifth Friday morning the Morris caught fire and exploded in sunny, deserted, cicada-throbbing Pire Street. Burning newspapers and flaming petrol destroyed an open Riley, a fernery, a telephone box, an aviary of irreplaceable birds, the garage and veranda of number one, the cypress hedge of number three, gutted the sidecar of a Harley-Davidson outfit, and inflicted second degree burns on William's arms, legs and neck. The next morning Mary did the furthermost rounds with the toyman, and Tom and Percy billycarted those nearby. Mary managed to keep things going until the day before William's discharge from hospital, when she was overcome by shingles and despair. People were sueing, the bank was threatening, it had rained for a fort-night, the newspaper circulation offices were complaining and Edna caught diphtheria.

Mr Onslow, a short, middle-aged, jolly person, came to look after the shop and did so with some skill until William's brother, Fred, discovered that Mr Onslow was somehow making himself a lot of money and the shop none. This Wed-nesday afternoon the boys were in the haberdashery helping Mrs Cushion count needles when Mr Onslow ran into the shop and hid behind the counter. Then Fred ran past the shop. The boys thought he looked very fine and though not black a bit like Jesse Owens the runner. Mr Onslow, panting and wheezing gasped that Fred was having a fit, and Mrs Cushion went oh oh ohoh. The boys ran from the shop. Mr Onslow came after them, dashed into their shop and slammed the door. The newspaper truck pulled in and threw off a bundle of papers which the boys dragged into the doorway. Fred returned, asked if they had seen Mr Onslow, saw the closed door, put his shoulder down like a tough lock coming from a scrum, ran at the door and burst it open. They heard screams from the back. The toyman came in and made them tidy the shop and set out the new edition, a big one because of a crisis in Europe. Then he sent Tom into the toyshop and Percy to Mrs Cushion. Afterwards, Fred told them Mr Onslow had gone through. He had gone to New Zealand, Fiji, San Francisco. He had cut his throat, cremated himself with newspapers. He was at Bathurst, Gundagai, Wodonga, Launceston, Kimberley.

And they lost the shop, William was discharged from hospital, Mary left the nursing home and they all went to live with Fred over his two shops in the city. Fred often told the boys that life was hard, that grinders and smashers were everywhere. Mary spent most of her time at the hospital waiting for Edna, and William and the boys helped Fred in his workshop. One of the shops had been a milk bar with a long refrigerator with many holes in which Mrs Brim the housekeeper made enormous iceblocks in cups with broken handles and great cubes of icecream she cut into animal shapes, her cows not replicas but rather miniature suggestions of cows. She always referred to Edna as That poor little mite and the boys could not understand how a small sick child could also be mite, which must mean mighty, so they asked Fred and he told them it did not mean mighty. It meant a small child or a tiny portion or a white insect.

Mrs Brim was cutting a cow from very hard icecream. Crystals scattered about her and as Percy peered at one it lost its hard insectal whiteness, became moist then wet and finished as a spot of milk. He asked Fred about Edna and was told she was doing poorly. She was very thin and hot and ate lots of icecream. She's a poor little mite, said Mrs Brim. That evening Mary, William and Fred went out and when they returned William began shouting and smashed a chair, and Fred went into the boys' room, switched on the light and told them Edna was dead and though things were tougher the grinding and smashing were over for a while. Edna was buried near a pepperina in the section of the cemetery below the railway embankment. The shadow of a stock train passed across them as the minister spoke. Mrs Brim and the boys waited fifty yards away in a lattice roundhouse. There were five cars and the hearse. There were twelve people round the grave. There were forty-seven headstones and many more. The train had nine trucks. The engine driver and the fireman stood on their footplate holding their hats against their chests and in the doorway of the van the drover picked his nose. The mourners left the graveside and went to their cars. Cattle bellowed in the saleyards. Mary cried out when friends took her arm, and Mrs Brim said Oh God, the shingles and everything. Percy left the roundhouse and wandered towards a small stone gateway. A red cow squeezed through, followed by a white. They stared at him and shook their heads. A black beast entered. Black so therefore a bull. Snort. Mgrrmm. He jumped behind a gravestone. He looked back and saw Tom run to his father and clutch him. His father screamed and shook him off. The gravestone was warm and because he was learning to read, he read about the glorious beyond, just as Mrs Brim called him to the car.

At Fred's place Mrs Brim set out cold chicken, corned beef, whisky and lemonade. The Browns drank quickly and wept, Mary took medicine and went to her room, Mrs Jones drank glass upon glass of lemonade muttering It's the gas; Mrs Tomson displayed the wishbone, and regretted it, and William kept telling Fred he would repay every penny he, Fred, had put into the lapsed newsagency until Fred shouted that he had written it all off and did not want to hear another word. William said he was going to make a new start in the country. He was going to work for a farmer, and to eventually buy a place of his own. Jesus Jesus Jesus, said Fred. I don't care what you say, said William, It's the only life. You can only begin afresh away from the city. The country's only good for holidays, said Fred. I'm going to do what man was meant to do, said William, Farming's in my blood. Your blood'll be

in farming, said Fred. Our grandfathers were men of Lincolnshire, said William. OK, said Fred, But we grew up in towns.
We lived in towns. I've made up my mind, said William. If
I'd known this, said Fred, I wouldn't have arranged the holiday in the bush.

Two hours later Fred drove them to the railway station but
did not wait to see them go off. At five the next morning they
were woken by the guard. The train stopped but the guard
signalled it on a few carriage-lengths and they were able to
step down onto the short platform. Through breaks in the
mist they saw clear sky. The station was built amongst rocks,
tree ferns and bushes. The stationmaster took their tickets,
and asked if they liked his garden. Did you make it? asked
Tom. With the help of the Lord, my predecessors and the rain
forest, said the stationmaster. Beautiful, said William. Wonderful, said Mary. Spooky, said Percy. Mr Humos drove them
to his guesthouse. In the week they were there Mary's shingles
disappeared, William removed his last bandage, Tom learnt
to ride a pony and Percy lost his fear of the rain forest because
he never saw mist again. There were tree ferns he could not
put his arms round, vines as thick as his wrist, birds with
incubator mounds, wallabies the size of geese, flowers like
orchids. He did not like the snakes. Sometimes he walked
along a track used by tractors. Now and then he came across
bullock teams. His father said This is the life, and his mother
said Couldn't we live up here, near the coast? and he said No,
it's not our kind of country, we're going South.

JOURNEYS AND EMPLOYERS
(& obligatory bushfire)

This is the seat, this is the floor, this is the window; that is the
mountain, those are the rocks, there is a cave; this the compartment, there the door of the compartment. I mean this is the
window; there are the rocks, there is the cave with the tunnel
and down you go feeling the slide into the hollow mountain

where it's dark in the day and light at night; this is the seat, this is the carriage, one of three passenger and four goods and a guard's hauled by a train making sooty smoke that gets in though the windows are closed; this is the window, above it the water bottle between two glasses always to be rinsed and wiped before using, the chain on the stopper tinkles on the bottle, the wheels click, the carriage creaks; another mountain and hollow inside and a spring of cold water, cold clear bubbly water; this is the carriage and the water bottle is empty; we'll be there in a minute; that must be a coal mine, so that's a coal mine, with wheels on a tower, sheds, huts, broken iron, coal trucks, rust dead trees and mountains of dirt and stone; this is my mother, this my brother, this is me, these are our things in the racks and in the guard's van we have more; she says in another five minutes; five cows, four calves, a dairy, house and inside people arguing, people being sent away, people shouting, someone . . . a whip, an iron trough with snail silver and bird poop, moss, green slime, three oyster shells, two ha'pence and one English farthing; this is the seat and this the floor and this is what we've been reading; and soon we'll be there and he'll be waiting and we'll load up and drive to the house ten and a half miles away though I think it'll be closer to nine and three quarters for he said he was never again going to be more than ten miles away, and she said a mile and a half so as to make it less to us, so it'll be nine and three quarter miles (which'll be nearly as much as the last place, and there are hills and it'll be push and ride, and bro will be the rider and I'll be lucky to get a dink); this is the window and there's a bubble in it, a glass cave; that is the railway fence, that is the ditch, that is the road; a hundred sheep and as many lambs running, running from the train; if they don't stop they'll hit the stone wall, fall into the paddock with rotted stooks and broken sheaves, with the ruined house in the corner with Norfolk Island pine behind a seaside tree; it shouldn't be here, though he said the sea's not far, twenty

miles off, and I thought he said there were cold winters hereabouts so why a Norfolk? He's waiting for us at the station
with the car, she said; and he himself had said this morning,
If I had a truck we'd do it in one trip but I haven't so I'll go
ahead, unload, and meet you at the station and we'll all drive
to the new place just a hop from town and a school bus passes
if it's wet and you can't bike, and don't forget I'm looking for
a second bike, and you know what I'll do when I get the
bonus? Get a couple of horses for you, and a ute for your
mother and me, how's that sound, eh? And I neighed, and
galloped along the veranda, dismounted, and drove the ute
back and opened the door for them; and she laughed, then
said wearily, Careful, don't count your chickens, and he said,
If we have to, we'll start a poultry farm, and she said, One
thing at a time. No no no, he had said, Many things at the one
time and one at least'll hatch; and this is the window and this
the glass bubble. I've seen cock tread hen, I've seen red hen
big as a long warm day, white at night, always moving, the
greatest traveller ever, moving from day to day, and each day a
little quicker, each day a little tireder, longing for a perch;
this is the window, here are houses, this is the town. I, Percy,
my brother Tom, our mother, and waiting, our father with the
Essex in the station yard, which is somewhere ahead; the train
has stopped, I must get out, I could walk along a rail to the
station, doing my Houdini trick, but why? It would be a waste
hurrying to the station to see him and pack the car with luggage for the drive to the farm, the third we've had, the fourth
address we've had, I wonder how many birthday and Christmas letters are following me.

I have, I have a feeling he will not be there, that the Essex
has a flat or its brakes have gone and only the spare wheel and
number plate are visible in the side of a haystack for I have
seen this happen in films; or he is doing some job for the landlord, or has quarrelled with the landlord; he could well be
waiting in the station yard with the Essex reloaded and no

room for us; perhaps he'll have bought a trailer, and will make room in the car for Mum and Tom and let me ride in the trailer.

Is the place we're going to owned by an Englishman, Mum?

Yes dear, but he's nicer than McKenzie-Dart.

Why do we always work for the English?

We don't.

My brother looked up. That's right. We've only just started and I hope we stay with the English, they've been doing things longer than we have. They're better at it. And there's the Royal Navy.

I don't like them.

Your father thinks they've got something Australians lack. He gets these fancies, remember.

The landlord will be an Englishman or be like an Englishman, with a moustache, baggy eyes and a straight back even though it hurts him like it hurt McKenzie-Dart at the last place who slipped mounting but said he'd been thrown, wearing tweed coat and jodhpurs. It was a hundred and two and the tramp he'd gone to order off was only three feet inside the gateway and out with sunstroke. Throw him out, Wort, he ordered Dad, The man's foxing, he was walking well enough along the road, I was watching him, and as soon as he saw the farm he developed beggar's stagger, and he didn't see me—go and put him off, Wort; and Dad said, In this weather he wouldn't be foxing, I'll take water down and maybe bring him to the house; You will not, said McK-D, The man's a healthy vagrant; Dad said, Mr McK-D, it's my day off; You are trying my patience, Wort, he snapped and wheeled his horse; and Dad said, There's never much patience on a day like this, anyway I'll go down, and you won't object to my taking a water bag for my own survival, will you? No, Wort, and I shouldn't rely on a canvas water bag for survival, either, as he urged the horse away. I was sitting under the veranda boards beside the water bag; Dad, I said, Are all Englishmen poops like Mr McK-D? What? You watch your tongue, Percy, Mr McK-D is a gentleman with too much of the sun on him, the English are all right but they can't take the sun; the rain they're used to, it's the sun what's shrinking the British Empire. Mum called from the house, You're right there, old feller, the sun's the shrinker, you can hear what it's done to McDash's brain; it rattles like a pea in that iron skull of his —and what about taking that water bag down to the swaggie; Dad pulled the bag from the nail, I'm going now; Mum called, That's the idea, water the shrunken colonial, and if he doesn't revive first splash wet the ground with the rest to soften it for when you dig him in; Dad said, You want to get us thrown out of this place? She said, No, love, you'll do that, as you did last time and you'll do again until you've this admiration, this misfounded admiration for pommy squires out of your system; he said, Gwen, it's too hot to quarrel; she said, It's too hot, yes, and for the poor bugger down by the gate; this isn't England. Why are you always on about leaving here for better things? Better things are now, so go help him.

He stood watching the room of her voice, the window half down, the brown blind moving gently as though breathing with her, the water bag in his hand, swinging, the water bag dry on the outside, like a nut, with stopper and handle the stem; I said, Me too; he said, No, wait here; she said, If you go wear the straw hat—did McDash go down? you better hurry, he might be trampling the man; he said, Jesus, and to me, Wait here; and he set off.

She said, You still there, Perce? Put your hat on; I said, I'm here; she said, Well put your hat on and go down; I said, Would Mr McK-D do anything? She said, There's no telling what this weather will do; I said, Will the man be dead? She said, Noooo, he's probably resting like McDash said; I said, Would he ride over him? she said, Nooo, that was only me and the heat; I said, Mightn't he get angry if Dad throws water on him? she said, Well he might swell a bit.

And I saw the man swell, throw shade and roll onto Dad

and I went to pull him free but couldn't and the man blocked the gate then flattened the fence and rolled onto the road and the bus came and bounced into him, and Mum ran down and we picked Dad up, he was ten feet wide and thin as paper and his split clothes fell from him and Mum pulled and hugged him and we walked him home.

When Dad got as far as the woolshed I followed him, sometimes on heels for the burning, I touched my hair, like hot soft wire, I put the hat on, and by the woolshed wall I turned my face from the bars of iron heat, and stubbed a toe, Ouch, and hopped; I turned, down through the smell of woolfat of shearings long past (I've never seen full shearing only a bit of crutching). Past the shearers' huts, the yards, to the pines by the gate, carefully.

Dad kneeling, holding up the man, giving him sips, words, another man huddled, no, it was the swag; Dad pouring water over the man's head, Mr McK-D riding up the drive to his house, the man mumbling, Dad saw me, put the water bag on the ground, said, Well, bring us the bag, taking the man under the man's arms and pulling him back into shade over the needles, propping him against the lumps of hardened white pine juice in bark.

The man about Dad's age, unshaven, with white stuff on his chin, in an old brown suit, white shirt and black boots. I gave the bag to Dad; the man put his hand to his neck, opened collar, nodded; Dad shook water down his back; he saw me, he winked, he tried to speak, grunted, then said, Oh the birds and the bees and the cigarette trees—got the makings? The name's Bob; Dad said, William; I said, Percy.

Dad said to me, Nip up to the house and get the baccy. I set off.

I saw McK-Dart among the oaks, standing by his horse watching Dad and the man, I stopped, then stepped behind a pine, picked up a cone, waited for him to leap into saddle and charge down to the gateway; I remembered marbles; in a bag on the veranda, and wondered if I'd have time to get them to throw under his horse, or hit him in temple; he was waiting. I saw Dad lift the man to his feet and start to help him up the track; I saw Mr McK-Dart slap his hip twice, seize the reins and begin to mount; the horse stepped away and Mr McK-Dart fell and the horse reared and dragged him until he got free. Dad shouted to him; he shouted back, Nothing at all, get that man off the property, get him off, turned his back and limped away; Bob gestured for Dad to let go but he wouldn't, even when he shouted, it was as though they had to hold onto each other to survive, as though parting would be ruinous, and I begged them to stay for if they fell apart McK-Dart would gallop from the trees and drive all of us off and onto the road till we found another place owned by an Englishman . . .

An englisher Englishman, a Major Something-Poop with a Great War poster moustache, a couple of jollying sons, a pair of curtseying daughters, and a Great War wife, an ambulance driver, knitter of sox, candidate for parliament with jackerooing nephews, croquet and polo, and afternoon teas on the lawn, where they are kind to the farm people and Tom and I are scrubbed and brilliantined; We take Bob swaggie with us; and the afternoon tea is a disaster because I break the teapot and Bob farts in the sugar; and I go down to the gate and find two swaggies there; and we are all ordered off and onto the road. On to a place owned by General Tweedledee-Lee-Enfield who wears medals on his jacket, ribbons on his jodhpurs, a revolver in his belt, a monocle in his eye and his wife, the attractive side of homely in appearance, has a commanding manner and knits scarves for the benighted of Arnhem Land; the sons, Roger and Basil; the daughters are boarders at a ladies' college.

And the Tweedledum-Lee-Enfields, to show they are not standoffish hold a New Year's Eve tea party for their employees on the lawn beside the rose garden, in front of the drawing-room, and the swaggies, the three of them, pinch the silver, stuff the ladies, ram medals, ribbons, school blazers up the gents, organize the employees and their families into choirs for God Save the King, bring on Leicester rams for the stud merino ewes, put the place up for auction, and vanish. We, the family, are then sent by an agency to a great property owned by a hard man who looks like the swaggies, the fences are electrified and around the notices, Do Not Touch High Voltage, are mounds of corpses, the bottom ones quite rotted away, the top ones crow-pecked, and the manager, Mr Master, resplendent in navy singlet, white jodhpurs, sandshoes and digger hat with dangling corks black with blowies, orders everyone, in beautiful English, to work a little harder for the owner, Mr Lord, who sends his love, and the epilogue: Keep it up friends, keep your heads clear, your arses clean, I'm watching, I'm marking your papers.

MEANWHILE, back on the McKenzie-Dart property . . .

Dad had Bob's arm over his shoulders. Bob looked back and Dad caught a wiff of him and closed his nose with his lip. What is it? I asked. He shook his head. Bob winked. Go on up and tell your mother to put the kettle on. I said I'd carry the swag but when I grabbed the straps found it far too heavy so rolled it under the pine. We'll get you a cup of tea, Bob. Don't want to impose on you.   It'll be a bad day when I can't give a sick man a hand.   I wouldn't want to put you in the shit with your boss.   No chance. He's a good man. Heat's got him a bit rattled.   Bit high and mighty.   Not at all. Tough but fair.   You're lucky.

I jogged up to the house and when they arrived Mum had tea ready. I'm very grateful for what you're doing for me, Mrs Wort.   It's the least I can do, Mr, Mr-er-er.   Bob, Mrs Wort, just you call me Bob.

A yell from outside, Jack, the other man.   The boss wants me and your Dad at the windmill on the hill, it's stopped. Mum told Dad he was mad to go. Bob said McKenzie-Dart should fix it himself. Mum said it was working. Jack said it had stopped and he hadn't time for tea. They went off. I wasn't allowed another cup so went for the milk billy. The hessian sides of the cool safe were almost dry. I stood on a box and felt in the bowl. It was dry, so I added some water. I heard Bob: It's not much I'm asking. My pleasures are minor nowadays. I've been on the road too long, you dry up.   I don't care, my God you've got a hide.

They faced each other across the table.   The safe wet, dear?   Not many things better than a drink of milk.   Would you like to show Bob the farm?   It's too hot, Mrs Wort. Later, eh?   Later, Bob?   I should have a lay-down.   The best treatment is to keep moving. He frowned, then shrugged. May as well.

So I took him into the garden.   Orchard?   Mr McKenzie-Dart's. Do you like peaches? We'd have to be careful.   Crime, retribution and salvation. He hoisted me into a tree and I dropped peaches to him, and when his arms were full he stretched on the grass and ate them, sometimes lobbing pits at me, and I, a fussier peach-eater, flicked skins accurately but did not dare hit him with stones after one had struck his neck. A faint, exhausted hen cackle made him sit up and lick his lips. We heard Dad and Jack call their farewells.   The old roosters are back.   Yes, I said. He stood up.   I'll be off now. Say thanks and goodbye for me.   You're not coming back? No, I'll get the swag and be off.   You're not staying for tea? Aren't you hungry?   Matter of fact I am.   We'll have cold lamb and salad.   Ugh. Chicken's what I fancy.   We had one at Christmas.   I bet you did.   I climbed down.   He was staring at two hens a few trees away.   How would you like to get me a bird?   They're Mr McKenzie-Dart's.   He'd never miss them. District's full of foxes.   I couldn't.   Bit scared, eh? They're not mine.   It must be five so I'll be off. There's a patch of scrub a half mile down the road, I'll make for it. There's a trough there. You know it, eh? I'll be there with the big billy. Chook-chook-chook-chook. I watched him climb through the rails. I walked to where the fowls had been and looked for eggs.

So . . . I turned and almost fell. Mrs McKenzie-Dart. The tallest woman in the country. Wearing a wide straw hat over her narrowed eyes, big mouth and long floral dress. So you've been having a feast. And a most unsavoury man. As though I'd eaten him. As though my gulp of fear a belch of indigestion. Well now. The birds would have eaten them. She pushed her hat back a little, widened her eyes, pursed her lips. Not that that excuses you from not asking. I shook my head. Wind flapped her fat, rustled leaves, made fruit fall. You have only to ask, you know that, don't you? I knew that. I knew that I had only to ask for fruit, drinks, cake or even ice blocks from her refrigerator and she would give what I asked for. She turned to go. And by the way, that man, he lifted you into the tree. You must never let men, strangers, especially his kind, touch you like that. She bent towards me, eyes wider still, hands on hips, and sang, or rather chanted, My mother said I never should, play with the gypsies in the wood. And she left me. Gypsies? play? wood? what was she on about? Sun had got her. I ran towards home then doubled back to where Bob had disappeared, slipped through the rails, ran down the track until I could see where his swag had been. Then the heat took me and I lurched into the pines and dropped to rest. The heat. Sometimes gusts overwhelmed the resin and brought smells of woolfat and dag from shed and yards and something dead. Mr McK-D? Bob walked along the road towards the scrub. Perhaps he was already there with his big billy waiting for the fowl for which he'd need fire and a fire on such a day would turn the country black therefore I shouldn't go to him; also, there were the gypsies playing in the wood. Still, when I felt better I returned to the orchard, stalked a hen, grabbed it, stuffed it into a sugarbag and set off. And was only two hundred yards along the road when McKenzie-Dart drove up alongside me, opened the door and said, Get in boy. He turned the car and drove towards town with me every now and then squeaking, What is it, Mr McKenzie-Zart, where are we going, Mr McKenzie-Fart, are we? and so on, and hoping, begging the bird to be still and silent, which it did, and we stopped outside the police station. Of dark, eighties brick and lichened slate. I'd never been in one before. I was awed but not terrified. McKenzie-Dart took the bag and limped alongside me into an enormous room which reminded me of a school. He spoke to the policeman at a desk, then pushed me through a door into a small room with a bench and a high ceiling and closed the doors. I heard his voice raised and his steps approach the door, halt, then go away. I pressed against the door and listened. Dead . . . respect . . . thief killed it . . . only a kid . . . criminal of tomorrow . . . vicious . . . vagrant . . . leave him . . . firmness. Someone left the room. I sat on the bench. The door opened. The policeman said, What have you to say for yourself? He's pretty angry. And the bird dead. I howled and swore I hadn't killed it. Shut up. Grabbed my shoulder, shook me. Did he touch you? He got me into the car. He did it in the car? What did he say? Nothing, he just drove. Drove where? Here. He shook again so hard something slopped in my throat. I'm asking about the swagman, not McKenzie-Dart. I told him everything, more than twice. So the man had put you up to it, the livestock stealing. I hadn't regarded it as that, in fact it took a while to work in, livestock stealing, it sounded reform school stuff. Jesus it's hot. I stared at my feet. Jesus it's hot. I didn't like his language, I thought it pretty filthy. Then he shook me again. I said Jesus it's hot. I looked at him. Does it always get as hot here? Yes. Come here. He pushed me into a cupboard and closed the door. I thought of rats and insects, paper dust and glue and, after a while, suffocation. Then the door opened. Come out. Mr McKenzie-Dart limped into the room, saw me, stared, and said Ha, and I was going to say hello or something when the phone rang and the policeman held it out to him and he took it and said Yes, yes, on my way. Yes, and tell Wort to collect his son from the police station, oh, yes, right away. No. Look I'll bring the boy. You'll need his father there. By now the policeman was standing at attention, overruled by McK-D's manner. I, too, had responded. To both. Like a schoolboy before headmaster and inspector. He then told us about the fire. The policeman said he would get things organized in the town. Good. Was this his first country posting? Yes, but he knew the procedure.

I followed McK-D to his car. I expected him to leap inside and drive off furiously with horn blaring; however we went sedately through town. He asked me if I was sore. No. Then how many did you get? Get? Straps. None. What did he do, the constable? Put me in a cupboard. My God. And then he drove faster. He drove with the bucket seat set well back so that his arms were almost straight and I didn't like this style because I felt he could easily sweep out and hit me. Damn, I forgot the bird. And I flinched. Then we drove over the hill outside the town and saw the fire, a few miles away. A few minutes later I could smell smoke. By the time we reached the farm I had coughed a few times. He let me out at the gate and I ran home. Mum was filling buckets and soaking blankets, Dad was fighting the fire and bro was closing the windows. Mum said, You wait till after, and put me to making sandwiches. Then bro and I set the ladder against the house, stuffed the downpipes with rags and bucketed water into the gutters. Stung by ashes and cinders we shouted at the smoke, and occasionally glimpsed orange sun. Sometimes he abused me for having stolen the chicken, and said I was sure to go to the boys' home at Parramatta.

By this time we had the ladder against the bricks of the kitchen chimney. Bro was about $3\frac{7}{8}$ inches taller than I, and very impressive he looked, one shoe on the ladder, one on the roof, and back to the bricks. There is a way out for you, he said. I'm finished. No you're not. You are if you don't do what I say. You can go and save the McKenzie-Darts and get yourself a bit burnt, and get a Sunbeam from the paper and a

40

Chuckler prize from the wireless and maybe something from the King—ooooor, you can fall off the roof and break your arms and head. It'd hurt. You want me to get hurt. I'm trying to keep you out of Parramatta. I looked at the ground, swayed, saw myself all broken, blood guggling into a stain like red velvet, and climbed down. Bro remained against the chimney, like a noble midget refusing to abandon his ark. Still, the falling and getting burnt advice apart, the suggestions had merit. I went to the big house to see if it was burning. It looked very safe; there were buckets of water everywhere, wet blankets, windows were closed and Mrs McKenzie-Dart on the tractor was chewing up a break with the rotary hoe. When I saw her determination I hid behind a tree. No low gear for her, she must have been in top. She had gone through lawn, flower beds, part of the vegetable garden, ripped out the side of the tennis court, gone wider and cut up the paddock outside the fence so that her pattern of salvation was something like a squashed eight. And she was wearing a wet, knitted cap, gum boots and a dripping overcoat. Her face was dirty and her teeth were out. I saw them on the tractor's radiator cap.

So I left her to it, went down to the road, and along to where I thought the fire was being fought. There was less smoke than when I was on the roof, so I started to run thinking, I've missed it, missed it, bugger, bugger, when, suddenly the country to my left was black, two dead trees were burning like flares, hot ash and cinders fell on me, I heard cracks like gunshots, a few of the blackened things piled along the fence bleated, snapping fence wires twanged, darkness swept over, and I fell. I remembered that I should get onto burnt ground or lie on the road if it is gravel or dirt, but never on tar because I'd stick to it and fry. So I lay on the road despite the gravel which had torn into my hands and knees. Then the heat and smoke went elsewhere and I was able to return the way I had come. I couldn't see the houses for smoke. I jogged on, sobbing, my face sticky with black paste. When I reached the gate the town fire truck with full tank and a dozen men aboard backed slowly up the rise towards me. A man jumped off and ran to me saying, We buggered the gearbox, are you all right? and rolled me in a wet blanket. I heard the truck pass, shouts, things breaking. Swagged in the wet smelly blanket I heard Mrs McKenzie-Dart chanting, My mother said I never should . . . over the tractor roar, I saw the man holding me become Bob the swaggie, the chicken struggled between my knees, I shitted myself, the man pinioned me, I was like a small roll of lumpy carpet, he held my head up and my shit ran down my legs, he turned me upside down and my shit ran down to my head, his face changed to the policeman's and I fainted.

That fixed you, he shouted as he unrolled me, Poo! as he held his fat nose on his young fat face with wide staring eyes under a hairless head. Then he ran off through the hole in the fence the truck had made. I shook with great shivers in my soot and shit and was there I don't know how long until Mum ran down and took me to the house. She put me in the bath and left me to soak while she took sandwiches to the firemen. The wind had died. I steamed in carbolic water. Heavy drops of rain slammed onto the roof.

I got out of the bath and watched the sooty rain. Smoky roofs and walls streaked clean. Our blocked gutters overflowed. Ashed, muddy water coursed down paths. The rain eased and the sound became a gentle hissing.

We left McKenzie-Dart the following week.

The train has stopped, it refuses to meet the station, the signalman has hanged himself from the green arm, the fireman is burning the driver, in the refreshment room the waitress boils in the urn, in the yard Dad is surrounded by a pack of hounds. In the next carriage soldiers walk the corridor looking for the Nosmokings, underground the coalmine burns, in the mountain the cavern collapses, our suitcase hinges snap, the ropes fray round our boxes, I shake in a wet shitty blanket.

This is our compartment in the carriage of the train taking us to the station with a yard wherein our father waits. And I am certain that he is not going to take us to the new place because already he has fallen out with the owner. My father is an Anglo though he has been in this country since the age of five. One day his unnatural affection for things English will turn unnaturally sour. My bro asked Mum, What's the difference between simple and compound interest? Money, dear, borrowing, it costs you more one way than the other. He went back to his studies. We have the compartment to ourselves. On the corridor windows are no smoking labels. Nosmoking; nos moking; nosm oking; quarantining labels; for the other compartments are quite crowded. Or we are refugees from Europe, the Nosmokings, and we paid for the space with jewellery and heirlooms; or we are being interned for the duration of what is to come; perhaps as mobile internees too dangerous to let loiter. We have been accused and found guilty of harrying the English. Dad: Your Honour, I am an Englishman. Judge: You are a pimple on any Englishman. Then I am an English pimple. Then, sir, you are green. Meadow green your Honour. Irish and alien, sir. At least I am not a blackhead. How dare you. I sentence you to be squeezed. There'll always be an England, etcetera.

The train pulls in to the station. Dad is on the platform. All smiles. We leave the train and our luggage does not burst. In the yard is the Essex with a borrowed trailer. I am allowed to ride in the trailer. The town has a pub and twenty buildings. We drive east, towards the coast. Trees give way to scrub. The road is sealed. The land is poor. We turn onto a dirt road. We have come nine miles from the station. The farm is at the head of a small valley. There is little grass and what there is is grey. A paddock of stunted millet and one of short maize. Our house is half a mile from the homestead and between them is a fallen house surrounded by dead lemon trees. Yards and sheds are close to our place, a bleached grey house with four

43

rooms. On the veranda beside table and chairs with beer and lemonade wait the owner Tom Green, a thin fifty-year-old Englishman and his thin wife.

Introductions. I wanted to look at the boards but made myself look up.

You got here.

Yes, you got Herr Nosmoking, member of the travelling Nosmokings, entrants in The Daily News Travelling Family Contest, and by the look of your property you'll soon be contesting yourself. Last week we saw the Harold Pounds who flew to an outback mine to look at schists, returned to the city by train, bought a new Buick, travelled to the mountains four consecutive mornings, returned each evening, on the fifth day went south to see a stuffed horse: they dead heated with: the Bill Smiths with: 30 hours on the big dipper, 11 in buses, and 50 in trains.

Tom Green declared: I've got a plan for this property and I've got the money to see it through. Mrs Green said, We're going to replace the lemons. Mr Green said, It's not good land but there's plenty of it. Mrs Green said, And we've a plan. Dad said (it being his turn), The true English spirit. Tom Green said, Anyone with a mind to could do it. Mrs Green said, What's this true English spirit? Tom Green said, The land was cheap, there's plenty of it, and I've a bit of money. Dad said, Only an Englishman would attempt it. The Greens said, Um.

Beside the fallen house I said to my bro, We won't be here long, it's too far from school.   You're beaten before you start. If we can't get to school we'll do it correspondence.   I found two bottles and broke them. Correspondence lessons would mean never leaving the farm. I said, Wouldn't you like to be back in the city?   No, I like the country. You learn things. Not as much as in the city.   When you live with your boss you see how he does things.   So what.   And I went to a broken sofa to get its springs.   What do you mean you see how things are done?   How he decides, how he gives orders,

44

that sort of thing. I was astounded. Is Dad like that? Yes, he watches all the time, but I think he likes the idea of English bosses too much. I'm going to be a boss. That's a good idea, but it's still a long way to school. School's here. I mean our public school, the primary. That's an extra. Who says so? Uncle Fred. You couldn't argue against Uncle Fred. He had money. He saved us whenever disaster threatened. Did he tell you about correspondence lessons? He took them himself. Does he watch English bosses? He's English and he's a boss, stupid. I know that. I know he fixes fun machines, but does he watch other bosses, funny bosses? You wanna fight? A couple of weeks ago I heard a man say he was going to get Fred. He's a poker machine gangster, and he said his boys were going to rub him out. Liar. You be careful, brother, because the man asked me if I wanted any protection. You stupid dogshit liar. You just wait. Tell your gangster where to find me. O.K., and then I'll tell Dad to look in the dam. You're a cinch for Parramatta, then Long Bay. If I get the rope collar you'll get the wooden waistcoat. You're nuts. He knelt and pulled out bits of metal from under a plank. I thought hard. I pulled a face and made him look up. I'm nuts; then, with gangster face snarled, And on the matter of nuts, what happened to my share of the twenty-pound almond haul? Eh? Ah you mean the almonds. Thought I'd forgotten, uh? They weren't any good. But you sold them. Sixpence a pound they were. I was lucky to get threepence. Liar! He scrambled to his feet. I ran backwards. 20 by 6 is . . . 120, ten bob. Five bob it came to and half that is 2/6 and 6d of that is for me for having the idea. Cheat. Anyhow, I'll take the 2/6 now. You can't. I invested it. Investment was very mysterious, it meant you did without in order to have much more in fifty years; it was to do with bookkeeping, credit, debit, cash not in hand and ledgers. I knew I'd seen the last of my money. How did you invest it? In a muscovy. The one we ate? Yes. It died, and I gave it to Mum. It died and we ate it? A heart attack. It dropped and we ate it? Died and I axed it. I'm going to tell. You do and everytime you see a duck you'll vomit. Tom Green had a flock and I'd seen them moments ago, and this recollection was enough to raise a stomach gob, so I went away, round the fallen house and climbed onto the broken cart on the flattened dunny and surveyed the dreary scene of ruin, poor country, industrious brother, marauding ducks, the three-legged pig scratching itself against a dead lemon, the frightening gander swaggering towards me, and I could not see the farm ever becoming the paradise described by Tom Green, with pasture and cultivation, windbreaks and dams, contours and copses, and wombats, wallabies, flowers and trees in thirty acres of gully. Nor could I see us, each morning, cycling along the narrow dirt road to the wider dirt road to catch the school bus, and in the afternoons, leaving the school bus to take the bike from under the wooden lean-to and ride the grid home; bro on the saddle, me on the bar, over the culvert, over the ford, on grey dirt and white gravel to work in the garden and fowl run, to listen if lucky to serials, to help in the bails, to have tea, rote learn, write exercises and read, and go to bed. On this grey farm in poor country near a town with a picture house where matinees showed Tom Mix, Jane and Tarzan, Judy Garland, Dad and Dave and serials without end if Dad decided to drive to town on Saturdays. But never on Sundays. So we were out of the grasp of Sunday school, a penalty whichever way you looked at it because if you were in town you endured it and if you were beyond its reach you were out of town.

In the tilted cart on the flattened dunny. In the sun. Swaggering gander. Bro scratching for metal. I recalled newsreels of King and family, of kings and families, refugees, things burning in Germany, might of the Navy, aerial dogfights, Prime Minister, dog rescued from drain, suicide winched up a cliff, riot in girls' home, air raid precautions. The tilted cart about to slide under the waves with the battleship of the fallen house, Abandon, abandon ship, the bro swims clear of

46

the wreckage. A couple of miles away a destroyer spumes to the rescue. I blinked. Had I entered the newsreel?

Bro carried a bucket towards our house. The gander stepped away. The destroyer became a plume of dust, now less than a mile off, not travelling so fast as had at first seemed, but lots of dust, more than one plume, at least two, as though trucks raced side by side, a dozen wheels or more, onto the treeless stretch. It is one truck, an odd-looking greeny vehicle, a *tank*, gee, a tank, here, is it war or practice for war? It races past the gate to the farm, if it goes much further it will have to demonstrate its off-the-road qualities. It goes on and suddenly its cloud is monstrous as wheels lock, slide and angle, it won't be able to stop, it won't; it stops; the dust hides it. Bro drops his bucket and runs to the road. The tank reverses from the dust, turns, drives to the gate and stops. It is not a tank but some sort of armoured transport. Men appear and call to bro, who opens the gate for the vehicle which then enters. The Germans are here already. I crouch in the cart and watch my mad brother talk to the men in the cabin. However he cannot speak German nor does he throw up his hands in surrender; instead an arm appears from the window and gives him something; then doors open and men climb down, one of them wearing a familiar steel helmet, one of ours. Mum walks towards them. The men follow her to the rainwater tank and wash while she returns to the house. I run to them. Mum reappears with towels. More men jump down from the rear. I halt and watch from a distance. Bro waves for me to approach, but I stand off. Suddenly the men are back aboard, the vehicle turns, drives to the road and goes. I stroll over to bro. The men had lost their way, they were on manoeuvres. Bro swaggers, displays an army badge, the sun forever rising. Why didn't you come over—frightened?

I went back to the cart. In half an hour it would be in the shadow of the hill. I threw a stone after the gander, and dispersed the ducks. I lay in the cart in the sun cleaning my fingernails.

The lengthening shadows were the colour of muscats or sea under a cliff, the ducks were gulls, the Greens' house a sunken hulk, the valley a submarine; dead lemon trees kelp, the breeze a current; unbalanced seahorses, prone seapig, school of seacows; the hills are hollow, filled with merpeople; the road is the track of the kraken.

I stumbled from the cart, examined the tracks made by bro's visitors, pissed on them and went in to tea.

Tom Green and William Wort often discussed intra- and inter-state trade, international trade, agreements, embargos, gluts, famines, drought, flood and fire, pestilence and acts of God. The destruction of a cotton crop in Texas by a tornado of mice aroused some scepticism, as did the news of a variety of French wheat said to be bomb-resistant, the progeny of a mating of pig and sheep at Nevertire and the edibility of sausages of pinesawdust, maizemeal and oniondust.

The boy Percy delighted in these conversations, and was often accused by his brother Tom of always hanging around Dad and Tom Green, of snooping, of spying. Percy was always surprised by this latter charge, even when told why: he was learning to be a gangster spy.

One day Percy heard:

Tom Green: You can do what you like with this land.

Father: All it needs is water and fertilizer.

TG: The more it produces the better for us all. A sensible division of prosperity.

F: Pity there aren't more like you, Tom.

TG: With luck we'll set an example.

F: Publicize it.

TG: I wouldn't go so far as that.

F: Word'll get round. Of course some bosses won't like it.

TG: Nor a union or two, because we'll bypass the System.

F: It's a wonder it hasn't been done.

TG: Oh it has. Lots of airy-fairy schemes, dreams, Utopias, Utopia-No-Where.

F: I don't think the Australian character is capable.

TG: Look at the Russians.

F: Communistic.

TG: Kiss my arse or down the salt mine.

There was no rain, the ground cracked, the grey grass became grey dust. The rabbits increased so the poison cart was used. Somehow rabbits died in dams and spoilt the water. Tom Green was angered by a rumour about the army wanting the land for a firing range.

Fred came down.   Jesus, Will, this place is like a desert. All it needs is craters and it's a firing range. Come back to the city.

I've been thinking a change would do us good. But not the city. I read somewhere last week of millions of acres for nothing if you build a house. In the Kimberley.

Jesus, Will, sand, saltbush and solitude. Have you told Mary?

Well, as a matter of fact I haven't yet. Another thing: if I do go up and the land's not what it's made out, I could go to Broome, Darwin, places like that and sell a few of your machines.

To pearlers for their pearls, miners for their gold, squatters for their animals, eh? Give 'em good weight, eh?

No, Fred, not the scales. Those other machines of yours, the g-a-m-b-l-i-n-g machines.

Will, I have six g-a-m-b-l-i-n-g machines. Six is a good number. I don't want them up there.

Your housekeeper's got you where she wants you.

I've got her where I want her so we're equal. If you want to piss off up to the Kimberley don't expect me to mind your family and bring you back.

I could make my fortune up there. There are camels too. There's money in camels.

You've got to leave this farm, it's getting you down. It's the grey dust, it gets in the lungs, clogs the brain. You *go* to the Kimberley. You'll get camel dust and from that camel-trachiosis, the ruin of many a fine Arab singer, not to mention

49

singers from England travelling through the Suez Canal, and singers going from here to there, Melba for instance, had a touch of it in her later years.

There's also the matter of the Jews. They're on the grab again.

What Jews? You leave the Jews alone, Will, they'll eat you, kosher or not. You leave them alone.

They want to take over the Kimberley. I read about it. McKenzie-Dart knew about it. They've asked the government in the West for permission to settle. It's the thin edge of a new Palestine. It means that foreigners are going to pour in and take our heritage; fill it with temples and mosques, grow oranges where they are alien. Grapefruit even. Balls of lemon, orange and green up there in Will Dampier country. Pearl, gold, sandalwood and turtle territory. And the government said yes.

State government, yes. But it's a matter for Canberra. The Commonwealth won't let foreigners into the country, especially for an isolated horror like the Kimberley. Zionists don't want it, they want Palestine. Canberra wants immigrants to be assimilated. You and I are being assimilated, whether we like it or not.

I'll always be an Englishman.

That's your problem.

I never thought I'd hear you say that. There's going to be a war, Fred. There was a war from 1914 until 1918, Fred, much of it fought in the Middle East. The camel was invaluable, it did sterling work for the Empire. Lawrence of Arabia, Fred, you think he ran over dunes in sandshoes? And do you know the camels in this country are in the hands of the Afghans? Asiatic people, Fred, like the Japanese and they've always had an eye on this country, they want it for their teeming millions.

I'll weigh them all.

Flippancy's not the answer. I regard it as my duty to keep the Camel Corps out of the hands of the Afghan.

The Camel Corps disbanded years ago.

You can't fight in the desert without camels. You only need a water bottle, hay, dates and burnous.

If you must go to the Kimberley, open a store and have camels as a sideline and sell to circuses, or hire out for camel safaris.

There's something else.

Go on.

The Government plans to make an inland sea up there, so I'd like to get in early while there's money in camels, get myself established as a cattle man. A channel's going to be dug from the sea. There'll be yachts, Drake's drum, cockles and whelks.

The crocs will get your cows.

Crocodiles?

Yes, they'd come in with the water, get under the house, eat your dogs. You'd have to walk on stilts. And they roar at night. You'd have to keep a ·303 by the door. White ants too. They're worse than in Queensland where I knew a man had an ant hill start under his house, eat through the floor and grow into the room, and he thought, well, they're here so I may as well let them build me a chimney, but of course the ants were every-where and the house fell down.

Onto the crocodile, I suppose.

No crocodiles there. But the best pair of heelers in the state.

I've got to get to the Kimberley, Fred, alone of course, and when I get settled I'll send for the family. I need a break. I've got to get away.

And he went away. Tom Green was annoyed (All our plans, You're chasing a mirage, and so on). Mary and the children returned to the city and stayed with Fred.

In November he wrote to say he was coming back. It was great country, no doubt about it, but no good for the small man. The climate was either dry and abrasive or wet and steamy. They wondered how he would like the city because November had been dry and abrasive and December hot and sticky. Moulds grew on walls, shoes turned green and cockroaches fell from the kitchen ceiling.

Two thousand miles he travelled home and when he arrived he was hardly recognizable. Sandy-blighted, humped like a camel, his skin like camel leather and spotted with skin cancers where clothing had not protected him. Stripped-off he looked like a starved camelopard. Sand. S and. S &. Sampersand. Sam Persand, a pity his name was William Wort. He had a long moustache, a squint, crow's feet, and a bend in his nose as though it had been broken. The pockets above his collarbones had deepened, the left a little more than the right. The skin thin and wrinkled. Those pockets. Percy knew them well. Having been a small child he'd been carried round in them. His mother carried him inside, his father outside. An early life of cavities and projections, womb, nipples, lips and collarbone pockets. A wonder he didn't join the kangaroo totem.

Mary groaned and set about stuffing him with food. For three days he stayed in bed with the blinds half drawn and everyone tiptoeing round, and Fred and his mechanic moved into the yard and worked there, as though William had tetanus and the slightest sound would finish him. On the fourth day he got up and shuffled about in Mary's kimono and on the fifth went downstairs in the evening and sat with Fred in the yard and Percy and Tom lay in bed in the upstairs room and heard them yarning. Sometimes he laughed, a dry chortle sort of sound, and once he went on for ten minutes, the only words he could get out being . . . And then . . . and then I . . . you should have seen them . . . while Fred kept asking, Look, Will, a stout . . . have a glass . . . you sound so dry . . . and Tom fell asleep and Percy listened and saw himself in the shoulder pockets, moving from one to the other as he pleased. William had travelled by train, truck, ship, aeroplane, camel, horse and donkey, worked in a mine, with sheep and cattle, had entered a garden in the desert and left it . . .

52

So the richness of the late 1930s. Rich in human experience, that is, for the late 30s were anything but materially rich. What with scientists devising new khaki and navy dyes for uniforms, extrameat from sawdust and maggot paste, armour from kapok and aluminium foil, radios to be worn in the hair, ways of hardening lead, how to swim for three days and not fall to pieces, how to make soap from skinny corpses, how to make a one million degree bomb and new inks to stop people forging identity cards.

In the Kimberley there was little of this sort of thing.

I set off for the Kimberley twelve years later. Simply to see what was there. The Kimberley had not changed much since my father's trip. He had made it sound rather dull and uneventful. When I got there I realized the strength of his understatements . . .

WILLIAM'S TREK

William took slow trains to Adelaide, stayed a few days then set off for Port Augusta and beyond. His postcards came in batches, as though saved for bulk posting and were sometimes of the All's well, weather fine sort, but generally they informed us of such things as . . . The man beside me has just fainted but we got him round with a nun's barley water, he was starving she said . . . An Abo sat next to me and a shearer told him to get out; I told him to stay; the shearer said I was a —— pom and tried to push both of us out but an old man pulled the cord and the guard took the shearer to First Class . . . Evangelists after me; Mormons, I didn't know they were here . . . Two well dressed young women gave all men buttonholes and leaflets about militia and army . . . Bought Illus. Lond. News today & v. homesick . . . Today I saw a MOSQUE what next! there are only 2 in the country but thin edge of wedge . . . Abos get a poor deal here and am proud English are diff . . . am returning to Adelaide to take ship Fremantle; got

53

lift with Abo shearers in V8; they were doing well and offered to get me job but no; in pub we were ordered out . . . Heard woman blaspheme that Jesus could change colour like lizard . . . Policeman cursed me when I reminded all men are bros . . .

Fred said: I don't like the sound of his trip. Mary said: It'll do him good. Fred: The way he's going he'll join the Salvos. Mary: He's making the trip to clear his mind. Fred: He could have stayed here and cleared his mind. Mary: Well, you know, Fred; distant pastures; don't forget you both came twelve thousand miles to here.

In Perth William applied to an employment agency for work in the Kimberley. The interviewer was a big, suntanned, no-nonsense man who opened up with a speech about the Empire, Boy Scout Movement, Perils red and yellow, Abstinence, Unionism and Defence. William presented himself as an Englishman eager for Kimberley experience, a married man preparing the way for his family, a man well endowed with character references, born in the saddle and lately immured in the vast Eastern wen. The interviewer urged William to bring his family West as soon as possible because the golden West was about to secede from the strike-ridden, Jew-run Commonwealth. Are you with us, Wort? snapped the man. You have come West; now, are you man enough to go North? The Jews wanted the Kimberley but I kept them out. They belong in Palestine where they can be watched. Chew it over, I can spare two minutes.

William recalled his conversations in the East with Fred and others, his adventures on the way to the employment office, the Afghan, railway, camels, family, newsagency, rural, metropolitan, tenant, landlord, Mormon, New Palestine, Empire, menaces, taxation, fishing, rowing, swimming, desert, gardening, shoe-repairing and other questions. The interviewer strode from the office with folders of applications, commands, confidential memos, shopping lists and wills under his arm. William wondered what he was doing in Perth. He looked round for Mary, heard a tarnished bugle blow, saw the flag at half-mast and thought, No. (At least one hopes he thought this way.) He answered the questions concerning Jews, Afghans, camels, Mormons and so on with: But they don't bother me. Then he heard Fred announce: I knew you'd be back. So William thought he may as well give the Kimberley a go.

He told the interviewer that he was eager to go North, especially if fares were paid. The interviewer, whilst disappointed, was prepared to arrange this. William elaborated on his earlier, all too briefly-listed talents; his mechanical, agricultural and office abilities; he demonstrated his health and strength by lifting one-handed, a heavy chair by the leg. The interviewer sniffed, removed his coat, dislocated both his shoulders, took a piece of rope from a desk drawer and tied a running bowline. William stood on his head and slowly pushed himself from the floor. The interviewer bent over backwards and whipped his ankles with the rope. William tried to remember shipping and railway timetables and wondered if the interviewer would produce a revolver if he ran away. The interviewer made a hangman's noose. William did several one-legged squats. A pigeon alighted on the window sill and the interviewer picked it up. My God he's going to eat it. Raw. But the man removed a small cylinder from the bird's leg. It's a sad day when you can't trust the post-office—where are you staying? (In a telegram tent with money-order stretcher, with honeyed stamps for breakfast.) In a telegram—, began William, Sorry, I'm at the Workingman's Palace. Get out of there immediately—it may already be too late! It has an evil reputation and everyone's watched.

William worded a telegram to Fred. Wire fare care Perth GPO Kimberley unsatisfactory. He hummed the opening bars of an American spiritual, Going Home. The interviewer threw the pigeon out the window. The door opened and his secretary handed him a file. The tang of here is sharp and malignant, muttered William, So fine it chokes, so coarse it cuts, I must away to the East and a new business from scratch, or a minor partnership with Fred, the loving bosom of Mary and the adorable embrace of my children.

The interviewer reset his shoulders and sat at his desk. Orebul Downs, he said, is the place for you. Kimberleys. Sheep, cattle, wonderful, loyal family, excellent climate, the best of correspondence education for children, flying doctor within hours, courage, pioneering and Opening up the North. House cows and garden to tend. Right? And William, to his immediate horror, answered Yes. Pride drove him towards the lions of the Kimberley. A satisfactory berth was available aboard a ship from Fremantle. However, he refused to move from the Workingman's Palace where the shared rooms were clean and tolerable, the cabbagie food bearable (and a little like Home) and the tariff low. The interviewer, whilst regretting William's decision, thought him man enough to cope with Palace dissidents.

William left the office and went straight to the Fremantle Cemetery for the burial of a man who had died in the Palace. Sandy blight, scurvy and dissipation. The sea, William guessed, was blue, fisherman fished, sharks ate, lobsters gnawed, trains sped East over the desert, swagmen swagged, hags hagged, the bottom held, time swaged and yes, we have no bananas. A fellow-mourner afterwards described Orebul Downs: Terrain sunbaked in Summer, sometimes frozen in Winter, bathed in minimal rain, where hateful grasses grew sparsely among stones, where rabbit warrens led to the mountain king, salt patches dazzled and burnt the sight and salted beef on the hoof, where sheep grew steely wool so magnetized it could not be removed. And so on. Such as: William, the ill-fated cameleers Burke and Wills, the King taking the Salute, the Australian Workers' Union, universal suffrage, drums along the Congo, Darwin or Cape Horn, Mr Chamberlain, Mr Menzies KC, H. G. Wells, the polar ice caps, the Royal Show, colostrum, cabbages and lobsters, Henry Ford, the Dalai

Lama, the China-Japan war, Guernica, 5,000 dead in cyclone, Haile Selassie, the quintessence of family life, and fish and chips in Fremantle.

William purchased a brown pith-helmet, a water bottle, a canvas holdall and took ship for Broome, 1,500 miles to the North. Twenty-foot tides, pearls, turtles, sharks and shanties. Passengers, stores and horses for ports as far as Derby, then back again with cattle.

Or so we were led to believe. For he was falling out of the postcard habit. I suppose the ship could have gone on to Timor and he with it, for now and then even now he mentions the Indies and ponies. The ship stopped at Carnarvon, Onslow and Cossack. Farther and farther from Fremantle, from the East, from home. From Onslow he sent a postcard: It will be a testing time. Bugger him, said Fred to Mary, if only he'd get himself arrested and deported—or whatever they do up there—and sent home.

I suppose he was lucky to get beyond Onslow because as the horses were being driven onto the jetty there was trouble and two went into the sea, William with them, and someone shouted shark, and William mounted one and just as he was hauled into a lifeboat a shark took the horse, a valuable one, and William was cursed by the owner for selfishness. It was all on the postcard Fred received, together with an anonymous pencilled PS under the address: If he can't take it, take him back to the city. Fred wired fifty pounds to the next port of call but it arrived too late and was returned to him.

Broome. He did not really believe it. Luggers, diving suits, Japanese, Koepangers, Malays, Chinese, Binghis, Manxmen, Scots, Tasmanians, Texans, Englishmen, Bretons, Capetowners, and so many others he thought he was being sent up. Glaring heat, mudflats, big hats, long hair, short hair, frizzy hair. The lot. Transport for Orebul Downs within the week. After a few days hanging round he met a man with an aeroplane. The pilot was bound for Darwin. Would William like a lift? Really? very grateful etc. He saw the plane and wanted to change his mind. It was a sort of old Walrus amphibian. He did not mind a biplane provided the wings stuck out from the fuselage, but this one had its wings stacked above it, as though by afterthought. The propeller of the single engine seemed horribly close to the passenger cockpit. The top wing was fastened to the bottom wing by bits of stick and wire. What's all that between the wings? he asked the pilot. Stays and struts, he said seizing his arm. You get a beautiful view through them, a glorious pattern of lines against blue, like these modern paintings, but with the wind of course, ha-ha. Could I sit in front, asked William, Away from the engine and noise? Afraid not, said the pilot, I may want you to do something to the engine, besides, the controls are up front and that's where I've got to be. Have another drink? Thank you, but do you think we should? I certainly do, there's a third of a bottle yet. Is this your first trip up here? asked William. Yes, a Singapore company, Imperial Nippon, want me to have a look at some country they're interested in, the clever devils—what did you say your line was? Camels and gardening. Very good. Wasn't there something else? To have a look at some land, to see if it's worthwhile. A few of us are thinking of settling. Jolly good. Now I'll show you how to start the engine, the magic word is contact! He climbed onto the fuselage, grabbed the propeller and turned it. Me! cried William, You mean I'm to do that? Wind it? Quite simple, William. There's no need to move away, it won't start till I set my controls. I've seen it done in films, said William, And I've seen men chopped. Nimbleness, William, that's all.

They took off at dawn. The pilot wore leather jacket, helmet, goggles and a long yellow scarf William thought was bound to get caught in the propeller and pull his head off, provided the blades didn't cut into his own head. William wore his navy blue suit, helmet, goggles and a long red roller towel which the pilot thought very jolly and excellent for not showing blood, ha-ha. They made repeated passes over particular stretches of coast, sometimes at two thousand feet, often at twenty. William made notes and marked maps. He didn't like their sea landings because of sharks and he wasn't keen on the land because of trees, stones and animals. Two days later they landed on what they thought was Orebul Downs, where they spent the night playing cards with the beautiful black mistress of Gumption Springs. Her husband was thirty or even seventy miles away tracking a white dingo which the previous week had stolen his new riding boots as he swam in a dam. She was shuffling at dawn, when, suddenly, she dropped her cards, drew her revolver and shouted Get 'em up. William fell backwards, the pilot raised his hands, the door opened and a respectable jackeroo stepped through with hands high. William and the pilot stood and were introduced to: MISTER Robert Pelman, my husband's new jackeroo who has been sent back to spy on me. Where's Charlie?   Charlie, shouted Mr Pelman, and they heard someone sliding down the roof. Charlie clumped over the veranda and entered. He was six and a half feet tall, straight backed, brown as leather, looked very light footed, tripped over the carpet, looked up at her and said, Martha, I'm ashamed to say I thought you had a flying gentleman caller. Indeed, she said, These gentlemen, aviators, just happened to be passing over. They then drank three bottles of rum. Before going to the plane Charlie presented them with thirty pounds of steak in two pieces, which William hung from hooks each side of his cockpit. The hosts returned to the homestead. As the airmen climbed aboard they heard shots. Mr and Mrs Territory and Mr Pelman came onto the veranda and waved farewell.

Later that morning, as they flew low over a billabong they went through a flock of duck, thud thud, and the engine missed, backfired, the plane lurched as the pilot grabbed at a duck. The engine stopped, William opened his eyes, saw two ducks caught in the wing wires, pulled them into his cockpit, fastened his belt, looked over the side, saw the meat, fainted and came to as the plane braked in a raft of water lilies. They cleaned the engine of other ducks, started the engine and motored to the shore, where they ate roast duck, baked lily roots, drank rum and fell asleep. For the evening meal they had duck soup, fried duck and watered rum. The next day they adjusted the engine, swam and played cards. Our idyll must end at dawn, said the pilot. It already has, said William, slapping at flies. The Territorys' meat, it'll crawl away with the plane if we're not careful. Jugged beef, said the pilot. The maggots are in my cockpit, said William. They'll blow away old chum, make us a wriggly slipstream, an act of God to anyone below.

They took off at dawn (again). Five hours later, the pilot slapped the side of the fuselage, pointed down then dived low over homestead, buildings, yards, patches of green and an airstrip, in a wide brown valley ringed with low hills. Dogs and sheep ran all over the place. A man ran from the house, pointed something at the plane, the pilot banked hard right, William hit his head on the mattock handle and read OREBUL DOWNS painted in big white letters across two roofs. He saw something falling, a piece of meat, it hit the ground and dust ringed it. When they made their second pass they saw two figures struggling towards the homestead. William dropped the rest of the meat. The pilot flew down a third time for a closer look at the airstrip. William stared. Had he come across the final resting place of Australian camels? He saw a great heap of bones, piled high in beautiful architecture.

As they taxied along the strip a station hand galloped over and directed them to a building near the homestead. He was a great horseman. He circled the plane. He went under the wings. William thought he'd go through them. He galloped ahead, turned tight, came head on. The pilot stalled. William stared at the heap of bones a few hundred yards away. The pilot shouted at the horseman who shouted that the dogs were upset and unless calmed would savage the newcomers. The pilot apologized and said he liked dogs. The heat was dreadful, William got out, removed his borrowed flying clothes, put on coat and pith-helmet, took up his holdall and walked beside the pilot to the manager's quarters. The horseman was Ted, who said the plane looked pretty good, hoped the boss had missed, and not to worry. Nothing like ground fire to sharpen the senses, said the pilot. You were lucky, replied Ted, The first shot's always a warner. He'd have got you with the second only his missus grabbed him. It's best to radio beforehand. He always shoots at strangers; he's worried about the reds. And who isn't? But we're all mates here.

William kept looking over his shoulder at the heap of bones. Fallen cathedral of Australian deserta. Oh shame. O ossuary of self. Ossiferous earth. What mortality there must have been. Tigris, Mecca, Babylon, Alexandria. From Cairo I rode to Ghizeh to visit pyramids, those places of sepulchre, and now I come to Orebul Downs to your resting place. *Le Chameau, par sa sobriété et son endurance, est l'animal le plus utile au desert. Le roi du desert.* Dromedary, with your single hump (now gone the way of fat and flesh), Bactrian, with your two (gone twice the way of all fat and flesh), I come to save your kind from the Afghan.

He tripped. Watch it, mate, said Ted. He had tripped over a bone. He stumbled sideways, aghast. I like your hat, mate, said Ted, But you ought to tilt it back and shade your neck. The bone, cried William, staring. Everywhere, said Ted, Like a sandblow I knew on the coast, used to move a chain every breeze, and bones you never saw the like, wombats big as cows, roos like giraffes and Professor Jones with his emu walk pulling bones from dunes like it was a great sandy jaw he was de-toothing, scratching with trowel, brushing with brush, numbering each bone, he didn't pay much, but by the hour, so we used to let the bones disappear. You might have heard of Ossie Cocsiks (and it was too, on the dangle it was six, and he'd done all kinds of peculiar things to get that way), well Os died when a giant skull hit his head: the question was had it rolled down the slope or had the Prof tossed it at Os? The Prof's idea was that the Nor-West had been a great garden

61

until the blacks unbalanced things (with their burning and hunting ways) and made a deal with the black Dutchmen of the Indies and created a precedent of magnitudinous disloyalty. They let the Dutchmen take sandalwood, *bêche-de-mer*, and pearls in return for the Dutchmen's dogs. Which: wirrigul, warrigul, warrigal, worrigol, worigull or feral canis. Or dingo. So the wily Javanese and Timorese exploited our precious pearls and so on and left us with what became known us the wolf of the antipodes, scourge of the kangaroo, emu, bandicoot and so on. Had the marsupials and emu not been worried by the dingo there would be many more today. There would be many more blacks to hunt them. There would therefore be a great quantity of reasonable labour; there would be marsupials etc. in sufficient numbers to be worth the while as commercial items. And you may ask me, What is this shit you are on about? To which I say, hear me but do not smear me.

Anyway, the Professor and Os had words and the latter was afterwards found with his head broken, encased within the skull of a giant roo which was, you might say, a reversal of what generally pertains, that is, the situation of the kangaroo within OUR heads, the kangaroo being our unique creature, our country's contribution of bizarrery to the universal zoo —Oops, up you get. Ted dismounted.

For William had tripped yet again, on a bone. On all fours he looked under his left armpit at what had brought him down. His bag lay in the dust, the pith-helmet also.

You all right? asked Ted, anxiously. Here, keep the sun off. He replaced William's helmet. William watched the pilot enter a shed a couple of hundred yards away. He looked at the amphibian, hundreds of yards behind. It began melting in the heat, wings drooped, spread wide. Suddenly it rose, grew into a slender tower of narrow wings, struts and wires, it bounced as though hiccuping, leant to right then left, collapsed into horizontality. The bone that had felled him joined ends, straightened, twitched a couple of inches. The great mound of bones, the Cathedral, the ossuary, had vanished. He stretched out in the dirt, off fours; on front, tips of shoes, right side of face, exhaling air, blowing craters in the dust, helmet off head again. Hey, Will, cried Ted, You can't lie there. Here, keep your hat on. Here, I'll give you a haul up. No? Your head's bad? Wait a sec.

Bones, aeroplanes, heat, Professor Jones, Hands up, said Mrs Territory, You're wearing my husband's boots, you dingo, you swam here from Timor and you thought you'd swim back eh, with his new boots eh, when you're not half the man he is, why the tops come all the way to your elbows, on him they'd come to your wrists; all the way to Timor eh, well I'm going to let you have the steak; get it into you, go on, the lot, and if you bring it up you'll lap it up, how's it feel down there, like triplets eh, and you thought you were going to put it into me eh, well you're not putting it in me again when I've got Charlie and MR PELMAN, flying doctor, vet, pilot, several kinds of inspectors and the KING.

Here y'are Will, said Ted. Water splashed on his face. He was in shade. Ted spun the umbrella. Twirling shadows of rib-tips. William groaned. Stop. You took a turn, said Ted, Here have a swig, take your time, the boss is not going any-where.

Now, as I was telling you. The kangaroo has a special place in our heads. He is on our stamps, fitting because of the way he stamps his tail on the ground when irritated by something important as for example, a governor-general, prime minister, owner, or union rep. He is on our coins, often shaping up to the emu like he wants the emu's egg for his pouch and the emu saying what you are after's unnatural. He is on the national coat of arms, a proper dexter supporting the shield, with emu proper sinister, the lot on a platform in a wattle, so he's a kind of tree kangaroo. New South Wales, now, has a shield supported by SINISTER kangaroo with dexter lion rampant, both gold. Victoria has an azure shield with white stars, supported by a couple of sheilas, one with a bit of bare tit and holding like it was the end of your prick a cornucopia, or it

63

could be she's scratching the head of a swan, bringing him on, giving the old cob a tickle, and you know what happened to that Leda sheila who got stuffed by a swan—

A swan? said William through his fingers.

—Some shrewdie passing himself off as god-in-a-swan. Skinned himself a swan, dressed himself up and did her in the rushes; he was clever all right, liked a bit of fancy dress, fond of the old dick, and knew a thing about physiology in that he water-cooled his balls—

Where's the pilot? asked William, Don't let him go.

—Anyhow, on top of this Victorian shield is a kangaroo from the chest up, holding what looks like a golden bird cage which is really a crown. Our state, Western A, hasn't got an official coat of arms. And what there is hasn't a single roo, nor even a roo paw, and they think they make up for this short-coming—nay, this lamentable lack—BY using a black swan.

Black swan, eh? Leda there, too?

William, I find such remarks atrocious. Poor taste. JESUS if I ever found a black up a white woman I'd have his feathers for pipe cleaners; *shit*, I'd have his skin for a tobacco pouch. Let me give you a little advice: the blacks up here are fiends incarnate, fiends in blackface, indeed. It's the food they eat. They fuck themselves noncomposmentis, which means every year there are more of them—

Ten minutes ago you said that if there were more the Kimberley would be a better place.

William, have you got a black woman somewhere?

My wife and children live in Sydney. I am an Englishman.

So was William Dampier, the first Englishman to touch these parts—geographic parts primarily—but also the velvet. And did not William Dampier, though a buccaneer, write in his journal in the 1690s of the blacks that they were: The miserablest people in the world. The Hodmadods of Monomatapa, though a nasty people, yet for wealth are gentlemen to these. Did he not?

I don't know.

William, don't get up, rest a while. Will, get off your hands and knees, you'll break the umbrella, it's the manager's. Stop and have a blow won't you? I love a yarn.

I'm dying of heat, exhaustion, flies and bones. Stop. No, no, go on, the water's nice. Splash a drop more. Don't let the pilot go, will you.

The Kimberley region, Will, was named for the Earl of Kimberley, a Colonial Secretary; there are 120,000 square miles, of fertile beauty and arid ugliness, of droughts and sweeping rains, of fifteen to fifty inches the year, hot as hell, cold as charity, of iron and gold, of mountains you can't get through and plains you can billiard on—Will, stop. This is pioneer country, you don't go on your hands and knees—

Then enough of the tourist gab. Hey—get off. Off I say, I'm not a horse.

Orebul Downs was founded fifty years ago, it is steeped in history and tradition, and we are making a ceremonial entry.

So William went on, dragging holdall and coat, with Ted astride holding the umbrella, and soon his hands and knees bled, and flies crawled in ears, mouth and eyes, and as he neared the shed he passed near a swarm of flies over what he guessed to be a piece of meat, and when Ted lurched on his back he lost his sun helmet and a fly crawled inside his shirt and buzzed against his wet chest. He growled and reared. Ted sprang off and ran away with the umbrella. William managed to stand. He tottered into the shed. At last, William, he heard the pilot say. Jesus, mate, you had a fall? said another. He could not see a thing. Someone helped him into a chair. William, this is Mr Eden, the manager. A bald, thick-set man, who asked, Water? and handed him a glass. The shed had a concrete floor, desk, rows of pigeon holes and several cane chairs. William drank his rum and fell asleep.

Mr Eden shook him awake. I'll take you to your quarters, said Mr Eden. $\frac{1}{4}$s, $\frac{1}{4}$s? hind$\frac{1}{4}$s of steak, hide, umbrellas and honey ribs? no, pouched fibs, get back to the bibs, no $\frac{1}{4}$s. What's wanted's a circle, a tube, the cockpit with neat little wind-screen, comforting safety-harness and friendly propeller. And the nice friendly pilot's head a few feet in front. Been sleeping in the chair, something's happened to my neck, I must get back home. My clothes, my God, what a mess; oh Christ my knees, my hands, flayed and dirtied, oh I do not belong here, I am a city man, I should be in England, where Elastoplast comes from, and Dettol. And this man—Eden?—the colour of kippers, is he waiting to jockey me to $\frac{1}{4}$s, to stable me?

William bent to pick up his holdall, coat and helmet.

Johnny asked me to say cheerio, said Mr Eden, He said to let you rest. William scrambled out of the chair and staggered to the doorway. He could not see a thing for glare. He dropped his things and pressed against the jambs. Mr Eden pushed him as though to pass. Are you ready? he said, Come on. William peered through his fingers at the shadow of the shed then slowly looked up, to where the shade ended, and beyond into the fierce light. The plane had gone. Here and there were bones. Far away was the heap of bones, and beyond, the low brown hills.

He trudged behind Mr Eden, past buildings, homestead, boxes, tufts of grass, bushes, small trees and bones to the garden, a few acres of fruit trees, lucerne, millet, vegetables and flowers, and was shown his room, a concrete and wire netting structure ten feet by ten, and the cowshed, a concrete and wire structure twelve feet by twelve. As gardener-cowman, this is your responsibility, said Mr Eden, You know your job so I'll leave you to it. Mrs Tyme will have a word with you about this and that. Come, I'll show you the cows. That one's Candy Blossom, and there are Flowering Cherry, Rhodo-dendron and Walnut. Why? asked William. To remind Mrs Tyme of the South, replied the manager. And the camels? enquired William. The what? No camels? The boss takes care of camels and donkeys, said Mr Eden, who then took him to the dining-room where he met a few men. You can see the blacks later, said Mr Eden, and went away. Jim the cook

66

questioned William and gave him a mug of tea. William returned to his room, unpacked, changed and wandered over to the heap of bones. At tea time he met seven men. They played poker. William lost 37/6. Five players criticized him for being an Englishman. O'Brien stood up for him, saying Wort was a very old name, old English at least, probably Scandinavian and that the Celts and Scandinavians had much in common. The big Swede jumped to his feet. No, he thundered, Invasion paths vos different, and we Svedes outflank dem. O'Brien said he'd shoot him. William stood up and fainted across the table. Glasses spilt onto cards and a bottle fell onto the cook's dog. Give him air, said Jack. Jim poured two small measures of rum into William's ears saying, It's the aerial wax from high altitude travel. He was then placed in the cane chair. The dog crept under the table, quickly nipped his ankles, and disappeared. He shrieked (falsetto, they later told him, questioning his manhood). Your friend the pilot, said Ted, Was very fond of dogs. Jim poured rum into the slight punctures on the ankles. The cards you stuck together, shouted the Swede, Wid de quick acting rum. O'Brien ran from the room. Stop him, cried Ted, He's going for his gun. The dog ran after him and they heard a yap and a curse. The Swede ran out the other door. O'Brien returned waving his revolver. The dog returned, leapt in for a nip, and caught its teeth in the back tab of the riding boot, and O'Brien spun with the dog on his boot, trying to get a shot in. That's it, shouted Jim, Get him on the run. Faster went O'Brien. And the dog kept up. Whenever the revolver swept the bystanders they flinched. He fired. The bullet went through the wall near the door. He fired again. They heard a scream of rage from outside and the Swede cursed in the warm Kimberleyan night. O'Brien slowed, and tottered, trying to swivel his insides to counter the spinning. The dog dragged along the floor. O'Brien fired again, roared, lurched across the floor, hit the wall and fell in a heap. The dog, freed, staggered across the floor and bit Jack, who then brained it with the bottle, a clear glass receptacle, $\frac{1}{2}$ IMP GAL. O'Brien lay against the wall, one hand hard on leg, the other pressed to breast, quite soundless. In fact a silence almost dead reigned. William sat silently in the chair. O'Brien looked with hatred at the revolver, the dog, the men round the upturned table, at the stuffed black swan on a rafter, at the tree kangaroo with branch of wattle on its platform above the rafters, at the rum-glued cards, at the calendar with the King. And from the pellucid, warm Kimberley night came the deep doomish voice of the Swede: I knows you wait, so I, too wait, and by the milk of the Holy Mother of Thor, Woden and other Northern gods I will get you Irish swine and your English, ah ya, your English, ah, English hog.

Friends, I say, came a voice from the kitchen. A sharp though gentle voice. Sssssshit, hissed Jim, He's awake. William turned, and saw in the kitchen doorway a tall, thin, white-haired man with hands clasped under his chin. We're buggered, whispered Ted, not bothering to turn. Grrr, growled Jack, I hate Irish, Swedes and what they've woken. The remaining men concurred. Bejesus no, shrieked O'Brien removing his hand from his breast and hiding his eyes. Sheet, groaned the Swede, He is risen.

The man entered the room and began righting the furniture. Everyone hurried to assist. With the exception of O'Brien and the Swede: O'Brien tried to rise but fell back rending the tidying shuffles of the saintly one and his helpers with moans of: Shot, I'm shot; to which the hidden Swede replied, Shot, uh, another pig Irish trick. Jack picked up the dog by the hind legs, trotted towards the doorway and threw it into the balmy Kimberley night. The Swede roared. Jack ran back and got behind the saintly white-haired man, saying, You don't mind, Red? honestly, I didn't know he was still out there. Jim got behind Jack. Ted got behind Jim. Bill got behind Ted. Sam got behind Bill. The Swede stormed into the room, a broad-axe held to his chest. William tried to look winningly at him but could not, so got up and stepped back until he stood at Red's side. The Swede had not noticed O'Brien who was carefully reaching for the revolver. By God I am mad, said the Swede, And vy should I be mad you may all ask? First, the O'Brien, second, the dog, third, the Kimberley, fourth, the dust of wild ochres and fifth, meat three or four times a day.

Dear friend, said saintly Red, You are staring into my eyes. Do you see your list of grievances there? Red then turned to William, and offered him Good evening. Good evening, said William, noting that the Swede's eyes had not followed Red's. Someone in the line behind said of the Swede that he was in one of his berserker moods. Red then gazed at O'Brien who had been reaching for his revolver. O'Brien caught the gaze, squinted as though to whistle Mother Macree or some such ditty, then actually touched the revolver and pushed it away, and Red nodded, then returned his immediate attention to the staring Swede.

Henrik, dear friend, he said, Why do you rage? You I told, everybody I told, said the Swede, I saw my grievances in your eyes (as you said I would), and berserk I am, with axe in hands, rage in heart and evil to combat. But Henrik, friend, said wise Red, You are not berserk, you may have felt that way, but not now, you are not a berserker, who was no less, a Norse warrior filled with frenzy and resistless fury at the sight of battle. You have not laid out with your broad-axe, you are not frenzied, you are not berserk. You are our good comrade, Henrik. O'Brien sat up, grimaced and said, Hello, Henrik, I am at peace with the Kimberley and we are friends. The Swede smiled, his hands loosened on the broad-axe shaft, he nodded, glanced at those before him, then over his shoulder at O'Brien, and the broad-axe fell, slashing the clothing right front, the blade thudding through his right boot and into the concrete floor. He screamed, and fell over.

He was attended to and made comfortable. He had suffered grazes to the body and a cut to the foot which Red skilfully sutured with needle and thread. O'Brien was then attended to, he having insisted on the priority of the Swede, for, as he said: The remorseless steel of the broad blade must needs be attended to immediately as was done in days of old on the field of battle for who knows what infection the blade carries? dung, beast-blood, germs and animalcules? Whereas my wound is from hot lead sterilized by explosion and velocity, and is, moreover, a mere graze. To which the Swede replied, But might there not be grazing on your skin germs and bitty animals? And O'Brien whitened and called for the antiseptic rum. After treatment the wounded men were made comfortable in cane lounges. The cook busied himself with a batch of scones and tea was made. The knowledgeable Red then touched on the correspondence existing between natural and spiritual things. Flesh, earth, fire and soul were mentioned particularly, the ferruginous Kimberleys; sheep, flora, man, freewill, fauna, transubstantiation, transmigration were touched on and, in reply to a query from William, the life of the camel. As they made their farewells William asked, Why didn't the manager come after the shooting? Red replied, No doubt he thought it came from the owner, Mr Tyme. Sleep well, goodnight, see you in the morning, keep your foot up Irish, you too Henrik, and other salutations.

William walked in the flickering light of the high-held lantern. A dog barked, things coughed and sneezed, something like a fox ran before him, someone laughed. Dots and dashes suddenly tracered the starry night. A message came to him:

Here tomorrow stop precipitation has been rare lately and the mind boggles at the evaporation stop it all goes up so where is it coming down stop of course you and I know where it is going stop the Americans and bolsheviks know and the Japs know stop we will hold out in the swamps and in the caves in the dunes and in the mountains stop you have said little tonight nothing in fact stop are they jamming your message stop do you hear me stop I defy them to come and get me stop I

am Geoffrey Manfred Tyme of Orebul Downs morsing to you
tamperers out there in the beyond and I challenge you to meet
me on my home ground stop badbye malignancies stop long
live the land and her gentry God save the King stop.

William placed his lantern on the ground, looked up, looked around, looked down. Why did I teach myself morse-code? Ignorance is bliss. Of bliss I have less and less. Looking about him as if, perchance, the mysterious morser, G M Tyme had left his key and crept outside and erected a pale of cla-vicles round the lantern bearer. William snatched up the luminary and jogged to his room. There, all was peaceful. He hooked the door shut and sat on his bed. The wooden oblong set in the wire-mesh wall looked comforting until he remem-bered it was a cage he was in. He got up and walked up and down until he remembered he was pacing. Oh gawdgawd-gawdgawd, he said, until he realized he was growling. He opened his holdall, took out his pad and wrote a letter home. Some small animal scampered over the roof. He looked up. With the exception of a dressed 3 x 2 the beams were rough poles hung with strands of bark and web. Burnt into the dressed beam was: *Arms and the Man.* He undressed and examined the burn scars. He saw again the mark on his thigh and shuddered at the closeness of it to his private parts. He praised the memory of his parents, who had allowed him to keep his prepuce, for had it been taken from him his glans would possibly have been scorched. He shouted: But what use is it here? He hunched, fearful of the noise. Still, the question remained unanswered. What was he going to do with it? Take it home. Look after it. Add a drop of olive oil each day to stop it drying out. And leave it alone. Solitary's comfort but leave it alone. Save it up. Better make sure it's all right. Never know what's likely to get at it in this country. Desert mice, crickets. He peeled back, gently, the prepuce, and a beetle fell out. He screamed. But it was a simulated-beetle of grey lint. He dressed in his striped flannelette pyjamas. He extinguished the lantern and got into bed. In the dark he was no longer displayed in a cage.

The heap of bones piled high in beautiful architecture alongside the landing field was, alas, no heap of bones. It was the remaining wreckage of a famous aircraft, the *Kleine Nachtmusik*, a Dornier-Wright Roc, seven years down and once the aerial repository of Baron Gunter Wasser and Count Adolph Schnitzel, the famous goodwill mapping aviators with two cases of hock, Wagner albums, Goethe in vellum, Protocols and illuminated Führer-endorsed addresses of friendship, expected at, indeed officially invited to, Orebul Downs. They circled thrice, and thrice they sprinkled Köln Wasser. Mr Tyme had drawn on his highly-prized gun collection and prepared a splendid greeting for the ambassadors of goodwill. However, as the Roc touched down a pair of wild donkeys dashed across the field. Mr Tyme, ramrod but for finger on the single-trigger multiple-firing-device, consisting of three Lewis guns, two Gatlings, two Vickers, seven three-o-threes, two Webley & Scott revolvers, two Lugers, Mausers, one each of Salimi, Petersburgh, Franco, and several others, fired.

Two station hands swore that the fusillade was actually an ambuscade carefully laid for the two aces, late members of von Richthofen's Circus, aces with twenty-seven kills to their credit. An international incident averted by the discovery of fur in wheels and engines, and donkey bones in the flyers' remains. Mr Tyme, however, had a job living down imputations, suggestions, hints, slurs and slanders despite motions of confidence, testimonials and friendly dinners. Eventually, reasonableness prevailed. Mr Tyme had the two disloyal station hands collected by the mounted police and taken to Fanny Bay thence to Fremantle where they suffered for their incivility.

Mrs Tyme came into the garden at sunset. She was tall, somewhat plump, with long black hair, a passion for horses and three children at school in Adelaide and Sydney. She took an instant liking to William. Within the week they were lovers. The lucerne patch the site of their amours. William gathered that the deceased flyers had hoped for her favours, having met her in a cattle pavilion at the Sydney show, but she had never really wanted them. What a waste, poor men, she murmured as William squeezed lemon blossoms on her nipples. What is it, William? she whispered. William had stopped his expression. For her murmurs had sounded like the soft steps of stalking, gun-laden Mr Tyme who had many reasons for hating him, e.g. William's relative youth, his shape and size, his flying to the station, especially aboard an amphibian, the machine's circling of the homestead, the dropping of two meat bombs which had later exploded with delayed fury into black and white clouds of flies and maggots, and William's inability to ride a horse on land though he had to admit, dammit, he had few peers in water. Mr Tyme fired a burst from his Lewis gun. William forced Florence flat on the ground. She complained bitterly.

She often brought him bottles of wine, and in return he presented her with daubings of his skin tonic made from the quintessence of Jersey cream and young lemon leaves, which when left on the skin turned golden, then palely rancid so that she looked to be sculpted from butter; and they took their pleasure side by side, though this was not always her wish. William kept a portion of the lucerne uncut for privacy, but this stage of growth always allowed some flowers, so that bees came, and several times stung them.

And so their idyll moved into the second month. Mr Tyme spent most of his hours on the homestead veranda, dismantling and assembling firearms. Sometimes he fired off every gun in his collection. Far worse, however, was when he sat, stood or walked clicking bolts and magazines, or ejecting shells. One day, after he had sent off a burst of machine gun fire, she murmured, He's entitled to feel upset, those Southern bastards refused to endorse him for the Senate, and all he's got is the guerilla group for when the reds seize the cities. William sipped his burgundy. But surely, he said, If they do grab the cities they're not likely to come up here. Wouldn't they get lost? No, she replied, They'd work it so the Javanese and Japanese came South; pincer, you know. Wouldn't they be likely to fight amongst themselves? William darling, what a beautiful idea! The Battle of Orebul. Orebul Field. You'd plough the garden and unearth skulls. Don't be morbid! Ssssh. Tibia in the beans. Do me in the lucerne, dear.

You know, said William, You could organize a camel corps. I thought you'd forgotten camels. Perfect for the desert. How many times do I have to tell you this is not desert? Dry, then. Lawrence of Arabia. *Seven Pillars of Wisdom.* I knew I shouldn't have brought you my husband's books. Lawrence was peculiar, you know. Are you suggesting something? No no. Put it in again. How do camels do it?

Mr Tyme fired a signal flare. Pale in the day. Like a faded kangaroo paw. William and Florence watched it vanish. Rest a while, she whispered. Mr Tyme went back to clicking breech mechanisms. Florence dozed off. William heard an explosion, and a shriek of rage. Eldritch, thought William. A bottle, smashing. MT or more scotch in the sand? Blastid, blastid, blastid, William heard. As though whispered. Then he realized that they were shouts, the words struggling against the wind, which meant the wind had changed and now carried from the garden to the homestead bruised scents of lucerne, fluids, and voices dulcet. He lay very still. The way he would lie after a burst of fire. Bloody and splattered across Florence. She was a nice woman. She was more than that. She was all right. But Mary was thousands of miles away, and that was where he should be. With Mary and Percy and Tom, and Fred, even, and his housekeeper, and Fred's machines. Tram tickets, ferries, planes, figs, fresh newspapers, squeezing into the bottle department at ten to six. Better still to be farming ten miles from the city. And the war had to be joined down there, and if it started tomorrow there would be no chance

74

of leaving Orebul because Mr Tyme, despite his patriotism, would refuse everyone the right to depart as he regarded war as an attempt to draw people to the cities so they could be easily managed and controlled. Mr Tyme would declare martial law, form his people into a guerilla band and shoot anyone who tried to leave. He never spoke to anyone nowadays, not even Florence or the manager, preferring to circulate terse memos and pin instructions to the notice board. Oh Christ, Oh Kimberley, Oh Cambrian. Pre-Cambrian, in fact. Mr Tyme's latest memo suggested crawling exercises. Make yourself small and you won't get hit. Already William had practised. Of course with Mrs Tyme he had become a skilful proner. He felt as though the sky had lowered, was pressing down. He needed a stick to insert between ground and sky, to keep things apart. His room no longer looked onto a paradisal garden; he had a cage in a too-green pen; the irrigation sprinklers were no longer fountains. He broke off a stalk of lucerne and sprinkled its leaves on Florence. And without questioning his action he stood, from hips up clear of the lucerne cover.

Mr Tyme sat in a gun chair on the veranda doing something to a breech. William watched him a while then cleared his throat. Mr Tyme picked up the rifle and sighted it at the ground a few feet from the veranda. William opened his mouth to say Tyme, Tyme, but did not spend the word. He sank slowly into the lucerne. It was one thing to stand, quite another to rise to commit suicide.

The next day William climbed the tank stand to fix the valve. Thirty feet in the air and he felt the heaviness of the cloudless sky. He watched Florence leave the homestead carrying a bright beach towel. She walked through the flower garden, along rows of vegetables, between the two figs, stopped behind an orange tree, and waved to him. She undressed slowly, put the towel over her shoulders and crept into the lucerne. Mr Tyme carried onto the veranda a table set with revolvers.

Florence reached the sanctuary of the tall lucerne, spread the towel and stretched out on it. William sighted a pair of pliers against Mr Tyme and slowly closed the jaws. He dropped them and they fell with a soft thud. He looked around and saw: a dust trail a few miles away, a donkey skull, bones, the Roc ruin, a bullock hanging from the gallows, a flock of sheep a couple of miles away, an eagle high overhead, specks of cattle on brown hills, Florence, the sun which seemed larger and much closer. What? he said, What now? and, giddy with horror, teetered and would have fallen had he not pressed hard against the cold corrugations. Fallen, or was he about to launch, spreadeagled? Now hard against the iron corrugations. Probably barred, zebra-fashion. Florence with bars.

He descended, and went to Florence, who inquired as to the reason for his discomfort, but did not press him, offered sympathy and urged him to take the sun before the heat set in. Murmuring, There, there now, there, there, as she unbuckled his belt. Mr Tyme laughed loudly and fired a shot. Water spurted from high in the tank. That was stupid of him, said Florence. William hugged his knees to his chest. For God's sake, she said, it was just a shot.   I was up there, he said.   So what? Had he wanted, he'd have shot you. That's nice.   But he didn't. So he doesn't want to shoot you. I'm sure he likes you in his own way.   Does he know?   Of course not. He's an honourable man, so if he knew he'd shoot you.   Perhaps he half-knows and his shot was a warning.   It was an accident.   First an accident; what happens next? Stop worrying; Come on, we haven't long; Emir Rahman's coming.   Who?   He's a trader, comes through this way once or twice a year. You'll find him interesting. He's got camels.

Mr Tyme fired two shots. William looked at the tank. He missed it!   He didn't aim at it. William hugged his knees tighter. That spurt's coming from fifty tons of steel and water, heavy, like the sky. It's going to topple and squash us.   Well it's losing weight with the leak, maybe my husband's trying to ease your burden. Come on, she whispered, Get some sun on your poor pale body. For God's sake, what's the matter? I don't feel too good. The will snapped? Perhaps it's the sun. A few shots and you've lost yourself. The Afghan's coming. He's a hawker, not a rebel, this is Orebul Downs, not the Khyber Pass, and he's been converted to Christianity. A Jesus Afghan. Mr Tyme can handle anything untoward. If you can't please me, I'll please myself. She lay on her side, her back to him. He put his hand on her haunch. Piss off, she drawled.

He went to the shed, dipped a rag in tar, climbed the tank stand and plugged the hole. Mr Tyme sat on the veranda watching him. William decided he was being stared at. I say, Wort, he heard, See me when you've finished. I can see you well enough, thought William. He heard cries and drumming. Emir Rahman was galloping towards the homestead as though being born of a dust storm. Get down, Wort, shouted Mr Tyme, Get down or I'll shoot you down. William scrambled around the side of the tank, out of sight of Mr Tyme, crouched on a corner of the platform. The Afghan galloped past, shrieking and waving a rifle. Florence was dressing beside the orange tree. She nodded to him. What a woman, thought William, So calm, so composed. A pack of yelping dogs pursued the camel.

I'm going to give notice, I'll walk home, he muttered, as he clambered down the ladder. Mr Tyme ran along the veranda, crouching behind every post, holding his hand like a revolver, shouting Bang-bang! The cameleer reappeared, sighting his rifle one-handed, pretending to shoot. William jumped to the ground and ran to Florence. What's happening? It's all right, dear, it always happens, it's a game of theirs. Bye, bye. The cameleer galloped off in the direction he had come from.

Which was, ultimately, Afghanistan, a country in Asia, bounded on the North by Turkestan, on the East by Peshawar, and Sind, on the South by Baluchistan, and on the West by the Persian highlands, all in all an area of about 240,000 to 260,000 sq. miles, depending on political conditions and the state of surveyors, for if they are Afghans they tend to expand the frontiers, if they are foreigners they tend to reduce them, which is at least a deplorable practice for any reduction in square mileage means a diminution of land available for the breeding and grazing of camels which are exceeding numerous in such trade centres as Herat and Kandahar; agriculture is but imperfectly understood, but many grains are sown, with indigo and cotton to a limited extent. Without access to the sea, Afghanistan nevertheless has ships: ships of the desert of course, though there are no deserts of the Arabian sort. Poets, musicians and painters of miniatures are in good supply, as are the languages of this country, chiefly Persian, Pushtu and Turki. Fat-tailed sheep are kept for meat, tails, wool and karakul coats. It is a delightful experience to view these fat-tailed sheep grazing their rugged terrain, the Hindu Kush for example, that section of the Himalayas where shepherds intone to far-off Tibetan prayer-wheels: Graze or perish. Britain has twice intervened martially, and on the first occasion a force of three thousand officers and men were treacherously murdered in the Khyber Pass, resulting in mosaic retribution, reparations and Victorian satisfaction. The wily Russian lurks to the North, China is not far off, Persia but a verb away and India sends songs little diminished by terrain, if not enhanced.

The Emir Rahman did not gallop off to his homeland on this occasion however. He made a fine, full circuit of the homestead and ancillaries before reining-in by the veranda steps. William, concealed within a thicket, watched the cameleer leap from his exhausted beast onto the boards, as though refusing to set foot on alien earth. He wore turban, burnous and fancy American style riding boots. He had a fierce, hooked nose. He shook hands gravely with Mr Tyme who sneezed in the great, slow cloud of dust. Gardener! shouted Mr Tyme. William did not answer. He's gone, said Mr Tyme with satisfaction, I'd have shot him. They stepped into the house. William crept closer. Drilled him, said a guttural voice. Filled him with lead, cried a falsetto. Of course he's not a bad gardener, said Mr Tyme, However he puts me in mind of a poacher. A poacher! exclaimed the guttural one, We Pathans eat them. Good Lord, said Mr Tyme, I've shot one or two but I'd draw the line at eating them. Eggs, eggs! cried the falsetto. Thief! cried Mr Tyme, A poacher is a thief. And the Afghan stepped backwards onto the veranda, declaring in falsetto, What better subject for civilized discourse is there than food? Mr Tyme followed him onto the veranda, also stepping backwards: Elevated talk on the nature of food is the hallmark of civilization. He then took from the wall an elegant brass gong set in an elaborate frame of polished bones and struck it thrice with a fur-padded vertebra on a handle of polished shin. An attractive native girl in a long white dress appeared. Tell Mrs Grope, said Mr Tyme, To prepare Khyber à la Kimberley. From the the back of the house came, No, no; never, never. The girl reappeared. Mr Tyme sent her to the men's cook in the men's quarters. Mrs Tyme, in a white sleeveless dress patterned with rabbits and apples, bearing an elaborate silver salver with three glasses of champagne, stepped out onto the veranda. So good of you, said the guttural Afghan. They toasted Empire, prosperity, Khyber à la Kimberley and the King. From the men's quarters came a roar of refusal. One of these days, I'll shoot the cook, said Mr Tyme calmly. It would be wise, said the Afghan. Today, said Mrs Tyme, Insubordination is general rather than exceptional. Would you like me to prepare the meal? We have about ten in the refrigerator. Not nearly enough, said Mr Tyme, Eh, Sheik? So he telephoned the manager and ten minutes later a basket of four fresh sheep's heads arrived. Mrs Tyme brought another bottle of champagne. She walked to the edge of the veranda and called: Wort, Wort. William crouched ten feet away. She jumped down onto the earth. William eased from his crouch and lay face down in the thicket. Wort, she called. Wort! roared Mr Tyme. Ants crawled over William's face. The swine, growled Mr Tyme. Disrespectful, gutturalled the Afghan. He's worse than that, said Mr Tyme, He's undermining the place. William flicked dirt at the ants and scratched into the ground for better concealment. Wort! shouted Mrs Tyme, Wort, I want lots of parsley, lemons and thyme. He won't hear you, said Mr Tyme, He's loafing somewhere. Probably got a hole. A bloody rabbit, he is. Be down a warren doing things with his kind. Really, dear, said Mrs Tyme. He has a hole? falsettoed the Afghan, Then you need mongoose or ferret. Gas him out, said Mr Tyme: Wort, Wort, parsley and thyme. Mongoose, man, mongoose comes.

William felt an ant climb onto his ear, then enter it. The external auditory meatus was explored. Antennae and legs of the creature entered ceruminous glands stimulating the production of cerumen or wax. He heard the glands chuggling wax, which rose like golden lava. Would the creature reach the tympanic membrane or would it be embalmed in the aureous secretion? He wiggled his ear and both ears wiggled, an unnecessary duplication. If he could perforce put all the wiggle into the offended ear he would thereby double the deterrence. His body control was faulty. Some people could wiggle one ear, flare one nostril or raise or lower a testicle, so what had gone wrong. But why was he worrying about meatum, tympanic membrane, tympanic cavity, cartiliginous auditory tube and the rest? Because of his St John's Ambulance Brigade training. Order of St John of Jerusalem. To aid sick and disabled. To fill yourself with the arcane mysteries of the body. The tympanic cavity or middle ear leads to the auditory tube thence to the nasal part of the pharynx. The Order had its origin in Jerusalem in the 11th C. Initially a monastic order, it later became militarized and its Knights fought the spread of Islam. A firearm was discharged. Not the familiar report. The Afghan had joined the shooting gallery. The Order of St John became militarized and its Knights fought alongside the Crusaders against the spread of Islam.

80

Afghan was Islam. Mosques at Maree, in Adelaide. Soon to be at Orebul Downs. Prayer towers. Muezzins shrieking from towers. Registered religion. Polygamous, like the Mormons.

Book of Mormon. Revelations written on golden plates found by a Smith under dung on a hillside in 1820s after two heavenly messengers with breast plates of Christ's crystallized tears, loin cloths of white samite (mystic, beautiful), and anklets of foes' toes commanded him: JOIN NOT THE OTHERS, START YOUR OWN, PREPARE TO BE PERSECUTED, BUT DON'T WORRY FOR IF THY ENEMY CHOPS OFF (IN ORDER/TO ORDER) THY TOES, FEET, SHINS, KNEE-CAPS, FINGERS, HANDS, NOSE(S), EARS, SEXUAL ORGANS, NIPPLES, LIPS, TONGUE, REMEMBER YOU WILL BE RE-MEMBERED IN THAT CASTLE IN THE SKY AND AS YOU (AS SOUL) ASCEND YOU WILL OVERHAUL THE AMPUTATED PARTS AND FLY AS ONE OF GOD'S CHOSEN (YOU'VE SEEN A FLOCK OF SWALLOWS HAVEN'T YOU? WELL, THEN, YOU'LL BE A FLOCK OF SOUL (IMMORTAL) AND SOULISH TOES, EARS, BALLS, NIPPLES AND OTHER SAINTLY ETCETERAS).

ORGANIZE   ORGANIZE   ORGANIZE   MR SMITH   ORGAN   ORGAN   ORGAN . . .

Mormons met in Adelaide. Join us for the sake of your soul. Join us for material comfort in later years. We are persecuted therefore we must profit. In Salt Lake City, Utah, our fellows are rich. We are Christ's capitalists. Not today, thank you, I'm on my way to the Kimberley. Are you indeed, you've a long journey ahead, join us and go to the Kimberley as a missionary. Kate and Ron Bloob, accredited Mormons, spreading the doctrine of the Church of Jesus Christ Latter Day Saints. Kate; slender, well-washed face, fair hair in a bun like a rabbit's tail, fair under the arms, cunt fair, waiting for the reappearance of Christ who will reign a thousand years, turning back the cock's three crows, cockadoodle-oooooo three times, into two (more splendid) into one (still more splendid), the cock for Kate, whose thousand-fold (every cranny a delight) cunt shall take the thousand-times cock (every vein a

81

mountain range) for one thousand years. Which is this, this and that. Which is tomorrow WILL BE better. Which is tomorrow IS better.

Hold onto today, mumbled William.

The falsetto Afghan. What? said Mr Tyme. Will—, Wort, called Mrs Tyme. Jesus Christ, thought William, the Arab heard me. Ants explored both ears now, the left nostril, hands, legs and the right armpit. I fainted, decided William, I hit my head and the sun did the rest. He groaned. Louder. He rose to his knees. Look! it's the gardener.   Wort, what're you doing there?   He is the one?   Wort, I asked you a question.

William raised his head but kept his eyes closed. Open your eyes, Wort, ordered Mr Tyme. William knew that if he did he would look into a gun barrel; however, if he did not, something would emerge from the gun barrel and hit him or the ground close by. Perhaps the sun's got him, said Mrs Tyme. Put a ferret under him, gutturalled the Afghan. Open your eyes, Wort, commanded Mr Tyme evenly.

Meaning, retract your eyelids, the muscular skin-curtains lined with conjunctiva so that the eyeball, that hollow spherical organ consisting of such parts as cornea, scela, iris, retina, be exposed to the horrible veranda tableau. Turn a man to stone. The bullet through the head; the body limp, then stiff; interred; into worms' dinners; then the remains bone hard, stone-hard; disinterred; ground; broadcast on garden or made into mortar. Ants crawling over eyelids.

He heard Mrs Tyme approach. Careful, said Mr Tyme, He might be dangerous. Mad and biting, said the Afghan. William groaned, forced open his eyes and croaked, The sun, oh the sun. The men on the veranda were unarmed. Mr Tyme jumped from the veranda, saying, Too much sun, Mr Wort? Then come into the shade. He grabbed his ankles and dragged him into the shade of a bottle tree saying, Now don't kick, you're sick y'know, keep your eyes and mouth shut and you won't fill with dirt. In the shade of the bottle tree William was eased onto his back by his employer's well-polished riding boots. You gentle darling, laughed Mrs Tyme. A good employer, he replied, Is firm or gentle according to the need, and every response is rewarded. The Afghan stood over William and he saw the champagne glass tilt and he closed his eyes before the liquid bubbled over his face. The men returned to the veranda and Mrs Tyme went to the garden for parsley, lemons and thyme. Mr Tyme set up a portable cooking device on the veranda and ignited the charcoal. William was advised to sit against the tree. The Afghan placed a heavy chopping block on the boards, split the fresh sheeps' heads, extracted the eyes and placed them in a bowl containing parsley, lemon juice and thyme to Mr Tyme's helpful commentary. A chilled bottle of triply-acclaimed rosé was drunk. Mr Tyme sounded the gong and asked the serving girl if she would care to join them. No? He told her to extend the invitation to his cook. From the back of the house came the strong female voice of the cook singing Abide With Me. He then telephoned the manager, who declined. The girl was sent for the men's cook. His distant refusal was heard by all.

The two men skewered the eyes onto three skewers. William did not count the skewerings, but he saw the first. The idea that Mrs Tyme would eat such food disturbed him. He was surprised when he heard her excuse herself and go into the house. He heard his name called. He stood unsteadily then mounted the veranda steps. The unsmiling Afghan handed him a skewer of eyes and the beaming Mr Tyme presented him with a glass of cold rosé. William dropped both, doubled over, was sick over the cooker, staggered, was sick over a row of revolvers, fell against the Afghan, was sick down the bore of his rifle, knocked Mr Tyme off the veranda, overturned the cooker, staggered into the house, was sick over a rare rug, crying: Not again, no more: then realizing how empty he felt, lurched backwards onto an elaborately carved stand of ivory, bone and wood containing the Orebul collection of assegais, knobkerries, javelins, harpoons and pointed sticks, just as the revolvered Mr Tyme burst into the room. Mr Tyme fell with the points of several weapons in his head, crying as he hit the floor: We are attacked! Insurrection and disorder! On the veranda the Afghan uttered his terrible Khyber cries. Sounds of disorder came from the rear of the house. William crept to the front door, peered out, saw the Afghan stalking away from him and when he disappeared round the corner William snatched up a rocket pistol, which went off as he brandished it, the projectile bursting through the library window and exploding inside. He dashed inside, knocked the points out of Mr Tyme's head and dragged him into the shade of the bottle tree. The Afghan, wailing a plaint of Kabul, reappeared, untethered his anxious camel, leapt into the saddle and galloped behind the side of the burning, historic homestead. Ammunition began to explode. Broken twigs and leaves fell upon them. A salvo of rockets erupted through the roof, long fingers of smoke exploding into punches. The Afghan galloped away with something across his camel. Mrs Tyme drove up in a truck, got out, ran away and the truck exploded. Now and then William caught glimpses of people. The camel train left quickly.

When the homestead had burned down and stopped exploding everyone came out of hiding. The saintly Red tended Mr Tyme. Mrs Tyme and the manager drove to the nearest station, Mt Grasp, forty miles away, to radio the Flying Doctor. At dusk Red came to William in the garden and told him of the death of Mr Tyme. When they reached his death-bed they found that O'Brien had revived him with rum. Next day the Flying Doctor flew low overhead then went off, and returned two hours later. The pilot had spotted what he thought to be an ambush and so returned to Mt Grasp where Mrs Tyme jumped into the plane, held a revolver to his head and ordered him back. The following day a De Havilland chartered by a newsreel company and a newspaper arrived and when it departed William went with it in a mailbag. He was discovered, stamped on cruelly and put down in the hinterland of Broome. Here he laboured and starved until October when he rescued a prospector from a horde of wild donkeys and was rewarded with maps, samples and two fifty-pound notes.

William returned to Sydney and encountered on the way: Mormons, Jesuits, Aborigines, Jehovah's Witnesses. He spent two days in the saddle of a bicycle belonging to a traveller named Uppermann and two days in the trailer behind.

They ran into trouble in the form of a prone policeman on the great dotted line known as the South Australia-Victoria border. He was conducting a grasshopper count. Would they amount to a plague? It was the policeman's task to find out. William cycling, Uppermann in the trailer. They ran over the policeman's bag of grasshoppers and the man himself, and he arrested them on these two charges and: driving an unroad-worthy vehicle, overloading, lack of due care, disrespect, dishonouring the dotted line, damaging said line by joining with mashed insects two dots of said line, not sounding a bell, offensive whistling, seditious utterances, vagrancy and roguery. Because of said injured foot he was unable to escort them on his bicycle. They refused him conveyance in their trailer. He was compelled to limp behind pushing his bicycle and carrying said bag of squashed grasshoppers. At the Station, William produced two ten pound notes and pur-chased their freedom. Free to loiter they purchased lodgings for the night. A pensioner painted their adventures. Three militiamen discussed their beliefs. William decided to hang himself. He changed his mind. At midnight he rose from bed, dressed, unhitched the trailer from the bicycle and set off for Melbourne. An hour later he changed his mind, rode back to the hamlet, re-attached the trailer, walked to the railway station and caught the mixed goods, arriving in Melbourne midday. The following morning he reached Central, Sydney, and, wildly extravagant, hired a taxi to Fred's place. Reunion.

Joy. His appearance aroused cries of consternation but joy was relatively unconfined.

Mary rubbed his leathery skin with olive oil daily until Fred, hinting at the cost, persuaded her to use machine oil. William filled out, grew two chins then three, wristlets and anklets. Fred put on two men. It was coming Autumn. Fred registered a new company, Wort Precision Engineering and told William he was negotiating the purchase of a small piece of valuable real estate which he would like to register in the name of his big brother, William. But you're the big brother, Fred. Only in age, Will. Don't sling off at my weight, Fred. Soon, Will, you'll need a sling before you can move. It's the force-feeding Fred. There's no stopping Mary. You're like a brown seal, Will, you'll go well in the Navy. It's city life, Fred, and being within sniff of the sea, Fred, it's the urban unnaturalness. I thought you'd rid yourself of rural bliss, Will. It's the quiet of the trolley buses, Fred, they'll run me down one day.

Three days running William lumbered with his two sons round the wharves at Pyrmont, Erskine Street and the Quay. Mary wailed about their schooling and William said he was showing them the workings of commerce. Percy wanted to stay behind with his mother but his uncle Fred ordered him out. Out, out of the place, go with your father. I'll look after Mum, Percy said. I can look after her, said Fred. Go on, dear, said his mother. Percy was a bit tired of his father's behaviour. He was not the same man who had gone to the Kimberley. He had lost the interesting pouches in his gaunt shoulders and was now simply a plump trespasser.

William generally left Percy and Tom with the gatekeeper while he sought people on the wharf or aboard ship, but now and then they followed him over plank and up gangway and were presented with lemonade, ginger, chocolate, indecent photographs and winchdrivers' gloves. They escaped dray horses, cargo from a broken sling and two bouncing steel hooks. They always filled their pockets with spilled grain.

The sea is very healthy, said William as they stood on a wharf beside a battered tramp at the Quay. He repeated himself as the boys stared at the unhealthy looking ship. He left them and went aboard. Tom pointed across the water to the enormous stone warehouse. I'm going to become a manager and run a woolstore and if you're all right I'll give you a job in the wool. Thank you, said Percy, But I don't think I'll work there. You will, snapped Tom, Or you won't get anything for your birthday. Then William came happily down the gangplank.

William disappeared the next day. Mary stamped round the house snarling, No more chances, he's had it, I'll get a separation order and maintenance. When Fred had calmed her it was his housekeeper's turn to stamp round the house snarling, I've had him, no more chances, he's had it. But she stayed on and for two months the household hummed with accord and the workshop thrived. Then the housekeeper packed her things and got out of the effing place. Oh? enquired Percy. Funny, said Fred. Futile, said Mary. But things went on fairly well.

Three months to the day after William's disappearance Mary received a telegram from Townsville. It claims to be from William, said Mary, But how do I know it is? Any William can go into a post office, call himself William and send a telegram to anyone. There should be a law that you use your full name or use mister, missus, master, miss, or sir, baron, lord, squire, or reverend. I shudder for the poor soul who receives a telegram:

ARRIVING TOMORROW STOP LOOKING FORWARD TO STAY STOP KING STOP

All right so it comes from King, but what if it's from George King? THE king, you think?

It's from William right enough, said Fred holding the telegram to the light and sniffing it. I can tell it's from

William by the lightness of it—don't you see it lacks an ı and an A—that it has an apostrophe M instead? 'M. WILL'M. Our uncle Ethelred called William WILL'M three times to my knowledge. I deduce that this is a code. Therefore he is in trouble. He's always in trouble, shouted Mary. This time it's enemy agents, snapped Fred. Why else would he send

AM BACK FAIR HOMING WILL'M

Meaning, said Mary, he's coming home peroxided—well, I can put up with a wanderer but not a wandering poofter.

Mary, I should be careful. William is my brother. Also, there could be other ears nearby. Are they eavesdropping? Why don't they leave us alone? Mary, dear, they don't know, sit on the scales there, eh?   Surely you know my weight, Fred?   I do indeed Mary.

He then took from his overall pocket the treasured calipers and struck a note on a temporarily incapacitated I-speak-your-weight machine and sang: Eight stone ten pounds: the final note very low indeed. Your weight is always right, Mary—should we go for a gallop? She sighed. No, Fred. The telegram has made me uneasy. How would you interpret it? Fred declared: AM BACK = he is, well, back, but from where I don't know; FAIR = fare, not faire; HOMING = he is on his way here, to do with homing pigeons; WILL'M = the way our Uncle Ethelred addressed him three times (to my knowledge). Uncle was a pigeon fancier who dealt in sugarbeet. Therefore William has arrived in Townsville from somewhere, is short of the fare home, has had dealings with Americans (sugar meaning money), is reminding me of his delusion that Uncle Ethelred left us a legacy of emergency money, and so on. And notice the number of words in the telegram. The minimum. The cheapest rate. He is penniless and beset by foreign agents. It couldn't just be the post office made a mistake—a drunken operator, say? Or that Will was rum'd when he sent it? Get the silly bugger home, Fred.   Leave it to me, Mary.

One morning three weeks later William turned up with a

rolling gait, grey hair and a mouth empty of teeth. Fred laughed, was shouted at and chased through the workshop into the back lane. William had taken so long to travel home because Fred had sent him a box of carrier pigeons. William had eaten them then set off on foot. Mary sent him to the local turkish baths where, hearing of a good thing for the afternoon races, he won forty-nine pounds. He bought a smart navy suit, a fine borsalino and some teeth.

Where had William got to during his three months?

WILLIAM TRAMPED

He had shipped aboard the coffin tramp he visited at the Quay. Bound for Palestine to see what was happening there. The new society amid oranges, ruins and camels. Camels? Yes. But never again. We don't want to hear your camelshit, yelled Mary and Fred. In that case, retorted William in high dudgeon, navy suit and borsalino, I'll save it for my memoirs. Your memoirs! shrieked Mary. Oh god, ha ha, chortled Fred. Yes, growled William, Of how I shipped out on the *Kelp* one foggy morn, supposedly for Jaffa but really for Tahiti, with Edward G Robinson skipper, H Bogart first mate, L Howard bosun and R Valentino cook, and J Harlow, B Davis et al as passengers; of how I was confined to the bilges for asking what was going on, of how Bogart said Hi pal, every watch, of how I was fed marmalade and toast by Howard who was very decent and British, of how the drunken Valentino spent his time throwing pots of marmalade out of portholes, of how Robinson went mad drinking seawater with his rum ha-ha, ha-ha, eh?

William then did impressions of the people he had mentioned. He continued his tale: Yes, I know all about life in the bilge—it's like being in one of your pin-ball machines, Fred, half-awash in oil and water in the fifty-yard pool at the baths, with a gang of roughs playing and a mad superintendent shouting to himself in a cane chair on the side.

After days of this I was transferred to the for'ard hold, the sides of which were coated with raw sugar which fed the cockroaches, which I pelted with sugar, nuts and washers. I became deadly accurate. Until the mounds of putrefying cockroaches began to unhinge my reason. Do you know that sugar-coated cockroaches are a delicacy to certain base palates? Some of my victims mummified. These I fastened to the sugared sides and achieved designs of horrendous interest. It is an insect and shares its order with crickets, locusts and whatnot. The second day of my enholding several planks were removed from the cover. Ah, thought I, They are not devoid of elementary decency, this crew. Each morning two buckets, one with water, the other empty, and a basket of food, were lowered to me. On the third day I noticed the camera. The fiends were filming me. I tried all corners of the hold but could not avoid the malignant lens. I stopped cursing and prancing. I reasoned that the film would be produced at court as evidence of my mutinous behaviour. I therefore altered my behaviour and acted in a mannerly way. However the pryers were too much for me and I often misbehaved. I would place Charlie—a medium-sized cockroach I had tamed —on the back of my hand and converse with him. This is not good enough, I told myself, I am simply pandering to their camera. I took to staying awake at night and sleeping during the day. One afternoon Miss Harlow was lowered into the hold. She is a remarkable woman. The next morning Misses Ross and Hareem joined us. Both handsome forceful persons. The ration basket contained only dry bread and water, which the women fought over, though they did not look at all famished. I resented their greed. Have you got worms? I asked. They threw dead cockroaches at me. The cameramen chortled disgustingly. The next morning C Laughton was added to the hold. He was charming until the bread basket arrived. At noon a hamper containing cold chicken, thin white loaves, pâté de foies gras, aspics, jellies, sauterne and champagne was lowered. The others removed their clothes.

Yes? demanded Mary. Will? said Fred.

They danced chastely around me as I ate.

Fsssh! hissed Mary. Will? said Fred.

The remainder of the hatch cover was removed and a second lidded hamper lowered to us. The rope was yanked, the basket fell on its side and a horde of rats squeaked from it. You can imagine the consternation. The next day the ship stopped at a small island port. I was paid off. Eventually I reached Cooktown. From there to Townsville was an arduous journey.

What about the hold, Will? asked Fred.

He then related how he had spent innumerable hours in deck chairs watching open-air pictures. He had been unable to satisfy his craving. He swept floors in return for free seats. He lived on fallen sweets and chocolates until, suddenly, he had seen enough.

Mary brought stout, bread and cheese. Fred went on an errand. William started into the second bottle of stout. He told Mary of a desire to go to the turkish baths with a few bottles. He then compounded his desire. Would she come with him? He knew it was somehow illegal but she could wear his clothes and in the locker room slip into a commodious shift and the two of them find a steamy corner, eh?

Fred arrived with the doctor. Old, stern Doctor Skye examined and questioned William about his journey. William told him, concluding with: A good story, eh? ha-ha, ha-ha. The doctor called in Mary and Fred. William was all right but he needed a change in the country; he had seen too many moving pictures lately from the front stalls, a region bad for the eyes. Mary took the doctor to one side and told him about William's turkish baths proposal. Doctor Skye's eyes glittered as he told her of the Turkish Baths Act. Before he left he asked William: Howard, Bogart and Harlow, eh? remember, back stalls only from now on.

William secured employment as a sharefarmer near Picton, about fifty miles south-west of the city. Thirty milkers and ninety thousand rabbits. Steep eroded land where fences were always tight and wires droned in perpetual wind. The land wrapped in fences to stop it going away. Hills scrubbed by every shower. The five acres of flat by the creek so rich in silt every summer it grew maize jungle. Unless rain and silt washed it out or buried it. Cows cantankerous from contending with rabbits. Cows so accustomed to slopes they leant as though diseased when standing in the bails. A little snow in winter. Very pretty. Cars stopped to admire the view. Cameras often produced. The Worts on sideboards, in many albums. Mary wore sound gumboots, William's leaked and the boys went barefoot to toughen their feet. William supplied labour and shared a few costs. The owner, Bob Atler, supplied land, herd, house and rabbits. Rabbits were frequently consumed. Rabbits were trapped, excavated, dogged and ferreted. Pelts were sold, rugged, slippered, caped and capped. On cold days large furry bipeds roamed. Bob Atler joined the army to escape. Rejected William stayed on and held things together (helped by the fences). Fred Abbotslee, a neighbour, rejected by the navy, cut his throat and rolled down a hill plainting through windpipe, during a dry spell too, so the blood remained and the flies outlined it into something like a quaver. Alan Choice, thirteen, who lived two valleys away, tried to join the army, was refused, so hanged himself from one of the few remaining trees. London was blitzed and William prayed for the bombardment of Picton and the strafing of the farm. Pearl Harbor was bombed and William rejoiced. William and Mary decided to rise earlier, at three-thirty, so that Mary could make camouflage nets and William could train with the VDC, change road signs and follow strangers. William managed to join the army.

It was decided to combine the two Atler herds and use Bob's dairy. Mrs Atler and her children Tom, Ted and Jill, and Mary and her children Tom and Percy, combined and every morning and evening dealt with the mob. The children often fell asleep at school. Percy fell in love with Jill who liked his brother Tom. Percy, to show how much he cared ran errands for her mother. Jill was nice to Percy because he was Tom's brother. Her brother Tom hated Percy and his brother Tom. Percy found Jill's ribbon. His brother Tom grabbed it and gave it to the dog. Percy let the dog lick him.

Mary caught shingles. Mrs Atler sold the cows. The rabbits ate the garden. Mary recovered more or less and got a job as housekeeper on a good farm towards the coast. On the Creel farm there was plenty to eat but little money so Mary sent their clothing coupons to Fred who occasionally visited them and gave them money but as they hadn't coupons for clothes they couldn't buy any except on the black which was too expensive. Fred's manner and clothes impressed everyone, though Mrs Creel thought him somewhat flashy. The army had William travelling between Darwin and Wyndham and in both places the Japanese tried to kill him. Because of his knowledge of the Kimberley he was made a corporal and although Brigadier Tyme was a thousand miles east he stayed away from Orebul Downs despite Mrs Tyme being in Sydney. Sometimes his censored letters were intelligible, sometimes not. Mary and the boys wondered if their letters were censored but could never find out because William's replies were censored. The boys took turns to write to him. Sometimes Tom asked Percy to write a joint letter. Mr Creel wrote to William offering him a job later on. Mary wrote to William telling him he was not to accept, that as soon as he was discharged he was to take them away: Mrs Creel was often bitchy and though Mr Creel was a gentleman she had to force herself to stay, mainly because of the boys and their schooling.

Mrs Creel often took to her bed and would become very charming and ask for the boys to visit her. At such times Mary became edgy and tried to keep the boys from seeing her.

Mr Creel would then give them money for sweets and comics. Mr Creel liked Tom and often helped him with his homework, especially bookkeeping and English.

We grew to be a pair of sturdy rustic youths. Tom affected the town manner, I the rural, but as my style was the stronger our average rusticity was quite high. He walked as though to the pavement born, I tended to plod. He was the office boy, I the farmer. He could not avoid my rural effluvia. One day while I was helping Mr Creel cut up a dead calf in a cow Tom turned up, stepped into the scatter of dismemberment and hurried off bloodied and bitter. Grass seeds would miraculously attach themselves to his clothes, mud stuck to his boots. Our high school had us two years apart with Tom a commercial pupil, I an agricultural, he played with the seconds, I with the thirds as second reserve.

One Wednesday afternoon when we the thirds had a bye, our broadminded sportsfiendish coach arranged a game against a district Marist Brothers' team. They generally played League and we were Unionists so the question of thirteen players or fifteen was tossed for and they won, having God on their side. Four of our team developed ailments and I was drawn in to do battle with the devoted servants of the Virgin. I looked forward to pitting my rustic protestantism against rural justice catholicism. The game took place on the Marists' field, literally a field for despite the goal posts and concrete cricket pitch under a sixteenth of an inch of gravel screenings, there were ruts where bogged beasts had lain, discernible furrows, cover of rye, clover, couch and thistle stubble, dried pats and fresh land mines, traces of afterbirth, a filled-in warren and lots of bones; literally a field of Mars. What appeared to be the entire Marist order packed the sidelines blackly. We had only our broadminded sportsmanic coach and a reserve. We thought it the end of the world. The day had given twenty minutes of sun, then fog again, the sort of day when it's ten m.p.h. over Razorback and cops wave torches where trucks have gone over. Our red and green stripes to mask blood and grass stains. Where there were not Marist brothers there were Marist brotherlings, and three nuns with three girls. We had a single reserve to their multitude. They even supplied the zambuck, a priest with brown attaché case containing oils and waters for extreme unction. The nuns played with their beads. We tended to play with ourselves. A senior Marist saw us playing, forgot himself, and screamed Filth, filth, stop, then staggered back into his crowd, and many boys took his place, staring incredulously and us so embarrassed for our several pullers. We all sat on the icy ground in a circle, until one of us broke it and went to the dressing-room for three rugs which he draped over us. Then the perceptive, filth-crying Marist returned, saw us huddled and rugged, and screamed again: Again, the filth under cover! and would have hurled himself onto us had not coach returned, and with extreme courage fronted up to him.

We won the toss. As we kicked off an arm of mist reached out from the dressing-room. They had the habit of kicking high and each time the ball soared the mist blessed it and made it inaccessible to us pagans. At half time the coach hated us so much he begrudged handing out oranges. A polite brother came over but was repulsed by our sullen silence. They won by something like 43-8.

A truck was supposed to take us home but did not arrive so we wandered, bedraggled survivors, through the town. In the milk bar I saw the three girls who had been on the sideline. One had red hair drawn tightly into two plaits, a haughty kind of nose, big green eyes and a mischievous mouth. I fell in love with her. She giggled with her friends and one of them gargled milkshake.

The mirrored walls and ceiling of the Parthenon Milk Bar and Deluxe Restaurant turned the twenty or so customers into a great crowd. Because of what had happened to us on the field we were not at all boisterous; we were a collection of sober

95

thoughtful boys determined to avoid a discussion of our fiasco. We talked about the reds who were taking over the city, pictures, first grade football, the recent and forthcoming test series, elements of algebra, girls, the American civil war, rationing, properties of hard and soft water, the mysterious qualities of the much publicized radioactivity, venomous snakes, rabbit skin prices, jerseys and ayrshires, australorps and leghorns, wet dreams, a tattered magazine containing nine photos of film stars with enormous thrusting breasts, curbs on snake life in the exhilarating 1940s compared with the 1840s when there were only scattered settlers, lizards, kookaburras and the omnivorous Aborigine, and the urgent need for the introduction of the mongoose, wild boar and any other snake eater, cow-milking snakes, snakes in dreams, girls, french kissing, palm-stroking, poofters, jobs on leaving school. We mentioned teaching, bank clerking, shopkeeping, apprenticeships, stock and station agents, accountants, pharmacy, policing, flying, gospelling to the heathen and farming. Favourite impossible occupations were then discussed. Yes, yes, someone said. But what are we really going to do—I mean what do we want to do? I had never told anyone of my wish to be a doctor, nor had I made known my interest in medicines and the workings of the body. Suddenly I was asked the proper name of the bum bone. Coccyx. They thought this hilarious and made many jokes about tonkseven, pricksix, doodlenine etc in hoarse conspiratorial whispers. Of course I contributed. I was then told I fancied myself as a doctor. Why. Because I seemed to know a bit about sprains and was sometimes snooty, my mother had told someone's mother I was going to be pushed into a profession, in a science period I had known the name of the Greek doctor Hippocrates, and knew of such things as testicles, vagina and other wonderful parts. The evidence piled up. I was able to mount the evidence and look down on my companions. Then the captain —a future banking man—announced that though I might at a pinch qualify as an ambulance driver I would never become a doctor. Oh? Because I wasn't doing Latin. Down I tumbled from my vantage of testicles, coccyx and penicillin. Ever so horribly true, my lack of Latin, and I'd known about it for months. I'd thought of overcoming my lack by studying privately but had never got round to it. I was aware that prescriptions were written in a degenerate Latin. Oh, I said (languidly) to the captain, You mean pig-Latin. Grunt grunt. Of course the captain's father had a Berkshire stud. The captain stepped in front of me setting his chin on my head. Father and son known as Bigrasher and Littlerasher. He stood on my toes. Surely, I said, If pig-Latin's good enough for doctors— and chemists—it's no offence to a pig? He stepped off my toes. I told them I had been enrolled in a pig-Latin course (I almost said herd) in the city next holidays. The captain said, In a sty, I s'pose. This was considered very witty so he moved away from me. I then told the boy on my right about my father's close relationship to the Flying Doctor Service; also, I had been promised a position; also that I had personally been on a mercy flight over the western part of the state with an injured ram fighter suffering from broken scapulas and a leaping fontanelle. We had flown low over the great Western Plain, steering round trees and literally sand-planing up dunes, praying the while there would not be a fence for we knew if there was we would be catapulted back and every minute was precious to the injured ram fighter, a famous, absent-without-leave American Negro actor-philosopher-general who had flown from China to confront a notorious merino. My companion told me I had sheepshit on the brain. A pellet pressed through my fontanelle into my frontal lobes. Once again I had exaggerated a story! And to a boy the son of man with a few sheep. Bosovis, a dairy farmer would-be grazier, whose cows existed to provide shelter for crossbred ewes. Boy Bosovis moved away from me. I recalled an essay I had written a couple of years before.

CATTLE: mammal, Bovidae Bovinae, mammal, Bovidae or hollow-horned ruminants (or cud-chewers) descended from Bos primigenius, the great, speedy and often mad beast of the steppes etc. The female is not so large as the male and has less hair on the body and has the usual udder while the male has only rudimentary nipples but big balls which the cow lacks (even small ones). The dairy kind of more importance than the beef. Melba of Darbalara gave 32,522 lbs of milk and 1,614 of butter in 365 days, a pity it was not a leap year for then she would have done even better, especially if the leap year in question had an extra full moon for the relationship between milk and moon is well known. Dairying is the mainstay of the Australian economy and without it bands of dispossessed dairy farmers would roam the countryside laying it waste here and there and eating the sheep of rich graziers (see *Waltzing Matilda*), and workless city milkmen would become early morning desperadoes with one or two jack-the-rippers thrown in. Also abandoned herds would run wild and a menace to man and beast. They are also known as hoofed quadrupeds. Also, oxen, buffalo, bison and the yak.

Jersey, Guernsey, Ayrshire, Australian Illawarra Shorthorn or AIS, Friesian or Holstein, Devon, Aberdeen Angus, shorthorn or ordinary, Devon, Kerry (tiny and milkers kneel). I am informed that in the natural wonderland of the Jenolan Caves there is a long-legged marsupial cow in limestone and scientists keep quiet about it as it does not fit their theories. The Jersey is a mild, small, fine-boned, rich-golden-milk-yielding cow which is more than you can say for others (bar the Guernsey). However the Jersey bull is another thing (altogether), being sturdy, compact and mean, and if you read of a farmer being gored you can bet it was a Jersey horn that punctured him. Bob Lyons-Bowles departed this vale of tears through peritonitis (inflammation of peritoneum) in 1932 because he laughed at his neighbour's bull, and when the owner refused to kill him the widow, Mrs Lyons-Bowles, speared it with a crowbar. (Much of the preceding story derived from gravestone and hearsay.) The Ayrshire is a good type of animal and has fine graceful horns curving upwards like the frame of a lyre (note use of letter Y in words ayr and lyre), and I have seen them strung with web of a dawn and dewdroppy too, and between horns I have seen five taut web-lines, like a staff hung with dewdrops like crotchets and quavers and it is an interesting fact that beasts following her lowed pleasantly.

On the other hand (hoof) the Friesian or Holstein, from Friesia and Holstein, is not musical, despite the pleasant yodelling traditions of places mentioned. They are large beasts and produce great quantities of weak milk. They are black and white and when seen at a distance resemble magpies with heads low, and magpies amidst a herd of Friesians re-semble midget calves.

The Illawarra Shorthorn is Australia's own breed! Pleas-antly hued in red it is a fine sight on pastures green and an even finer sight is Florence Spryte leaping from the backs of her father's herd. Handstands and somersaults are also in-dulged in. Performances on the back of Magnificent Sprytely Percy III are uncommon though not rare. Her dancing angers her father, Noel Spryte, who says she teases the bull. She is a slender girl and the cows, though not the bull, are accustomed to her antics and she will do well with the circus. I lived near Florence three farms ago. She had seven double-jointed fingers and her father had a hole in his throat from gassing on the Somme. Summing up I would say, Bovidea is here to stay.

My teacher, Miss Dry, tried to amputate my fingers with the edge of her ebony ruler. An affectionate classmate, Sarah Nightingale, afterwards rubbed the ruler with dog shit in the hope that Miss Dry, a ruler-sucker, would get worms. How-ever Miss Dry in her Morris Ten was run down by a G-38 locomotive named Whippet. The incident changed Sarah's attitudes and she became deeply irreligious.

The many mirrors of the Parthenon suddenly produced grotesque reflections. The captain and his cronies saw it first. They fell silent and looked at the floor. I looked at the floor to see what was there. I noticed the shape of a large trapdoor in the green linoleum. I pointed at it and gasped, We're doomed, it's opening—aaaaahh—down down into the green slimy pit —aaaaahhh. I then looked up to see the grotesque Mr Parthenon pointing a malted milk spoon at me. I could not return his glare so stared at the malty gun. Mr Theodurulis, late of Alexandria, was a noted writer, singer, democrat, caterer, weekend farmer and marcher in Greek national costume and over the years had devastated more than a hundred jeerers who on seeing him in his costume of slippers, pantaloons, tassels, skirt and pleats had declared him to be (for example) a poofter, olive fucker, arse oiler, acokolis, cuntopolis, as he marched the streets of towns on Greek days. A leonine face, lean though, as though starved of prey, tawny haired, slit-eyed. And wearing a sunshade. What do I look like, boy? he demanded. I was joking about the floor, Mr Theodurulis, I whispered, thinking: Oh let the trapdoor open and take me. So I look like a joking-about-the-floor, uh? he hoarsed. His voice a roar-whinney, double-mouthed, like a lion on the back of a wild horse. You kids are driving customers away—what do I look like, boy? A lion, sir, I whispered. That pleased him. He lowered his spoon, leant back and told us, All right, boys, less noise, OK?

We discussed, in a quiet civilized manner, the game. We would do much better we agreed next match, when we met them on our home ground, a decent oval drenched with victory. Not a paddock or slaughterhouse pen. Local ground. Local? I could hardly call it my locality for I had not been there long and there was no knowing when I would leave, it all depended on my father's migratory instincts. Would his service in the North have curbed them and make him want to stay in the district? I doubted we would stay more than a week or so after he returned.

I watched the girl and her images. I watched her past other faces and backs of heads, and had to keep moving to keep her in sight. I borrowed a shilling and moved towards her. From Mrs Theodurulis I ordered a sixpenny malted. Twice the girl glanced at me. A large silver cross hung between her breasts. No wonder her head hung forward. Once she laughed and threw her head back and the cross dazzled me. A demon thwarter. But I did not quail. Should fly to rest on breast. My pubic stubble (a reaping to make it grow). Then she stared at me for at least a second. Oh leaping heart.

The coach strode in and ordered everyone back to the truck. The team began drifting off after him. I took my malted to where the girls were. One said something unintelligible, then: Was it bad? My girl said, His scapula was torn. I had taken a sip of milkshake; I let it run back into the glass. My God. A torn scapula—no wonder the Marists were standoffish, if not surly. You can't go round breaking scapulas. Tearing one is infinitely worse. Barbaric.

Poor creature. Out for the season. And every season thereafter, twitchy with internal draughts as they sweep from heel to poll reviving winter wounds. My theory of internal draughts needed several more years research. I had thought of it two weeks earlier whilst wrestling with Kay, Ron and Syd Couch. In the kitchen. Mr and Mrs Couch were over a hill burning a cow. Syd had a headlock on me, Kay had a scissors on Ron who had an ankle lock on Syd and I had a full nelson on Kay. Knots of barbarism and affection. My hands clasped over Kay's nape, my face pressed between her scapulas. Under the kitchen table. Syd yelled, kicked against the ankle lock, screamed. We fell apart. He cried and hobbled from the room, slamming the door. I told them I had heard the beat of the artery of Syd's arm. The pulsation, explained Kay. I told Kay I had heard murmurs in her back. She described a hole she had in a shoulder blade. Incredible. Birth of theory. Gestation would be complete by the time I entered medical school.

Overjoyed professors allowing me to compress three years of study into one.

In the Parthenon Milk Bar and Deluxe Restaurant the girls ended their discussion. Carefully placing my glass upon the counter I turned to them and said: I had no idea it was as bad as that. From my girl, blankness; the others tittered. The winger or five-eight, sprigged or fractured? I asked. Eh? said a girl. I explained. The girl told me a scapular was an item of clothing worn by officers of the Roman Catholic Church, and she was prepared to tell me more but my girl cut her off with: He's being rude and nasty—just what you'd expect from a high school boy. I replied: We'll beat you next time. They left the milk bar. I finished my drink and set off after them. Along the railway viaduct where the terrible fog stank of coal smoke. The two girls turned off and mine continued alone. She couldn't go much further for the town was not big. I had a brilliant idea. I caught up to her under a light. She was startled, then a bit snooty. My coach, I said, Told me I should apologize in case you thought I was being rude. She agreed that this had been her reaction. I explained my confusion over spatula—no not spatula, I mean scapula. Again? she hissed. No, I protested, Spatula is a blunt knife. I've got spatula and scapula the bone mixed because I'm going to be a doctor. You—a doctor, gee.   As a missionary. That's why I was so interested in the priest with the first-aid kit.   Are you? she yawned, then: Look, you're just after something, aren't you? A stammered denial.   You can walk with me but no funny business.   Still, we walked hand in hand through the horrible wet air towards a faint light until I walked into a fence and she nipped through a gate. She kissed me so quickly I didn't have time to close my eyes. Even in the gloom I could see her eyelids (palpebrae). Extraordinarily pale. Pale as mammary gland (or breast). I whispered for her name. She shook her head. I begged a kiss, she denied one; I demanded a kiss, and she relented. My arms held her, she struggled, I touched a breast, she grunted, she pushed free, managing a knuckle uppercut, hissing Raper! and called for the dog, Blue. Determined not to hurry I picked up the kitbag, bade her a sweetheart's farewell and stumbled onto the road. I decided to undergo Instruction in her faith, a curious though popular one. I understood that you were only allowed to put it in according to strict rules. Covering it with a letter was even worse. Tit and fingering were permitted provided you apologized afterwards.

I jogged back to Main Street. The truck had gone. I had been abandoned. In a foggy unfriendly town where three girls were spreading hostility. I cursed the coach and team and vowed never to play with them again. I lashed a pole with my kitbag and tore it. Coach would excuse his departure with: Your mates have got to get the cows in—they work hard off the football field—not like someone I know who hates any kind of work. I decided never to return home. I went to the railway station but there would be no train for an hour. I walked along Main Street. Outside a pub I saw a sideshow truck and trailer. Several children played in the cab. Two women and a one-armed man came from the pub. My town and the next one were mentioned. A woman cranked the engine. I went to the trailer, climbed aboard and got into the cockpit of a whirl-a-plane. The runway was unnecessarily long and too crammed with buildings for comfort, cloud ceiling perilously low—and when I breached it what would I find? Night fighters. I shivered with apprehension, not fear, and decided to use the full length of the runway and burst through the ceiling seventeen miles away and take them by surprise. Victory aerobatics in the cold clear night. (In time runways will link all airports and aircraft will not have to fly.) We drove right through the old home town but I managed to bail out at the crossroads two miles on. At home there was hell. I had decided to embroider my account of being left behind by the evil-minded coach and team with details of injuries suffered i.e. wrenched patella (knee-cap); bruised fibula (or outer (splint) bone of the leg) and an overabundance of synovia (joint-oil). I had kneaded and rubbed the knee into rosy prominence. I lurched into the kitchen. Where have you been? Take that and that! Oh I fell heavily. My feigned injury forgotten I scrambled across the floor. My brother watched coldly. I was force-fed hot soup and sent to bed. Bro said to me: You're a liar. I'm going to find out what you were doing. A player told me you were eyeing girls in the milk bar —it's a roman town, you know, and tykes and prots don't mix.

I named her Pat. I perched on a confessional box and heard a stream of trivialities. Incense almost overpowering wafted round me. Candles flickered about the altar. A choir excelsiored. In the steeple the pigeon friar released his messages. In the vault the nuns nunned. In the vestry the radio brother spoke to the Pope. The confessor's tongue frenched through the grill of the confessional. Pat listed her enormities. What are they doing to you, Pat? How can you believe this hocus pocus? Did Henry Eight act in vain? If in vain then Thomas More also? He who out of pride wrote a story, *Utopia*? Leaving behind Church of England, story, and head in basket. *Utopia* (no-place), an imaginary history of an imaginary republic so governed as to secure complete happiness. I am suspicious. I prefer Topia. Even in Winter.

Wintering with Pat. School years, football, basketball, marriage, family, old age . . . Never out of wool. Wool, Vicks and cabbage. Surely there's some alternative? Yes. Alternatives are controlled by a department which embodies the best of former departments i.e. manpower, production, police, defence, commonwealth, blood, you name it, it's somewhere. Pat, let me take you away from all this. To live in a secret valley. When your teeth go we'll melt your crucifix for a silver mouth, when we're shot we'll make bandages from shirts, when the kids are born I'll uncord with glass, when my knee goes bad you'll take my leg off with bottle and tenon, and when I die endung and enleaf me (not that there'll be much left) and grind my bones to toothpowder (for the silver),

104

(ground bone the great abrasive); silver egg-spoons discolour, therefore Pat, eat not too many eggs lest I abrade thee. We'll have lived in a cave and had a good time, stalactite to stalagmite, stag to stal, ssst to ssst.

Caves have so far featured several times in this series of recollections. (Caves of recollections joined with one another by passages sometimes long and narrow.)

I once spent a day at the Jenolan Caves. Got there on the Norton. Bugger of a road. Caves House for Accommodation and Teas. I had two teas but could not bring self to be accommodated. Arrived there with left leg dripping oil from broken oil-line. My coat, my splendid don-r coat, the coat of a bringer of great despatches to generals, the sort of coat worn by helmsmen rounding the Horn and cray skippers between Flinders and the Prom . . . my coat, its beautifully faded brown canvas, with buckles and flaps, zips and buttons (not a true don-r coat but a don-r/flying-suit combination) this coat, on arrival (outside Caves House) was daubed with green, red and yellow lacquer as though I were wrapped in the flag of a fools' army, the vanguard of an army of one. And over everything splats of mud. I dismounted and drained my boot. I then hobbled into reception to confirm my phone booking. Phone booking? I'm afraid there's nothing here—and we're booked out. Busloads of tourists any minute.   Oh yeah? And busloads of refugees fleeing the radioactive city I suppose? Contempt and fear. To show my anger and contempt I stamped the floor with my foot. I slipped and went arse over. My God. Nothing like castor oil for lubrication. And from entrance to reception an oily trail. (Clerk, I could make you suck my boot—do you know what's in it?   Foot, sir?   Clerk, do you know the meaning of the colours on my coat?   You are re-enacting an episode from the Old Testament, sir?) You mean I can't stay here?   Any other time, sir, but today cripples from Korea, an American admiral, Rotarians, missionaries and unspecified guests. Bland. Oh the creature so bland. And with the full resources of the Govt. Tour. Office behind him. And a Labor Government providing solid support. Filling the House with warmongers and businessmen. Warm ongers and busi nessmen. Outside, to puke, to puke, to machine! The workers' underground playground sold out to mammon.

Sir, before you leave would you mind removing your boot —it's messy. Puffing away, the clerk, on a de Reszke, a cigarette of distinction. I off with the boot. Held it high. Clerk's apprehension—assault? I touched with my tongue the oily upper. Horrible stuff, but I smiled sweetly.

Castor oil, I announced, Have a lick, and held it out for him, but he declined. Have a lick, you look a bit bound-up, it'll loosen you, do, do have a lick.   If you don't leave I'll have to summon the manager.   Oh do, do, do summon the manager.   You are creating a disturbance.   Then let me tell you that the castor oil I have just tasted is this very instant creating a disturbance—nay, a tumult—in my bowels, and I am leaving here, now, with seething bowels, and do you know where I am going? Off to the workers' limestone underworld where I am going to fart, fart, yes, fart, and do you know exactly where I am going to fart? Beside the Gem of the South which, as you should well know, is in the aptly named Moloch's Grotto. And my farty hydrogen sulphide will discolour old Moloch. The chemical equation being: $H_2S + CaCO_3 \rightarrow CaS + H_2CO_3$: CaS calcium sulphide, the dreadful sulphide—and do you know what it does in the dark? It does not, like you, masturbate—no, it glows with phosphorescence. Truly, truly, truly you have decreed for the govt. tourist bureau a fearsome Moloch.

With that I left. I was so exhausted I could barely operate the kick starter. Before I departed I cast onto the barren drive the brochures I had been given.

So much for caves.

The colours on my coat had come from an unpleasant incident at Katoomba, gateway to the Three Sisters, mountain resort sans excellence. No, I'm being unfair. The air's good. I had made my way into the good air of Katoomba with a beautiful pillion passenger. Moira. Perce, the vibrations make me feel funny. Me, too, Moira. Oh, they made me feel funny all right. Moira, let's go to Jenolan Caves for the day. Terrific. I have to make a phone call, Moira. I phoned Caves House. Double room, please. Yes, sir, certainly, sir. Get to the Caves; then . . . Moira, engine trouble, we can't return home today, have to stay the night . . . At Katoomba we sought refreshment in the Mountain Devil Panorama Cafe where walls and mirrors are festooned with those eared and snouted woody fruits pipe-cleanered into devils, a major industry thereabouts. Toasted raisin bread and tea under the devils. Your hand, Moira, your waist, your leg. Cut it out, Perce. The owner, the omnipresent Greek: OK you two, finish up and get out. We quarrelled. I'm not going to Jenolan with you, you sex maniac. Oh, Moira, Moira, I'm in love with you, we must make love. I'm not that kind of girl, you want that sort of thing you get a Bridge Café slut, don't come near me. And off she went to the garage round the corner, to Norm, the mechanic. I struggled into my coat and followed her into the repair shop. No Norm. Round and round the cars. The greasy apprentice whistled at her and winked at me. Her fury. My blunder. Life's dull, Moira, we've got to colour it. I said this outside the paint shop. Oh blunder, blunder. Here's colour for you—splash, splash. She then ran off to Norm's place. Who the hell was Norm? Norm was the boss, the giant speedway rider with plates in his head. Round to Norm's then. He and Moira were on the veranda. That's him, she yelled. He took a deep breath from a tin of racing fuel and plodded towards me. A younger girl came from the house and stood beside Moira. Ijit, Norm, she yelled, Ijit. She pushed a box of pistons off the veranda. Norm turned and plodded back to the house. The girl slammed the door. Moira shouted to me, You wait there. I pointed to my painted coat. Pity it wasn't your face, she shouted. I waved £2: Your train fare home, Moira. She ran down to the gate: Norm'll drive me home, he's a gentleman, well-brought up. That's obvious, I said, Born with a silver plate in his head. She snatched the £2. For refreshments, she hissed. (Women in anger often hiss, I find.) The front door opened and Norm reappeared on the veranda, beset to left and right with engines dismantled and shrouded, boxes of parts, tins of oils and mounds of cotton waste, wires and tyres, and, high on a post a broken crimson crash helmet serving as a pot for a feathery-leaved plant very much like rue.   S'long, Moira. Don't let him sniff any more fuel. 'Bye, Normie.   He picked up a tyre and cast it at me, as though playing quoits, and by god he almost pegged me. Bidding them farewell I made my colourful way Nortonwards.   Hey there.   The ijit girl from Norm's. Rose.   Gee, this your Norton? Give us a ride?   A thin girl (with long fair hair) made bulky with sweaters.   Go on, give us a ride, I know the sights.   We came to the end of a road but were able to ride along a path until a woman sooled a dog onto us, so we went upstream above the falls where we left the bike like a rock under my coat. As we sat on a rock watching garbage float past she plaited her long fair hair into a topknot. Hugs and kisses, rock hopping and teetering. Contact with the stream would be dismembering. My hands under her sweaters. I'm not sixteen so you can't. I didn't want to. I desired her lips, neck and waist but could do without them if need be. I would take her to Jenolan and sleep chastely beside her . . . protect her and save her from her silver-headed brother the speedway star. She never missed a speedway meeting and showed me little scars from flying stones. She loved the smell of Castrol R and racing fuel and sometimes she got Norm to start the engine just to be able to snuff up the stench. Norm had had dreadful falls and col-lisions. I gathered that Norm's time was nigh. When he fell finally, fatally, the steel pins in his bones would shoot out and nail her. Let's have a real burn, she said. But I put her off between the garage and the house to her jeer: Fuckin' yeller, even yer coat shows it! Off, off on the winding road to Jenolan and debacles fresh.

(My bro is very keen on caves and I have reason to think he has at least six in the mountains. Difficult but not impossible of access, each one contains drums of water, food, fuel and clothing but no firearms. He plans to sell them on war eve. Bro is a positive thinker.)

Because I had let down the side, i.e. missed the truck of vanquish, I was dropped from the team. People told me I was taking things badly. So, buck-up, cheer-up, smile a while, apply yourself, work hard, strive, shoulder to wheel, don't let the team fire die down. Being out of the team didn't trouble me. No, I was in love with the distant Roman. In the workshop I found a small piece of iron like a crucifix. I looked at it a lot and it must have been seen by bro because it disappeared from my coat pocket. The twinge of concern I felt soon gave way to relief because I'd even thought of constructing a harness so it could hang against my balls. Just a thought. But what a thought; I must have been an eerie creature in those days. Bro did well to steal it. The symbol of Christ on my cock. Perish the thought. I could have fallen over and gelded myself, died even, and been buried in that unprepossessing, insignificant town not far from the similar town where Pat lived. Question: Was it the single Pat I loved or was it Pat and her mirrored images? Question: Did I really have such thoughts as an adolescent? I think so, but without the present floweriness. (She was keen on Scotch thistles. I picked one for her when I returned to the town the following weekend. I pierced my fingers, she shrieked with laughter, I tried to bloody her, but half-heartedly.)

I suppose that in those days I'd have eschewed floweriness

and got straight down to plainness. The basic language of sauce labels: Made only from fresh choice tomatoes; Ideal for lamb & veal & hogget & yearling & mutton & beef & fish & eggs & veges (even the glorious fresh tomato itself is enhanced by a few drops of this tomato sauce); Kiddies more and more (no we are not suggesting our tomato sauce for roast kiddies) but kiddies in ever-growing numbers add it to ice-cream and for a party treat what is more intriguing than tomato sauce in your party sherry? Nett contents 26 fl. oz. Glory, glory to the tomato, a species of plant of the natural order Solonacae, whose fruits when green make a capital pickle and when ripe and rosy are unexcelled raw or cooked; within its firm skin vitamins swim midst essential seeds and pulp par excellence; scientists have proven its tonic effect upon weak eyes and R.G.C. of Vic. uses tomato ointment on his suppurating buttock bites. The tomato, known in olden times, as the love-apple, induces copious flows from Bartholin's glands, blood engorgement of the penis and a fruitful swelling of the testes; so—down this sauce, farewell remorse, our good advice to you; the natural course, without remorse, our good advice to you; take a Bex or Vincents in a teaspoonful of tomato sauce, add it to Eno's effervescent salts and watch the delectable bubbles; buy six cases today for your fallout shelter; and brides-to-be—use it to placate your suspicious betrothed; *pace in terrum tomate* 26 floz 26 floz 26 f loz 26 flo z oz fl 26 ozl f26 ozlf 26 . . . the tomato requires a rich loam but it is inadvisable to manure heavily at time of planting which should take place when there is no danger of frost; we recommend Rouge de Marmande, Grosse Lisse, Potentate, Bonny Best and innumerable others depending on local conditions, pests, diseases and frosts; beware the wilt and the voracious thrips or they will inherit your realm . . . *Deus ex Tomate*.

Pat. Did I pine for her, moan and rant in sleep, was I wan and did I palely loiter? To the first I do not know, to the others, no.

The following Saturday Mum, bro and me were driven by

Mr Creel to Pat's town for a surprise. Eh. Oh. Ah. We separated. But not before being told to be at the station to meet the train or else. I walked past Pat's house several times and then went to the Marist's oval where I saw that my earlier impression of it as a boney paddock was correct, and noticed on the dressing-rooms two memorial plaques to three Irish names, but whether donors of money or lives I cannot say. In the Parthenon I came across Pat and her two companions. I hurried past and they followed close behind me. Loverboy, Errol Flynn and similar epithets reached my ears. On a deserted side street I turned to them lecherously and asked to be taken to the nearest haystack. Taken by surprise they became affronted, giggly, flirtatious, overbearing, seductive, rude, crude and so on. Poker? asked the plump one. Of course. Pat dashed off for cards and her friends led me to a hayshed on the edge of town. They declined to enter until I had declared the loose hay free from snakes, rats, mice, possums, bats and beetles. I jumped up and declared the hay pest-free. Pat arrived and we began our game of modified strip poker. They egged each other on. Before long I had lost everything but trousers and I suffered considerably. Pat had lost two sweaters, yet had at least another to go, the plump girl had lost shoes, sox, coat and sweater and the redhead sweater, blouse and shoes to reveal another sweater. My goose pimples were larger than their breasts. I gave up my trousers and burrowed into the hay. Pat lost her final sweater and showed her breasts under a woollen singlet and so distracted me I played the wrong card. The girls averted their eyes as I ouched and removed my underpants in the painful burrow. Pat named me Adam, I called them my Eves, the redhead cried Oh yair! the plump one blushed, the redhead pulled Pat's singlet and showed her breasts, a straw ran into the eye of my prick (or urethral opening) and I cried out. Pat and the redhead seized my clothes and attempted to make off with them. I sprang from the hay to oohs and ahs and we wrestled, often roughly, always amorously, exchanging kisses, caresses, headlocks, nel-

111

sons, hair pulls and slaps until I spunked copiously. Gosh, gee, Sorry, Urrrh, beast, pig, Don't let it get on you, and the town clock chimed. Pat and the redhead dressed quickly and, tight-lipped, hurried from the shed. The plump girl asked them to help her gather the cards but they ignored her. I heard them break into hoots of laughter outside. She found all but two cards. She asked me if it had hurt, the, you know, stuff. She asked could she touch me. We made love for about three seconds. Veronica. We brushed each other down. I combed my hair then she asked me to comb hers. She had large round blue eyes and the longest lashes I have ever seen. Her small chin had a dimple like a tiny navel.

As we moved away from the shed what was only to be expected happened. I had led the way furtively, looked left and right, listened carefully, sniffed the air like a fox on a jaunt. Then: the fog lifted, magpies carolled, the roofs and streets of the town below shone like polished lead and to the North a tremendous rainbow arched the railway line to the city.

Can't say I approve of such incidents as just described so I'll avoid them. Or dodge, dummy, feint or forget.

Percy got to the railway station several minutes before the time set by his mother. She washed his face in water from the bubbler. His brother shone with cleanliness. Mr Creel stepped along the platform then back, endlessly. The train arrived and William, Mr Wort, stepped down. Everybody was polite and restrained to the point of tension, though Mary and William rocked in a tight hug. William's uniform abraded the boys. William and Mr Creel shook hands firmly. Mr Creel made William a profit-sharing proposition and William nodded gravely. He did not mention camels, Afghans, Kimberley crocodiles or his brother, Fred. Percy felt easier for a while until his father mentioned several cases of wives who had run off the rails. William spent days in bed and the boys seldom saw him. Why had he taken so long to return from the

112

war? William had been engaged in something called special duties.

A fortnight later the Worts left the Creels for a better place.

It was much, much worse than Creels.

I did not belong there. I was brought from a desirable place near a pleasant town where I mingled with young Catholic ladies, played exciting games of football and led, generally, a wholesome life. Transported to a dreary forest—sic ho ho—land where pathetic cut-into and burnt-out specimens of bloodwood drew a sub-existence from leached soil (as though it ever had anything to lose, a thin skin over shale, a corruption of sheol if ever there was one) where my abductors, my parents, put me to hard labour before and after school to make more money for themselves without working extra hours in order to save enough for a place of their own. I asked them why they did not get a repatriation loan and was told they were not after charity—and there was prejudice against the English. I was a wage-slave under a pair of sub-sub-slave-masters, share farmers who voted Country because they were on the Land and to uphold the figure of C. H. Slug, grazier, farmer, investor, A.J.C. Committee member and landlord. I'm not suggesting he went into the voting booth and held their hands as they ticked his name. There was no need. They were born to follow such as he. So long as I was small my abductors were safe. I could not get away because of my short legs. I was determined to escape without resorting to wheeled transport. I forget why. On the other hand my captors wanted me big to get more work out of me. This dilemma—I did not know such a word existed and had I been told I'd have guessed it to be a forked lemon—this dilemma occasionally worried them but not enough to halt their nomadic drives.

We moved again. Eastwards towards the sea. As though they somehow had the lemming spirit. To rich land this time, not far from the coast. Mountains behind, to the West, Pacific to the East, steelworks to the North and to the South a middling market town. And more cows than ever before. Beasts placidly grazing, walking, cudding, sprawling. Reddish cows mostly, and a fair size; the remainder were fine-boned small things. They took the bull placidly. The terrain was flat to undulating. Cows everywhere. Moooooo. Not a beefy beast in sight. Never a sheep. And the damned, perpetually blue sea, not that we went there often.

One day neighbours took bro and me to the seaside for a picnic. We drove up the coast twenty miles then down about forty. I had to admit it was an exciting drive what with coastal strip, ocean, mountains, forest, steelworks, mines and houses beginning to spread all over the place. After lunch I went with Tom to an enormous ship high on the rocks. Very rusty, the red paint nearly all gone, a great hole from the wrecking and others where steel had been cut out. It looked as though it had been trying for an overland route. We got aboard and Tom climbed down into the engine room looking for bits of non-ferrous until he hit upon the idea of having me descend while he stayed on deck ready to yell when he saw the tidal wave. Damp, rusty, echoing and trembling with wave slap, I clung to the rusty ladder in the biggest bog in the country. I can't go further, I shouted. I can't continue, I screamed. Got much? he called down to me. I looked up at him framed against the sky, and very impressive he looked, too, and knew it, in captain's hat. There's nothing, I shouted. Open your eyes, he yelled, Go deeper and don't come up till your pockets are full.

I wanted to give him a whiff of fart, I wanted to make the biggest of my life, a gloom-shattering, metal-ringing, face and mind shattering fart or, better still, one of great lightness and nonflammability, a bowelly helium, not toxic but musky music-making, bells, miniature harps, a lone violin, and be borne upwards, knocking arse-over the caricature Bligh and be carried far away . . . Just be my luck to be dropped in the middle of Main Street Wollongong and arrested for indecency with shorts round ankles, or into the Cross and be buggered, or be hit by a plane. I found several brass nuts and bolts and headed for the ladder.

As I climbed the ladder I meditated on recent events. Such a stirring period. The great war over, another looming, the silver of Broken Hill going into medals, newsreels changed twice a week, repaired cripples appearing on the streets. I wanted to join the navy to sleep in a hammock, have tots of rum and fire a flare pistol; Verey, I think, that's all I wanted to do, fire those signal or distress flares, and if they were only to be used for this latter purpose then I wanted to be permanently distressed, firing brilliant lights into the sky to the captain's chant, Abandon ship, Abandon ship; and as I stood on the upturned barnacled hull driving off the swooping fighters. Only I had no real interest in guns, torpedoes or mines, only rum, flares and a hammock. And I wasn't really a rum drinker either. I could only tolerate rum in tiny quantities in pudding and cake.

Come on, bro urged, and we scurried over the deck. We found a dozen brass nuts and washers, though not a bolt and why not? I was always stopping and trying to figure it out: fishermen would have visited the ship and they were always on the lookout for nuts and washers as sinkers: so what would they want with bolts? I asked bro. Cap'n Bligh again. Fishermen do not use nuts and bolts because they are easily caught amongst weed and cunjevoi. Cunjevoi? Rock animals like enormous warts that squirt water. Here? Everywhere. Oh, terrors of the deep. Oh unfortunately unrare deep and W. Shakespeare's play, *Tempest*, recently read in comicbook form; full fathom five your father lies.

Bro's idea was to salvage as much as possible before the blowtorch crews came down from the steelworks. He thought they were due any moment so wasted much time peering over the side in the direction they would have to take; this line of boilersuited men pulling gas cylinder trolleys, stopping now and then to brandish torches; these men from the horrendous hostels near the furnaces. The ship had been there a long time. Waves broke on the stern and surged through great holes and although we were fifty feet above the water whenever a wave shuddered and echoed through we expected foam to sweep the deck. The sea was calm but looked doubtful. As soon as we decided the tide had turned we hurried to the bow and escaped down the rope ladder. We didn't trust the sea; we were not coastal folk. A couple of hours earlier, miles up the coast I'd seen a bombora a few hundred yards offshore, a mound of water swirling sea and kelp which every minute or so shot up a wall of spray. Submarine kelp gave me the horrors. You had only to swim against it and you were grabbed. Even after it had been torn loose and cast ashore it was sinister. My father had mentioned that as we were not living near the sea we would be able to gather seaweed for manure. English masters, camels and perpetual motion were not enough for him, oh no; he now wanted to turn his temporary farm into a stranded Sargasso Sea which would catch vehicles the way the Sea caught ships. I thought about this as I came down off the wreck. I wondered how I'd come to take a fancy to navy life which was simply a matter of sinkings, kelp, sharks, depth charges, exploding boilers and keelhauling. Ships were steel boxes, floating caves, the evil counterparts of the good ones in mountains. Proper caves had bats and you'd never find bats in a high and dry wreck. Bats I liked.

I once set bat nets in an orchard, but somehow caught an alsatian and when I found him he'd been netted for hours; black net, grey soil, grey dog and apple trees heavy with green fruit. The dog nipped me. I tried to wash and swab the punctures secretly, was discovered and had to lead five indignant adults to the scene. Hello, it's Davis's dog.   Sheep killer.   Apple eater.   Good pedigree. Is that foam?   It is, and wouldn't you be?   Why'd you set the nets, Percy? It *is* foam. Get a mattock. A gun. Get David. Bats, he, Percy, set it for bats? Let him alone.   And so my attempt at natural history ended in a brawl with people tripping over the net,

being bitten and punched until reason returned and someone saw the dog had been squashed unconscious and could be
safely unnetted. There are probably sea-bats in sea caves
which eat fish. My nets would have caught flying foxes rather
than bats because there were thousands of them camped in
trees, by a cliff, which when disturbed rose like ash then fell
back. There were foxes, too, with brushes like feather dusters,
always after poultry. Also: foresters, walleroos, scrub wallabies, pademelons, wombats, ringtails, gliders, bandicoots etc.
(I should have paid more heed to natural history. I would
then be finding my present situation quite interesting and
watch the fauna and spend less time scribbling.) The people I
mixed with in those days knew fascinating things about
flowers and animals, earth and sky. Some were fascinated and
sought to know more, and were sparing with axe, gun and
plough; the others did what people have always done.

When we finally got back to the picnic they were about to
send out search parties. Naughty boys were we. However they
understood, they knew what it was to fall in love with the
sea. Did we have enough salt water? Salt water? Certainly—it's essential, here, fill these bottles. What sort of
rite were they involving us in? Silly boys, you need salt
water for the anemonies, sea urchins and fish you've collected.
But we haven't. Then what were you doing? Anybody who
is new to the sea collects them. Well, said bro, look what we
found. Good Lord, it's nuts and washers—were you on the
wreck? Ah, what mercenaries we were. I dug into my pocket
and found an oyster shell I'd thought could be with pearl. I
was a double mercenary inlander only interested in plunder.
While we'd been wrecking they'd been jamming their car
with beach litter, shells, bags of shellgrit, dried kelp, miles of
barbed wire taken from collapsed beach defences and fish. On
the way home bro and I were squashed among their harvest
and assaulted with songs I didn't know. Our hosts tried to
teach me the words and went through them endlessly. I did

remember a few and began to feel less of an idiot child on an outing. Bro was much better at it than I. The Ramseys, who knew everything in Gilbert and Sullivan and the Methodist Hymnal were delighted and every now and then pierced me with beams of their joy. I also recalled something about a singer who had knocked his head while on the way to a concert and lost all memory of what he had to sing. And there was the explorer who set off for Cape York and returned to Moreton Bay with his pockets stuffed with Sydney tram tickets. So I made up a song about a wreck in which a ship bearing nuns, missionaries, camels, wheat, dried milk and a hermit, is swept over a bombora, ripped open and cast ashore; the grain swells, rises and covers the decks with puffed wheat, the missionaries are trampled by the camels, the nuns group on the forecastle, sing and take a collection, the dried milk is shaken into froth and the milk-sodden hermit wolf-whistles the nuns. I then ran out of words and was trying to bring in the crew when bro made me aware of the awful silence. Do you think it'll be printed in the *Boomerang Songster*? I cried, There are more verses—The nuns grab the hermit and kick him up the backside . . . Mr Ramsey glanced over his shoulder. Mrs Ramsey stared. No, I cried, The nuns don't kick him up the backside—it's the anus. Well, now, said Mr and Mrs Ramsey. Two of their four children looked away and two smirked.

At home bro told Mum who told Dad who flew into a rage and belted me so hard something happened to my eardrums which put me into a coma for three days and bed for a month. Bro suggested to them that I had been kicked by a heifer, and this was what they told the doctor and, later on, me, so that I could tell the doctor I had been kicked by a heifer. He prescribed medicines, rest and sea air. Twice a week I was hauled to the ocean to absorb its goodness. Feigned relapses did not save me. I had to sit in freezing winds and look at kelp. The trips cost them dearly because they had to slave on the farm to make good lost time. My father began to see the ocean as the great healer of things animal and vegetable. Oh.

Bro would sometimes sit by my bed and tell me I needed an interest, something positive and fulfilling. I did not know what he was talking about. He told me that as I was not a sincere church-goer, genuine scouter, keen cadet, adequate sportsman or potential success in anything by nature I would have to cultivate something. Oh, what? He did not know. However, he soon would. In the meantime I should abandon all thought of doctoring. Perhaps I could try teaching. He brought me exercises and books from school and, I suspect, exercises he had set himself, involving bookkeeping and how to manage employees and employers, in order to get the opinion of a man in the street, man in the bed or average person. He was by this time buying his own clothes, banking money and dealing in rabbit skins. He was tall for his age, thin and wiry and generally had several pimples on the left side of his face. There was I, a convalescent schoolboy with nothing in my spirit. Ah, Spirit, bag of seething breath, nay, nay, bags of breath—mouth bag, lung bags, the former the opening in the head which inhales air, receives food, utters sounds and indicates affections, the latter those two spongy, greyish-pink, cone-shaped (?) bodies in the chest which complete the process of turning air into spirit. Eh, eh, St John, leave me in peace. Or is it that having once absorbed the tenets of his ambulance association one is forever stuffed with data of the body? Childbirth. Application of the roller bandage. Circulatory System. Respiratory System. Poisons. Bites. Wounds. Rigor Mortis. Resuscitation. Pseudo Rigor Mortis. Premature Burial. I have plenty of spirit, the trouble is it lacks lumps, coagulations or clots, those bodies of agitation, drive, performance and belief.

One day bro announced that he had been invited to edit the next issue of the school magazine. I offered to contribute a poem.   Huh, I've got poems. I suggested a short history of

119

the cow in Australia. Moo-oo-oo, he replied, and went to welcome a guileless child who had brought rabbit skins.

On Mayday, 1788 (I could have told him) there were two bulls and five cows in the colony of New South Wales, and hardy beasts were they, all the way from the Cape of Good Hope, later famed as Rorke's Drift, after Rorke, an English adventurer who, with many friends, insulted the local inhabitants who then surrounded them and assegai'd (speared), clubbed and generally robbed of life the whole bunch under a fluttering Union Jack. There is a big painting of this incident in the Sydney Gallery and it appears to have been done on the spot. This could not have happened though, because the artist would have needed a scenic lookout, on a knoll perhaps, behind the attackers, and this they would surely not have allowed, gentlemen though the Matabele be. So perhaps the painting was done by a Matabele. Alas, no, for the style is not in their manner, it being obviously more in the Victorian style, with noble suffering English faces and savage Matabele ones. Also, the painter's name is something R.A. Rorke's death and the loss of his Drift happened a long time after the bulls and cows were taken aboard at the Cape for the long journey Eastwards to New South Wales under the command of Cap'n A. Phillip, R.N., but I mention the Rorke painting because of a recent visit to the gallery with members of 3E.

The trip to the gallery was a hard day for all concerned. Three hours on the train there and three back, with the carriage doors locked by the sour guard on instructions from a pent-up teacher, pent-up because he had already lost Bruce and Brian Jones to a refreshment room after a mere twenty miles: Only a third of the way there, he cried, And already we're two down. Yes, pent-up was the teacher and well might he be with the prospect of losing another three to the terrors of the train and its way (ahead lay long tunnels—and what if the lights failed . . . ?) And all of us desperate for at least a cup of tea (the carriage water bottles were dry and dusty; was dehydration the intention of the guard?). The torture increased as we trained by enamelled advertisements on fences: Griffiths' Tea 50m to Sydney; 43m, 35m and so on. Between Redfern and Central, Kingsford Bruhl declared that the buildings alongside the line were definitely made of coal not sooty brick and that when coal is scarce people creep out at night, knock them down and take pieces home to burn. And for his effrontery (shouted Mr Cilly Chosis, the Commerce teacher who had shares in mines) he was whacked over the head and had his ear twisted. As he fell back he called our names as witnesses. Can cows eat coal, Mr Chosis? asked Ted Way, and he too got whacked but shouted back, The Germans turned coal into bread and sausage so why not cowmeal? Mr Chosis sarcas'd, The Lord turned water into wine and one fish into many but that was religion whereas the German method was the scientific transformation of minerals, oils etcetera into ersatz protein and much good will come from this and subsequent enlightenments especially when the red Russians start their tricks—and Way—from what did the Germans make coffee? Hot water and Turban essence, Sir? replied eager Way. Way, respect me, Way, respect me, Way . . . As though in tune with wheel clack. Way left the compartment and Mr Chosis sat down saying, Acorns, they made it from acorns, was that not a splendid achievement? From home-grown materials. They freed themselves from the tyranny of African and American sources. I saw a Griffiths sign 1m to their tea (would it be in a great teapot or would they cater to the spirit of bushmanship with a billy the size of a gasometer?). Tea, sir? I asked, Tea from acorns, too? They do not drink tea, boy, he replied and as he was tired he eased himself by simply kicking me on the shin. We're almost there, someone cried, the someone being Blue practising his many voices. Oh God, said Mr Chosis peering at the soot outside, Remember, all of you, today is an educational outing, so keep together or take sixes when we get home or on the spot if the spirit moves me, and do not gawp at tall buildings, keep out of air raid shelters and

121

amusement (sic) arcades for we do not want to be recognized as country bump— as ah, country visitors. We have come to see the Art Gallery and Museum. Do not fritter your time gawping at exhibits in which you fancifully detect elements of smut but pay heed to instructional paintings and practical models. It is our great misfortune we'll not have time to visit the great Technological Museum in Harris Street where true knowledge lies—that of applied science; paintings, flora and fauna are the stuff of hobby; applied science is the way to riches and power. As we left the carriage it was found that three of us were missing. Mr Badge raged and Mr Chosis peered at the roof and under the carriage. Blue threw a moan among the wheels and Mr Chosis nearly fainted. Ted Way pointed at what seemed to be blood on the wheels at the front. Railway men came running. Here they are, someone yelled, and we turned to see Brownie, Thomo and Reg Constable walking towards us. They had escaped through a window and made their way to the end carriage. Messrs Badge and Chosis took them behind a stack of boxes to administer what is known as summary punishment but a porter followed them and threatened the teachers with dismemberment between two engines. When we got to the ticket barrier there was trouble with the tickets and the collector shouted at Mr Badge who is a returned soldier. Mr Badge put up his fists and moved in like Rocky Graziano, the middleweight champion, forcing the collector into the back of his box until Mr Chosis brought calm. During the disturbance six boys escaped to the magazine counters (Gordon & Gotch Ltd) to annoy the attendants by perusing, disarranging and not buying comics and illustrated salacious papers. Alfie was sent over to bring them back but had his foot run over by a luggage train, his yells echoing from the lofty iron roof until Mr Chosis threatened *him* with six so he hobbled with us to the tram, to the quay, and up to the gallery and Rorke's Drift. We had lunch in the gardens (Botanical) then walked along Macquarie Street behind Messrs Chosis and Badge, past Sydney Hospital, Parliament House (parler, to talk, + house), the Mint (where we sucked noisily), the Rum Hospital (where we staggered), with Saint Stephen's Pres. Church over the road (we clasped hands in prayer) to Hyde Park with the Romans' cathedral, St Mary's on the left (v. big, and rich with strains of mumbo mass and whiffs of incense sniffed even over a road and a hundred yards of park so that we were compelled, some of us, to walk as though crucified), we circled the Archibald fountain twice (imitating Theseus fighting Minotaur and the poses of the naked women). We then entered the Museum and examined stuffed whales, bears, kangaroos and seals, spears, clothing and other items. The journey home was without turmoil.

(End of essay my brother refused for school magazine.)

The next time he came in to see me, he mentioned teaching as a vocation. No, I told him, not for me. You, he told me, Don't want to be helped. I denied this, and asked him to think of other occupations or callings. He was then called to the door to finalize a transaction involving fox skins, bicycle tyres and .22 cartridges.

One day I heard Mum say, Will, let's get away from here and return to the city? No, he replied, That would be running away. Will, Will, we've been on the run—or at least the move —for years. Look, I've traced our comings and goings on the map, from farm to farm, and the pattern's like a number puzzle and the result's a giraffe. You really mean, he shouted, A camel, don't you? You don't want a man with ideals, you want a stodger. Will, I know what a camel looks like. God knows you were like one yourself when you got back from the Kimberley, remember? I had to stroke and knead you back into shape—you wouldn't have got on a bloody tram the shape you were. Every time there was a knock on the door I thought, Ah-a, who is it? vet, RSPCA, Wirth's Circus or the health inspector? There, there, dear, he soothed, We've had good times, and now we're getting money in the bank.   Then let's get another newsagency?   After what happened to the other? he shouted, You need to be rich to live decently in the city. Yes, she said, And I'd like to be rich—and maybe a little indecent.   Mary, *this* is the life: natural, organic. Anyhow, we'd never get the money for another agency.   Fred would help us.   Bugger Fred, he shouted and stamped outside.

She is on my side, I thought. Bro is doing well skin dealing so he's with Dad. Two and two. My condition rapidly improved. I was allowed to sit in a canvas deck chair on the veranda. The quarter-acre garden was enclosed by five-foot netting and six-foot poles, a reminder of the days when there were roos. There were ten fruit trees if you counted the loquat, rows a chain long of rhubarb, celery, cabbage, broad beans, peas and carrots, several rows of potatoes, a patch of strawberries and one of everything. One chain of rhubarb was ridiculous. More than six clumps of rhubarb is ridiculous. Of course he did plan to sell it but this was ridiculous. His plantings were an attempt to deny his migratory instinct. The sharefarmer who took over from us would look at the garden and say, Poor buggers, the Worts, only here long enough to get the garden going; or, They've left us a fine garden and a farm in good heart—there must be something wrong with the owner, otherwise why leave?

After a couple of days I was allowed to go walking, but only in pyjamas, dressing gown and gumboots, as though to restrict my movements in case I decided to run away. I noticed new quirks in my father. On a hill at the back of the house he practised deep breathing whenever the wind came from the North-East or South-East. One day he saw me, came over and asked could I, too, smell it? I couldn't smell anything unusual. He winked, rubbed my hair and went off laughing. Ozone, he shouted back. He had been sniffing sea air on the North-East wind. There was certainly sea in that direction but between us and the sea lay the thumping, smokey steelworks and I could not even smell that. I knew then that we would soon be on the move again, to somewhere closer to the sea. He had the lemming spirit alright. One day he'd take us on a picnic. We'd go over dunes, through scrub, sight the sea and—wham, splash.

It is now time to ask a question: Why did I put up with all that pushing and pulling around by my parents? Here, there, get your things packed; Hurry, or you'll miss the train (or bus or whatever); Come on you'll like where we're going; You've got to learn punctuality if you're going to work in an office (oh yes, they'd chosen deskmanship for me, and didn't mind if the desk was a three-ply one in the middle of a thousand acres of tillage, a construction of coal slabs against a pillar, or a steel thing flanked by lathes in an engineering shop—it didn't matter what or where it was because the thing about that first desk is that it's the bottom step, see, of a deskway to heaven). Perhaps they slaved, dragged and messed around simply to fill me with horror of a life such as theirs.

My brother's bullying was another thing; he was aware of his role as exemplar. When he found out about my wish to go doctoring he was terrified. Doctors rate higher than accountants. He gave me hell even to the extent of learning a little Latin; *cave canem, caveat emptor, centum, contra bonos mores*; he was prepared to go right through the C's—we once visited a house and as he held the gate and ushered me into the garden called out *cave canem*! and when the horrible little dog whipped out at me, slammed the gate on me (To stop it escaping and frothing) shouting, You idiot, I warned you, now look! And so I looked, felt and retreated. At other times he developed ailments and limped, moaned and coughed (but I managed one effective treatment, with a pin—buttock acupuncture). Oh I was a quiet, deferential lad. I did, however, get my end in long before he did. And I wrote . . .

A TALE FOR CHILDREN

On a farm in a fertile district about a dozen miles from the sea lived a farmer named Bray, his wife and their four chil-

dren, Dick, Ruth, Helen and John. It was a well set-up farm
with a herd of good cows, a small flock of handsome sheep,
half a dozen stately draught horses, four splendid pigs, fifty
busy chickens, an agile cat and two dogs (one jokey the
other aloof). The animals were coloured brown and white,
pinky-grey, chestnut and white, black, marmalade, brown
and ginger. Oh, and there was Sandy, who was yellowish. The
grey weatherboard farmhouse had a red iron roof, the milking
shed had a green roof, the tub silo was black, and the hay and
machinery sheds were weathered-wood colour. And there were
three well-built stacks of sheaf hay.

The farmer hoped to buy a farm three miles away for his
sons, and his daughters were going to hospitals to train as
nurses. The four children shared two bicycles and every day
two of them would come straight home from school to help
with the milking and the next day it was the turn of the
others, so that everyone shared in the work. However, despite
all this the farmer feared that his good fortune would not last.
He worried about the rain, the wind and the sun. Every few
years the flood would come, slowly inching up the walls, and
they would have to put furniture on trestles or move things to
higher ground. Sometimes there were long dry spells—but
never a drought—and everybody would be out distributing
hay, silage and maize. Still, he had a good farm and did not
owe the bank much money.

One day he heard that city people wanted to dig a deep hole
in his farm and in those of his neighbours and take away what
was under them. The following day a powerful corporation
decided to bring lines of electricity cables on huge pylons
across another part of their land. The mining engineers began
flying over the valley taking photographs. Then the first
electricity pylon appeared on a hill and soon there were four
down the hill. One day the engineers' aeroplane taxied into a
cow and the smell of roast beef and other things was strong
for two days and when a pylon collapsed detectives were

brought in to find out if the hole under the foundation was natural or criminal. The detectives declared for the former. The farmer hoped that the pylons would soon be completed and cables slung because he saw them as a huge web across the valley and the replacement aeroplane as a fly. One Sunday morning he received a call from a neighbour who told him the mining company had abandoned its plan for the valley, and in the afternoon he heard that the towers had been mis-routed and were to be dismantled. In the evening everybody went to the Shire Hall to celebrate with supper and beer. As they drove home the farmer admitted to his wife that he felt a bit let down after everything.

Over the next fortnight the farmer trembled during the day, and spent nights without sleep. He found footrot in his animals and treated them secretly so as not to have to report the disease. He made everybody wear gumboots and allowed them to come off only for baths and bed. Three times a day they had to dip their feet in formalin water. Visitors were discouraged by two new dogs, fierce alsatians in rubber boots.

Came a Thursday afternoon, cold, clear, with a delicate sun, with willows streaming into mirrors, wattles goldenly motionless, magpies strolling augustly, crows enthroned know-ingly, water hens stepping discreetly and ibis stalking pro-foundly in the lignum and reeds of the small swamp at the foot of the stony hill on the western side of the valley. Dick and Helen were walking home from school as was their right every second day. They came to the old well near the ruins. The boards which covered the well had rotted and the weatherbeaten warning notice had snapped its post and smashed through them. The children had a plan. They also had Sandy, whom they had taken to school for a pet showing. They had previously measured the depth of the well with a weighted string and from the sound of dropped pebbles deduced that the well was dry and half filled with bottles, iron and probably, treasure. The windlass had been repaired and this Thursday afternoon they were ready to explore. Dick put his feet in the loop of rope and Helen braced herself against the handle.

You think it's all right? asked Dick.

Yes, be quick, I can't hold you all day.

Dick peered into the space beneath him. There wouldn't be any snakes, I suppose?

'Course not, she replied impatiently. Look—you lower me down, girls are lighter than boys.

I'm stronger, he said, And I don't care about snakes—lower away. And just before his head disappeared he called good-bye to Sandy.

Go on, Sandy, said Helen, Say goodbye. And Sandy slunk to the well top and put his paws up on the wall. Most people said his eyes were red but there were many different ideas as to what was meant by red. The newsagent called them orange, Mr Green the storekeeper called them reddish, Mrs Dunne the postmistress would never say because she closed hers, Mr Carney the teacher said they were yellowish and the Kays said they were paleish. Everybody was agreed about the colour of his fur though, it was definitely yellowish.

Dick reached the bottom. Helen looked down and watched him shining his torch. He shouted out the inventory: Bottles, old iron, a car battery, a crystal set, and then . . . Pull me up, up, *quick!*

What is it? she cried.

A skeleton!

Oh dear, she'd had an idea there might be something awful down there. Then, Don't bother, he yelled, It's only a funny sort of skull.

Oh! My! she was annoyed. No skeleton.

There's a bike frame, he shouted. Helen did not reply. It was bound to be a boy's bike. She stepped back and let the sunshine warm her face. Words came up the well but she could not tell what they were.

She could see his torch shining. She aimed a small piece of rotten wood at the light. But there came no answering cry from Dick. She called to him but there was still no reply. The silence frightened her. She ran off to get help, then ran back. She ran around the top several times followed by Sandy. She leant over the well, tested the rope and got ready to slide down.

If you're joking, Dick, she said, I'll pee on you. She had an idea and ran to her schoolbag. She wrote a note and stuck it under Sandy's collar. She tied their second rope to the well-rope and dropped it down. When she was halfway down she looked up to see Sandy's little head.

Go home, Sandy, she cried. Bread and milk, bread and milk, liver, liver, liver! He disappeared. She went slowly to avoid burning her hands. Her feet touched bottles and iron. She was surprised by the amount of light because from the top it had seemed dark.

Sandy ran off. Although he was a well-reared pet he was not the children's slave so he allowed himself to be diverted by a rabbit burrow close by, and forgot all about bread and milk and chopped liver.

Helen heaved Dick against the side. She shone the torch into his eyes. She rubbed his face. She stood him up but he fell as soon as she let go. She pulled the loop of rope over him, fastened it under his arms and set about hauling him to the top. He was nearly there when, suddenly, she felt very weak, the rope started to slip through her hands and she felt like vomiting. She managed to loop her end of the rope round an iron frame and tie it there and the last thing she saw was Dick, high above, dangling, spinning slowly against the clear pale sky.

The exit of the rabbit burrow Sandy had explored was twenty feet nearer home than its entrance so that his underground journey was not altogether a waste of time. He wiggled his shoulders and Helen's message poked out further

129

from under his collar. He darted across the hill, stopped, sniffed, moved on. He felt hungry and looked forward to his bread and milk and chopped liver . . .

Young Tom Kay saw him. He was looking for pieces of the meteorite he had seen fall the month before. Tom bent and picked up a stone. It was heavy. He stood very still. Sandy stopped fifty feet away, raised his little head and sniffed, but as there was no wind he did not smell him. Tom got ready to throw. He turned the heavy stone in his hand. Sandy came closer, stopped again and scratched his neck with his hind paw, but did not dislodge the paper. Tom saw Sandy simply as a savage, wild ferret, one that killed poultry, ate the eggs and fledgelings of ground-nesting birds and killed bandicoots and goannas. Suddenly Tom saw Sandy's collar. He called to him and stamped the ground, knowing that a ferret's eyes are not the best in ordinary daylight. So Tom went over and picked him up.

Why are you out, Sandy? asked Tom, Where are Dick and Helen? Then he saw the piece of paper under Sandy's collar. He put Sandy down and ran to the well. He managed to haul Dick to safety. He could see Helen in the torchlight. He wondered how he could get down, decided he could not, and tore off for help. But only got a little way before he ran back, pulled the loop of rope off Dick and dropped it down the well. He slid down so quickly he burnt his hands. He quickly put the loop under Helen's arms, leant her against the side then squiggled up the ropes to the clean surface air and hauled her to safety. He lay Dick on his left side with his left arm against his back and his right hand cushioning his cheek and threw his coat over him. He gave Helen artificial respiration and when he thought her breathing would last he covered her with his coat and attended to Dick. Then he leant one against the other for warmth and dashed off for help. He remembered Dick's father's fierce alsatians. He turned and headed for his own father's farm.

A Chapter for Tots

Tom's Daddy and Mummy were in the milking shed hand-milking their cows. They didn't have a milking machine because they had so many children they didn't need one. The work kept the children out of mischief. There had once been lots of mischief when a man persuaded Tom's Daddy to try a milking machine. Wasn't there trouble then! You see Tom's Daddy had a maize crop which looked like being the best in the district if not the world because the tassells were twelve feet high. There was even talk of the maize pullers wearing stilts to reach the cobs. Well, when the machine was installed the children had idle hands and do you know what they did? I'll tell you. They dug these tunnels under the crop of twelve foot maize and one night there was a noise like a deep sigh, and when Tom's Daddy went a-milking in the morning, do you know what he saw? He saw that his crop of maize had shrunk to eighteen inches, in fact all he had left was a crop of tassells a-blowing in the morning breeze. He was ever so angry. He made them walk up and down the rows a-pulling-up maize plants. However, there was rain that day and the tunnels filled with water and the land subsided. Well, Tom's Daddy threw out the milking machine and went back to hand milking.

Anyway. Tom ran to his Mummy and Daddy to tell them about Dick and Helen in the well. His Daddy shouted: You lazy pigturd, I suppose you've been mooching for sky iron?

Tom said, Yes, Daddy.

Tom's Daddy roared, Don't give me that Daddy poop you little bigmouth! You call me Dad—now, grab that broom there and get into the shit.

Oh, dear, sobbed his Mummy, Don't be hard on the boy—perhaps he'll become a sky scientist.

Yes, roared Daddy, And start calling you Mummy!

If he does become a scientist, she sobbed, He'll be able to tell us what the weather is going to do.

Everybody back to work! roared Daddy.

The cows have gone dry! shrilled a child.

Tom, dear, asked Tom's Mummy, What were you saying about the well?

Dick and Helen fell down it, he sobbed.

Well, well, said his Daddy. And why did you have to run to us with this horrible tale?

Because—because, sobbed Tom, I'm frightened of Dick's and Helen's Daddy's rubber-booted alsatians!

Tom's Daddy paled at the mention of these dreadful animals. I'll go and tell him, he snapped. All right—everyone back to work, get that milk down! And with that he went to the house, got his shotgun, filled his pockets with shells and drove to the well where he gave Dick and Helen more respiration, wrapped them in blankets, sat them on the front seat and gave them a great deal of brandy. Then he drove them to their Daddy's front gate.

Mr Kay, hic, What are you, hic, going to shoot? managed Dick.

Not our Shandy, Mr Kay? slurred Helen.

Yes, he shouted, that horrible little ferret of yours—and those alsatians!

Mishter Kay, said Dick, I'll give, hic, you their boots inshtead.

Boy, there isn't any footrot around here, it's in your Dad's mind.

All three looked for the alsatians but they were nowhere to be seen. Mr Kay opened the gate and drove to the house. The children's Mummy and Daddy were overjoyed to see them. Mr Kay accepted a glass of Christmas port. The alsatians had been given to a hawker that very afternoon who had promised to make them gentle. Indeed, he had demonstrated his way with them by dancing a threesome at the gate.

And there's no footrot, cried Mr Kay, What you call footrot is something that happens hereabouts every thirty-seven years and now is the time it vanishes overnight.

132

At that moment who should peep round the door but Sandy! He was given a hero's welcome, and all the bread and milk and chopped liver he could eat. As Mr Kay drove away the children's Mummy phoned the newspaper and told the editor what had happened and he promised the item *a good spread* and said that he would whisper in the proper ears and see that Sandy's heroic deeds received a just reward from the King and his S.P.C.A.

A Chapter for Herbal-Minded Children

Farmer Bray, once a downcast gloomer, became a joyful optimist. He retrieved the bicycle frame from the well, had it restored, and bought another so that each child had one. He bought the hero, Tom, a restored telescope and he bought the hero, Sandy, a mate. These cases of generosity are not, of course, indications of optimism; however, they were in that direction. He saw life blooming. Elsewhere people were being bombed, burnt and starved but all that was about to end and be replaced by universal brotherhood. His cousin was killed in action so he undertook to pay the widow and her children an allowance he could little afford.

We beat the mining company, the electricity and we are defeating the enemy, he often said.

The earth murmured with Spring growth, the air buzzed with fecundity. His wife urged him to remove his rose-tinted spectacles. One day he said to himself: By God, things are rosy. And when he stepped onto the veranda to go in to lunch he fell in a fit. The doctor prescribed rest and tonic wine. But his condition did not improve. So his wife took him to a specialist in the city. The specialist prescribed tonic wine and a high altitude.

But I live on the coast, cried the farmer. And the specialist nodded sympathetically.

The farmer and his wife strolled gloomily through the city. They came to an old-fashioned, galleried arcade with numis-

133

matists, philatelists, shoemakers, saddlers, barbers, dental mechanics, sandwich makers, a library, a pharmacy, a news-agency, milliner, chiropodist and many others. The floor was marble, the roof curved glass and in between was a floor with cast iron railings. The farmer stopped and told his wife: I am not going back the way I came. I am going to have my feet done. So he went to the chiropodist who did wonderful things to his feet, and his wife went to the milliner's and bought a hat. In better spirits they continued their walk through the arcade.

Suddenly he seized her arms, crying: That's what I need! People looked at them. From above a voice thundered: Are you all right, lady? From a man in a bowler leaning on the railing of the upper walk. The farmer led his wife into a shop filled with bags of seeds, meals, barks, leaves, juices and milks. He explained his symptoms to the intense, elderly man behind the counter. His wife humming nervously. The man gave him a bowl of cold porridge, a glass of spinach juice and a box of assorted seeds, meals etc. for which he paid three pounds.

Three pounds! gasped his wife, that's thirty gallons. The man then gave them goat's milk *on the house*.

On the train the farmer ate many, many seeds. Four days later he was *brimming* with health. He became an *advocate* of the natural diet. He did not insist on the abolition of meat from their diet but he persuaded them to eat no more than Sandy, the ferret. (And he fed Sandy more and more bread and milk, yes he did.)

Finally, a Chapter for Children who Appreciate
Fine-Wrought Prose . . .

What are they, Dad? asked John, the son who had not gone down the well. The farmer gazed at the tiny creatures, crawling and smeared, on his big, rough, though splendidly-mooned thumbnail and, after deep and patently obvious cogitation, replied: I do not know. They are not aphids, bean fly, false loopers, plague thrips, grape-leaf blister mite, onion fly, carrot fly, leafhoppers or leaf-lacers. They do not appear to damage anything in the garden, and so far as I can ascertain they are not depredating pastures. However, they do possess an ominous quality. They do not suck, nor do they bite.

John admired his father's calm for he knew that these minute animalcules had pestered him almost to breaking point. If only they would chew, suck, smell or make sound! All they did was proliferate. Was the creature to inherit the earth? Father and son parted and went their separate ways. When they met several hours later, the son was twitching with apprehension; the man's eyes glowed with joyous comprehension for he had consulted an old almanack, or rather, the remains of an old almanack, for the ravages of time, a long sea journey and ravenous silverfish, slaters, earwigs and other things had taken their toll (and whatismore the almanack spoke of troll and these, too, could well have ingested fragments of wisdom). Although he was aware of the need to contain and eventually banish superstition, the farmer referred to the aspects of troll as related in the almanack. Indeed, he laughed as he told his son, who, however, was quick enough to notice his father's gaze as it swept his creature-burdened garden before coming to rest, fearfully, on the headless gnome beneath the brass tap of the 44-gallon drum cum tank of rainwater from the meathouse roof. Meathouse! Now a shrine to their meatlessness. That eerie if not dread structure in the garden, forty feet from the house, a warped weatherboard eight-foot-cube topped by a steep pyramid of shingles, and lined inside with flywire, and just above head height, a ceiling of beams hung with meathooks—beef hooks, mutton hooks, lamb hooks and rabbit hooks, no longer used.

The almanack discoursed on the benefits of seaweed, of its iodine, bromine, magnesium, potassium, nitrogen and oh! so many others—indeed it spoke glowingly of ocean essences generally.

The farmer had decided to experiment with seaweed. If it

135

did not destroy the ominous animalcules it would at least invigorate the plants in his garden. Bulk, harvesting and distance from the sea were the only disadvantages the farmer and his son could see in the idea. Unfortunately they would not be able to carry much on the back of the utility they had made from an old Buick sedan.

One overcast Saturday morning they set off for Five Mile Beach, about an hour away, but after twenty minutes the farmer turned off the road saying, We'll visit Pleasant Downs, to see a machine they've made. It's said to have an ingenious system of irreversible banjo-strung pulleys.

The road ran between fine pastures, rows of short and tall windbreaks, haystacks, dams, cultivation, fine-flanked milch cows, sturdy-sided beefy ones; pigs with deep, well-let-down sides and level and even in the underline. The pigs so captured their attention they stopped the Buick and appraised the animals with the usual skilful ease of the man on the land. They noted one especially: a medium-sized head, broad and fleshy, wide between the ears (pricked and inclined forward, fringed with fine silky hair) and eyes (bright and kindly) with an even-dished face and healthy friendly saliva dripping; and the skin! smooth, pliant, scurfless, free from wrinkles, lice, tumours and cancers; ribs were well-sprung and broad; action was distinguished, smart and active; loins were full and wide, powerful and not drooping; and the chest was deep and full; the hams were broad, long, deep, and fleshy down to the hocks.

Not bad, eh? said the farmer. However, it is not for us. We have forsworn meat.

He's good all right, Dad, but his colour's wrong; he should be black with a white facial blaze, white feet and tail tip.

My god, you're right! exploded the farmer. This one's rusty . . . Still, it's a Pleasant Downs pig and they do peculiar things here. Ordinarily I wouldn't let you come here, but today you're with me.

Although Pleasant Downs was regarded as a large farm, it

136

was really a village built around a square with a fountain, troughs, benches and two flame trees. There were eight trim houses, each with a tiny garden, a common orchard and vegetable garden, two big wooden sheds and an office building. The farmer parked the Buick near the office, and was inside only a minute when the door flew open and he reappeared briskly stepping backwards, as though driven out by the noise within which suddenly became intelligible to John.

It's *ours*. We invented it and our patent's pending and we're not showing it to businessmen disguised as farmers—we've been laughed at for years—now we've got SOME-THING—get out, get out—where's that watchdog—yes, we've got one—though never thought we would—got him yesterday.

The farmer turned and walked slowly towards his son who saw three curtains move in three houses. A thin man wearing overalls and a beret came to the office door. He gave a piercing two-finger whistle. The farmer hurried. A dog dashed from between two houses. It was an alsatian! John picked up a wrench from between his feet. The alsatian ran at the farmer, who had whipped off his coat and wrapped it round his arm. They recognized the dog, and cried, Blitz! Blitz relaxed a little, even gave half a wag. Blitz! yelled the man, and the dog crouched low, snarling. His new owner walked from the office.

I thought you were peaceful here, shouted the farmer.

The door of the nearest house opened and a woman strode over the veranda saying, It was too, until Chairman Herbert here puffed up like a frog—there, see him now, puffing?—and told us we had to plan like BHP, a B, an H and a PPP. Bloody Herbert Prism.

Mr Prism, not looking at her, said: That our community was threatened from without, we all knew; it was up to me to disclose the inner threats. Such as yourself, Mrs Gilmore.

Mrs Gilmore, a tall, thin middle-aged woman wearing gum-boots, short dress and red and green beret sang: The Co-opers'

137

flag is red and green/When tyrants come we fight them clean.

Bravo, Mrs G, exclaimed Mr Prism, But it's not necessary for you to entertain us with your songs. Just be sure all your belongings are packed ready for the van. Mrs Gilmore sang: Hark, hark the dog does bark/There's froth in his mouth to put out the spark/But it won't spit out and he'll drown in cark.

Mr Prism addressed the farmer thus: Mrs G is a deranged lady poet crammed with archaisms like cark. I've heard it before. It means anxiety.

Cark, cark car car car-rrrrrr, croaked Mrs Gilmore. You bloodless businessman.

Another metamorphosis to Mrs G, cried Mr Prism, Excellent. She has such a wide repertoire of animal noises that during wet spells members see our houses as eight arks moored to the fountain, so please forgive her.

The crow's wiser than the businessman, Mr Prism. Remember the maize planting? To the farmer she explained: A tribe of five crows here, doing untold good, took as rations a titch of seed maize. So Ledger Prism has to lay poisoned seed. So, crow eats, finds it not to his fancy, and retches into pig paddock. So, we have sick pigs. Eh, Prism, wizen, eh? Ca-aaa, caaaa.

Said Mr Prism to the farmer, You are witnessing democracy at work. She has her free speech.

Free speech? screamed Mrs Gilmore. This is my last one —you're evicting us, you scrawny pervert.

The farmer looked over his shoulder painfully and called to his son: She means prefect. John nodded, and thinking he was in class asked: A synonym, sir?

That's it, boy, shouted Mrs Gilmore. Pleasant Downs is dominated by p's—.

We were, interrupted Mr Prism smoothly to the farmer, A communistic community until altered social conditions compelled us to change our ways. We still believe in the Commonwealth, sexual liberty—

Liberties, you mean, Mr Prism, with boys, men, calves and sheep and the once-only mock-it with us women.

She is quite beside herself, said Mr Prism. The farmer said: Couldn't I have a quick look at your—.

You do not have to ask, said Mrs Gilmore, slowly, He waves it unasked.

No, snapped Mr Prism, The machine is not for viewing.

Oh-ho! trilled Mrs Gilmore, So it is now a machine, eh?

Go away, bitch! shrieked Mr Prism.

And with that the unpleasant man sooled the crouching alsatian on Mrs Gilmore who, however, threw a rug over him and dragged him into the house. The farmer told Mr Prism that such treatment of the dog would bring on an attack of nerves or distemper. Fallen pizzle even, oh oh, a complaint not unknown amongst humans (he had lowered his voice) which requires syringeing five times daily with a solution of bluestone in rainwater (Mr Prism looked anxiously at his informant and pressed his knees together, tighter and tighter), and if this does not clear it up then you've got to slit the pizzle and drain the unwholesomeness.

Is that all? shrieked Mr Prism.

No, said the farmer, It spreads to the liver which turns pasty. Mr Prism fell to the ground clutching his crutch and making noises like many sheep coughing.

An unhappy property, said the farmer sadly as he drove back to the main road.

Hello, said John, What's that over there?

My goodness, said his father, Those pigs, I knew there was something the matter with them.

They were rusty, said John.

Colour's the least of it, said his father as he braked the Buick. They've got someone down and though he may be a communist he's still a human being. You take the mattock, I'll take the axe.

Me, the mattock?

Would you rather the axe, son?

139

I'd rather the crowbar.

No, you're not going to spear or lance—they'd run off with it—it's a good bar, so take the mattock—we can bury things with it.

As they clambered through the taut fence John suggested that the bundle of rags might simply belong to a scarecrow. His father sternly urged him on.

We'll soon see.

The superbly proportioned though miscoloured pigs ignored their approach and went on circling and darting in on the bundle of rags. The farmer cut the top of a pig's head off, John belted one on the snout and the remainder squealed off, after one with the head-top between its jaws.

The bundle of rags was a dishevelled maiden of breathtaking beauty. Her name was Rosa. She had talisman hair, rosy cheeks, bloodshot eyes and scratches on her pale skin. She embraced father and son. She had been sketching pigs at pasture and been taken by surprise. It was her seventeenth birthday and she had the day off.

You mean Prism is so generous? asked the farmer.

Yes, she sobbed, It's one of the rules he hasn't been able to put in his hip pocket, and bend. And he mustn't know about what's happened—could you take the pig and eat it?

I'm afraid not, said the farmer, We are vegetarians.

Fuck it, she cried.

Ahem, coughed the farmer. You want a bucket?

Oh, let's take the pig to the windbreak and bury it, she said. So they dragged the carcase to the trees and the farmer set to work with the mattock he had so positively ordered his son to bring. Rosa asked John to accompany her to the other windbreak to retrieve the head-top.

Among the paperbarks she hugged John, tenderly, then impassionedly and they fell down.

Isn't this like a fairy tale, she whispered. I was about to be turned into pig when you rescued me! John peered round a trunk and saw his father digging.

140

Turn me into your lover, he cried.

What a beautiful thing to say.

And she pulled up her ragged dress, untied her black bow, kicked off her gumboots and opened her thighs. John pulled down his trousers and got between her legs. She shook her head and spread her hair (talisman) and away they went, but not far because she gasped: Your boots, you're not doing me with your boots on? and she pushed them off with her toes.

John looked round the trunk.

How deep is he? she whispered.

To his knees, and he's among stones.

Then we'd better get back.

When can I come again?

Oh, you won't—anyway I'm going to the city next week.

So they returned to the farmer who had by this time half filled the hole. They told him the pigs had eaten what they had set out to bring back. He had little to say. John and Rosa replaced the sods he had so carefully cut out. Until all that remained of the place was a grassy bulge. The farmer wiped his axe and led the way back. On their way down the road he said, Were you kissing and that down there? and John stammered and his father said, Well, I suppose it'd be natural to snatch a kiss after what happened. And that was all he had to say. The two of them drove on in silence.

Soon they were driving through coastal heath. Then the track went round and over dunes covered with banksia and pigface. They crawled up a steep pinch and stalled on the high crest in slow mist. They heard sea thunder from the southern cape and John thought he heard gunfire. The track ended beside a lagoon through the seaward dune near an abandoned gunpit like the bottom of a silo. Barbed wire flagged with seaweed sagged between bent steel posts. Mist came from the sea in waves, slowly in highs and lows. The sea was gentle and there was no sound from the cape. In front of the barbed wire seaweed banked knee-deep and on the thirty yards or so of sand lay strange mounds.

Seals? whispered John when he saw them.

Weed; nutrition and health, corrected his father addressing the sea. Various peoples would consider us wantons for intending to utilize it as manure. To some it is a staple of diet, as in say, kelp mince, wrack rissoles, sea-lettuce salad; while elsewhere vigorous local industries wrest invaluable iodine from the seaherb; there is also the famous seaweed derivative petroxymol of carragheen, the key to the universal efficacy of wonderful Bonnington's Irish Moss, that extraordinary decongestant and general internal salve. You go off and have a good look round while I get the weed ready. Keep your eyes peeled for ambergris. Cuttles too.

So John walked down and along the beach. He went cautiously; close to the water, on hard sand, he was surprised to find tyre tracks. What he at first took to be ambergris turned out to be a rotten flitch of bacon. He filled his pockets with cuttles. He saw something dark in the shallows and stood still. Somewhere a sea bird piped. He crept towards the object. It moved. He thought he heard an engine far off. The shape splashed, grew bigger and staggered into deeper water. He darted closer. It was a man wearing a tweed suit. He called out. The man turned.

You all right? asked John. The water rose higher on the man. You're going the wrong way, he called, but the man went on.

John splashed into the water after him, grabbed his sleeve and the man turned round quietly, followed him to shore and fell down. John held him under the arms and hauled him to the tideline.

You were going the wrong way—what happened to your ship?

Ship? I'm not off a ship.

He was an elderly man with a white beard and a gingery moustache. His suit though wet, smelt of greasy wool.

Do you always swim in your suit?

I was going from paradise to paradise lad, and paradise roots you. If you don't think so read this—no, take a dozen and separate them when they're dry. He took from an inside pocket a wad of paper.

A cry rose from the dune behind them: Sa-ammmm!   Shit, muttered Sam. Through thin mist John saw a figure walk down the dune. He noticed the path through cut barbed wire. A tall middle-aged woman in a long navy coat and floppy maroon hat approached.

There you are, Sam. Thank you for helping him, young man. Here you are, Sam, take a good swig.

John took one arm, she took the other and they staggered up the dune, and over, and down to an old Austin Seven at the end of a track. She undressed Sam, wrapped him in rugs, put him in the car, shook hands with John and drove away.

He returned to the beach, looked at the tracks, felt his trousers wet to the knee, removed his boots, emptied them of water, sat on the sand and shouted to the sea, Yes? He then followed his footprints along the beach. He heard the engine again. The noise grew through gear changes. He ran to the barbed wire. A motorcycle cut through the mist. The rider in leathers.

John ran back towards the beach and met his father, who sniffed and muttered: Motor cycles—where there's one there's more—let's go! They loaded the last of the weed and went home. His mother hung his coat over the kitchen range, went through the pockets, found the wad of wet paper, lifted a ring and tossed it onto the coals.

His mother turned away and like lightning John reached in to the stove, and retrieved the wad of smouldering papers. He did not burn his fingers, did not even sear them or singe finger-hairs. He was quick-fingered. He was inquisitive. Why had the old man been lurching in the shallows? Why had he been swimming on such a day on such a beach? Clothed, and in high risk of being run down by a crazy speedster on a motor bike? In mist, too. Had he been struck by the machine his clothes would have been a hindrance because the aider on

143

the spot would have had to have cut them away to attend to the wounds and torn them into strips for bandages, tourniquets, ligatures and the other uses to which clothes are put.

He took the papers to his room and carefully separated them. They were leaflets and brochures, sometimes in triplicate, by Roderick Skitart: *A Journey to the Edges of the Mato Grosso, Through the Straits of Magellan, Report of an Attempt to Cross the Merino with Guanaco, My Discovery of Machupicchu Years Before the Yale Expedition 'Discovered' It*, and oh so many more. It was a wonder his mother had been able to press the wad into the stove, and little short of miraculous that he had been able to extract it, especially the two outer publications, printed on material resembling blotting paper. The first, *An Interesting Social Experiment on the North Coast of NSW*, was about the somewhat plausible doings of a Mister R. Russell, a communalist, sometime pro-Boerist, a regulator of sexual passion, a slight man whose long hair went to the shears of a deranged patriotic shearer, a cyclist of great achievement who once, when refused conveyance by a Miller's to Milson's ferryman, leapt into the harbour with his bicycle and crossed so hindered; a man who established a thriving though short-lived community whose production of broom millet and subsequent manufacture of brooms brought about a significant decrease in the general death-rate—and how did the life assurance companies respond to this lowering of the death rate? By supplying the knives plunged so treacherously into the by then hapless Russell. The second paper, *A Refutation of Russell: A Postscript to an Interesting Social Experiment on the North Coast of NSW*, dealt with Russell's horse dealings with Chile and Argentina, his hairiness-is-beyond-godliness, his manipulation of the co-op he had set up, his surrounding himself with virgins, his downfall and the probability of his becoming a martyr in the eyes of the impressionable. So many sheets of words. And not a single pound note. So the lad took the papers to the fire and burnt

144

them. He asked his father about the beach incident. The old man—Skitart?—had been going to commit . . . ?

No, the old man was a bit senile and had got away from his nurse. Don't occupy your mind with such incidents. Beaches are happy open places, not thickets of despair.

The next day, Saturday, the father borrowed a horse float and went off. The mother wrung her hands and went around murmuring Oh my god, not again, I've had about enough. He returned mid-afternoon with a camel in the float. To the children it looked old and scabby. The mother watched, tense and cursing, from the window. Suddenly, she changed and took a tea tray onto the veranda. The father was trying to coax the camel out.

Leave him/her, called the mother. Have your tea, and afterwards there'll be a packet of dates for the—the beast. The children would not go near the float.

The mother said to the father, Look, I didn't mind you going to the Kimberley to look at camels but why bring a camel here, where it doesn't belong? Mrs Steel is seven months gone and she might see it. And see how the chooks and poddies stay well away. The cows'll go dry. And there's no market for camel milk or cheese—I'm assuming it's a camel cow. So, why dear husband, why do you want a camel?

Some men, he replied, have sought the holy grail, the perfect double, the ideal udder or the magic number. My search is harmless to others and probably of benefit to me. Had I not taken this beast it would have gone as bait. Years ago I saw the camel as a mystical beast worthy to stand with the lion and unicorn or displace one of them. As a boy I saw my first camel—leading in line of four—striding along a fen dyke one misty afternoon, late, in Cambridgeshire, owned by a local squire, who had been in the desert. I rode along a lane on my bike. The squire rode the leading one and the others had sou'wester'd men in the saddle. Oh yes, they certainly looked funny, and self-conscious, but they were well paid for their task. Then they began to gallop and the squire led them round Ely Cathedral, which is a great, awesome building plonked in the middle of flatland with pretty well no buildings around it. They galloped and the squire tried to lead them inside, down the aisle, but vergers and two policemen on bikes stopped them. I never saw them again. They have remained in my memory. I, however, do not intend anything of a similar nature. This is not Ely. I have only one camel. I have a mind to organize camel trips along the big beach in summer.

I was going to give you a packet of dates to help you get him/her out of the float, said the mother, But I'll not encourage you. Listen to the poor dogs, and you an animal lover.

The father tried to unload the float without dates. He tried raisins, sultanas, bananas and apples, and once, when it seemed he might succeed, he was bitten by a dog. He then called his son and they drove, with the camel, to the beach, to exercise it and soften sores and lumps.

It was misty there. The camel left the float as quickly as possible. The father led the camel off into the mist. The day was much the same as when they had made their previous visit. The lad wandered along a little and saw an old man—Skitart?—wading in the sea. Then the woman and two men ran down the dune and dragged the old man away. The motor cycle spat through the mist. It came back and stopped near him.

The rider was a middle aged dark man who asked: You seen anything funny on the beach?

The lad replied, There was an old man trying to swim.

He's always here, said the rider.

What are you doing riding up and down the beach? asked the boy.

I used to be in rodeos and troupes, said the man, until I decided I was getting a bit old for it. I decided to get into the speedway business but the going round and round made me dizzy, and as I couldn't sell the bike I decided to get a few quid having a go at the world speed record. I'm on 16 : 1, cams of my own, secret design, methanol nitroglycerine. You're sure you didn't see anything funny on the beach? I hope you did, otherwise I'm seeing spooks.

I am ashamed of my father, thought the lad. Then, How fast do you go?

About 167.33.

It must be cold. Do you ever hit birds? There are albatrosses here.

The man made a menacing gesture. He bump-started and streaked off.

The lad grew cold so jogged along the beach and when he came to what reminded him of a marine bunyip he turned in his tracks and went the other way. Sooner or later he would come across his father.

And did, half a mile away. He lay on his side a couple of chains from where the bloody neck of the camel stained the sand. Bits of head were here and there. The father groaned for several minutes before he sat up. He said he was all right, that all he needed was a snooze, the damn camel had kicked him as he pressed his shoulder to its rump to get it up, it had given a terrific belch and that was that. The lad took him to the car, covered him with blankets, gave him the thermos then ran back to the beach. The rider was two hundred yards from the camel, in the shallows, head under the water, broken-necked, and dead. The lad set off for the car again, to get a shovel to bury the rider and camel but half way there turned back to check the tideline. Already the rider was moving in the current. Only the handlebars of his machine showed above water. The lad went back to the car. To where the father snored. He got shovel, crowbar and rope.

The camel had become a groyne against which the rider was pressed. The lad dragged the rider half out of the water and set to dragging sand from under the camel and when he thought he had taken enough tied the rope round its hind legs and tugged seawards. He fell several times but with each

147

fall found the camel easier to drag and when he could no longer manage the waves he ducked under, untied the rope and surged ashore. The rider had vanished. He ran through the shallows, with the current, and when he guessed that he must be well ahead of the body ran to the high tide mark and dug a grave a few feet deep. But he could not find the body. So he tiredly gathered up the rope and tools and stumbled up the beach towards the cleft in the dunes, looking over his shoulder, seeing nothing but wads of mist, hearing nothing but the faint plash of tide and now and then a murmur of sea on the far reef.

He pressed on for two paces and was cast back into his trail. The old, sagging barbed-wire fence. Arrested on many points of law. Between mist and sand huddled this wet shivering blob on its many-printed trail. Something doomed to scrabble from sea to dune. So he took shovel and rope and filled the hole he had dug above the tideline and as he retraced his steps to the car dragged the rope and obliterated the trail.

On the running board of the car he once again became a wet shivering blob, exhausted morally and physically by his exertions. I.e., he thought, An attempted burial. Grave digging on the strand. If caught, it's the reformatory because I've disposed of evidence, cast away a corpse, burley'd the sea for sharks, dug an unauthorized grave on the strand, and—he now got into the front seat—drove away from the scene with no intention of notifying the police.

To make his escape decent and proper he stopped, dragged his father into the front, removed his overcoat, wrapped him in two rugs, dressed himself in the overcoat and woollen cap and sat on a cushion to appear taller and older. He drove with style but took a right turn, went through a familiar township with a small boat harbour, noticed that the car behind seemed to have a policeman at the wheel, and kept driving north until he came to the outskirts of the steel town. Wire fences, rusty scrap, shacks, hostels, smoke and stench, coal and coke trains, steam and grit, lagoon and swamp, houses and overhead wires.

The father looked up, peered, and mumbled, We're here? A good town for a business; am thinking of unfarming and businessing instead; because this is where the sick are, the poor reeling urbs in need of herbs; on the farms, us rurs are fit and able and have it too good. I'll open a health shop here.

The car still behind. On to the big town. The car behind disappeared. Now and then his father sniffed or mumbled. To the left the town's suburbs straggled up towards the escarpment. He knew he somehow had to turn the car, go South then West. If he kept going he would come to the pass. The Buick could not climb more than halfway before stalling and running backwards and over the side to join the other wrecks. He had a chance to turn left but had to take the right. He drove three times round a block and as his father began to stir began a fourth circuit but had to go on when people began pointing. He drove towards the high suburbs. Red and liver brick, cream weatherboards, low fences and hedges. Along a road leading to a brick church with a big arched open door, the churchyard thick with pines. He braked, and muttered, as his father slid forward, It's god's arsehole.

His father banged his head but did not complain beyond a Jesus! He pushed his father back, got the car going, turned South, had to turn West then North, West again and found himself in a dead end with the church a mere hundred yards ahead. His father looked up. Aaaah. The stubble of gravestones, the cicatrice of crucifix.

They got away, onto the escape road which soon led them to the steeltown where the father, his head against the door window, began sniffing at the stench seeping inside and he opened his eyes, looked up at his son (who glanced down at him), looked through the glass/pressed his nose against it and looked out and said: How many years have I slept? You've grown into a tall lad, have I been in hell, and are you rescuing me—no, we're still there from the look of outside, so I'll keep quiet till we're clear. He pulled a blanket over his head. Murk smeared the windscreen, the blast furnaces choomped.

A bit dirty out there but it looks interesting, said the lad.

The father pulled the rug from his face: In this locality health food would prove too much for the inhabitants—or it would heat their blood and cause the steelmasters to disallow it for fear of uprisings—or health food brought here would turn to ashes—or it would have to be processed, sliced and wrapped—or it would be allowed in only for holidays—the complications are an unknotable net. He withdrew to the sanctuary of the rug. Enfolded, he added, I have gone right off health foods. Stop at the butcher's and we'll get some steak.

When they left the steelworks behind the father began to heave, so the lad stopped. The father leapt from the car and saw the camel float. He looks somewhat like a bedouin, thought the lad. The father smote his brow, breast and right shoulder, and spewed raucously. He sounds like a camel, thought the son. When empty, the father climbed through the fence and grazed on the fine pasture.

The day after they reached home the father announced that it was time they moved. The mother, glad that something had been done about the camel, took the announcement calmly.

All right, she said, Let's go North.

(Conclusion of Children's and Adolescents' Tales.)

William Wort saw an ad for a share-farmer at Peeny, many miles to the North, a region laved by fringes of monsoon, frost-free, not far from the sea, where share-farmers quickly became owner-farmers, where roads were sealed, passion fruit grew wild, pineapples grew in forty-fours, maize had to be ring-barked and the Country Party ruled. Mary refused to let William drive the car. You'll keep going right up to the Cape, I know you, she told him. She carefully calculated his expenses and allowed him ten bob as pocket money. He went to his son, Tom, and asked for a loan. Tom, who was against moving, spoke of falling rabbit skin prices (due to the arrival of hare skins from Queensland or worse), the state of the money market (particularly unsworn debentures), the death of W H Conylapin the skin tycoon (ill-fitting dentures) and the rise of rural standover merchants. William needed money so he signed an IOU. He returned four days later with the share agreement. He hadn't touched the borrowed money but Tom demanded interest all the same, saying, How do you expect me to understand the business world and get on if you won't play fair?   My god, said William, I've bred a banker.

The new farm was on the Merther River flats, four miles from Peeny: Welcome to. The farm was one of five owned by tiny, eighty-year-old Jasper Screw, who spent his declining years riding from farm to farm hacking tree seedlings because they robbed the soil and were a hazard to aeroplanes. William had never had irrigation pumps to play with before, and after a little while he had all the silage and hay he could use. Then he had to sell most of it to pay the water pumping bill. The weather stayed beautiful and fine. Then it became dry. Drought is no problem here, he told his family, There's always the river to pump from. But as the river flow slackened, tides came further up the river and soon the water was too salty for pastures. Twelve inches one weekend finished the drought. On Monday morning at sunrise Mary said, We are truly roofworts with a houseboat. Percy said, Mum, You've a dry sense of humour. He shrieked hysterically at his joke and fell into the flood. She jumped in after him and when they regained the roof, clipped his ear, and he fell in again. With a bitter smile he swam round the house several times. You're tedious, shouted his brother. Percy was very impressed by this expression and said it to himself many times. Come up here and get out of those wet pyjamas, yelled his mother. Don't yell, dear, said William, With all the damp around you'll croup. It was your idea to come here, she snapped. Let's move, eh? he replied. Up, into the hills, eh?

And so, at Uppersass, the Worts gained altitude, their own farm (give or take a mortgage or two), a sense of community and the dignity of near-poverty. Tom stayed at school, got his Leaving, and started work with the Peeny auctioneer, who also owned the newspaper. Percy managed his Intermediate, worked with his father for a while then went to the city as a clerk for a vegetable wholesaler . . . six months later he came home. Sacked? they shrieked at him. Resigned, he lied. He rented ten acres from Jasper Screw and planted onions. Onions! everyone cried. People came from afar to look at his rows and rows of onions. One hundred and thirteen rows, he told them. Sometimes he pulled a top and cried for them. Sometimes he had fifteen people working for him and occasionally they bumped one another over and cried into the bruised tops. He worked very hard and often drank at the Merther. In two years' time I'll have three hundred acres of onions, he told the shocked bar. Peeny people had something intangible against onions. He was beaten up twice. He cleared £3,000. People were aghast. This Uppersass hillbilly had dared come down on the flats like a fox upon ducks (eagle on hens, dingo on calves, Jap upon Darwin were other popular similes).

Jasper Screw refused to rent him land. He couldn't buy land because he had given his father £1,500 to pay off a mortgage.

Peeny people, from the lowest (pensioners and the three Ab families near the cemetery) to the highest (Screw, the Mayor, and Grutt) planted onions. Percy worked the family (and bank) acres. Whenever he went to or through Peeny he marvelled at the onions.

The onions died of allium mingies, a disease which causes the plant to swell, burst and putrefy, all within twenty-seven hours. The stench of corrupt onions all but overwhelmed the flats and general watershed of the Merther River. When Percy went to town pensioners spat at him, the sergeant followed him, the publican gave him dirty glasses and the bank people refused him clean blotter.

He discovered a very thin paper called onionskin upon which, after some practice, he was able to write without tearing. He then wrote letters to every adult and onion-growing minor in Peeny and the flat land thereabound, notifying them that their onions had died of allium mingies, a disease which causes onions to swell, burst and putrefy within twenty-seven hours. After this essay into publicity he did not visit the town for two months.

Percy then went to the city.

IN FLIGHT

I am still in my wortarium, though if my nature were suspicious I'd have gone half an hour ago because if Matters can find me, surely Tom can. I thought I'd travelled without tracks but he found me easily enough. A bruised leaf or a bent grass stalk is enough for him.

How did you find me? I asked. I saw from the road, he said. Your smoke signal, as though you wanted help. The wood, I said, is smoky. The local tribe could manage it, he said. It didn't save them, I replied, Where are they now?   Here and there, in mills, fishing, peas.   He offered me a smoke.   Perhaps we should step this way a few yards, out of sight—not that you'd be out of mind of anyone on the road.   He helped me move my gear.   With all this stuff they'd see you from 5,000 feet. Baden-Powell's likely to ask for his badges back.   I paid for them.   I didn't want to get onto scouting and my patrol leader days for *he* had been outed for some unstated offence against a guide and claimed that genuine scouts were poofters owing allegiance to a foreign queen.

I asked what bro was doing.

He told me my brother had tried to have me certified or outlawed, that it wasn't the money I had cost him but the humiliation; that the denizens of Peeny hoped that I would be exiled at least, that the police had been brought in, that there was rumour the Army would be asked to help.

I asked him to have a look at the Norton and fill the tank. He said he would—but what about roadblocks? I was shocked. I hadn't expected that sort of treatment. I said I'd use back roads. But would I be able to get to the city on a full tank? What about the punt over the river? And wouldn't the disappearance of the Norton alert everyone? Couldn't I borrow or pinch a car? I realized I was a novice. I wondered how he had come by such knowledge.

He said he'd do what he could, and went off.

In the city, I bought a jeep in a pub on Parramatta Road.

I was in the public drinking rum and cloves for my sore tooth when a fat man eating fish and chips from newspaper walked through saying: Anyone want an excellent, fully reconditioned vehicle, twelve months' registration, new seat covers, comprehensive tool kit, total range of spares and equipment for getting out of holes our government has had put in our so-called roads? He stood in front of me a few seconds and I read the front page, the news. It seemed new but was somehow familiar: Uncle on Carnal Knowledge Charge, Troop Movements in Korea, Kelpie Bites Rescuer, Lottery Results, Joanne Smith, 17, Catches the Sun at Bondi, Radioactivity Not Harmful, and Mystery Buyer (pays £40,000 cash for vehicles at auction). It was the latest edition.

In the lounge, he said. How much? I enquired. £350 to £770, he replied, offering me a chip. I winced. You reckon you can do better? he demanded, Then let me tell you this: I cannot be bettered; furthermore I am not interested in selling you a jeep. I would not sell a single item of jeeper's clothing. And he stepped away. It was my tooth! I called after him. Your tooth? he said, I would not give a tooth from a ruined crown-wheel. Look! I commanded, and he was compelled to turn. My face steady, unwrinkled, unsmiling, relaxed yet not loose. I opened my mouth. As I opened it I thought to myself: I am opening my mouth: and a twitter of nerves dressed as a moth all but came out. What would he have done? Controlling my all too random thoughts, I opened my mouth. And no moth flew, and I was pleased and permitted a slight smile of pleasure. Into my mouth I inserted my right index finger and removed, from the left lower molar region, a wad. What is it? he enquired, stepping forward. Oil of cloves, rum and paper handkerchief, I replied. The ailing tooth reasserted itself so I plunged the wad into my rum glass, and replaced it over the faulty enamel whose very flaw permitted the easing rum and cloves to penetrate the pulp cave wherein lay sickly nerves and blood-vessels. I had a mind to tell him all this, but his chips were cooling.   I'll come in, I said.   Please yourself, he replied, and went.

Did I need a jeep?

Two months earlier Percy wouldn't have paid a fiver for one. £400 would have bought him an Inter Norton, a 500-knocker for milkbars, pubs and burns over the mountains to Panorama. He was working on an assembly line tightening nuts on tractor diff housings in a re-fronted corrugated iron shack built to handle a tenth of the stuff they got through. Great clumsy tractors with headlights for nights in the wheat belt. Lines of tractors with eyes on them like grasshoppers. And music while you work on full volume to overcome clatter and screech. And voices over screaming, Mr Valve to the Manager, please, Mr Valve to the Manager. And bonus, bonus, two-three-four bob a day. Two bob yesterday because the stupid shit down the end let a wheel go over his foot. And during smoko, St George will do Norths and Mulley's a cinch, and so long as we've infantry we don't need tanks, it was the same at Bougainville; but Bougainville was tropical, this time it's snow. And so on. Then back to the line. Then lunch and longer debate. Then through to four. Then on to overtime. Je-sus. Overtime. Time and a half. What'll you do with it all? How you like the city, Perce? Saving up for a place of your own, Perce? Yair, Perce's saving for a place of his own. You'll never make it, Percy. Percy sometimes had these awful thoughts: that he would never make it.

One day he thought he would make it; not alone, but in company; say, three or four, five or six; married couples; one big happy family; the only possible combination of idealism and realism; of today and tomorrow. With costs so high individualism is impossible; therefore, pool resources. Show the singles the right way for today. Probably annoy—anger—them, even. Socialistic bastards. Coms, even. No need to marry if the feelings are right. If not, then a simple severance, no bad feelings. A community of affection. You mean the free-love place? They do themselves silly, no energy for work, it's the place with the weeds.

A bolt he was tightening snapped, he fell backwards against a man who had one end of a length of flat bar and dropped it which made the other man drop his end on his foot and stagger into a welder who burnt himself, whose torch cut into an electrical cable which blew all power which stopped the machines, the bundys, and all was quiet except for music. The battery-powered musical offering went on and on, and everyone heard the current favourites, news flashes, ads, and cheerio calls and declarations of time; and the manager fell out of his elevated office box quite beside himself, indeed most of him went into his shadow and the shadow paled in the unlit tractorium. And. And the flock of bonus-birds roosted on the girders and shat over everybody. Filings of coins and snippets of notes. Indeed the eagle was that day constipated and would not be shitting properly come payday. And, The p.a. summonsed The Manager to his office, please, The Manager to his etcetera, to his darling glass-walled den where he performed to a large audience the managerial telephone jig. And.

In the meantime, our Hero, P. Wort, had gone to the aid of the stricken employees, particularly the one who had been forced to drop the merciless grey steel on his foot. Percy cut

156

away the man's shoe, despite his protest that it was half a new pair, a treasured gift from his dear wife. I should say, diagnosed Wort, P., That you have sustained a fracture of the phalange; I can go further than that; the metatarsal phalange. Bugger me, said the victim, You a Zambuck? In my day, yes, replied Sir Percy (KRAOstJJ), Many's the pot of salve I've applied, many the crêpe wrapped and much balsam of that famous, honourable gentleman the nameless Friar have I libated. Glory, Glory, Glory, rang from beam and rafter.

The burnt welder refused Percy's offer of assistance, and waved threateningly his fiery brazen wand. Leave him, murmured a voice, The flux makes him cantankerous. A double-certificated nurse arrived from a nearby manufactory of evil and bloody repute. Percy was bitterly reproached. A first-class machinist stumbled by jabbering, What about the starving millions, what about the bonus, hanging's too good for industrial saboteurs, and disappeared into the noisome corner known as The Lavatories.

And Percy Wort was transferred to the storeroom. Because the leading hand informed the foreman, who declared to the manager that this Wort, P, number 199, had broken his last stud, had broken, moreover, seventeen studs in two weeks which surely indicated heavy-handedness if not worse? Worse. For what had the leading hand been doing to allow this heavy-handed wanton wrencher sixteen chances? Henry Ford would not have allowed it. Dearborn would have been aborted and Henry Ford II exposed on a hillside and there would have been no Henry Ford III. P. Wort demanded his pay. He left.

Did I need a jeep? I had money now. I had been one of a prize-winning lottery syndicate, and what is more was sick and tired after two months of working in Invoices for East Coast Pastoral and Wool Limited (ECPAWL), established in 1847, head office London, sub-head office Sydney, main store in Pyrmont not far from where I lived, at Glebe, branches and stores wherever there's wool; selling wool and shipping wool, chemicals and machinery, with stations here and there. If ECPAWL had its way the jolly swagman would have been pulled out, never been allowed to suicide in the billabong; he'd have been pulled out, resuscitated, taken to Martin Place and hanged, drawn and quartered for two days as a deterrent to potential sheep thieves; ECPAWL disapproved of the eating of sheep flesh—unless the animal had died of old age or disease. The fleece was golden, ergo the bearer of the fleece was precious.

There was nothing I liked better than a plate of lamb chops. Each day as I checked invoices I thought of lamb chops, roast lamb, stuffed lamb and shoulder. I had heard of kebabs but had not eaten them. My lambophilia could not last, and I had a feeling it would end with lamb's fry. The general manager, Mr Eynoh, even looked like a sheep, especially when his nose wrinkled in irritation; his mouth and tongue resembled lamb's fry. He was always circulating memos like *How much will you Pay to Avert World War 3?* It hadn't registered the first time I saw it. Then . . . 3? and still I hadn't got the message until I turned it into III. I'd pay everything I had. Until I saw the full edition of his memos. *If by working a little harder and a lot better . . . if by joining one of the armed services for part-time activities . . . if by encouraging your friends to support the armed services . . . if by giving generously, knitting scarves and sox—you, in common with all good, loyal Australians could help avert World War 3. Would you? Of course you would. Let us bleach the Red Menace.* He'd served his country. Where, I didn't know. He wanted me to go to Korea to patrol a frontier. I'd have gone in for one reason only: to be eligible for a land ballot.

After his World War 3 memos came the Wool is Peerless series. *Wool is good . . . is without peer . . . is naturally healthy . . . is cool and warm . . . is THE fashion fabric . . . Wool clothes armies.* Yes, I thought, ours and theirs. Atomic preparedness dresses in wool. The small gold merino ram he wore as a tiepin was replaced by a larger one. He was sometimes seen scratching his crutch as though burred or flyblown. In the eyes of his secretary, accountant and many other employees he reached apotheosis when, sighting a buyer he took to be Japanese, he lowered his head and butted him thirty feet. The unfortunate man was French. However he was not an important buyer so it didn't much matter; besides, the word went around that Eynoh had slipped on the lanolined, greasy floor.

Somewhere, in Melbourne I think, there is a courthouse made of roughface stones like parcels of wool; it is a minor court, the first stomach of the essential beast, and there are others, each with a specific task, each subject to parasites, subject to treatment, endurance depending upon whim, tickets for the journey are available on date of issue subject to subjectivity and objectivity of inspector at moment of inspection.

ECPAWL paid bonuses to employees on completion of three months of service. At an ECPAWL employees' film night I had touched the right breast of Marj Oates who in fright dropped Eynoh's box of chocolates. The next morning he baaed that I was a disgrace and should leave; also, that my invoicing was faulty; I encouraged the clown Rogers; I had been observed on the showfloor, wearing a white coat and mingling with similarly garbed important buyers; was suspected of planting foreign matter in opened bales, that I had fondled the bosom of Miss Peach (a former employee of this company) in the lift and that I was frequently late.   But if I leave now I'll lose my bonus, I cried.   You should have contemplated that, he said.   All right, I said, If this is what you want. I'll tell my father to send his wool to an opposition firm. Eynoh blanched but refused to withdraw my notice. I left the building immediately. In the bar of The Colonial Shearer I celebrated my departure. I decided not to tell Mum and Dad. They would want me to return to the farm, to recharge my batteries. To be reborn, away from the dreadful city. To put

159

my agricultural high school expertise to proper use. To cease frittering in the city. To return to a sound, basic, agricultural subsistence. To rejoin the pastoral symphony of moos, oinks, clucks and earthings. All of which I liked. Loved, even. But not as a definite future. Alternated with factory, warehouse and junkyard, yes. Junkyards gave me hope, for if I could cope with scrap and rubbish I would endure. Perhaps I could open a junkyard on the farm? I ordered a schooner, hailed the froth and drew it off as a toast to my idea.

Anyway, I bought the jeep for £400. Put down twenty deposit which the fat man stuffed in a paper bag and with another buyer went with him to his car and we drove to the jeep yard, collecting on the way four buyers from a pub at Granville. My jeep had a full range of spares all right; engine, diffs, wheels, stacked on seats and floor and sitting behind the wheel was like being in a spare parts store. I fixed things with the bank and set off to where I was staying, in Glebe, but after a few miles I stopped in the early winter dusk outside a pub. Heavy rain began and I tried to put up the hood. It jammed halfway so I went inside for a drink. A beer and a rum and cloves in the crowded noisy bar.

When the rain stopped I left by another door. The hood was down and a woman was lifting something from the jeep. Need a hand? I asked her.   Hello, she said, You left the hood down and I was trying to get things out of the rain for you.

She was thirty or so, small face, reddy-brown hair in ringlets, green sweater and baggy cotton army trousers tight in the seat, with lumpy rolled-up cuffs.   Everything's wet, she said. That's rain for you, I said.   See you around, she said and walked off. The spare axles, wheel chains and shovels had gone. I saw the side gate of a little semi jammed open with one of the shovels. She walked past the house without a glance at it.   Give me a hand, I called after her, I'll have to get the gear back aboard the jeep.   Upya, she called back.   OK, axle-arse. I then began replacing things, and had made two trips when a man ran down the path shouting. He snatched a

160

shovel from me, raised it high over his head and brought it down like an axe, missed me, fell off balance and went down, striking his head on the side of the jeep.

The woman ran back.   Is he all right?   Yes.   A pity the animal didn't die, he's pissed and nasty.   You know him? He's my husband. We carried him into the sparsely-furnished house, rolled him onto the bed and went to the kitchen. Sorry about trying to knock your stuff off, she said.   It's nothing.   What do you mean, it's nothing? What sort of man are you if that's nothing? Selling the furniture's nothing to my husband.   Were you going to furnish the house with shovels and axels? I asked, That'd be something.   Of course it'd be something.

She poured the tea and although scalding I sipped it so as not to speak. She began talking about leaving her husband. She asked me what I wanted with a jeep load of spares and I told her I wanted to journey north, into the dry country, and perhaps north-west, beyond Capricorn. She said she had once headed there herself to work as a cook but her husband had sent a telegram declaring his imminent death from injuries at work and she had returned to find him with three stitches in one arm and the accusation that she had only returned to collect his worker's compensation, a thought which had never occurred to her but on thinking about seemed extremely sensible so that for a week she was consumed with conflicting wishes that the wound become infected and kill him, or that he recover quickly and be made a better man in the manner of dissolutes in sunday school tracts. He being, basically, a good man. A solid, gentle man, firm to the touch yet soft, a proddable man now overlaid with flab and only thirty-two, given over to sherry and lemonade, never mixed in the glass but taken by the bottle, always bottle then bottle, followed by jogging to mix them, the stomachal fermentation foul and obvious but to a new friend, Lee, down the street, meadowy and intelligible, for the gases spoke.

She noticed my frown. The gases, she explained, were released through the mouth, nose and, probably, ears, unintelligible to all but Lee, medium, whose understanding of the sounds improved, according to Lee, with the passage of each day, at least until the previous weekend when she had thrown Lee out of the house for interpreting a wind and word session as: There were three of them, skeletons, covered with blotchy faded brown paper, stuffed with dried guts; the sherry's all right but the lemonade's too sweet, have tried sodawater but the acid's too much for me; the papered skeletons wore loin cloths with messages like I O Tom £50,000 and Afterwards Everyone Must Work a Little Harder and Yank Owes Us £5 mil and There is Goodness Despite This and Herewith My Will and Testament; perhaps I could take sherry with bicarb; the skeletons though wearing Englished loinclothes weren't our kind so I felt easier when they died and were dropped in a trench onto others and covered.

Three raps then a clout on the front door. Repeated. We made no move. Did you, she whispered, Get all your stuff from the side?   Yes.   And did you slam the gate?   The wind did. Three raps and a clout. We heard the letter flap open. Ssssh, she whispered, listen.   I know, I know you're there, I know you're there, and I know Harry's there, and the air in his belly's gassing, but I'll be back because Harry needs me.   The voice careful, clear and flat. The letter flap rattled shut. Lee? I asked. Yes, she murmured, it's that sort of voice, isn't it, but it won't be back tonight. Lee's got a house down the street though he doesn't live there. Again the letter flap opened.   Harry's message is important; if he doesn't tell me tonight, he will tomorrow but he'll need more to drink and you know how he'll feel. She jumped up, ran from the kitchen, came back, seized the teapot, ran along the hall, threw open the door and let fly with the tea. At nobody. I brought her back inside and closed the door. I led her into the yard then down to the side gate then into the pub and then to a Chinese place next door then back to the pub, then to her house where we lifted her husband from the bed onto a couch then returned to the bed asking, Do you want to? Yes, but . . . Seems wrong, doesn't it? So she went to bed. I said I'd stay a couple of hours. She tossed me a blanket. I slept.

. . . a big brown parcel spoke through the letter slot. I couldn't hear it but the brass flap moved with words. The door was glass. Harry cut the string with a shovel. The paper tore, sand and bones fell out onto the doorstep. I drove the jeep along a track between dunes pocked with rain marks, stopping twice to listen for anything at all, but there was nothing. The next time I stopped I heard rustling, as of windborne sand on sand only there was no wind. I drove on. The ground was cracking, green shoots pushed out, becoming creepers, covering the ground. I drove on. The windscreen flat, the hood down. I stopped, and listened to the creepers, quite noisy now, covering the dunes. The sound of a great brass flap closing over a slot, and a voice: shovel into the sand and let me out: and part of the dune to the right started slipping, as though into a hollow beneath and it soon stopped, and liquid oozed from it, sweet-sour and bubbly, and ran into the shallow ditch alongside and the voice said: Out it comes, I'm leached, leached. I drove on. The creepers moved onto the track which suddenly became a narrow bitumen road. The creepers burst into scarlet pea-flowers and the ones on the bitumen I squashed and the ditches ran red and I drove through red mist. The dunes flattened out and I came to a plain abounding in white, pink, and pink and white stones like heads and the ground covered with tiny daisies. Soon I came to a dazzling white salt lake from the centre of which protruded turrets and truck cabs and the sticks like rushes I soon saw to be barrels and bayonets. The steady ticking was intolerable. I came upon men cutting slabs of salt from the lake. Further on they were shaping slabs into figures and faces. At the end of the lake were statues, all of them familiar but none identifiable. Suddenly the jeep veered off the road, drove onto the salt, smashed a few statues and sank into the salt crust . . .

He had me by the throat. Ann had him by the neck. The light was on. I twisted free. He staggered back and sat on the bed. Ann stood against the light switch. I sat on the arm of the couch rubbing my neck. She shook her head, saying, You're a real bugger, Harry. I had a bad dream, he said, and laughed, I thought I was Lee: how's that? and to me: I hope your neck's all right: and to Ann, I'm going away a while. He pulled a suitcase from under the bed and left the house. Me too, she said as she pulled shut the iron gate, First thing. Let's get into bed.

When she woke me, at dawn, she had her case packed and breakfast made. We drove to Glebe, where I tossed a few things into a haversack, and left a note for the landlady. Most of the spare parts were left at Fred's factory. We drove west, then north, and 1,200 miles from Sydney, in dry, sandy country in sight of red dunes, we stopped beside a pisé ruin and quarrelled over money. Petrol had proved inordinately expensive and I thought we should return to the small town twenty miles back and take jobs for a month. Did you sign the book at the garage? she asked. I had. Jesus. Oh? Well, who wants to be remembered in that hole? Perhaps it's that they like a record to know they've not been forgotten. Oh yair—only cheques, receipts and letters need your name— keep it out of visitors' books and petitions, O.K.? To my surprise she produced £20. I pointed out that it would not be enough to get us through. She clawed my face, bloodied my nose and gave me a thick ear. I blackened her eye and hurt her wrist. I turned the jeep towards the town and when she would not get aboard, drove off. A few miles on I turned back. I searched the ruin for her, I drove towards the border, I returned to the ruin and as it was dusk lit a great fire in the remaining room. It was bitterly cold outside. Carrying the pressure lamp I pushed through scrub and saltbush calling her name. I fell into a well, filled to six feet with rubbish and sand. I scrambled out and almost fell into another. I tripped over a root and smashed the lamp. The camp fire had died

164

down and I could not see where I was. I cursed her. Something scuttled from between my feet, I fell against a stump and my nose bled again. So I decided to wait until light. Even crouching against saltbush I chattered with cold. I tried to sight the ruin against stars near the horizon but it must have been too low. I had stopped calling for her.

I woke at one under a sky bright with stars and when I stood up I saw the fire in the ruin and a lantern on the wall. I gave her a fright when I stepped into the light for sand and leaves stuck to the blood from my nose. She had been back hours, every twenty minutes sounding the horn, shouting, and had even driven along the road until a plane flew low overhead. A what? You were asleep—a plane, a small one, with a searchlight. She had taken fright, driven into the scrub and cut the headlights. I told her I had not heard or seen a thing. She told me I had certainly been dreaming; and in dream I could never be woken, short of physical attack. I told her she did not know what she was talking about. She told me I was the deepest dreamer she had ever slept with. How did she know? She knew, she could tell. Then what was the nature of my dream beside the saltbush? She counted on her fingers: a journey, a salt lake, armies, satanic and celestial mills, the St John Ambulance Service. I told her she had herself been dreaming. Was I calling her a liar? I examined the wall through the fire, I wondered about our journey, I saw the lantern on the wall, I saw the bonnet of the jeep through the doorway, I thought of the tractor factory, of Korea, of the war, of my father in the Kimberley, my brother in his office, of salt lake and sea, of Harry and of Lee. No, I told her, I'm not calling you a liar: I think there's more you can tell me; and I'm frightened. Go on, she murmured, and shoved me. We made toast and tea. We huddled under the blankets, let the fire die and talked. I remembered the lantern on the wall and made to retrieve it but she said not to bother, that they knew where we were. They knew.

Our ruin was not far from the security zone where rockets

and bombs were to be tested or had already been tested. There was no way of knowing, for secrecy ruled news. The plane had come from the zone. Travellers were suspects. I thought we should pack up and get away. She disagreed; they knew our location and if they wanted us all they need do was block the road ahead and behind; they had followed our progress through every town, had photographed us and lodged reports. The border of their millions of acres of secret zone to the south-west pushed out fingers of territory to enclose us wherever we went; if they wanted to lay hands on us all they need do was declare us employees, subject to their regulations.

Are there still sheep out there? These ruins once the homestead of a million-acre run? A sheep every hundred acres. Fleeces heavy with sand, tick, ked, fly-maggot, grass seed and burr. The government had done everyone a service in clearing out the sheep. Though they could not have got the lot. Bound to be wild ones with uncast fleeces dragging along behind. Great country pioneered by great people who would have done better elsewhere but could not, so now it's done, and scientists are in. There are lesser and greater infortunes. I said all this to Ann. I was not sure she could hear me for I suspected she had fallen asleep halfway through; to be sure I hoped she was asleep because I had thought, halfway through, that she would think my monologue peculiar. But no, she was awake. What a lot of garbage, she mumbled through blanket, So you know a little of what goes on around here, so you learnt a bit about sheep at school and the woolbroker's and you think you can go all philosophical; where does it all end, this golden fleecing of yours? Fleecing, I said, You mean it two ways? Yes, she said. When we started I thought I was off with a ram but you've run out of stuff. I am an ordinary jeeper, I said, I am a tourist. Come under here, she said. Two wrists? I asked.

A bitter wind from the south-west woke us before dawn. I robbed her of a blanket and got a map from the jeep. She got the fire going. I thought the sandy air would put it out. The

166

only thing to do in such weather is go before it like a ship in tempest. While she made tea I stowed gear in the jeep. She complained that I had not left her enough but there was sufficient for a billy of tea which we drank as sand scoured the windscreen. I could see the track disappearing. We would lose it and drive in patterns through desert (marginal country, was the map's euphemism) until wild sheep and dingoes got us or we went into the banned lands and were rocketed or gunned. I turned the jeep.   Hey, she said, north is our direction. South, I said, Then north-east, then north.   You carry a compass? she asked.   Road signs and bottles, I said.   No, she yelled, Let me out.   It's just a little detour, I explained, Because of the wind; if you get out here you'll be knocked by a plane or petrified. I only want a short detour, that's all.

So we went one hundred miles or so south-east, then headed north. Along a terrible track through beautiful dry country. Some days we stopped every hour or so for a meal or billy. It was the only way the driver could enjoy the scenery. Sometimes we were lucky enough to score a waterhole or creek. Perch and yellowtail, duck, pelican, cockatoo and ibis. Drive on. One town, Ronga, had an abandoned mission, store, pub, police station and three camels. And half a dozen houses. I couldn't see the reason. Two bottle-trees and five coolabahs with wire guards. What was there to do apart from watch the camels? Not that the three people we spoke to knew much about them. The cop was curt and suspicious and wouldn't put a saddle on a camel though he looked as though he could. The weather was nothing, meaning I can't remember. We drank a lot of expensive beer. The publican asked us to sign his visitors' roll.   No, said Ann.   Where is it? I asked. It was a patch of white wall. Names, addresses, remarks.   No, said Ann. The pub had a wonderful bottle heap out the back. Four feet high and fifty long with sand banked to windward. Beer bottles and wine and spirit, and sauce and ink, chutney and scent, blue, brown, red and green as though a rainbow had tumbled. I went to pick out a few. I selected about forty.

Ann left the pub and raged at me, so I chose three. The wind blew (there was wind) her voice to the cop who had probably been watching us and he strolled over and said wasn't it time we moved on? We drove on. A mile on, a bush beside the road stood up and waved us down. His name was Jack Pongo. Why do you let them call you that? we asked, What's your proper name?   No proper name, he said, But I wanted to change it only the policeman wouldn't let me. He played on his mouth-organ. After fifteen miles he asked to be let out. Near a horrible sandhill.   Why here?   Got a job.   Here? Jesus, man. Ann was driving.   No, she said, Wait till the track widens. Three miles on she was able to stop by a clay (or something) pan and drive back. Jack kept saying No, no. On the edge of Ronga the cop stepped onto the track, stopped us and ordered Jack out. The cop said, Now turn and get off. Jack disappeared. The cop cursed him and us. He demanded Ann's licence and while he examined it she pulled out £40 and said, This says we can't be vagged.   Thank Christ, he said, I don't want you here. Move on. A mile out a bush beside the road stood up and Jack got in.   Call yourself Jack Proof, said Ann.   The policeman, he said.   Move away, she said. It's my country, he said.   Jesus. Twice we were stopped by sand. On the outskirts of Poona he got out and thanked us. Poona had two stone buildings, seven iron ones and thousands of goats. We stopped outside the iron pub and a khaki cop strolled over. Where's the blackfeller? he demanded.   What's your name? I demanded.   Where's your licence? he growled. The pub had a bottle heap fifty feet in diameter. We had a few beers then drove back, took the turn and drove towards Alice Springs.

Yes, I have decided to put it all down. Or am I bringing it all up? In both cases, no. Because of faulty memory and the stress under which I write, the latter rising (or falling) out of bro's pursuit. Thomas, you should have been called harry. If he catches me I don't know what'll happen though I can guess; tyre lever'd, twelve gauge'd or strung from a wattle. Several times he told me I'd end hanged and though the idea delighted him he had a massive misgiving for he would suffer in my fatal publicity. He would have to change his name. He told me: Percy, jesus, it's not like some Jones, O'Reilly or Brown being hanged—these names are everywhere—but who's ever heard of a Wort getting it? Perce, the least *you* can do is change your name before they get you—and do it properly, by deed poll, don't just pick another one out of the phone book because the papers always print aliases—and you've used so many. I don't want you spoiling the family name. I've come a long way and I'll soon be a manager and then won't I show my colleagues that figures are scrums, not coaches' blackboard lectures. I am going to make the name Wort respected and, if necessary, feared.

My brother Tom. A figure with lumps on. Ticketed, too. What is known as a fine figure, Tom. Five feet ten inches tall, barely eleven stone, well-built, on the slim side, neat features, somewhat thin in the mouth, brown hair barbered weekly in conjunction with a shave—a mind-shaking extravagance I have never been able to accept as a reasonable act. I have never been shaved by another's hand, I would sooner get into the chair and ask for an armpit trim.

My memory has been triggered: I *have* been shaved. That time when I went down to the city. I wore the suit and the dark red rose in my buttonhole went admirably with the subtle dark and pale stripes of the material. I did not feel completely at ease because I am not a confirmed suit-wearing man. However I had to look my best for Uncle Fred, the family industrialist. I got to the station soon after dawn and was greeted by the Assistant Station Master.   Pretty flower you've got there, Perce. Have a good piss before you board the train.   Oh? I replied.   Yes, Perce because if you go to have one on the train a poofter'll get you. Have you all taken to wearing flowers up there? As a target for cops? We're peaceful rose-wearers. Bring your daughters up one day.

The ASM is about forty-five, tall, thin, sandy-haired, pale skinned apart from rosy cheeks, nervous and fearful of us hill people who practise abominable realities amongst ourselves and animals; he only goes into the hills to *do a bit of hunting*. But this is his excuse; he really goes into the hills hoping to be ambushed by a horde of nubile women who will mount him to limpness; he will then massacre them and return to his NSWGR house; here he will realize that as he has created a shortage of women in the hills, the hill men will be forced down to the flat lands; and the ASM has five daughters. Three of them nubile but only one desirable. She is the one who will never enter the Miss Show Week because she is so thin. His station is littered with ferns and staghorns in buckets, tins, tyres and bark baskets.

I fidgeted with irritation through trying to muster a witty reply. I finally settled for a leer at a basket of maidenhair fern and: How's the family maiden hair? This worked very well and his rosy cheeks vanished in a general rubiness. I narrowed my eyes, snorted through flared nostrils, turned my back on him, settled my case on a handy truck and pushed off to where the first carriage would stop. But he followed me, hissing: You hillbillies are going to get it, see? *They're* going to take over your lousy hills and use them for manoeuvres and the pity is *they'll* move you all out beforehand—but at least you'll be gone—and where? Into a camp if *they've* any sense. We had conducted our exchange in low tones, and none of the six or so people took any notice of us. Why do you hate us so? I beseeched. Because you give us a bad name. We're going to give the Queen a good welcome when she comes through here. And what happens in the hills? Some lunatic *peasant* writes to the paper saying he's a Republican. But the Queen's going through here at fifty, I said. Five, you moron. Here's your train, I said. Don't miss it, he snapped. You have a

170

wonderful, thin daughter, I said.   Keep off and piss off, he snarled.   I could have said, I'll get under or skirt round. But there's a limit, a railway station can bear only so much sourness and tediousness. Any more and the loco's fires would be quenched. I remembered his advice and stepped over to a maiden fernery under three tree ferns along the platform fence and pissed into two baskets. The train came in very slowly, as though he had warned the driver there was a hillbilly on the platform likely to pull a sleeper from his pocket and derail the engine. As I shook the last of my water I called out: Hey, ASM, and he rasped back, The sergeant'll have you, feller. I then boarded the train. The journey was uneventful.

Uncle Fred would not lend me the £300 I asked for, despite the barbering I had undergone at Central. He mentioned expansion, the need to cut one's cloth according to one's yard, the banking situation, the ascendancy of R G Menzies, the forty-hour week, the profitability of the dairying industry and the dire straits of metal trades employers. He then extorted three days' labour out of me. I didn't want to stay but I did owe him ten pounds, so it wasn't a bad exchange. He offered me a permanent job and hinted that within a few years he would need a couple of directors for what he called Hmmm the hmmm board. Expansion was imminent. Would there be much money in a directorship? No, but directors would be permitted to buy shares. Buy? Well, buy at discount, perhaps. If I undertook to become a director in a few years' time could I have £300 in advance? No. Why did I want it. For something at Uppersass.   I wouldn't give you money to sink into that place. To syphon money from Wort Engineering into Wort Uppersass would be like screwing a good bolt into a brummy nut—you spoil the bolt. How's your mother—does she want to leave the place yet? Take that brother of yours; he knows what's happening, he's got his head screwed on the right way.

I told him that though my mother enjoyed the farm she was fond of the city and regretted she could not visit it more often.

My brother, though apparently prospering, had already had ulcers and a twitch in the right shoulder; he was screwed tight, probably with a screw loose somewhere, a grub screw; he was assembling his own money machine; this he would later drive inside the district political machine; his trojan horse into a larger trojan horse. Uncle Fred was interested to hear all this, but regretted my bias. He urged me to take a leaf from Tom; otherwise I would be *wrenched* into reality; strong talk would do it—something along the lines of a sentence; it should be remembered that the Law was aware of my existence.   Oh? Yes; the previous year a pair of extremely pleasant gentlemen had visited him; officer types in almost identical clothes, one a bit thinner in the head than the other, and they had asked about Percy Wort who had driven a jeep through classified country with a Mrs Ann Flabb, a woman known to the authorities. Said Ann and Percy had, moreover, supplied aborigines with alcohol. In several towns on the way we had paid particular heed to bottle dumps, which made me an accessory before the act because Mrs Flabb was known as a person interested in the construction of offensive fire-bottles and was known to have suggested their use to certain disloyal and/or mad blacks in the outback.

I pointed to about fifty dirty milk bottles in a corner and suggested that he, Fred, also had an interest in fire devices. He shouted that they were there because he had dirty workers. Nothing more. I told him it seemed like a case of poor management and that it was the likes of him who caused the milk industry its crippling overheads; and one morning he would come to work and find the place filled with hybridized lactic moulds, greenish bubbly growths often attributed to the general rise in radioactivity. Not only would it entrap his workers when they arrived the Monday morning but, also, get into lathes and millers and gum them beyond repair (and if he managed to establish another business, worker's compensation/compo and general insurance premiums would be

172

ruinous); I had seen what one milk bottle could do in the desert . . . Back, back to your bloody cows, he shouted.

I did not go back to the cows. I took a job which did not last long but I had little trouble getting another. I successfully lotteried *again*. I shared in a one thousand pound lottery prize with my boss, Mr Loane, Miss Likke of the mail-desk and Mr Barb, the western traveller, all of us employed by Agrarian Substances Ltd. I had gone on an errand and bought a paper because of a crisis headline: something about fifteen-year-olds to be called up for mini-turret duties in small jets and sixteen- to twenty-year-olds wanted as shock troops, but it all turned out to be a rehash of hitherto secret Nazi documents. Released and reprieved I turned to the lottery results and there it was, our number. In my astonishment I dashed into a pineapple shop for a glass of juice. Very casually I asked the owner if there was money to be made growing pineapples. He assured me there was, though growers suffered greatly from scratched ankles, while he knew of one, a shortish man named Lowe, who began a tall pineapple plantation, and he, you'd never dream it, poor bugger, suffered terribly on the hips, and had to sell out and go into passionfruit which was to his benefit as he is now big in pulp. I then went into Fred's Sand. Bar and ordered a lobster sandwich from Marlene, a pretty, plump girl not cut out for sandwiches.

You really want lobster—you win the lottery? Not exactly, I replied suavely, But near enough. One lobster on the way, she cried. Fred the Sand, the owner, three operators down the bench, looked up from his lightning slicing and snapped, Marly, get on with the job. She is, Mister Fred, I said, Excellently—and when I open up my sandwich palace she'll be manageress. And you'll be broke in a week, snapped Fred. You mean spread, Fred, I replied. What? The way he could continue a conversation while his hands wielded knives, spreaders, forks and slices of fillings fascinated me.

173

Spread, Fred, not broke—I won't have an egg in the place.   It was a weak rejoinder but the operators glanced at Fred, and he knew it, and he was aware that every time they looked up from a task it cost him threepence ha'penny. Marlene was picking out the choicest pieces of lobster. Fred was horrible but he did know all about lobster sandwiches, in fact he was now salivating and had to suck back to keep his bread dry. I asked Marlene to be free with the worcestershire and tomato sauces.   What? yelled Fred, and in that cry of nausea he cut his thumb and bled onto beetroot and pressed ham.   You, he shouted, You don't like my sandwiches, I've seen you, so why do you suddenly come to ruin the lobster special?   His hatred must have turned sardines and corned beef. Marlene dropped my sandwich as she tried to bag it.   You're fired! he screamed at her, and to me, Get out, and never come back here again. Everyone was shocked. Then Marlene told him he could stuff his baked beans, one by one, and I asked if he was going to charge extra for the blood. He clawed coins and notes from the till and paid Marlene off.

We went to the Mirror Bar where milkshakes were extraordinarily expensive. We entered a curtained booth. She drank hers very quickly and as soon as she finished licking her glass, explained that she was all het up, and though she wasn't in any union she was going to the Trades Hall to get them to sue Fred, and—Could I have another one?   Yes, but wait. I went along the street and withdrew a tenner from my savings book. When I got back she apologized for finishing my drink. I ordered again, this time Mirror Specials, doubled. Doubled! said the waitress, Nobody has ever had a Special doubled. A pair of specials doubled, I said. Other waitresses passing our cubicle glanced in.

Five minutes later two waitresses brought out our specials, doubled, which had to be spooned into the champagne glasses. There were linen napkins and a small basket of wafers. The spoons had hollow handles for sucking.   You won't get it up, said a waitress shaking her head. And I wouldn't take too much in the mouth at once or you'll choke, I once saw a man die on a blancmange. This nearly deterred us but as soon as the woman had withdrawn and closed off the cubicle with curtains we set to. We spooned, kissed, locked ankles and sighed. She squeezed into the space next to me but I soon realized she had done this to hamper me. There imprisoned we swelled with double specials and tumescence. Suddenly I began to cough like a fox and in between spasms I heard the waitress come running, crying, I knew it, I've seen it happen with blancmange. But as soon as she threw open the curtain I stopped. A nice trick, she said. It wasn't, I said, I jammed on a cherry. You were doing things and howling like a male wolf, she insisted. Marlene dropped her hand onto my thigh. There! cried the waitress, I saw your face. Marlene said to me: Your turn first—what should you be doing now? I said, Thinking about what I should do with my life, something that never fails to gloom me: study, go to sea, become a drover, work in a library, buy a truck with my winnings, do something marvellous and secretive on the farm, become a stockbroker or write a long poem about ferrets. Marlene was delighted: Write a poem! Lovely. You know what I should be doing? Looking after my Dad who's sick. And she burst into tears and her hand squeezed my knee. There it is again! yelled the waitress, The look of a male wolf. You know what I should be doing? I asked the waitress. I should be delivering invoices and thinking of my future with Agrarian Substances. The proprietor arrived, said we'd had enough and suggested fresh air and sunshine. So we went, leaving our unfinished specials, doubled, and much of one of them splattered on the dividing partition.

Seeking to ease Marlene's distress I walked her across the street to where the sun shone, and a tram nearly got us. What could I do? I asked her to look several years older and when she succeeded I escorted her up the stairs to the ladies' lounge of the Golden Emu. Old people bleared at us as we trod the deep pile. From a secluded, blown-bulb corner I strode forth,

175

put on years till I looked like a ruined strapper, accosted the waitress and asked for lemonade, double, with a dash. Of what? Of, er port. Still, we were brought our drinks and I tipped lavishly.

Two drinks later the lunch crowd arrived so we left.   Take me home, she said. By taxi we went to the other side of the city, where strained sunshine soaks into soot, asparagus fern hides gas meters, stained moss cloaks southern walls and pigeons wheel in pall. Into the house of her ruined Dad. From the hall she stepped into the front room, his, and motioned for me to pass silently down the hall and wait. I pushed through the velvet curtain and sat at the kitchen table feeling very sick. My invoices! Agrarian Substances would be scouring the casualty wards looking for them. Marlene lurched in. Her Dad was asleep. We went to the phone box and she rang my boss, Mr Loane, and told him it was Sister Mercy calling about his clerk, Mr Percy Wort, who had come in with the trembles, been treated and sent home. We then returned to her place for tea and rest. But where, where in that tiny house?   Jesus, Percy, not in my sleepout, no fear, not that.   We are both of us sick, I mumbled, and in no condition to put in and receive. Enough of that talk, she said.   Marlene, look, you get into bed and I'll sleep under it.

Three hours later, shrunken with thirst, I crawled from under to see her sitting up holding a hammer. I brought her a glass of water, and climbed back under the bed. Hours later her brothers and sisters came home and crashed around but I slept on till six in the morning when we both slipped out, me to work, she to seek work.   Never again, goodbye, she said. Don't be silly, Marlene, we're going to open a sandwich bar and buy a Morgan sports. I have to tell you something, Perce —I'm only fifteen.   Marlene, you're confusing carnal knowledge with business practice.   Not after last night, Perce. Sweetheart, all we did was kiss and tit a little.   We were tongue kissing, Perce.   Marlene, let us swear to each other to be proper and sell only meatless sandwiches.   It's too late,

176

Perce, she murmured (sadly) and with a chaste kiss on my cheek, left me. I boarded a tram, left it, took another, and another . . . and zigzagged across the city to Agrarian Substances upon whose mighty hand-carved doors I hammered until admitted by a cleaner.

I brooded over invoices, statements, reports and cables. What was wrong with me? Every time I put foot to rung of the ladder of success, every time I tried to ascend the ladder of achievement, a rung broke. In fact I stood in a heap of broken rungs. Would it be my fate to turn the ladder upside down and climb from inverted success to a rungless void?

I had no faith. I was like a perforation in an invoice. My father and brother had faith—was it that there was only a limited amount in the family? The boss, Mr Loane, was preparing to take over the rural communications of the state and had promised me lessons in rapid elocution so I could become chief announcer with a free choice of commercials, music, market reports and wise rural sayings. Lavish expenses, generous remuneration and service to the public.

By the time the others arrived I had circled news items, filed reams of invoices and compensated for my absence. Mr Loane was terse. The ministrations of Sister Mercy the nurse, I told him, had saved me from a lengthy absence. I suggested that Agrarian Substances make a small donation. They are wonderful people, the nuns, he said, In fact, if there were more of them the Communist menace would lessen—have you seen this morning's paper? They are inventing their own atom bomb from stolen secrets! Though I am anything but a religious bigot I feel that all hospitals should be run by the church, or, if you like, churches. Communist patients would then appreciate the facts of life.

At eleven I went out on an errand, collected the lottery cheque and had it changed into fivers. Great was the joy and envy when I distributed the shares although it all proved too much for me and I fell to the floor in a shower of fifty fives. Shock, someone said.   Excitable, said another.   Hayfever and note allergy, said a third.   He should go into a trust account, said another, loosening my tie and fanning me with a superphosphate ledger. While behind fluttering eyelids I thought of sunshine, sand, Marlene, the fluff under her bed, spring, champagne, chicken with trimmings, flowers, birds and Miss Wedge. Miss Wedge! How did she enter my thoughts? Then . . . I, who am two hundred and fifty the richer (in fivers) will take a sickie today, and not lose a penny of pay . . . Oh cunning creature. I will ice the lottery cake with another day snatched from the firm.

My elated partners insisted I visit Sister Mercy with a group contribution. I declined the accountant's offer to turn my fivers into a safe, crossed, not neg. cheque, and wandered weakly from the office.   Be at the pub at five-thirty for a celebration drink.   Chicken with the trimmings, champagne etcetera . . . Was that all life had to offer? Be better up on the farm, money in mouth, body in harness, pulling plough. Oh Uppersass you have such a name—who would not sing your praises?

As soon as I stepped into the sunshine a kind of madness hit me and within two blocks I was fifteen fivers down, tense and tight-faced. I passed a flower stall. I went back to it, bought a fiver's worth of flowers, decided I had too many so handed half back. Peering and sniffing through colours and scents I went into the post-office, took one of their doorless booths and telephoned Australasian-Texas Alliance Incorporated and asked to speak to Miss Wedge.   You may not, Percy Wort, said the telephonist.   What, what—who, who? I demanded. Profuse apologies gushed from the switchboard spy, Miss Dobb.   Doctor Mackenzie here, I gruffed, Who is this Wort you mistook me for?   He was sacked for banistering, doctor.   Banistering? I gasped.   With a girl, doctor.   I allowed a medical grunt.   Miss Wedge immediately, please, it is a matter of the utmost and completest importance, and no more about this ruffian Banister . . . Miss Wedge? So good of you to speak to me—please come at once. To cool your ardent relative. Eh? Well, Miss Wedge, we are relative.   Not today, said Miss Wedge, It is you isn't it?   Aye, it's me, Dr Mac. You can be had up for posing as a doctor, you know.   Miss Wedge, you have foolscapia and running mucilage. I'll meet you by the colonnade newsagency and take you at once to the solar laboratory. (Was Miss Dobb listening to our conversation? If so, disconnection.) Miss Wedge, I insist you consult me within ten minutes. I am a busy man and happen to be in the locality only because I am in transit between the braw hospices of Mater and Luke, and as I am here—my Daimler chuggles at the kerb—I wish to make a braw muckle from many mickles. So pressed am I for time that as I speak I am checking the instruments in my massive black bag: catgut 00.000.0000; needles fine and infinite; forceps vulsellum, artery and nez; bandages crêpe and roller; catheters and holy rollers; the latest in sulphas and the most ancient of Aberdeen unguents as immortalized by Rabbie Burns!   I'll be there, said Miss Wedge, But not for intimate consultation. I won't be accompanied by Miss Di Fram, who for some reason you think is my constant companion.   Miss Wedge, said the good Doctor Mac, Would the gracious telephonist have overheard our conversation?   Little, if any, replied Miss Wedge. She is trying to engage our manager in trans-Pacific dialogue with our president in Fort Worth, Texas.   Then ring off, Miss Wedge, and put me through to the good switch lady.

Doctor Mac thanked Miss Dobb for her courtesy, and she was a little frosty through having missed so much, though satisfaction from having connected manager and president was some compensation. She did apologize for having mistaken him for a Mr P. Wort who had recently resigned from Austral-Texas.   Did he suffer much from this banistering? asked Doc Mac, Is it infectious? Miss Dobb excused herself because Fort Worth was calling.   Falling? cried Dr Mac. Fort Worthy, that bastion of international finance? Goodbye, I must phone my broker.

The booth was one of a row of ten. It was truly a flower

booth. I looked out at the curious and the counter where forms were stamped, received and issued. Post-office machines clicked like mechanical bees. Miss Wedge knew I had flowers. Not, however, by the telephonic transmission of perfume but through the nature of my nectared hebridean words. I embraced my flowers, went to the newspaper stand and awaited Miss Wedge.

At Austral-Texas there was a man, John Rigg, two years older than myself, easy-mannered, knowing, languid and handsome, knowledgeable in the ways of women and business, who had regarded me as a competitor though I don't know why— unless he saw clumsiness or comparative clumsiness as an attractive alternative to his own winning ways. He joined Austral-Texas not long before I did, and is still there. I have two pleasant memories of the firm: the heaps of loose sulphur we imported from Texas, and Miss Wedge.

John Rigg called me Our Rural Expert and a few times hinted that I'd had ewes, poddies and ducks. Once I thought he was going to say rams, but he went into one of his pipe-smoking chuckles.   Any great danes where you live? he added when he was able to unpipe his mouth.   Fewer than you'd have corgis, I said. Before we sat down at a staff dinner dance he took me to one side and told me my passion for Miss Wedge was obvious but that she was no cradle-snatcher; moreover she thought me a fool; however, if I cared to follow advice he had gathered from a smuggled book, the snowy valley of her thighs would open and the ginger brush receive me. I asked him to repeat it. As he did so pipe ash slowly trailed down his incredible velvet evening jacket. He said it a third time adding that at the head of the valley the secret cwm flared with burning bush from which came her nether voice. By this time I was looking around to make sure we were beyond earshot.   Follow my advice, he panted, and you'll explore Caitlin's virgin territory. (There! the office lothario had denied his own boasts.)   How? I murmured.

180

Listen—you take a rose, tuck it under your nuts, do a few vigorous dances, take Caitlin onto the balcony and hold the rose under her nose.   Well, well.   You don't believe me, he said.   It's not that, I replied.   You'll never get her without it, he said.   It could work, I said, But it doesn't seem fair— why don't you try it if you're so sure.   I'm not after Wedge. You'd be wasting your time, eh?   Wort, you and Wedge are virgins and terrified.   Let's be rational, I said, We'll both try the rose treatment.   Without bother we took roses, he a white, I a talisman, and retired. Back to the dancing. He danced gracefully with his partner, a tall, plump brunette. As Miss Wedge was with someone else, I went with the manager's daughter, Jane, and we managed well enough in the tango because I was able to race along the floor a yard out from the tables. Parallelity was what I needed in the tango, otherwise I tended to lose direction, zigzag and fall over.

Then the scream. Followed by gasps and lots of little screams. What—, Is it—, What, what? Poison? Sniping? Appendicitis? My mentor on his knees tearing open his flies. Of course the ladies withdrew. He was taken to the cloakroom. He ordered everyone out, saying it was only a cramp with complications. When we returned to the dance floor the band looked shattered and was muttering, and didn't want to continue. But on we went. On with the tangoing! Like South American dignitaries with a revolution outside. I was possessed. Should I pluck my rose from my crutch and press it upon Jane, the ravenhaired—would talisman colour match or mismatch quim, cwm, cunt or con? I noticed a couple staring at my feet; in fact so observant were they that they blundered into others. I ignored them. My body movements may sometimes be stiff, but my feet are ever nimble (in my role as Doctor Mackenzie, the Aberdeen sculptor of flesh and bone, I could sword dance and operate at the one time). Then someone nudged me. Several people were watching. Jane, as befitted the manager's daughter, ignored them, though she did drop a hand to hip to check she was all there. At a turn I fell. Slither, crash, thump. Rose petals everywhere, two of them my downfall, others stuck in my shoes. Carried to the cloakroom and left. My mentor had gone. Both felled by thorn and petal. Had I carried a pencil I'd have written Life is Rosy or some such time-honoured saw on the wall.

The office atmosphere on Monday morning was slightly tense, but a shipping crisis quickly quashed talk about the dance. At eleven o'clock I had to go two floors up to see someone about sulphur insurance. (Sometimes the heaps burn; blistering, sulphurous gases are produced and if there is dampness in the air acids fall; I should like to see a heap burn, it would look like a yellow volcano.) There I met Wendy, bold typist, sixteen, slim, blond, tennis and taunting. In a marble corner where a light had failed we kissed, groped and caressed until steel on marble footsteps parted us. The stairs went round a well six feet square. The lily-patterned bottom was eight floors below. She threw a leg over the banister and slid down. I followed cautiously. At a turn she slipped over and hung, cursing. I pulled her up. We hugged and rubbed together. Oh my god how we rubbed. Then we climbed onto the banister again. I said I couldn't because my cock would ignite the wood. She told me to go first, she would follow and quench any fires. So I went first and when I slowed on the turns she came down, my face burrowed under her skirt and I nosed her crutch. We went down, down, down, oblivious to where we would finish. On the third floor I looked up and saw twelve or twenty faces peering down at us. From her floor a finger wiggled, beckoning, and from mine a hand gestured peremptorily. Up we went, full of fearful disdain. Chop, chop. Week's notice but go now. Cast out infection. Be fucking on the marble next and messengers with crucial papers slipping in semen and slip, fractured skulls and falls down stair well. Miss Wedge watched me leave thoughtfully, (Is she thoughtful, I wondered). I waited for Wendy in the street.   Mum and Dad, she sobbed.   Let's take a ferry ride?

Is that all you can think of? Let's have a drink then. I don't. And off she went. Finish.

Coming from the country can be a great advantage when applying for a job because it is possible to obliterate a disastrous past by implying or stating that the vacant period was spent on the family acres, or property, if it is desired to create an impression of munificence. Thus was I able to erase my connection with Austral-Texas and join Agrarian Substances.

Anyway, I waited at the newspaper stall for Miss Wedge. I did wonder if the telephonist, Miss Dobb, had given my call a second thought; if so she would think nothing of telling the boss who would forbid Miss Wedge to leave or allow her to go but have her followed. When I saw her cross the street I stepped behind a column. Titian hair in bun, navy twin set with pearls, tweed skirt and teeter heels to make her tall. I wanted to embrace and soak her with juice of bruised petals. Instead, I greeted her calmly and made a presentation of bunches and posies. Are you all right? she asked. Rather anxiously, I thought. Good fortune. What were my intentions? Did I want to examine her for general health or a particular chest disease? Oh Miss Wedge! Let's go on a ferry trip but first—book into the city's leading hotel. I haven't a nightie, she replied demurely. Her body packaged in nightie? And I don't want to have a baby. Wedge oh Wedge I'll enrubber my cock, balls too, I'll buy you the best foamers, a diaphragm of silk and rubber, silken sheets, a gold nozzle syringe . . . and so on.

We bought many things and a tooled pigskin suitcase to carry them in, and went to the hotel at four. Food and drink were brought to us by discreet and lascivious servants. At three in the morning she insisted we return to work that day. I didn't hear clearly but agreed with her. I then asked her to say what she had said but did not catch it the second time either because I fell asleep or she did not answer. We were

183

like that. At six we were brought grapefruit, tomato juice, cream, porridge, and coffee. Forty minutes later we had a bottle of champagne. At seven-thirty breakfast proper arrived. I could barely chew toast but got it down after dipping it in milk. She ate a rasher of bacon slowly. Suddenly she began to sob. I comforted her. She could not manage the rinds, hence the anguish. She adored rinds. I fed her scrambled egg. I even gave her my parsley. I went to the bathroom and examined my slack honourable member. He rose like an overworked cardinal. I baptized him anew with cold water and he relaxed. I lurched into the bedroom and managed to get in without waking her. She stirred, I moved closer so that we touched and felt myself sink into the growing street noises. Then we were making love again. We murmured drowsily. Then: she suggested I was perhaps—perhaps insatiable?   Me?   I thought you were a little that way.   How many times did we do it? Beyond number.   Pints of us inside, and outside.   You thought I was insatiable? You thought I was insatiable. Which means that really we haven't known one another.   I suppose you could say that—you could also say we are mere beginners. Beginners, yes, but you still don't know. No outburst of petulance, no weeping, no brittle humour. Simply exhaustion and unknowingness. So we dressed, packed what we had in the pigskin and told ourselves we'd better hurry if we were ever going to get to Austral-Texas and Agrarian Substances. We then opened the window and looked down on people streaming to work, jammed traffic and two men on a platform winding themselves up the face of a building over the way.   Lecherous window cleaners, she said, Always peeping.   They do it out of boredom, I suggested. Would you ever get bored up on a platform, everything to see and everyone watching you? The wonder is more of them don't fall from skiting.   As we watched they slowed their ascent and crept up to a ledge. Suddenly a bird dropped out of the sky and skimmed close, making them cower and setting the platform swinging like a pendulum. One of the men produced a pole and tried to dislodge

184

something jammed against a gargoyle. The bird dived again.
It's a hawk, she cried, And they're smashing its nest—turds!
Leave it alone! One man looked round, but had to hang on.
She left the window, ran into the bathroom and came back
with a tumbler. I grabbed it from her. She went to the case,
heaved it open, pulled out the syringe, yanked off its nozzle,
went to the window and let fly. It hit the poleman, bounded
off the building, hit the other man in the face and dropped
into the street. We heard the platform grating against the
building. The bird swept past them again. She threw a tube of
toothpaste and it burst over their heads.   Piss off! she yelled.
They saw us and almost wept with fear and rage. She threw a
cake of soap. A few people seemed to be looking up from the
street. The men shook their fists at us as we closed the window.
Better go, she hissed.   Caitie, I said, Are you really going to
work?   Sure, I'll say the examination was exhausting. We'd
better hurry or there'll be an interrogation. Are *you* going to
work? she asked.   Yes, I'll say I was celebrating.

   We dashed out of the room, ignored the lift and ran down
the stairs, gaining momentum floor by floor until we were
nearly running. I stumbled, lost the case and everything
spilled.   They'll take you for a pox doctor's clerk, she panted,
and we giggled crazily and the desk clerk glared at us. I paid.
Ever so much. She gave me her tortoiseshell hair clasp, I gave
her the case and we rushed out and stood on the pavement and
watched the men winding themselves down the face of the
building, The Saint Paul's Trust Chambers.   Goodbye,
said Caitlin.   I'll see you in a few days, I said.   No, she
said, Lay off—promise me I'll be the one to make contact.
Yes, I said.   Don't phone me at Austral-Texas, will you?
No, I said.

   Agrarian Substances greeted me coolly. I breathed peppermint over everybody, explaining that the nuns advised it as
an after-care. Sister Mercy has a welded tower of seven earth-
filled 44-gallon drums with side openings for herbs, which
are tended by her from a ladder, a splendid sight, this herbal

tower. And when the excellent nun ascends to tend her vegetative charges a young novice plays the flute and patients in the children's ward laugh and cheer.   She is a saint, said Mr Loane, And I'm sending her more of my win.   Me too, said Miss Likke, and I'm sure Mr Barb will do likewise when he returns from the desert.   Not desert, Miss Likke, corrected Mr Loane, There is no desert in New South Wales—Mr Barb's territory is low-carrying-capacity dry country.   The picture of the nun up the ladder compelled me to add that I, too, would make a further donation to the hospital.

At lunchtime I went with Ron and Pat to a small coffee house. I could not understand why I had not given notice or why I had bothered returning or why I had asked for the holidays due to me so I could go home for a few days. As though I wanted only a short respite from invoices, dips, advertisements and drenching guns. As though the small but growing Agrarian empire of rural weekly, radio stations and stock and station agencies would fall if I stayed away too long.

Ron said, It beats me why you're not leaving. You're a wage-slave. Pat said, Put a deposit on a house or buy a block. Ron said, Take it to the races for increase or loss. Pat said, Go to night school or get a title to land. I said, I might lend it to the old man. That would be nice, they agreed. Well, not all of it, I said. Mmm, said Pat, Your father's in the hills back of Peeny, isn't he? If you make him a loan make it a condition he move elsewhere. Yes, said Ron, Up there you work for the bank or live rough. That's not so, I said, There's good land there, and the locals stick together. That's because they hold to each other like drowning swimmers, said Ron. Nonsense, I said, It's traditional and comes from the memory of a man, Russell, who was there fifty years ago.   I suppose they stay on because they're in debt to his estate, said Pat.   Not Russell, I said, His estate went for grabs when he was overthrown. Overthrown? said Ron. He was some kind of socialist, I said. Ssshh, murmured Pat, If that was his way no wonder the place has a bad reputation. Percy, said Ron, You'd better spend some of your win on books to find out what you're letting yourself in for. Why bother with books, said Pat, When all he's got to do is open a paper, listen to the wireless or see a newsreel to realize where it all ends. I showed them my ticket to Peeny. They were pleased to see that it was a return. I told them that while they struggled to work the next morning I would be sitting beside the driver of the milk truck climbing into the hills towards Uppersass.

But I didn't catch the train. I spent my days in libraries, museums, and bookshops as though trying to remedy neglect or stuff myself with what would be unavailable at Uppersass. I went to parties with strangers I met in pubs. I lived on fillet steak and oysters. I awoke, one morning, alongside a fat woman in a mucky room near the wharves and another time in a room packed with snoring drunks. I stuffed a bony girl behind a sofa. I visited a brothel in Darlinghurst and argued over thirty bob (extra for a strip). As I left the place the woman, Rosie, shouted at the crowd to send round the hat, fellers, he needs his fare back to the bush, tee-hee-ha-ha. I was glad I didn't hurry away. If you do her, I told the audience, cover her head with newspaper. I was ready for a spell of unpleasant banter when, suddenly, my arm was forced up to my shoulder blades and I was run out of the lane with the crowd parting like wethers before a beaten ram.

I met a tiny twitchy man in a pub and bought him a beer. He told me to put a fiver on Low Flyer. A short fat man heard him and cackled. The tiny man cursed him and had beer poured onto his stitched pate. I urged restraint. The man shoved me along the bar demanding my name. I recalled the name of a notorious gangster and said Percy Grudder and the shoving ceased. The barmaid jeered at the man and asked me about my Uncle Bert. I told her he had bought a farm and that I was its manager. Low Flyer, said the tiny man, I can see you know horses. So I went to an S.P. and laid a tenner on the horse and it came in at 33s. I went back to the pub to reward the tipster but the tiny man ignored me and the barmaid said my uncle had got it bad. The gunnies did him. The fat man stood in an evil corner with two businessmen. I fretted for the wad of notes in my pocket. I told her I had backed Flying Ooze, which the jockey had pulled but he was going to get his. Uncle Bert's going to be cremated, I said. He's not dead yet, said the barmaid. Lead septicaemia, I said through the corner of my mouth. And he's Catholic! cried the barmaid. Everyone stared at me. I'm his heir, I snarled, and swaggered to the farthest door, not wanting to but feeling that a careless exit was demanded.

The next morning, Saturday, I went down motor bike lane. Riders roared up, they roared down. It was risky crossing but I had to, I zigzagged my way from showroom to showroom. The enamel and the chrome! Engine fins, wheel spokes, brake drums, saddles! I planned a visit to Europe for the racing season. GP and TT. Mad. Instant madness induced by an unplanned short cut along motor bike lane. When I reached the bottom I went through the arch of the railway viaduct to the smaller street of showrooms and Chinese cafés and disposal stores. And here I saw the five hundred Norton. My god! A genuine black and silver projectile. Splendidly second-hand. Sober, nothing flashy about it. Overhead cams, big brakes, monstrous carburettor . . . So on the Monday, instead of returning to Agrarian, I bought the Norton.

Never daring to get out of third gear into top I rode out to see Fred. He disapproved of me and the machine but warmed a little when I told him I had bought it outright and the money had come from a wise investment. In the thirties he had owned a Rudge; he knew that the Norton was a fine machine but was it comfortable and safe? I explained the reasons for the machine's general superiority; steering and suspension were so good one could eat a plate of bacon and eggs at one hundred miles per hour if one did not mind them cold. Yes, once would be enough, otherwise indigestion would ensue and gas and gripe overcome the superior handling qualities of the Norton and what would an ambulance crew make of a battered rider covered with eggs and bacon? why they would stuff them into the nearest wound thinking they were replacing entrails.

That's enough of that talk, Percy, I don't want you coming here disturbing the men.   Sorry, Fred.   That's all right, Percy, you mean well.

Seven hours later I was home and drinking tea. Oh great relaxant, tea. Oh whitened tea—supporter of the dairy industry. I needed essential tea. Because I was almost a ruin. Seven hours of being lashed by wind, dust, spit from cars (thrice), rain (once), grasshoppers (twice—like being hit by a piece of wood), and jarred by bumps, corrugations and potholes. The miraculous smooth-riding suspension a salesman's lie. When I dismounted to open the gate I fell over. Wonderful return of wandering son.

IN FLIGHT AGAIN

Before the beginning of this present turmoil I lived a quiet enough sort of life. Of course there was the onion disturbance, my jeeping and nortoning. I was a fairly contented farmhand. That's not true. I was sometimes fairly contented. I didn't know what I wanted. I liked the city—for short spells; likewise the country.

I have few friends. I like women—I think. My doubt is perhaps due to my lack of experience. Now and then I have stood in paddock or on city corner—I exist at this instant to write my impressions. And to complete them and go on to do what I have set myself on my thirty acres. My brother loathes my thirty acres; my parents disapprove; a few locals would be with me, while most would shrug their shoulders and get on with their own business.

I have thirty acres of Uppersass. I own it, something I never thought I'd do, expecting to be a lessee from cradle to grave. It's not what anyone would call good land. I am, however, expected to improve it for pasture or cultivation; what I appear to be doing strikes most as simpleminded wantonness. I think I would like to be simpleminded. Well, for a few minutes, to see what it's like. I am being conceited. I am.

Aaah, the delights of Uppersass, the glories of dairying, parents, bro, and so on. There. The mere mention of my brother is enough to bring down awfulness or its promise. Perhaps he's pursuing me because of our ends. It is a pity he has a greater range of ends to choose from. That is something the philosophers seldom discuss, quantities of means. The rich have many, the poor, few.

Zzzzooooooom. It was quite low, the plane. I heard the engine two seconds before the shadow passed over. Had it been lower my wortarium would have collapsed in the draughts and vibrations.

I am certain bro is aboard. His zeal is frightening. It is even greater than his love of money because plane hire would cost £10 the hour. Unless he has persuaded the flying club to join his search. For that matter it could be his own plane, the beginnings of Wort Airways, its inaugural flight the hunting down of a Wort.

Maybe I've been outlawed—he thinks I tried to kill him.

He has renamed me Gelly Wort. Wanted for attempted murder. Jelly on the run needs more crystals—crystalline gelly however is hypersensitive so that's no answer. I should stop running and stand firm. Become a standard plug. The Gelignite Kid my alias. And here I am without even a detonator or length of fuse. Armed only with my faithful thirty-five-shot Remington, I doubt I'll ever hit the target. More nuisance than asset.

The plane returned, tilted this time. Was it bro behind the pilot? I felt like waving.

Referring back to my tales for children and adolescents: they are, I think, a little complicated. Years ago I told bro the one about the ferret, only then it wasn't half as long (the tale not the ferret) or nearly so (turgid?). (It was all bone and sinew, but lacked skin to keep the blood in.) He said he liked the plot but not the wordage. On hearing about the camel on the beach, he called me Percy Wort-Wells. For a week, until he dried up.

A minute ago the plane again flew up the valley, as though joyriding or surveying a new route. I think I could very easily begin to hate my brother. By this I mean constantly, on and on. Though I doubt it. Persistent hatred must be a burning, destructive thing and it would soon eat holes in me and let the wind in. Unless I destroyed the object, and I can't see that happening because he doesn't really get me down that much.

The plane has returned and gone off. I am not certain the man behind the pilot was bro. Perhaps it was the police. Or Forestry Commission. Or Army, even though it was not emblazoned with badges, or camouflaged. Lately, rumours have circulated to the effect that five hundred square miles of this electorate are to be given over to military manoeuvres. Also the Air Force and the Navy, believe it or not, though what the latter will do up here in the mountains is anybody's business, unless they send their frogmen on motorized surf floats to find the sources of streams so that the Air Force can bomb them, thus striking as it were at the origin of things wet. Clouds to be dyed and shadowed with searchlight patterns for gunners to gun at. Rain to be persuaded to fall as large hail, each piece coloured and numbered. And those Uppersassians who refuse to move out to be hunted down.

All this, however, is highly unlikely because there is one thing Shire Councillors, even the most patriotic—and by God, Eureka, Deakin, Darcy, Phar Lap, the Statute of Westminster and other sacred oaths—there is *one* thing hereabouts stronger than patriotism and that is roadism. Councillors' attitudes towards roads—no matter how minor—and bridges—however small—are one thing; that is, unique. They would never allow anyone to damage a road or a bridge. The Road is above all. The Army could argue that its tanks exert less pressure on the road than a farm truck, and probably be correct—but to no avail. Too many councillors have seen too many films of tracks churning up ground to be otherwise convinced. I do not know how this local sentiment came into being. Many if not all roads form property boundaries, and roads are essential for the transportation of produce but these reasons savour of the materialistic whereas I feel there is a strong element of mysticism in the people's attitude.

It is known hereabouts that Robinson Wentworth, the venerated pioneer, proposed an east-west highway one hundred years ago, and while he did not build it or for that matter do the blazing or start it, it's said his ghost can sometimes be seen. Even I have seen something odd, and not only on his road but also the side road, the one nearby, the Uppersass road. Robinson Wentworth was a resourceful, courageous, proud, family-loving murderer, who rid his lands of blacks by means of clichés: poison, gun, club and mastiff. Everybody knows this and everybody is at least a little ashamed though so desperate are they for a local historical figure that they are willing to overlook his crimes and say after all, it was the way they did things those days, things were rough, like, and old Robinson had put a lot of money into his seventy thousand sheep and cattle.

There is another local of historical importance but nobody away from Uppersass will have a bit of him, and there are many who deny he ever existed: R. V. Russell, the man who set up Uppersass on his return to New South Wales after a short spell at William Lane's disastrous Utopian colony in South America in the nineties—the New Australia where racial purity was demanded, and communal ownership of production, distribution and exchangio; where there was monogamio, equalitio of the sexios, and nonreligio and teetotalico. Hombres in disagreement with these ground rules will be sent homio.

Russell stumbled right at the start. He lost his interest in racial purity a week after he arrived there and soon earned

192

himself a nickname which in English becomes small-cock-with-big-head-and-heavy-stones and fathered five children; he became an Anglican but because there was no priest for five hundred miles would go to the Romans and confess (the colonists could take a lot, but Russell's confessions enraged them); and he built stills in the jungle (despite Lane's regular still-busting) but would not produce anything stronger than shandy. The year he returned to New South Wales, an uncle died leaving his money to his three children who died without issue and Russell got it all. £90,000. Ninety thousand pounds exerted tremendous pressure upon Russell. He shrank a little all round, and his shiny pate sprouted long hair. Russell Victor Russell became a smallish, bustling, glittering-eyed man who could hold a crowd of ten thousand and get at least half of them to follow him anywhere; but his attractiveness did not last more than two months and by winter he was lucky to draw fifty, even into a heated hall, and nobody knows what happened to his spell-binding ways, but his opponents were relieved.

So Peenyites reject Russell and accept Robinson Wentworth, who died in the seventies, many years before Russell. The Shire has Robinson Avenue and Wentworth Gardens in Peeny, and the now non-existent village of Wentworth on the highway. He died at Wentworth when he fell into a small but bottomless quagmire outside the inn when he strode from his horse to have bitter words with mine host, Zerox, our first known Greek. Something to do with straying cattle, or children. It was not long after dawn, with Zerox, family and customers deep in stupor, or, they were wide awake and heard the irate cry, Shantykeeper! and, not caring for the term or the tone let it continue, and so Wentworth sank. At least the story goes that he went into the mire. It is unplumbable and at certain times emits a foul stench.

Anyway, I do not think we'll see manoeuvres up here. What we have to watch out for are the national parks zealots.

Already this year a score have been sighted giving us the once over. They crawl through in jeeps or zoom past in Daimlers. They walk the roads and climb rock faces a local wouldn't go near. They eat picnic lunches of chicken and champagne or munch raisins as they walk. They are not so keen on Uppersass proper, it's the steep country behind they want, the ravines, waterfalls and fern gullies, but if they get their hands on that they'll want Uppersass as buffer territory. I've nothing against national parks but these people want to turf us out. Compensation of course. No doubt about it. The national park's needed for future generations—you Uppersassians wouldn't begrudge your grandchildren that, would you? and many of you will be required as staff—rangers, attendants and so on.

Peeny likes the idea of having big hotels for the tourists. And the ever problem of what to do with the hillbillies would be solved. Perhaps the park people would keep on a couple of families for tourists to gawp at. We could dress in skins, mate with beasts and probably manage a bit of incest. Perhaps I could be a guide. Get a crowd of Ab peapickers up from the coast to be my porters. Bwana Wort.   Jacky-Jacky, Bill-Bill—you'um go easy wid that'm sofa—and you'm Charlie-Charlie, stop fuckum Missus Bates when Mista Bates watchem. And every now and then we could drop some loath over a cliff to maintain the park's reputation as a place for those who dare. And with a bit of luck we'd all end up park rangers with no need to range.

UPS AND DOWNS

One Sunday, the morning still and clear. So much the former I had to stand on a post and clap hands to shiver things into life; so much the latter I wondered where the clarity had come from, so rubbed eyes and got peculiar dots like ethereal smuts before them. My god, up on the post clapping then rubbing eyes as a single unit of the world's population (a

194

unique fraction) acting as fraction god.   Hello! I shouted.
It came back. Then came other sounds. Steel dropping on concrete. Magpie. Moo-ooooo. Hoink. Cluck-cluck-cluck. All is
well. Hymn. Did I hear hymn? I did not because I was out of
range of wireless. The milking done with. Every day the
milking has to be done with. The demands of beasts. If only
they would have rest-days and fix for themselves.

Dad called me from the bails. I replied that I was going to
the road for mail. He came out towards me. It's Sunday, Perce,
Sunday, y'know? I agreed but pointed out that the truck
collected milk or cream every day. Yes, Perce, but Sunday is
never a mail day. I agreed with this but pointed out that late
or misplaced mail could be delivered Sundays, though I knew
it had never happened before; therefore, if it came this Sunday it would be a unique occasion and well worth meeting
the blessèd truck.   You're trying to dodge work, Perce.
Father, I have no intention of shirking any task no matter
how menial.   I cupped my ear.   Hear—isn't that the truck?
Percy, the job won't wait ten minutes, it's high, and what you
can hear is probably the Sergeant's Ford, or worse—and why
the hell is there so much interest in mail nowadays? Just you
let me go for it.   Father, are you expecting top-secret intimate mail?   Percy, if I'd ever gone on and acted this way
with *my* father he'd have brought the strop out. You've made
too much trouble down in Peeny and I don't know where else,
and one day some father, brother or husband is going to have
your nuts out.   I grabbed myself with both hands and
howled. He had made a painful statement and I declared that
if anything happened he would be held responsible for his
curse.   I didn't mean it that way, Perce.

So I wandered down to the gate. Would the driver stop on
the way up or on the way down, he's not long on the job so
perhaps he does it to keep us guessing on mail days so farmers
won't wait for him and he'll be able to do the entire run and
not meet a single high-countryman (he being a properly
registered low-countryman, someone not to be trifled with).

195

Perhaps bro put him up to this dodge. But I doubt it because bro does not drink at the Commercial. Unless there is profit in it. I held out my hands. Not that I would refuse graspable profit myself, especially as there is a limit to profit and my grasping some would leave less for him.

He stopped for the cans. There was no mail. Didn't I know what day it was? You're certainly out of touch, up here. Sinday? Eh? Sinday—the day we high country people roll about, grope and wail so why don't you stop over, eh, and have yourself a real EXPERIENCE. Eh, oh gee, what you getting at? This is our day. Hey, is it really like that up here? Like what? Aw, you know—but I'm engaged. Bring her up next Sinday. Watch what you're saying, Mr Percy Wort.

Why did I have to talk to him like that? What is the MATTER with me, why not leave well—or unwell—alone? I had converted another low-countryman into a superior being who would now be able to lean on the bar and swap Uppersass stories with the worst of them.

Yet, no matter how I regretted the encounter, I made things worse a few hours later when I went from the house to the gate to see what the people in the car wanted. The man had got out, walked round, then leant on the gatepost. The Chev was a shabby '47 model, seething and squeaking with life. I could guess the nature of the enquiries. Yes, as I strode down along the right rut to the gate this splendid morning, stepping over the pats, I knew. Yes, my friend, the Irish are always here Sundays. Not that I associate them with cow dung (we are the cowdungers), but they are trying to take us over, god knows why. It's the priests in the city and Newcastle and on the coalfields who are saying, Go north, lads and get the best farms, back to the land, lads, be worthy and fecund and soon all will be yours. But as they can't afford the best farms they come to places like Uppersass, where, if they're unlucky enough, they exchange the life of a miner or factory hand for that of a landed peasant proprietor.

He opened the gate and strode towards me, strode he

certainly did, between the ruts as though seeking cowshit for
his brogues (which are shoes patterned with holes for collecting shit to show your station according to the quantity you
collect). The sunshine beating about his head as though he
were all it had to halo. This place for sale? No. (An air of
communion and incense.) A friend told me it might be.
(Father Rogan, no doubt.) I was told there were rundown
places up here. (Insulting bogtrotter; mustn't let him talk to
Dad; rundown indeed, fences good, plenty of super, pastures
harrowed, manure spread, cows above average, a good bull,
silage pits, hay shed. Ill-mannered miner so accustomed to
looking at coal he can't recognize a healthy green. Poor bugger.) Your father home? (Jesus, he sees me as the boy. Wants
to see the master.) Your place or do you share-farm?
Ahearne's the name.

So I led him to the house. I had to talk like a lunatic to
head him. What about your family? I asked. They can
wait. As we climbed onto the veranda I heard Joe Tank
hoy. I turned to see Joe put his horse over the western boundary. Very elegant. It was one of his rifle bucket days, when
he straps them on with a couple of bottles to drink to the
memory of the light horse of '14, though he's about thirty and
went through the last war in destroyers.

A beautiful sight, said Ahearne, A bushman born in the
saddle. Tank cantered up in fine style, a man born in the city,
a plumber turned farmer. Ahearne asked Dad if he was
thinking of moving on. He had the idea that the further he
went into the hills the more shiftless and migratory were the
farmers; that on average they moved once a month and that
he, Ahearne, was the one to change this pattern, and put down
roots.

Did you pass any odd looking blokes on the way up? asked
Tank. He had not. I wouldn't have left your family in the
car, said Tank. And why not? Oh nothing—it doesn't
matter, there's nothing to be done now. Ahearne looking over
his shoulder at his car. The Morgans down the road, said

197

Tank, The place painted black, it's their time of the year, the
banana pollen blows from the coast and gets them, they go
yellow and jaundiced, wild.   There's a pea rifle in the car,
said Ahearne.   In the boot I hope, if not you're running a risk
what with kids nowadays, one of ours shot the cousin in the
back of the head, ruined the windscreen too.   Well, now,
better be moving on, said Ahearne. Tank and I went with
him.   The Morgans wear dungarees, bow ties and go barefoot.   Ahearne quickened his pace. Trying to turn the car he
bogged, so we got the tractor. His family scrambled out like
children released from detention. His wife, too. A small thin
woman with a nervous smile and a pink coat. As Dad
positioned the tractor the children swarmed over it so he cut
the engine, warned them about hot parts and got down. Mum
came from the house with oranges. When they drove off Tank
advised them not to stop for anyone.

Dad told me to finish the job I'd started earlier so I got
the pig from under the oleander and fired it with kero. This
very fine morning not a fortnight ago. Had the fleeing
Ahearnes looked back they'd have seen the pall and thought
it a signal to the dungareed Morgans.

Sergeant Smogton rang from Peeny.   What are you doing
up there? Terrorizing tourists—a good man, Ahearne, almost
clipped Mad Harry near the cemetery; if you want to be mad
in the hills put it in writing and I'll have you fenced off and
toss in every troublesome Abo and vagrant I can lay hands on;
my job's law and order and I've never fallen down on it.

Coppers are noted for their lack of humour, said Tank.
You go too far, said Mum. I do think we needle the Peenys,
said Dad. What do you say, Perce? asked Tank. We overdo it,
I replied thoughtfully. He's being thoughtful! cried Tank,
Watch out for him or he'll have the world on our necks.

Early the next morning I went down to the mailbox and stood
on the stand beside it, behind the cream cans, thigh-high,

full of the liquid wealth of the dairy industry, cans rich in antibiotics, the region's bonus to city folk.

Thigh-, hip- or knee-high to a man they are, depending on stature. One day when we've got it made and are sending down cans chest-high—when we're cream millionaires, I'll empty one, get inside and have myself transported to the co-op, or coop; coop, that's where you stand condemned.

I sentence this person to fifty years in the coop and when he is released he will be beaten with a gold watch, rubbed all over with butter, his mouth washed out with yoghurt liquor and a certificate of performance given him. Let this be a warning to those others who would masquerade as cream millionaires for such millionaireness is not for menial producers—nor, need I add for millenial producers (pause for applause): silence or I'll clear the court!—(*The Wit of Judge Blight*; Personality Press; £5)—milk, the fluid secreted by mammals, in this case bovines, is primarily produced for the sustenance of their offspring; secondarily for the growth and maintenance of the children upon whom our glorious future depends; and tertiarily (or thirdly) for the delectation of workers i.e. milkshakes, cocoa, etc. to keep them away from drinks of an alcoholic nature. Cream and milk producers stand knee-high—if that—to the full majesty of the law. When examined under the microscope milk is seen to consist of a great number of minute globules of fat floating in a clear liquid; it is, in fact . . . who was that! Ushers clear the court with the exception of this disorderly wretch who'll get a splendid curative sentence equal to five bovine lactations. You! you're the creature? and you say you merely cleared your throat? Oh ho, what a throat you have, ever tried the stage? Ho ho ho; I clearly heard you liken the Law to a globule floating on the clear liquid of the People, ho ho take him away for five lactations.

I must get away. Permanently. Returning occasionally to visit the family—if they're fools enough to stay; and they are —and friends—ditto.

I have gone away so many times. Mum and Dad do not depend on me, indeed they would not despair to see me go even though a departure would affect the garnisheeing of my wages. Mrs Page—sweet Emma—why did it have to end in such a manner! The animals got us. But pastures new. Hard for you with two. For me a weekly garnishee. Costs awarded against P. Wort of Uppersass. Why am I so fond of the spouses of uniformed men? Is it some martial quality I seek? I who have never worn a uniform except as a scout. Damn. Garnishee. Gone is she. To he. Of the uniform with two stripes. (A stripe a child.) He won't stripe her, by God, though he wanted to with his lanyard. Lanyard, would you believe it. I had one in the scouts, kept my knife on the end of it, against the wishes of Baden-Powell *and* the Governor-General, who disapproved of knife against chest, who stipulated instead the position on hip or in shorts pocket against groin or private parts. Corporal Page, and what a corpus, and what a mind; everything according to regulations, eating, emptying, drinking, speaking and—the imagination flinches at this— loving: Let's have a nordy, Emmie, put it in, pull it out, snore snore. But everyone has the geishas Emmie, Jesus Emmie, I'm a man, very clean they are, weekly inspections, they're trained for it Emmie, it's their job, their *job*, don'cha understand?

My immediate departure would invalidate the garnisheeing of my wages and possibly render my parents liable under the relevant Act, i.e. rendering assistance to offenders. The Act is riddled with references to the likes of me. Protection of Dependents of Members of the Armed Forces Act. Part 3: It is an offence for a civilian to fornicate with the wife of an active member . . . in peace time £200 and/or 12 months . . . in war time 5 years or the death and/or £400; Alienation of the affections to any degree particularly if the Judge considers such behaviour directed towards the eventual entry of the wife shall carry the penalty of 40 lashes and/or £100. Psychiatric evidence may be admitted at the discretion of the Judge.

The guilty one shall lose one testicle for the first offence if mental disturbance is proven, and a second offence shall carry away the other; in the case of unitesticular men the second offence shall be accompanied by brain surgery by a registered and fully qualified veterinary surgeon; in the case of tritesticular men a third offence shall carry away the third, such thirds to be kept in cool storage for presentation to National Service geldees on the first anniversary of their loss, or, if the organ be of inferior quality, kept for regimental ceremonials.

From such thoughts does derangement come. Corporal Page for example. Deranged yet fully employed. Got compassionate leave, flew back to his erring spouse. Tttttt. All those tongues going. Poor Page. But what bloody pagination. Whole pages gone. Chapters. The beginning screwed up, the end stuck back with pension glue.

Such thoughts on a day like this. Blue, calm, dew, benign. Nature. What'll she do next, nature? Emma. Twenty-two and two, Steve and Phil, G'day, g'day, two crumble bars, one for you and one for you, wrappers admission to your Mumma. Only it wasn't like that, they're nice boys, they didn't know the corporal, and if they came in with us at night they thought I was the natural thing there alongside or on or under their mum, their sweet mum, Emma, hair up to her navel. Course you shouldn't shave it, it's unique, a pity it's not up to your tits so that if we make a baby—course I'm careful—it'll come out of you and follow the hair. Kangaroos do. Back in the pouch, never an ouch, do it on the couch, damp cloth on the velveteen afterwards. Now your corporal punishment. Though maybe it's not like that. You're fond of him, he's fond of you, only fondness is not enough, my Emma, five feet three, nearer am I to thee than he. Nonsense. But a nice soft thought on such a memory morning. Once, she saw me out at three, to walk with me, to the Norton, under the willow beside the showground, three blocks away, the night full of stars, dew thick as mist, we stopped twice and not a sound and when we stopped thrice we did it again on the lawn by the baby health centre and she was quiet and I squeaked. I'd never squeaked before, I don't know where it came from, high in the throat I suppose, my squeak through her hair, and then only our breathing.

I heard the cream truck climb the pinch three farms away. Six pick-ups to go then back to the Co-op, weigh, test, tip-out, credit. Peeny Producers' Co-op. Peeny Shire. Two thousand square miles of low Peeny country, of valleys, of hills and ridges, to Uppersass, then up into the mountains, the rough country, the western boundary a road seldom used. Peeny Shire had tried to advance westward but the climb had been too much, the air too thin and the big tableland shire beyond too strong. Still, Peeny had tried, would try again, for the view from the top was quite splendid, you could see to the ocean on a clear day, and the councillors loved a view, though they were not too fond of some of the country they overlooked, the hillbilly or hillybilly of Uppersass, Wombat Falls, Stevens and like places where uncivilized elements periodically dissipated what worth they had. But Peeny could be magnanimous. It could be joyful. When it expanded it would organize a festival.

This fine morning I feel like a fête. I should sing. I should jaunt. I shall run. I shall dance down the road all the way to Peeny. Dancing I will go, combining the best of the modern waltz, the foxtrot, the quickstep, the pride of Erin, the schottische, the barn dance, the rhythm, laden with flowers for the women, apples for the men. Dawn would be the time, not now, it's too late. Dance through Peeny, get everyone up then watch them dash back to their still-warm beds, only the men, however, for the women will dance with me before returning to their spouses, and children will throw coins for my garnishee.

I can't get this damn garnishee out of my mind. Penalty for playing out of bounds. The balls bounced, the linesmen reported them, the umpire pronounced. The penile prowess of the Arbitration Act: whosoever defies a ruling on principles 1234567890 shall be tied to a Sunshine Harvester hauled by twenty sturdy geldings three times across a salt pan, then be untied and pelted with mill ends, reject SAE bolts and nuts, flogged with wool caps and finally buttered with frozen rejected-for-export butter.

I can't get away from punishment. Time to be positive.

The truck arrived. Ross was polite and asked after things, predicted a dry bitter winter, higher rates, the destruction of the newly repaired culvert, the imminent madness of the commo schoolteacher, a plenitude of women at the next Uppersass dance and an increase in Peeny's hatred of Uppersass. He then handed over the mail and a box of penicillin. See you later. He drove off. Three letters for me.

There was a letter from an enquiry I'd made of a group of people living on two boats two-hundred-odd miles away at Rushcutters Bay. An experiment in communal living, and they still had room for one more on receipt of £20 for the kitty. As I walked back to the house I looked at the red-crossed letter I'd signed for. From Tomas & Dout, Solicitors. I felt its shape, weight and texture. Rectangular, three ounces (two stamps) and crackly. The sort of letter to be left unopened. If not claimed by Percy Wort within seven days return to Tomas & Dout, Bridge Street, Sydney, NSW. Summons? Writ? Demand? By return mail despatch £500 and your testicles. So, eh? I decided to return it on the eighth day marked Deceased. Died intestate. Claim for damages to house rented by Corporal Page. Mrs E. Page, use of. Special tax on all residents of hamlet of Uppersass, etceteras, for being alive. Then a second letter from the lawmongers: You are alive though unwell so do not tempt the Law. Tomas & Dout Vigilante Service. Satisfaction Denied to Wrongdoers. Highly recommended by All Lovers of Legal Language. Highest average of hereforeto & hereinafter in the Commonwealth. Etc.

But I had signed for the registered letter. My indelible mark. Fingerprints too. And Ross Driver would say anything on oath. Stuck with it. Crossed with red pencil. Sign of the plague. Treat the plague carefully and survival is possible.

So I kept that letter for later.

I opened the third one. From Uncle Fred.   Perce, next time you're down come and see me.   That was all. Short and ominous. I walked slowly back to the house. Fred's worrying brevity. He was tight with his quids so why put stamp to a letter of seven words? To do with money.

Fred's letter and the one from the aquatic co-op. And the red-crossed missive. So, go down, see the coopers and Fred. Open the registered THING en route.

The letter I'd opened went on to tell me that the aquatic coop was two houseboats at Rushcutters Bay and I could join if I put a further ten pounds down and survived—their word —a week's trial. Communalism. Democracy. Everything put to the vote. Marrieds and singles. Go to work where you will or in the immediate vicinity teaching swimming, or painting and fitting out boats, or setting moorings, or go further afloat crewing for the repulsive rich or fishing like a Galilean if that's how you feel (though it should be remembered that the aquatic coop is not tied to Christianity or any other -ity). Your immediate reply requested.

All of a sudden, as I walked through the dewy grass this splendid morning (I feel that I have already referred to many splendid mornings in this short account of my life and doings —however most mornings are splendid; perhaps there is a case for reorganizing the calendar and splitting each day as we now know it into two of twelve hours each, giving an ordinary year of seven hundred and thirty days). Anyway, just as I was about to push open the garden gate, I felt this sharp, tiny stab in my right buttock. Not an ant. Chill from the dew perhaps? A clot of blood ascending fatally? Or something equally morbid? No. Simply an edge of the red-crossed letter reminding me of its presence. I sat on the edge of the veranda and looked at the envelope. I have received three legal letters in my life and each has attempted to doom me. One was from Emma's husband's solicitor, demanding cost of repairs to walls of said connubial nest wherein said spouse Emma and adulterer Percival the Wort did fuck and tear lino under bed legs, sofa legs and cast-iron claws of bath and thereinafter when the said Wort was apprehended by our client Corporal Stripes and his brothers hereinafter known as the Three Stripes said Wort did burst through walls of Stripe home to detriment of said wallpaper and veritable walls . . . and so on, almost ad infinitum.

I wish to have no truck with law companies but cannot resist opening their letters and feeling the heavy paper. They know this—that ords cannot but yield to the temptation to touch such paper. I've yet to score a communication on vellum. Vellum you can use doubled or tripled for soling shoes.

(IDEA: The dairying business being what it is—i.e. above poverty today but likely to be below it tomorrow—farmers would be well advised to turn their calves into vellum—indeed, it is the farmers' only hope for it's only a matter of time before some diabolist manufactures an artificial cow covered with plastic, producing numilk from seawater, soybean juice and sterilized sewage.

NOTE: have IDEAS book covered in vellum. FOUND Vellum Society to promote use thereof. HIRE gangsters to rub out potential artificial-cow inventors. CURRY favour among medievalists and RCs to secure return to vellum mss. WHEN I GET OUT OF THIS DREADFUL SITUATION I WILL HAVE MY WORDS TRANSCRIBED ONTO VELLUM. Two beasts or twenty? A bloody picture. Calves' heads drawn back and final, spurting mouths in throats. I think I eat too much meat. The north coast of New South Wales has a number of vegetarian Christian sanctuaries and I think perhaps I should join one and not bother with the aquatic coop.)

The legal communication still unread. It is on fake parchment. A vellum summons, impeachment, enfeafment or catchascatchcan should be handwritten by ancient scrivener. Typewriting would be at best tasteless. Even thumbnail dipped in tar would be acceptable. I think I should reply to this missive on reverse using thumbnail item. Such as: PERCE HAS GONE HE SPRANG LIKE TIGER FROM HOMESTEAD ON READING YOUR SAME AND OUR GUN IS MISSING   and we think he took it so look out you will not be safe anywhere though we doubt he has shells in which case he would use it as a club. There was certainly some movement on *this* station when *your* word got around HO HO HA HA.

That's the treatment solicitors respect, firm and registered.

I'd have no objection to a vellum inscribed Will, not that I wish death on any benefactor, tho if there's a will there's a way—indeed a veritable highway to sufficiency.

[I do go on about money. It is my situation. Here in this ruin, wondering when the next plane's going to drop a hanky with snot message I SEE YOU. Unless I'm careful I'll end up like bro.]

OPEN the letter for there is no escape from a registered letter once you've signed for it. A simple x'd be enough for the postmaster. x'ing your death warrant.

Dout & Tomas headed paper. . . . Dear Sir, we are in structed by . . . payment within seven (7) days . . . loan by Frederick Wort, Esquire . . . £100 . . .

You old swine, Fred. £100 in seven days. The piggy old joker. £100 loan to help me out. Dear Tomas & Dout, Your comctn. to hand and going to arse; tho yr. comctn. be unyielding am beshitting same . . . however . . . the £100 referred to was invested in improvements on locomotive machine, my internal combusted velocipede, to wit one Norton 500 cubic centimeter (cc.) motor cycle, International model, the scourge of varlets, vassals, barons, lords and sheriffs of the road. Said machine with modified cams, big piston and other alterations and improvements. Am sending in six days' time my UNCLE'S

206

share of said machine—wheels, front forks, rear suspension and secondary chain . . . I suggest he pedal slowly and have machine registered with proper authority . . . otherwise the might & majesty of the LAW will fall on him. Am fitting MY parts of said machine into reconditioned pram chassis & may elemental justice have mercy on your soul.

My poor Uncle Fred must be out of his mind. It's all that metal dust he's inhaled over the years, gone to his heart, turnings have wormed into his ears. An iron man trying to transmute himself into gold. Fred, you send me a letter asking me to contact you. Fred, you get your solicitor to send a letter threatening me. Perhaps the old bugger is broke—has lost a tender for half a million grub screws? In which case I would lend him £50.

HOWEVER. Reseal the letter, mark Opened In Error and change P. Wort, Esq. to T. Wort, etc. Gain a week. Flash down and see the man. Take sack of cowshit, call on salacitor and leave for window boxes. My repeated references to shit. Wipe them out.

I ran down to the bails. Dad had the hose running as he broomed the concrete, Mum stacked separator parts, the wireless played breakfast session and the last of the cows was about to disappear below the night paddock. I ran back to the house, got into my riding gear and readied the Norton. And remembered the gift for Uncle Fred, the old shotgun bought from Peeny Secondhand. Pitted and dented but a genuine colonial weapon, dismantlable for carrying, ideal for collector or romantic (suicide-prone) gunman, which I wrapped in chaff bag. One cannot depart (or flee) on an empty stomach, so cooked piles of bacon, eggs and toast, ate my fill and put the other plates in the stove to keep warm. Then I slipped down to the shed, got the tractor out, filled the tank and attached the ripper. Dad saw me from the separator room and waved. I filled the wood boxes. Mum and Dad stepped onto the back veranda. I slithered along the hall and out the front.   Hey—

where're you going? he cried.   Won't be long, I answered, giving the starter another kick.   Hey—you can't.   Won't be long.   You stay away from Peeny—they'll get you.

And the damned thing wouldn't start. So I pushed and bumped it, Manx-style, and went off side-saddle, bumping and leaping, off from the Wort pits for a record-breaking streak to the smoke, and to Dout & Thomas, licensed extortionists, acting on beloved Fred's behalf. The road still dew-damp so dust too heavy to whirl. I was going to arrive at destination pristine! Through town after town, over the Bridge immaculate! The toll-takers bow as I hand over my money! Song of the road limited only by my need to keep my voice low because atmospheric peculiarities can produce echoes.

Clean, and remaining clean—what a way to begin and end a journey! One has only to look at the old air cleaner on an engine after operating in dust to see what is taken in. Sometimes I use a damp handkerchief across my face when the going's dry and the resulting pattern is skull-like. Not to mention spit, garglings, crusts and ash cast from cars ahead. As for wet weather and mud and slush.

But this particular morning! Oh beauties of Nature! Sweet smells of forest litter, peeling bark, leaves and flowers. Intoxication! So—if intoxicated why not rest and drink in Nature's essences? Camp beside a beautiful creek, beneath a canopy of wattles and native willows, among perfumed shrubs, flowers and native mushrooms—hist! Chew one slowly and gargle the scented juices! Nibble a leaf of the wild tobacco, or the corkwood for its hyoscine and atropine (which has a stimulating effect on the central nervous system). However, who needs to chew a herbal stimulant when the senses are soaring?

Thus I mused as I motored over the damp dust.

I then considered the alternative: i.e., dry dust. An impenetrable cloud behind. Cosmos of whirling particles! The creation of matter aerial! The Norton Comet . . . I was quite overcome. I wept. I had to stop a moment. I held it. Fortune smiled (LET IT NOT TURN LEERY).

Dout & Tomas to be frustrated, Fred warm hearted, my Uppersass scheme successful, peace and etceteras reigning, the Rushcutters Bay aquatic coop spreading its halcyon influence! Blessed be my mother and father for conceiving me.

I INTEND MAKING THIS JOURNEY AS NEAR PERFECT AS IS POSSIBLE, I thought to myself. Would smile at everyone, succour the distressed and aid the needy. As I travelled south I would be the unfastener on the zip of the dashed centre line— behind me the line would open—its jaws unmesh—and radiance pour out! However . . . jaws? Letting the light out? Am I, therefore, inside a mouth, at the back of teeth, in some vast cavern? And, if travelling south, am I diving down a gullet? THIS IS PESSIMISTIC THINKING I told myself. Continue the journey . . .

Left, right, over culvert, across bridge, the twelve miles of it to Peeny, then Moneq. Farms on flats, small paddocks, irrigated, treeless, suburban farms once flooded-gum, blackbutt and cedar. Through Yerk Springs, over the Yulie bridge to the Tarah. Walls and footpaths wet from hosing. Two trucks with four by four's. Sweet noise from tappets and silencer. To the lift bridge. Whenever I approach it I wonder: will it rise today? It rises slowly to hootings and red lights while the coaster or drogha stands off waiting for passage: and as the steel deck rises I knock the Norton back into second, grab the throttle and snake for the rise. O dear O thrills, faster ever faster. Making turbulent the mild river breezes of the river. And we leap the great gap in G. Duke Works Norton style.

But this day there is no river traffic and the bridge stays down. I ride sedately along the poplar'd causeway until the engine stops. An empty tank. The racing star extinguished because he forgot to fill up. I get off the road not far from Taanish Village, and in view of its reputation, chain the wheel and check the pannier locks. I walk back towards Tarah. Soon a Morris stops for me and I get in beside a thin, middle-aged bristle-haircut driver. He didn't usually give lifts but after leaving Taanish Village he was so glad to see a clean young white man that all reservations vanished. He thanked the Lord —but then, who else?—the government had seen fit to situate the village a couple of miles from Tarah. Ten miles would have been better, of course, and a high barbed wire fence. Locating it on the highway was a blunder of great magnitude, and it would be interesting to know who made the decision, and who did well out of it. And now I'm going to tell you something. He stopped the car on the crown of the road.

See here, I am interested in charity work—in fact I manage my livelihood in between works of charity—and I have just come from that village where I left my usual gift of eighty cakes of soap made by my wife. Not plain yellow mind you, but coloured with cochineal and perfumed with rosemary. I took it to Sam Brothers . . . Mr Jones, he said (some of them speak very well), Mr Jones—back so soon—surely not another month has passed? I replied: It is the Lord's timetable I keep, Sam.   I heard someone within the house say something about His missus' rags. I said to Sam: Is that a reference to me? My wife in rags? Sam said: Of course not, it is a reference to a hardworking neighbour currently experiencing poor health, irregular employment and the depredation of his laundry by a pack of wild dogs.

By the way, said the driver, I'm Mr Bill Jones of Whalers' Inlet. Percy, I replied, of up the coast. I did not dare be more explicit for fear of visits or mail. Well, Percy, you probably don't know much about our problem here. Those small weatherboard houses I've just left were an attempt to lift up the Aboriginal people hereabouts and success is not foreseeable. The village is attractively treed, there are decent families—but oh alas these people have unsavoury relatives. I had always had high hopes for Sam Brothers but even he is not strong enough to resist beggarly relatives and their accomplices who are as often as not completely unknown to him.

I looked in the rear vision mirror and saw a great log truck bearing down. The truck braked, swung wide and went past with a cry of Something Galahs. Mr Jones shuddered then drove off the road. As I was saying, Percy, there was this disagreeable person in Sam's house. I heard loud panting and snorting and this fat ugly black man jumped onto the porch, shadow sparring. I ignored him. He took a cake of soap and pretended to eat it. Of course this had no effect on me whatsoever. He then rubbed himself with it, dwelling on those parts of the body one always takes for granted.

Look, I said, I've got to get to Tarah. Of course, of course. Anyhow this man then threw the soap into a tree and made obscene remarks. Such as Belt it, Stick it etc. I've heard of the place, I left my bike near it. You ride one of those . . . your leather coat. Dangerous things. I once heard of someone being smothered with a leather coat. O jesus weary. I stretched out. Your trousers, he said, Open. I'm hot. It's unseemly. It's not and I'm hot. You can't go round like that. You get a beautiful draught. You'll be run in, flagrante delicto. Fragrant, delectable? So long as I get a policewoman. He drove quickly across the causeway, the bridge, and put me out. I bought petrol, chocolate, and got a lift back with a man who talked about clouds. Two men were looking at the Norton.

Great bike you've got there. Speedo goes to 120. Phew. Gee. Gosh. Going back to the city? What about nipping back to Tarah and getting us a few bottles? You can keep the change. It's a bit far for us. So I went back to Tarah for half a dozen bottles of port. I said I would like to have a wash. The tall man said the village was full of soap, and the other man laughed. So one sat on the pillion, the other rode the mudguard till we reached the gates. They said I couldn't get in because of the you-know dobbers. They went in and a few minutes later a woman came out carrying a basin and a shoulder bag. She stepped lively, but she was thin. She was so thin, she was like someone freed from a concentration camp, with reddish hair, pale skin and dull enormous eyes. She had to get to her job at a city hospital where she was Doctor

Roger's special nurse. I told her that the bike had a slipping clutch and was likely to lose a valve within forty miles. She stared at the ground, mumbled and said, Pig's arse. Certainly no way to ask for a lift. She asked where I had come from and I told her I had a place up north. Cattle station? she asked. Yes, a station, I said. She said she had to get down and seeing I had such a terrific bike she thought she'd ask that's all, she'd missed the train and if she didn't get down she'd lose her job. Nance. She'd ridden pillion before, and knew how to lean. All right, so off we went. She could have been a feather.

I stopped a few miles on, fumbled with the cable and a screw and said, Clutch and carb OK. She seemed to be asleep so I touched her shoulder. Hands off, she said. Through hamlets masquerading as towns, and the town of Koolong, where, near a side road and abreast of the sign freeing traffic of restriction, we were ordered in by a cop on a Thunderbird. He stopped alongside so he wouldn't have to dismount and creak over in his smart leggings. Goggles pulled over his cap like Rommel. Bitterly disappointed he could only get me for 40 in a 30 zone. A truck passed and dusted his serge and lenses, but he remained very calm.   You get many bikes? demanded Nance. (Don't Nance, don't, you'll have him poking at the bike and bound to find something amiss, he'll ask questions I won't be able to answer because I've only a vague idea really of how the thing works, in fact I'm grabbed by incomprehension whenever I look at it, all I've got is a smattering of mechanic's jargon. Conrod and bumpy cams. You can't annoy a Rommelie cop, a man who sees a Norton and sees an enemy, for he can be outrun even with two up.) He stared at her: We've got a few bikes round here. And you reckon you fix 'em, eh? said Nance. (I am never going to get to the city. She was sent to frustrate me. The cop has only to go back to the village to find out I'm a port-runner and get me six months. I am a coward. I realized it with awful calmness.)

Then the two horsemen came down the side road. Father and son, beef men; once, perhaps, dairy men, but now risen in

212

the world, perhaps a thousand feet, where they ride stocky mountain horses with quick hoofs. Still, they said Hello, though the cop was taciturn. The son said, Officer, my horse wants to relieve himself, do you mind? And a cauldron of piss hit the dust, some of it splashing the cop's beautiful leggings and he straightened up, Rommel, half out of his tank. Move on, he snapped. You're not in Martin Place, said the son. Would you know where it was? said the cop. I once reported you to the Commissioner, said the father, And you were reprimanded. Never! cried the cop. Then he was your double, said the father. I never did duty in Martin Place, said the cop. Freemartin, said the son, He is innocent.

I am a coward, I thought, and what is about to happen to me will be my punishment, I'll be shot down, brought to earth, flattened in the horsey mud. However, if you go to the bottom there's nothing to stop you peeping up at the other players and exacting a final pleasure from the show. Do you catch many locals, officer? asked the son. The cop examined in minute detail my licence for the third time. Your sergeant, said the father, Is very keen on enforcing the droving regulations. I'm a motor-bike man, protested the cop, and my sergeant's in sidecars. A harrier of cattle and cattle men, he is, said the father. So much so, said the son, That before long we expect to see him and his sidecar concealed under a hide, the better to catch infringers—he is a frustrated cattle man—he can't have them so he persecutes them and their owners. You warn him, said the father, That while's he snooping and steering around he doesn't get jumped by a bull.

The cop returned my licence and seconds later was a hundred yards away. The horses pranced. He's got a piston for a heart, shouted the son. The only cops I can tolerate, said the father, Are the mounted ones in the city. Do you know the score? the son asked me. I'm from Uppersass, I said. What? said the son. Where? said the father. Behind Peeny, I said. Up where? said the son. Oh *there*, said the father, Cows? Zone? said the son. Now and then, I said, Mostly it's cream. Ah, said

213

the father with a mixture of superiority and sadness. I thought you said it was a station? said Nance. Station! guffawed the son. Easy there, said the father. The name's Black-Bouquet, drop in next time—and bring your lady friend. And away they rode.

Bring your lady friend my arse, growled Nance. I think he meant it, I said. You're a fool, she said. I kicked the engine over. Nance was a great passenger, a bundle of charm. You ready? I called back. Yair—but go down the side road a bit first. So I rode down until she pinched me to stop. She wants to have a leak. She got off, told me to put the bike on the stand, sprang onto the saddle backwards and lay back on the tank. Put it in, she ordered. Winking at me. My god, I muttered. Go on. Undoing the top of her dress. Can't you? Come here and I'll fix him.   On a bike—you can't!   There a law against it?   We'd fall off—anyway, I'm not that keen on the bike.   Frightened the copper'll come back?   No, I said, and I don't expect you to work your passage.   I can y'know. With her finger.   This is bad, I said.   Then bugger off, yeller man. And she hurled herself off the bike. It crashed on its side. She bent over, bared her arse, straightened up, grabbed her gear and strode toward the main road. I heaved the bike upright. You still want a lift? I shouted. She gave me one of those offensive gestures. So I rode away alone, but only to a store a few miles on where I had a drink. And didn't feel like continuing the journey. The way things were going I'd be lucky to reach the outskirts alive. I peered into the mirror and saw a coward's face. Without meaning to I put on one of the brother's faces. HOW HE WOULD HAVE HANDLED THINGS. Chatted up the cop about his bike, admired his leggings, asked about old sergeant so-and-so, asked about tickets in the police raffle, mentioned his work with the police boys' club, introduced the horsemen to him, offered to organize a rodeo with the proceeds split between police boys and hospital and, finally, bought fifty cows. Ride on, I commanded. What else? said the storekeeper's wife from the doorway. I took off like a grand prix hero. Doing eighty I passed a log truck and all but went into the safety fence on the bend ahead. A couple of miles to calm down, then wang! between two cars. On the long straight stretches beside the stringybark forest I had my chin on the tank at 105. Where the road looped I tucked in behind a Cadillac the size of a bus, it was the sort of car a baccarat gangster would use, and I dawdled a yard from the rear through gentle bends until the Caddie's wallowing made me queasy. I let it go and didn't catch up until the road straightened. Then he gave it full bore to burn me off, but I simply snicked back a gear and went past, picking my nose, bogies for his wipers. I WILL DO GOOD THIS DAY I told myself. Chastely.

Skirting dry, earthen road shoulders I sped south. I am sure many riders come to grief travelling the way of broken edges. The alternative is to hug the crown. Where head-ons occur. If you keep to the middle of your side then traversing marsupials bring you down. Even a mouse can do it. Jam the carburettor or rise and block the vision. Kangaroos and wallabies of course, destroy you with their furry walls. Once I hit a steer on the Uppersass-Peeny road. Slowly, in fact I was sliding sideways. Drumstick against taut side of skin over three ribs. I saw them with my left eye. Am not suggesting the beast had only three ribs. Simply all I saw before consciousness regained. Furry walls is a bit like hearts of oak and similar notions.

At the T intersection I stopped for a hitch-hiker with sugarbag swag and a long, thin, newspaper-wrapped parcel. A lay-preacher kind of man, with polished head. Sam. He rode like a bag of spuds. Keep still, I cried after I'd corrected an alarming wobble. They must be alive, he shouted. After a while I cried: What's in the sack? Din dins, he shouted. Sweet Jesus I had a caterer, and it wasn't a big sack. He was planning a loaves and fishes, this missionary of the Hunter.

We came to the river and rode straight onto the punt behind two army trucks. He prodded his sugarbag and something inside wriggled. Blood dripped from it. Rabbits? Yair, and a bandicoot. Why did you want to do that, I asked, glancing at his wrapped rifle and wondering if it was becoming customary for travellers to carry dismantled firearms. Not that my old shotgun really qualified. He whirled the bag a couple of times and smashed it against the railing. He unroped the top. Go on, he can't bite you now, he urged. I didn't need to see the huddle of warm wet fur. I suggested he ask the army for a lift, but he would not, he liked the fresh air too much. How would he cook the bandicoot?   Me eat bandicoot? It's for the fish trap.   We rode off the punt and he resumed his wriggling. They're touchy mean little beasts, still alive, he yelled, Pull up for a minute. Wait till I drop you at Sawyers, I shouted. I heard him fiddling with his newspaper. Stop or I'll fall off, he yelled, pressing close and prodding me with something hard. The rifle, I thought, he can still use it without a stock, and if he thinks he's going to fall he may as well go with a corpse to fall onto as without. Stop, he commanded, Get off and give me a hand.   I propped the bike and scrambled after him down the embankment to the fence, where he emptied the bag, kicked the bandicoot to one side, tore the newspaper from the rifle-breech and slipped in a bullet. Why don't you unwrap it properly and bolt it to the stock? I asked as politely as possible.   Eh, for *this*? He picked up the bandicoot, screamed, and blundered into me. Look at me fingers! The bandicoot clawed slowly through twigs and leaves. I picked up a stone to finish it off. No, he screamed, waving the rifle. I ducked. He grabbed the bandicoot by the back of the neck and threw it at the fence. Wait and watch, he snapped and with string from his pocket tied the bandicoot to a post. This is how guerillas work, you know. A man's got to be ready for the call—are you? Gotta live off the land and execute. Like first shot? You'll ruin the skin, I said. Hit the head, he said. Hadn't you better unwrap the rifle then? I'm a bushman though I live in a town, he snarled, I can shoot from a bike with a hat over me eyes.   I think it's dead, I said, but I'll hit it with a stick. Leave it, he growled.

(Oh Christ, he's screamed and snarled, and now he's growling.) You're mad! Eh? I pushed him as hard as I could against a dead tree, the rifle fired, he fell to the ground. Have shot a man. A nasty nut but no excuse. I rolled him over and found he hadn't been shot. He groaned, sat up and rubbed a graze on the side of his head. The bandicoot sagged against its bonds. I hit it with the rifle stock then threw the parcel into the scrub. Sam, squatting against the tree, mumbled something. I got onto the bike and rode off. Swearing to never again offer a ride.

But I soon weakened, along the river, where the drab, flood-marked houses are. Two girls with rucksacks thumbed rides. Waved as I passed them. Mine was a bike of fools and it was well there was room for only a single passenger at a time. I overtook a huddle of circus vans and briefly and desperately wanted to go back and look at the pair of camels. A couple of miles on I stopped for the driver of a Bentley. MY RESOLUTION! The snob in me overruled it. In any case it's not every day a gentleman asks for a ride. He was a genuine GENTLEMAN. Stupid of me to run out of fuel. Have to be in Crudd Street in fifteen minutes. Do you mind? Wouldn't he rather be put off at a garage? If Crudd Street's out of your way I'll pay. Lovely black overcoat he wore. I do hope he's not armed. Something about him. Officerly kind of man. I glanced at the pillion. Bandicoot blood but before I could do anything he'd leapt aboard. Looks like James Mason. I say would you mind hurrying. If they pull you up I'll fix it.

They? Suddenly I feel exhausted. Strain of the journey. All right, Jas. Mason on pillion & H. Bogart at controls. Look, rider, my business is urgent. OK, bud, I'll get you through. Tension, tension, tension. Ease it with fistful of throtttle. Whaaarrrrrrrrr. Quite a good grip this man. Zoooooom. Nearly sideswiped by big Riley. Into third and overtake him. Big squatter at the wheel driving from Scone to Newcastle to swap a coalmine for more sheep. Furious. Into top and the squatter's far behind. Swamp, mangroves, oil smears

217

and old tyres to the left and ahead, the steelwork's smudge. J. Mason rides well, leans properly for bends. A big Ford drifts out as I go to pass, so drop back, try again, out he goes. Pig-necked driver with V8 style. I say—shouted into my ear—I say, let him lead, we're doing marvellously. Marvellously for you, bud, isn't good enough for me. Change down into third. Feint to overtake, let him edge out, drop back, pass him on the inside, my god this horrible broken shoulder, write to the minister. From hospital. Past him at 85. I say— (Yes, breathless?) I say—that car scraped my leg. Lucky the cops aren't scraping you off the road, bud. Full of confidence now. Demonstration of fantastic braking for a detour. More traffic. Bog suburbs. Easier. Beautiful engine crackle. Crudd Street. OK, bud? White-faced and dried froth from mouth to ears. Twitchy smile. Tenner and his card. F. P. Boot Esq. Beautiful overcoat probably stuffed with them. Hails taxi. I follow. To a taxi rank where he changes cabs. Round the block twice then out and into a black Chev. Fantastic. Better than a film. I look over my shoulder and Christ if I'm not being filmed from Holden behind. Stop it, my name is Percy Wort, I'm a common farmer. I lose them down a side street.

Into a pub for the pause that refreshes. Grim atmosphere between flaking ceiling and match and butt littered floor. Suddenly I am surrounded by three big men. Why was I following Colonel Boot? *Mr* Boot, Fly. Yes, Mr Boot, Charlie. Me following who? Mr Boot. Yes you were following our Mr Boot. Mr Boot, we saw you. O Christ, the boot was after Russian spies and I was after the boot so my name's Rouble. All the fuss about the spy Petrov. I have fallen among secret agents. H. Bogart where are you? Here: Look fellers, Boot was my pillion passenger, had to keep an eye on him, right? I'm KZ 690, don't carry a disc, too risky, but here's my licence. KZ 690 is your bike number plate, how do you account for that? Ooooh, quick on the uptake these men: Of course, bud, it's my machine: must find Boot's card; am so careless; pocket, pocket, pocket. Ah, here. Mr Boot's card, right enough, Charlie. All right, KZ 690. Can't be too careful, KZ. See you around, 690.

I cannot take to the open road without hitting iron curtain or freezing in cold war. Coppers after you, love? A red-haired woman of about thirty. Broken nose and gold teeth. The cops got nothing on me, lady. Betty. Perce. Never leave you alone, Perce. They better leave me alone, Betty. You off a boat, Perce? Off the punt half an hour ago, Betty honey. Want a good time, Perce? I wanna good time filled with quiet, honey. I'll give you that, Perce. Gunna get me a pair of camels. They make me cough, Perce. Camel animals, honey, like a drink? She had a gin, I, a double Scotch. Listen, Perce—now stop me if I'm inquisitive—but why d'you want a pair of camels? You feed 'em capsules of diamonds, Betty, and when the danger's gone you collect. O lie upon lie. You're a liar, Perce, but I like you. Betty, the most remarkable things have happened today. I even saw an army truck stuffed with ruined straw dummies. You been in the army, Perce? I've got a heart condition, Betty. No offence, Perce. I saw Betty as a whore with mouth and heart of gold, riding a bicycle with a dress-net over the back wheel, her hair streaming behind, brilliant in sunshine, her gold mouth glinting, and stuck in this damned town, riding from slag heap to furnace to wharf.

Stick to the wharves, Betty, and don't let the wheels jam in the planks. Here, buy yourself a bike. And I gave her Boot's tenner. What's this, Perce—r'you one of those peculiars?

Back to the Norton, and away, away . . .

The rain began before I crossed the Hawkesbury bridge. Halfway across a squall hit, such a swirl I went onto the wrong side, where the whistling and groaning girders, the rain squirting under the goggles and hammering on jacket and oilskin cap, the shapeless spectres of boat and boatshed lights on water, oil on the road gulping colour as though to swallow, made me thoughtlessly toe the brake pedal and I skidded

219

easily towards flaring car headlights until I snicked another gear and weaved back to the proper lane and the car went past with blasting horn. Over the bridge the road was dry. Stopped at a stall and bought a bottle of oysters. Drained off the water, swallowed the oysters in three gulps, ate four rounds of buttered brown bread. She was a short plump woman with narrow eyes, straight sparse eyebrows, large mouth, full cheeks, small chin and straight jaw; short dark hair cut in a fringe; wearing white bib and brace, roll-reck sweater and a broken homburg.

I like your cap, she said. On the bridge, I said, It almost became a mug of brains. Eh? I almost collected something. You'll make me bring up my oysters dear. Do you eat many? Dozens of dozens, but never at home or by the stakes, only here, by the stall—here, have one on the house. And she deftly removed a cork. It's a German sort of cap you're wearing, she said, Afrika Corps. I bet there were plenty of messy caps then. The oysters I was swallowing tried to rise, swim against the fall, but I managed to get them down. This is more of a ski cap, I said, The Afrika Corps cap was cloth. I heard they're coming here, she said. What? Looking along the road, listening for tread clank. Not in their tanks, she said, they're migrants. Ah, I said, Can you imagine them in their tanks on the Nullarbor Plain? Better there than here, she said. Would you take to your boat? I asked. I would, she said, but first I'd get the couple on this stretch of water who were locked up in the war; there's a certain gentleman with a wharf who says that what the Germans did with their camps we might have to do here if the coalminers on the Hunter get any worse. We need all the coal we can get—if you put the miners in camps who'll dig the coal? He means fence the mines so the miners can't get out. The miners, I said, Would then put plugs of gelly in the coal for furnaces and house grates. The buggers would too, she giggled. I bought another bottle of oysters. She reached under the counter and produced a bottle of stout. Have a look for coppers while I

220

dunk these glasses in the bucket, she said. She opened a few bottles of oysters. On the house. More bread and butter. I squeezed quarters of lemon. She shook pepper. She rubbed the squeezed lemons over her hands and arms. We ate and drank. We spoke of tides, moons, fish, where to go when the bomb dropped and of a man in a plastic raincoat who might turn up, her husband, Ted, sometimes a bit funny with customers. Madge. Pleased to meet you, Perce. Oysters are great for starting friendships. Oysters and stout, Madge. The perfect pair, they stiffen yet relax. Here's another stout. Madge, you're the perfect oyster woman. You think so, Perce?

My god it was on again. If road travel is generally risky, then motor bikes carry 69%. She leant across the counter. Listen, what say I close the stall and come to the city with you? I can give you a good time.

What is it that triggers this kind of thing? Does a certain kind of woman think bike vibrations do something to the system? Or does the clasped-tight, rider-and-passenger image boring along a road set off ancestral urges? Or is it that riders, being leathered oafs, arouse ineradicable desires? By the stall, holding Madge's arms across the counter, I actually had these thoughts. But there was no consummation because all of a sudden this figure sprang onto me. Ted, she cried. He wore his plastic raincoat. A tall thin man with wide-open mouth. Watch out! she screamed, He's taken his teeth out. Yair, he yelled at me, Filling up with my oysters and stout and hoping to fill the wife, stand up and I'll show you. We jostled and wrestled. You want to dance, he grunted, Then I'll jitterbug. He was quite a weak man and his thumps and elbowings didn't hurt. I jabbed him a couple of times just to show I cared. I stood on his foot, he screamed and fell to the ground. You hurt him, she yelled. I ran round the stall to the bike and as I bump-started I looked back and saw them limping off together.

I rode carefully until I came to the suburbs. Showers. At

intersections I couldn't see well enough without removing my goggles. I tried to keep in second gear. As the light poles and neon increased my unease grew. I could not possibly reach the city without a disaster. At red lights cars and bikes screamed engines and slipped clutches as though green indicated the start of Norton-versus-the-rest matches. I didn't care. I let them go. Rain became general. From a high part I saw the city. I saw red smearing over wet ground, orange running along overhead wires, purple-set windows, an acre of road greened like a diseased lawn. But I did not falter (though my clothes were by now spongy with rain) nor did the Norton, though engine hissed with steam, and water sought the carbie. I kept on (the bike i.e. did not skid or topple on treacherous surfaces, and did not stop to shelter under shop awnings). I rode on through the night. I rode toward the Unknown (i.e. the real meaning of Uncle Fred's letter, and Dout & Tomas). I pressed on like a bearer of prescriptions through minions to U. Shancar (who lives with Arch Fountain).

I thought all this as I rode. I kept going because I was too damn frightened by what I was thinking about to stop. I did not dare stop. But the rain stopped. I rode down a hill into a wad of stinking smoke from a dump. The exhilaration I experienced on entering the murk was soon vanquished by dullness then nausea. Headlights became slowly moving bleary eyes of light. I had to stop. A car or van scraped my elbow. I sent out a message of despair on the horn, I shouted Hey, hey! I looked down at the dotted centre line knowing the crown of the road was the worst place to stop yet not being able to move on. And there was no traffic at all. In a moment the tentacles of a recently arrived Tipp would wrap round my ankles. O Madge, O Oyster Lady, if only I had dallied with you and been delayed. Then I heard muffled voices.

Outside, traffic had jammed against the smoke. Someone shouted, Fool. I stopped near a milk bar, and retched thinly and sourly into the gutter. I gulped a bottle of lemonade and gorged two cold pies. A mile further on I slowed for warning beacons. A policeman sprinkled sand from a bucket onto a huge patch of crimson. A burst drum lay in the gutter. Obviously a truck had dropped it. Simply spilt paint, but it was enough to make me realize that unless I stopped for a while someone would be hosing my blood away.

I went into a hamburger joint. One with the lot and a mug of tea. A swarm of bikes settled outside and the riders came in. Yes, it's my Norton out there. Vin's got a Rapide—he'll give you a go over the bridge. No thanks. Go on—he'll even pillion Rosie. No, I feel a bit crook. The motor's crook too I s'pose. No, but I've come three hundred miles. There were eight riders and three buns, Janie, Jill and Rosie. The latter said she'd like a burn with me, if Bill didn't mind. He did. She told him to stop being stupid. He said he'd split her face. He wore a long, scruffy leather overcoat of the sort used for bunning. Or smothering or shrouding. Rosie unzipped her leather jacket. Yair, said Bill, I'll open your face just like that. A mean-looking man, yet another creature full of Norton-envy. Is the bike worth the antagonism it generates? Rather buy a bicycle and a ute. A rider pushed through the mob and whispered to Bill. He twiched, looked at me, went pale. I did not know the reason for his confusion, but took immediate advantage of it to stare expressionlessly at him. They mumbled. I pushed through them and went to the bike. A pannier had been unbuckled and the wrapping on the folding shotgun torn open. The mob had spilled onto the footpath. I felt the barrels. Rosie left them and strutted towards me. Just once round the block, Bill, she called over her shoulder.

I'd got myself a gunmoll. Get going, she hissed, Don't let 'em see you're scared. I'm just being thoughtful, I growled. She got on behind me, so close her knees almost reached mine. Her prominent pubis (part of the pelvis; anterior portion of the os innominatum and overlaid by, in woman, the mons pubis, or mount of venus) pressed against my sacrum (or coccyx). She rested her hands chastely on her thighs. As soon as we were out of their sight she pressed her hands into my groin. I rode so sedately she started pushing me as though I wore reins. Haltered at traffic lights, I muttered that I was distraught.   What?   I ignored her and wondered why I had used the word. It was a new one. It did not fit my condition. I am not a distraught kind of person. I need a drink, I said, Where can I get one? Her mouth so close to my ear her warm words unthawed me. You want a club or a sly-grogger? Sly.   Go left a mile, right up the lane to the third gate. She wanted me to get a few bottles for a park tryst? I, who had sworn to remain faithful to intentions! I was being tested. I had to prove I could resist temptation. So I let Rosie direct me to the sly-grogger. Great—fantastic—holy shit—bore it up! She was quite breathless. He charges five bob a bottle—get half a dozen. (6 @ 5/-!) Still, I pushed the money into his grasping paw. Tight-skinned, as though rubber-gloved. All I could see of him, the rubber hand on the end of a khaki-shirted arm from an unlit doorway. Beyond, something wheezed and ticked like a broken clock. Rosie stuffed a couple down her jacket and the others into the panniers. Geez, a gun. The door slammed. You do much shooting?   Rosie, where I come from people have suffered greatly. We always travel armed. Gittout! something screamed from the slygroggery. Fix him, Rosie snarled.   Er, Rosie, er—you going to be my woman— gunmoll—you know, er?   Yair, yair—but gitim—then Billie!   No ammo, Rosie.   No shells! what sortova guneru? I use it as a, ah, club.   Jee-zus. Get away from this woman. Stand back, Rosie, let me start it.   I tried one of those leaps into the saddle and away, but crashed over with the bike on top of me. Got it upright. Smell of beer. Running from left pannier. Hey, whatsyername—what *is* your name?   Perce. Percy! Perce the worse. Perce, you going to get the glass out? Horrible noises from the slygroggery. Rosie put her mouth to the door and screamed Mug! We rode up the lane, her bottles hard in my back. She directed me. This way and that. Faster. Bore it up. If we fell off she'd have a masectomy. The bottles,

I shouted at her. Cold on the tits, she shouted, Makes 'em stand up. Cut 'em off if we fall, I shouted. Have 'em sewn on me arse, she shouted. Wonderful words for a quiet suburban street. Oh, why? I said. Be great when you do it dog-style, she shouted. I asked myself: Am I narrow-minded? I could slow down to a walk, suddenly accelerate and let her fall off and see how she liked the transplant. (Such a thought is additional evidence of narrow-mindedness.) To the park, she shouted. This way and that. But—to HER park—the gang's park—overlook the harbour—waves, lights, city across the water, ferries —and the gang in the shrubbery—the awful long leather overcoat—vivacious Rosie back to her bunning—and I, Percy Wort, fallen among desperados—BUT if I fall am I not perhaps presenting another desperado with the opportunity of saving me from death? Considering the nature of my thoughts it is a wonder I was able to ride without crashing. There, she shouted, pressing into my groin(s) (fold(s) between belly and thighs). Trust her. She's a tough girl but good underneath. I know of a better place, I said. Suits me, she replied. My fear displaced, I stopped the bike.

Down to the sea wall. Clink clink. Geez, they've gone hard—feel. I felt. Get the tops off, eh? You're a funny man! O harbour lights, splash, buoys, eternal sea! Bill and how many others running out of her? And me sworn to chastity! Still, I opened the bottles on the back of a bench and we drank one then the others, not quite breast-warm but better than cold. Empties into the water. The breeze cool. Not too much off, eh, Perce? I glanced back at the bike. I saw the gang coasting silently, unlit, down the hill. Here was I, the man who had been selected as bait to find the gangster samaritan. Me! Through bleeding eyes I would look up at my saviour as he gently remonstrated with Bill. Would gaze at Rosie and her girl friends as they writhed on the grass. Then would catch a glimpse of my would-be saviour as together we were hurled over the seawall. So I twisted her arm and ran her into the shrubbery. Her terror. Me a sex killer! I pointed to the gang. Push-bikes, she squeaked. A bicycle club on an illicit, unilluminated outing! Her guile! I warned her to keep quiet then sprinted to the bike. About a dozen cyclists pedalled past. Rosie, I shouted. Piss off, she replied. I ran back. She burst screaming from the shrubbery, with a stake. Get yourself a pushbike—you're no Norton!   I am a Wort, I replied though not clearly enough. I dodged round a palm. What?   Wort, I cried.   Wart! she screamed, getting between me and the bike. I darted off. She sprinted after me holding the stake like a javelin. Eeeh! she slipped and fell heavily. I grabbed her. She tried to bite and scratch. The cyclists returned. Next, the local band would march down. Then the Buffaloes and Masons. Newsreel cameramen. Editor of the *Peeny Gazette*, Tom, Mum and Dad. Tell 'em to go, she hissed and edged me to a bench. Tell 'em nothing, I said, And they'll go. Put your hand in my snatch and they'll think we're friends.   You all right, lady?   Get lost, she begged them.   She's answering under duress, cried the lawyer amongst them. They wheeled their machines to the footpath. There was clatter as they rested them on the ground. Jeezus, I know him, she whispered, He lives next door. Go away, I yelled. Don't let him see me, she begged. A few lamps were taken from bicycles and flashed at us. Give 'em a shock, Perce. She lay on her back on the grass and opened her legs and I got on top of her.   Phew, Hey! Look at that! Come away lads. Come a-way. Tony! Michael! A job for the police. Michael! Troop away!   Now for the band. Then the Buffs. Scout Commissioners and so on.

You can get off now, she said, I don't need you. Ignominy and shame were my lot that night. As we rode away I remembered the two bottles we'd left by the seawall. She said to leave them for the gardener and I dropped her on the corner of her street.

I booked into the Farmers' Plaza near Central. Brown lino, marble tops, china urns and brass bowls. Overlooking sooty roofs. I phoned Uncle Fred. Great to hear from you, Perce.

Meet you beside the Archibald fountain, eleven tomorrow morning.

Ominous. A fountain within a Hail Mary of the cathedral and a Guilty of the courts. City life is staying at the Farmers', avoiding trams, glancing in bargain windows, noting pawn shops, avoiding or succumbing to beggars, passing darkened pubs, walking through the park past down-and-outs on benches, climbing the steps to the railway and entering the grubby cavern of night travellers, indicator boards, railway pies, drunks, coal smoke and migrants worried by the familiar strangeness of it all.

Because of the horrors of the day before I slept until seven. So many dreams that when I awoke I thought the room was a stilled vision. I got out of bed. My shape two feet deep in the mattress. I'd been cast. A terrible scene. I looked round the room. Awful. I opened the window. The courtyard below must have been a cut-off chimney. Fried breakfast and burnt fat. I retched, spewed and almost went out with it. Set the pigeons wheeling. Got to the enamel basin. I covered it with a towel and smuggled it into the bathroom. Back in the room I filled the basin from the jug and worked up a pungent lather with the guest soappe. Closed the window. People in the courtyard but they missed me. Back to the bathroom where I showered until pink. Dreadful noises and stinks from toilets. Gossip at the shaving mirrors.   City's full of drunken women. Never like to see an inebriated woman.   City went to the pack in the war.   No, it'll get worse.   All the foreigners, too. But you can always rely on the Farmers'.   Yes, the Farmers' is a bit of all right.   What d'you think of the Farmers', son? The farmer's son had stayed in better.   Ooooo, come down in the world, eh?   Rock bottom and from now on I'm going up. No need to spell it out, son—and I think you'll find the roof slippery and sooty.   Back to the sleeping chamber.

A maid looked in. Were you sick a while ago? Her nostrils twitching for airs of vomit but all she could smell was soappe. Tried the roof? I asked. Sick, not pigeons, she snapped. Farewell, spew huntress, I go to closely examine my breakfast for same. My finest quality, craftsman-tailored, unbeatably priced suit had sad creases in it, my white shirt was rumpled and shoes and socks smelt of beer. Oh, miss, would you mind running the iron over my clothes. I drove all night. Have to see my bank manager—owner—first thing. You really want me to get out of them? But I like a warm iron. Not naked? Don't wave that iron at me.

The dining-room manageress stood at the door examining the face of every person for the paleness which would identify the upper-floor vomiter. Ruby from shaving with a grim blade I entered fearlessly. Nothing like a layer of grease on the gut.

As the early morning gasper had not been identified the cooks were punishing everyone with burnt, fatty offerings. The food was so greasy it should have slid down easily, but it could not because it was fried hard. I thought I was going to die on a piece of bacon. A man three tables away started retching, pushed his chair back and fled outside. The manageress leered triumphantly at the clot of cooks in their doorway. Suddenly, at every table, people began pushing back chairs and retching, and many were the table settings rendered disgusting. A woman lost her sense of direction and charged into the kitchen. I ran into the lobby, knelt before a brass fern pot and gave up my breakfast. Soon the place rang with cries of Food-poisoning, Get the health inspector, Ring the papers and you'll get a fiver, Foreign cooks, Seeing my solicitor, Get the cook, Knew the place had changed, and so on. Please, please would we return to the dining-room for scrambled eggs and copious quantities of coffee, dry toast and newspapers with the compliments, tickets in a new lottery and flowers for the ladies, please, won't you? No.

Slightly rumpled, and empty-bellied, I wandered in the pleasant morning sunshine. I bought papers and trammed to the business heart of the city. I bought a rose for my buttonhole and ate a leisurely breakfast in a grim, dear place.

At eleven I met Fred by the fountain. He announced that

228

he had cancelled my indebtedness. The week had been good to him and he saw no reason why he should worry about a small debt. And there was the matter of a new Will. I would, at the appropriate time, see what I would see, no less. Very confusing to me. Of course there would be conditions I would at once see to be just and reasonable. He then asked me to nip across to the registrar-general or someone and buy a duty stamp. This I did, springing lightly across the turf as befitted one with a light heart and fancy thoughts.

When I returned a quarter of an hour or so later I found hue and cry and general commotion. Fred and two others had been arrested by a policeman who, when I remonstrated with him, threatened to add me to his catch. I suggested that his hands were already full. He said he would call for assistance from the bystanders. I said I thought he was overdoing his authority and asked his reasons. Disorderly behaviour and others too dreadful to mention in the open air. Fred told me to shut up and follow them to the police station.

Some days later Fred said he would tell me what had happened.

We were in his factory, sitting on orange cases between the big lathe and the miller. We began by talking about dreams. Sometimes, he said, I have nightmares in which the lathe and the miller fight it out over the question of output. The machines' place of origin, South Bend, Indiana, puts the last horrible sweat on me. South Bend, Indiana! There's an awful finality about the place. It exists solely to manufacture machine tools, and is close to Lake Michigan, one of the world's great open sewers. Indians long gone, their human supplanters gone, and their place taken by machines of all sorts. Sitting as we are now, on these orange boxes, how would it be if miller and lathe moved together? Two south bends come to what sort of geological, geometrical or directional conclusion? Would we be milled, turned or made into energy —a tremendous flash?

229

I found his line disturbing and had to stand up. Nothing could have induced me to remain seated. His tremendous flash would come if something connected us, positive to negative. His factory is on uncertain ground, which is resentful of the machines he has set upon it, for they squirt cutting oils, earth themselves, vibrate, whine and tear, and the roof keeps weather away.

Fred told me not to be afraid of the machines, that once the power was off they were nothing but ornaments, and that at a pinch a man could take to them with a bar. I told him that we had quite a collection of machines on the farm. He hoped they were well tended because the last time he had seen them there were indications of neglect with even the splashes of red lead he himself had applied two years before well into the final stages of decomposition. Agricultural machines were peculiar things because they were in contact with elemental forces and these forces were probably nurtured by fertilizer, manure, animal and human contact. He, now, kept his machines under strict control and was assisted in this by factory inspectors, trade associations and unions. The factory was well maintained. Even the scrap drums were painted twice a year.

As already mentioned, he said, You're in my Will. What would you do if you came into money? Try to keep this place going, I replied to my surprise. Also, I'd help keep the farm going, and I'd make something at Uppersass. I did not want to elaborate, but he kept at me. I have an idea, I admitted, To do something with the bottles and scrap of Uppersass. I refused to say much more and he, to his credit, did not persist, beyond hoping that I would have a fountain. I had not thought of a fountain but agreed that one would go well there. Even an imaginary fountain. Or a big screen reflecting a film of a fountain. A milk fountain. A grass juice fountain. Endless possibilities.

I suggested he tell me what had happened at the Archibald fountain.

He had stood beside that fountain awaiting my return with the duty stamp. The Will needed a stamp and signatures. Witnesses. Any passersby. Surrounded by humanity. Hovered over by birds. Apollo, Theseus skewering poor old Minotaur, Diana of the tits and shaved mound. Spray . . .

Witnesses. Random selection. All these people to choose from and I had to choose him. Excuse me, sir, but I wonder if you'd . . . I wish to bequeath my estate. Fountain playing, water music, the messiah man, people eating early lunches or late morning teas, gardeners, the bells of St Mary's, whistler into Crosby song, oh dreadful piece, I hear they are calling/wailing . . .

I am going to meet my young nephew here shortly. A good place. Water and metal. Beautiful bronze, only wish it were cheaper and I'd use nothing but bronze, yes, tin and copper, I am in metals, yes. I am holding the document like this, sir, to shield it from spray. I do not distrust you, you look an honest man, I would not have stopped you otherwise. Against the chest is away from the spray. Like an extra garment though I am not cold. Port Jackson figs over there, fine trees, shade trees but surface rooters, free fruiters, so rather messy. Yes, sir? So you are a Baptist. Very fine people, Baptists. Yes, Baptists believe in total immersion. Yes, a fine, basic sort of ritual. Not a ritual? Ceremony you call it, no place for pomp and popery in the baptistry? You don't believe in it, eh? Yes, a simple down to earth creed. Oh. Me? Me, immersed? To get you to witness this document? No. No no no. Take your hands off me! How dare you. You want a brawl, sacred or profane, I'm your man. My God, ju-jitsu. Oriental influence in nonconformist Christianity. But Tokyo bear-thump no match for quick jab to chin and right cross to pectoral. Made of iron this man or sheathed in hymnals.

I am a believer in charity, d'you hear? Let me go and I won't press charges. Ow. Jab to the Corinthians and bust the glass lightly. Jesus and his aseptic immortality, fancy wanting

231

to sit on the right hand of the Dad for ever and ever amen, what's the use, what's the point? The D's made of nothing so you wouldn't even feel a knuckle of the right hand, however, as we're grunting about the great cosmic nothingness it could be you'd sit NEAR the right hand, that is, within belting distance, cunning adroitness, that of the Dad. Belted over the ear for eternity with perpetual choral backing. Forever and ever. 33^n revolutions forever. Do they—Baptists and the rest—ever think of it this way? They should be saved. Saved from themselves. But I'm not the man, I'm not the bloody man to do it. My skin shall remain intact, my bones unbroken, my mind clear.

And there I was wrestling with a Baptist beside the Archibald fountain near noon. If I don't drown I'll bust my head on the flags. Dying with Will invalid.

Perce, this assailant of mine was probably a graduate of one of those north coast grass-eating sanctuaries run by the Seventh Day Adventists. A man fallen among total immersionists. A complicated Seventh Day Baptist simpleton the sanctuary could not tolerate: so they sent him to the city, a pestiential judgement. I knew of his Seventh content early in the struggle because he dropped a packet of that unbelievable blend of grasses, nuts, fruits and grains, Helthbru. Crummy. I stamped on it, hard, with heel, and the crummy brownness shot over the flags. Like stunned ants. Lunchers, already disturbed by the baptismal fracas, stamped frantically. Reminded me of a troupe of Morris dancers. A policeman came running across the lawn, in fine style, hurdling in fact two amorous couples and a family picnic. A passing gentleman in sombre shirt, black suit with black armband, bronze chrysanthemum in buttonhole, a black haired, small-moustachio'd man, crowned with dark fedora-type hat burst into a totally abandoned dance of the tarantella sort. He was immediately seized by the policeman, a young, and usually, I'd say, mild-faced person but now pale with zeal. Then he grabbed me. The Baptist fled, I'm sorry to say, and in so fleeing ran along the rounded fountain surround, sped on his way by two or three blasphemous onlookers, one of whom was quickly nabbed by the law. The Baptist sped towards the St James underground.

The constable was very pleased with himself. He had captured three wrongdoers in one swoop. He had nipped in the bud a riotous display—if not an insurrection and averted the sacking of the city. He had in his grip a blasphemer, a dancer in a public place and a breaker of the peace if not worse.

I tell you, the Baptist had been been launched on a series of adventures he'd have turned R.C. to avoid. I met him later and he poured out his woes to me. Over the years his faith had undergone much persecution; however it had endured and flourished. The way our man rose to the occasion is worth telling.

. . . The Baptist, sparing not a glance at the normally tantalizing windows of David Jones across the street (the goods and models there always offended him), dashed down the steps to the station, cantered past the ticket windows and galloped past the ticket checkers. I ask you, is there a more appalling picture than that of a Seventh Day Baptist

1. assaulting me
2. avoiding arrest
3. threatening with his racing person innocent bystanders —and remember, his iron—or hymnal-bound body—made of him a projectile
4. seeking to travel without a ticket?
Questions:
   a. did he, while fleeing, take his Lord's name in vain?
   b. was he in fact fleeing me—seen by him as a manifestation of the Devil?
   c. was he distraught at the breaking of his packet of

Helthbru? (and had he seen the scattered product as ants—as I myself had done—did he regard me as a wizard, one capable of changing the exotic banal into the ubiquitous?)

d. did his temporary—we hope—condition as a projectile make of me a projector or firearm?

e. and if I could be regarded as a firearm, had I been discharged in a public place?

He reached the platform as the incoming train arrived. For an instant he contemplated leaping in front of it. But desisted. Train stopped, ssssss, clunk, clatter. He entered the carriage fifty feet along from where he had stepped onto the platform. And he was just in time because a bracered official appeared in more than hot pursuit. Too late, alas. For the NSWGR. But only just too late, for the official was tensed, one leg bent for the leap into the carriage.

(Ah, what an athletic day that one: the wrestling Baptist and feeble me, the hurdling policeman, the sprinting Baptist, the dashing railwayman. And the day anything but done.)

The Baptist secured his escape from the railwayman by the raising of his hands, palms together, over his bruised pectoral. The gesture finished the railwayman who, agnostic to the core, was unable to suppress his curses and blasphemies, and was winded. Unable to leap into the carriage. Suffered awful humiliation. Had lost a bylaw infringer if not breaker. But not through fear. No.

At the beginning of the tunnel a poster for Peck's paste. Fish, millions every day into paste for bread. Loaves & fishes. Into the tunnel proper; the roaring and swaying, the carriage lights on grimy walls, Jonah in the whale, any moment now misty spray then wall of water, punishment fully deserved for the disturbance created. He had done wrong. Grievous wrong. The sort of things others did to Baptists. Baptist creed, the glorification of God and the righting of wrong. The train slowing. Get off, go back, redress. Policeman, court, papers. *Truth*. Denouncer of errors, blazoner of horrors, *Truth*: Norton founded. Ezra Norton, Ezra, fine Old Testament name meaning . . . ? Help. Help Norton. The last thing I'd do. Who touches pitch is defiled.

Baptist Elder in Brawl, next to: Her 3 Lovers At Maroubra, above. Bookie Welshes on Live Hares.

The Baptist left his train at the next station, spoke to the ticket collector, paid his fare, surfaced and walked back to the Archibald, then went on to Queens Square, almost entered St James for a quick prayer, but passed for he knew it was too High. Rumble under feet a reminder of trains. He found the police station. He hesitated, then entered.

Bare boards. Uniforms. Defendants, plaintiffs, lawyers, officials. Summary justice dealt. Dispensed. One prescription listed three ingredients, and needed a fourth.

Fred, Marsalino the dancer in mourning, and Scrivener the blasphemer waited in a huddle in the queue behind jaywalkers, loiterers, offensive traffikers. Fred caught a constable's attention, and to the cold scrutiny said: *Je suis Fred et mon cousin est l'homme de TRUTH.*

The constable said: Speak English, I've heard you. Fred said: My friend here, Mister Marsalino, needs an interpreter. The constable said: This is Aussie, mate. And your fellow defendant will speak it well enough for His Honour. The constable then gave his attention to an interesting facet of the Law which was being polished by the magistrate, one R. I. P. Looms, sternest of the stern, the judge of all stipendiaries, who would shortly pronounce flogging for an unrepentant jaywalker. Said Fred: I'll have the front page of *Truth—Truth*—reserved for your case. The constable swayed. Despite his interest in the words of R. I. P. Looms, s.m., he had heard Fred's awful statement. Said Fred: My cousin handles that sort of thing. The constable stared at him weakly. Said Fred: the power of *Truth* matches that of Looms, s.m.

The constable left the room. Three minutes later he returned and nodded for them to follow him out. In another room another policeman reluctantly struck their names from the list. As they turned to leave, the Baptist hurried along the corridor. Always in a hurry, that man, said Fred, and looked round the door.

The Baptist entered the court-room at a jog, crying: I provoked them, the Lord forgive me.

R. I. P. Looms, s.m., was declaring: . . . and there has been an unprecedented increase in jay-walking; why not two hours ago my vehicle was struck by an umbrella . . . Who is this, what's the meaning of this hooliganism! Clear the court—arrest that man!

Fred and his friends were carried from the building by the press of evicted people.

They waited in the street risking charges of loitering with intent until Fred said: Another honest man gone. They walked to Usher's, had drinks in a bar filled with brown faced men in big hats, and tolerated their acres of resentment.

Fred suggested to Mr Marsalino that perhaps he could fulfil his role of mourning market gardener better on the north coast, and named Peeny as a suitable area, and to Mr Scrivener he mentioned a favourable position in a small electroplating factory not far from his own establishment. Each gentleman then purchased a round of drinks and set them up in threes. Representing: health, prosperity, longevity, virility, peace, honesty, truth, freedom from arrest, good weather. Fred proposed a toast to the continuing prosperity of the wool trade, the increasing demand for lamb, mutton and sheepskins, the development of pasture improvement and diminution of pests of all sorts. A few members of the grazing fraternity greeted his statements coolly. Fred, realizing that there should be drinks all round, ordered them and generously tipped the barmaid. The graziers responded with a round and returned to *their* triclaves.

As they left Usher's, Fred purchased the two afternoon papers. The Baptist, John Tremor, was mentioned briefly in the stop press of the *Mirror*. Bail had been granted. Fred remembered his Will, and his two friends were only too pleased to oblige with their signatures, the document being pressed against a shop window much to the annoyance of the florist within.

Fred consulted a directory, and an hour later the Baptist, John Tremor, received a telegram from a Fred Enth, who gave his address c/- the GPO: HOPE THERE IS NO ILL WILL BETWEEN US STOP MUST SAY I ADMIRE YOUR PLUCK IN CONFRONTING LOOMS SM THE SORT OF MAN WHO 300 YEARS AGO WOULD HAVE CONSIGNED YOU TO THE STAKE STOP. Tremor replied immediately and the next morning they met on the GPO steps at the corner of Martin Place and Pitt Street, a bright sunny day, 11.30 a.m., the Cenotaph with its laurel wreaths, the flower stalls and newspaper kiosks, people on business, strolling pie and sandwich eaters, men on the steps talking or staring into the sun. Fred waited across the Place outside the tourist bureau. Local colour's all very well, he thought, all this monumental, cityful, lunchful city-hobnobbing is all very well and I could easily lose myself in it. But what do I do? I come in disguise, in impermeable sweating disguise, like a lost codliver oil man; as though, still fearing total immersion, I do not dare wear shrinkable clothes when meeting this man. Fred saw Tremor and went across to meet him. They indulged in polite discourse about the weather, people, flower stalls and other local colour, and had a mild disagreement when Tremor suggested a choir of clean youths would add something. On the one hand Fred agreed that something would be added, but on the other declared that something would be subtracted, e.g. the pigeons would flee, and what little silence also, and perhaps money because of the collection and the activities of pickpockets and their ilk. Fred pulled back part of his impermeable coat and showed Tremor his hip-pocket-less trousers. Tremor then showed Fred his extra tract-carrying pockets. By this time a group of interested people had gathered. Fred was all for moving on but Tremor began to address them and in one sentence brought in drink, local colour, a discreet allusion to Jesuits, hot water as drink and cleanser, gambling and the Lord. Fred casually moved away from his companion and when the policeman suddenly appeared was able to observe everything with a certain detachment. Tremor refused to move on, and even played with the order. Move on—to what? Another piece of footpath? I have my rights. I have my convictions. Fred watched the martyr stride manfully away with the policeman. Tremor's plaint soon died in the distance.

At six in the evening, I went to see the aquatic coopers at Rushcutters Bay. A man on a jetty pointed out the two houseboats, and hired me a skiff. The first houseboat was simply a gross launch while the other was an enormous pontoon equipped with a marquee, several side tents, a couple of corrugated iron lean-to's, and a chicken coop. I tied the skiff to the stern of the launch and boarded. Someone said, Hello, fartface. He's a collector, shouted another. Hands seized me and I was hurled into the water. A row of leering, grinning and despicable faces watched me. If I drown, I shouted, The coroner will commit you all. One of them, a tall thin man, pissed towards me. Instantly diagnostic, I told him he was prematurely old, with an enlarged prostate which had projected into his bladder. His flow diminished and ended on his feet. A plain, middle-aged woman turned her back to me, lifted her skirt and farted. Piles like grapes, I yelled, And full of seeds—at least a morbid indication. A man, stout and young, thrust his face at me and shouted, Down, bourgeois, down to the bottom where bourgeois rubbish lies rotting and rusting! By now I was cold, rather weak and close to the boat. Your eyes are yellowish, I told him, They indicate a disease of the liver so you are jaundiced and infecting your boat-mates, and your teeth are rotten.

Are you a doctor? asked another, a beautiful girl, with long fair hair, Or are you a dentist? Have you got cramp? And she dived in and bobbed up beside me. Swim over to *Xanadu*, she whispered. Sonia. Can you manage? she enquired. Facing me,

238

her hands under my arms. Nice face. Wholesome kind of girl, with a band on her teeth. As we swam slowly towards *Xanadu* she said how pleased she was to meet me, regretted the circumstances, but was certain I would adore *Xanadu* to which she herself hoped to transfer as soon as she had severed her relationship with Steve, the yellowish man who combined the disabilities of working like a slave half the day with drinking the rest.

I ALL BUT SWOONED BEING SO CLOSE TO HER. I trod water and told her it was quite nice in. She grimaced, Superb! I sank. I rose.

THERE I WAS TREADING WATER WITH A GLORIOUS WOMAN.

For all I knew sharks circled. The thought made me shudder.   Are you all right?   I tried to say Yes, but my teeth chattered. Can you manage? asked this wonderful nymph. I smiled. I WILL INTERPOSE MY BODY BETWEEN HER AND ANY SHARK. The water is now too cold for sharks. Try and float on your back, she murmured. I did this and she placed her hands over my ears and pulled me towards *Xanadu*. I was able to watch the people on the launch. I waved to them.

We reached the side of *Xanadu* and bobbed together. I pulled a piece of seaweed from the band on her teeth. The woman on the launch screamed: You going to have him before or after tea, Sonia?

A man and a woman let down a rope ladder, and we clambered aboard. Xerxes and Amanda. Tall, slender, middle-aged people in floppy khakis. They were pleased to meet me. I was interesting. *Xanadu* needed a farmer to complete its heterogeneity. It had been decided to tap the sea's resources for chlorophyll and xanthophyll and I, being a man used to green plants, would understand. A third person, a man in khaki overalls, commented that I looked green enough for the job. Shame on you, said Amanda, I think you'd do better on the launch. I'm no greeno, bud, I growled. See how aggressive he is? said the man. I'm cold, I said, I've been assaulted and I've caught a chill—take me to your stove, please. Wait, implored Xerxes with a blessing hand, Entry by uninitiates to the Tent of Xanadu is forbidden.

I could see inside. Very snug with carpets, mattresses and low stools. To emphasize my coldness and impatience I broke into a discreet jog. Sonia went into a side tent and quickly reappeared, quilted, and carrying a pair of blankets. She told me to wrap myself up. I made to enter the tent, but Xerxes held up his hands and told me I was not to go in. Muttering, I wrapped myself in the blankets. No, cried Sonia, Get out of your wets. Here? Of course, are you shy? *Xanadu* knows many bodies, said Amanda. What about people on other boats and ashore, I protested. Are you ashamed of your form? said Xerxes. So I got undressed but before I could cover myself everyone, with the exception of Sonia who stood back smiling enigmatically, examined me closely. I was blue and goose-pimply and cock and balls had shrunk to infantile proportions. He appears to be quite clean, said the man. A pity he's not better hung, said Amanda. I am, I shouted, wrapping myself in blanket, I'm perfectly normal when I'm warm. Normality, said the man, Is what we are refugees from. Well, I said, I've been a refugee too long and what I want is a bit of moored cooperation. I told you he was aggressive, said the man. Fish bait, I snapped. See? he said. Shut your mouth, I snarled. Xerxes and Amanda shook their heads. Sonia dropped her quilt and dived from *Xanadu*. She was so beautiful I nearly fell in after her. My skiff had been untied from the launch and drifted close to the breakwater. She climbed into it and rowed towards us. Those people in the park will report her, I told Amanda. Not them, said Xerxes, but the ones with binoculars in the flats will. Sonia's rowing action was superb. You can't stay, said Amanda. You're not our kind, said Xerxes. Um-um, said the man. Sonia came alongside, her long narrow breasts touching her thighs as she lent forward. Her hair swung fairly, her ankle tendons stood out as she pressed against the seat at the stern. My heart pounded. See how he stares? cried the man, As though he's never seen nudity before. We cannot admit him, said Xerxes and Amanda to Sonia. She threw me the rope, leapt aboard, glanced at the coopers and went into the tent. See how horny he is, cried the man as he snatched away the blankets. Although I had lengthened a little and my bag loosened somewhat I was anything but rigid. I did not attempt to retrieve the blankets, but assumed an aggressive pose. Cold.   See how belligerent he is! the man chortled. Amanda stepped to my side murmuring, Are you a tense person—or are you impotent? Sonia, dry but still naked rushed between us crying, Go stuff yourselves! and gestured for me to return to the skiff. She grabbed our wet clothes and joined me. She sat in the bow and I could not see her gaze upon my back.

We returned the skiff to its owner and went to the bike. I could not properly fasten the clothes she had given me but the kitbag I carried hid any bareness. I took her to a friend's place at Edgecliff where we dried my clothes, made love and entered a single bed where we talked, made love, dozed and loved for hours.

Back at Uppersass Mum and Dad liked her and asked her to stay a few days. She had some knowledge of the district and knew the recently proclaimed city of Woopo quite well. Do you now? said Dad. As a matter of fact the name Collifon is similar to Collie, a family well-known there—are you related? Yes, but I never see them.   There's Collie the Legislative Councillor, said Dad. He's not such a bad man, said Mum. He's a Labor-Country Party-Conservative, said Dad, Who goes with the wind which at Woopo is a dirty, sluggish whirlwind. Oh, I know that, said Sonia. Collie, remarked Dad, Doesn't strike me as being a man, he's more of a grimy eminence behind party workers, who screen him. From us mugs. A person who emerges now and then with a firm handgrip, bright eyes and eager ruggedness! You make him sound awful, said Mum. He's done a lot of good. He's done that, said Sonia, but he fits Mr Wort's description.

Mum gave her Tom's room but she came to mine. She knew the milking routine and we were through long before the truck came. Mum apologized for our chip heater in the bathroom but Sonia thought it a marvellous invention. After she had showered she darted naked to her room. Mum saw her and afterwards spoke to me. She didn't mind of course—but was there anything going on between us? Yes, I said. Oh, she said.

During lunch Dad mentioned Collie the Legislative Councillor several times.

[Have just seen bro. Horseback. Quarter of a mile away. In a high paddock. What determination. And such a poor rider. His keenness indicates a shattered pride. He needs to find me. Or perhaps he needs to hunt me. The former would mean the beginning of a new phase. The latter a continuation of what has happened—and what a drag . . . However he was riding away. Time I moved on. No regrets to be leaving this first hideout. Pity I have so much to carry. I could bury some. I'll move on in two minutes.]

Collie. Sonia is his daughter!
  Dad: Eh? what? you?
  Daughter Sonia had been ordered from Collie household. Some scandal or other. Name never mentioned at home. Symbol of bad Collie. Went to city. London. Paris. Rome. My god a woman of the world. Who must return to the city on next morning's train. End of lunch. Afterwards we walked, talked, ran like couple in idyll. Visited the unlucky Grools, their house a repository of doctors', chemists', priests' and undertakers' bills, old crêpe bandages, crutches and other home-

242

nursing apparatus. Heard a loud breaking noise. Pop Grool: Is it the shed or, at last, long last, the sky?

Back to the Wort acres for the evening milking, tea, wireless, and euchre. To separate rooms. I go to her, the bed knocks (possum in the ceiling). The alarm clatters before dawn and we ride down to Peeny for the train. At the station, the bitter Assistant Station Master (ASM). Goodmorning, asm. Mr Spasm, the asm.

In his fernery I was specific.

Marry? Yes. Hello, lovely. Morning, lovely. Think about it. Have thought about it. The train.

As I went to leave the station Spasm the asm thrust out his arm and barred me. Ticket. Without a please. And not a question. A plain barren Ticket. I didn't leave the train —you saw me see a friend off. Ticket. No ticket. Regulations state that a platform ticket must be obtained by anyone not travelling before said person goes onto platform. Rule 99 Section B, I suppose? I'll allow you to purchase a ticket this time—but if it ever happens again you'll be prosecuted for trespass. So I bought a ticket and dropped it at his feet. Littering is a punishable offence, he said. You are destroying the railway system, I said as I strode to the Norton. Which would not start. Who was the sheila? asked Spasm. A friend, I replied coolly though with mounting heat from my kick-starter activities. I bet she's easier to start than the bike, drawled the asm. The Pervy Monster! However I did not allow him to excite me but replied, over my shoulder, She's harder than any of your daughters. A howl of rage and he dashed across the station yard like an overwound doll.

And what a morning for such goings-on! A touch of mist here and there, an occasional thump and clatter from the town, the sun soon to rise through low eastern cloud, a yellowing jacaranda leaf falling between me and the rampant asm. Who was not moving nearly so quickly as first thought. I dismounted from my recalcitrant machine, dropped into a relaxed ju-jitsu stance, cried Kazza! and then, Kazooom! which stopped the asm in full scurry. She's well-known—your Miss Collie, he hissed.

This asm was going the full gamut of animal noises. He had: growled, snapped, barked, roared, cried, howled and hissed.

Miss Collie belongs to herself, she is a free agent, I said, modifying my stance. He muttered and I asked him to speak louder. He made a similar noise. Ho—ho—hi! I cried and dealt the pillion seat a tremendous blow with the edge of my hand. Her father'll fix you, he whinnied.

The asm had been possessed by animal spirits.

I stared at him. You've dribbled on your coat, he sniggered. I had, too. From my kazza-ho-hi etcetera. His appearance! Eyes of a sly possum, teeth of a wild dog, the bearing of a brain-damaged roo. Her father'll have your nackers, he snapped.

Mr Assistant Station Master, I replied, Watch out or I'll report you to the RSPCA and you'll never become Rail Superintendent.

He howled (as was by now his wont). I un-standed the Norton, made a fine running start and left the yard side-saddle at forty.

Up into the hills to Uppersass the Eternal. Where I worked hard fencing until morning tea. When the phone called for me. Sonia, from Broadmeadows. I'm sorry, Percy, but I left the train. You'll have to forget our idyll. I met a man I hadn't seen for six years. I love him. He wants to give me the things I knew before I left home. He wears a hat and you never do. I don't want to go through life wearing a flying helmet, Percy. And I'd rather lose my right arm through giving hand-signals than halve my head on a tram. You do understand, don't you, Percy? Now I've got to tell Daddy our engagement is finished. I sent him a telegram but didn't mention your name. Bye, Percy.

Oh. I went to the woodheap and split a load of logs. Mum

and Dad watching anxiously from the back door. I had never before tried the chopping cure. I did not split with rage. I axed with a dullness which gradually changed to a sharp feeling of relief. Had I gone on perhaps I'd have sweated with anger. At ten-thirty we bundled into the ute and all went down to Peeny. And no funny stuff, said Dad. Don't nag the boy, Will, she said. Funny stuff? I said, Do you think I'm going into the Royal to make jokes about the Queen? Dad said, if you've a notion to act up I'll turn round and go back. Mum said, Do that and you'll fast for a week. Dad said, We don't need to buy their groceries, we're self-contained, everything we need is grown or can be got within a mile of the house. Mum said, I've books to exchange and you can't do that at Uppersass. Dad said, What d'you need, Perce?

Ten pounds of gelly, detonators and fuse for the stumps down the bottom I said. I wish you wouldn't, Mum said. Sometimes you've got to, said Dad. All the explosions nowadays are due to the wars, said Mum. One day we might need it for those Peeny people, said Dad. There you go, said Mum, Filling your son with ideas of violence. If those stumps and stones aren't broken, we'll be broken, I said.

Down to Peeny we went in our ute. Over the broken road and squirting culverts. Past the patch of flooded gum the Kennys have sold, twenty loads the mill reckons on, some of them single logs so huge the driver will curse and pray every corner, near-white the bark, and some of them with staghorns big as a car, and ferns so deep on the floor you can't push through, and felling'll begin when the ground dries and the Kennys can move round without gumboots and run their tapes over the logs with dry pleasure and tot up their royalties. I have never come across people with such aversion to gumboots, as though they believe sweaty feet rot the brain even though the only really gaga Kenny, Tiddy, runs around barefoot.

A mile before we left the hills we came upon a Chev with the bonnet up. When Dad and I got out a man came up and said he'd done his radiator hose. Lucky man. Dad is a believer in the universal efficacy of insulation tape. If diplomats would only carry rolls of tape the world would be a better place. He took from his insulation tape box a new roll of tape. It looks beautiful, said the man, I'm Oz, got the wife and kids and her brother with me. Touring? asked Dad. Peas, said Oz, And the picking's been good so we're out for a drive, though you wouldn't know from the in-law Jo.

In the car, around it and in the gully beside the road were nine people. The wife, said Oz. Jo, said Oz. While we bandaged the hose Oz opened a couple of bottles. Jo grabbed them for first drinks and Oz and the wife stared at the air over his head. Jo passed us the bottles which we offered the wife but she declined saying, Not in the mornings. So we drank and passed the bottles to Oz, and he passed one to Jo who drained it and passed it empty to Dad, who passed it to me, as I received the other which I drank from then handed to Dad who emptied it, and thus the Worts ended up with two empties. Two at a time's a principle of mine, said Oz. He shouted Bots! and lobbed them into the bush. The kids, I snapped. I warned them, said Oz, They dodge 'em—what I call preparation for life. Ah, Oz, said the wife. Oz produced another bottle which he passed first to Joe who passed it to Dad who passed it to me who returned it to Oz who emptied it into the radiator. The wife handed us a sugar bag with five pounds of peas.

On the way back to the ute Dad said, You know there was a time when I hardly noticed them, even in the Kimberley, but now I see them everywhere, and not because their families are bigger, it's just that I *see* them now. The peas were nice of them, said Mum, But I bet they're pinched. Pickers' bonus, said Dad. The pickers'll be pinched, said Mum, Especially if Smogton the sarj sees them. Smogton the sarj, I said, Isn't going to be bothered with itinerants while he's preparing for an assault on the Uppersass hills. Stop talking like that, she said. Just because we're withholding Shire rates doesn't give

246

him the right to treat us like criminals. We'll pay, said Dad, When the Shire fixes the road.

At that point we missed one pothole and broke a spring on another. We all got out and had a look. Dad got under and shook things. Mum went behind a bush for a leak. I went and pissed into the pothole. At that moment sunshine dissipated the haze, silvered leaves, steamed rare puddles, whitened new bark, fuzzed the old, wound up an old crow, freed a dozen mixed birdsongs, coaxed a frog to croak and other things I missed because I had to get in beside Mum.

Past the two sawmills, the cemetery, sanitary dump, tip, peeling paint and into Main Street and garages, signs, new paint and brick. We split up. For an hour of Peeny.

The Hon. J. C. Collie, M.L.C. will be in his rooms this day, 1-3 P.M.

In black and white, bold as you like, honied jesus christ, the colly, emelcee. Is back in town. Voters meet your representative, bring him your problems, air your grievances, exercise your right to be in a room with your representative, bathe in his presence, be reborn, a better voter, be gilded in his aura, seek the downfall of your enemies, cut government spending, bring business to Peeny, geld your enemies and god save the queen.

Much as I wished to see the Hon. J. C. Collie I decided to stride the sun-warmed pavements of Peeny to the newsagency for papers, magazines, paperbacks, indefinables and things suitable for a man such as I. And six postcards, black and white and coloured, which I took to the post-office and addressed to friend and foe. Woopo Town Hall. Big gums at Geege. Miss Banana with sceptre and skins. Mountain splendour. Rock pool at Bebe. Surf carnival march past. I paid ten pounds into my savings book. Dot dot dot dash dot dot dash dash dash dot dash. Hello, who's that morsing in the corner? It is Skunjher, post-office technician extraordinary; interceptor of telegrams, mismorser, opener of letters, smasher of parcels, secret policeman, militiaman, Peeny & District Horticultural and Agricultural Society stalwart, friend of Spasm the asm, six feet, thirty and shaped like a barrel (may his staves go, and bung fire straight into his associate, Collie). Skunjher, a rate-paying family man, captained the Peeny Tigers, has countless relatives in the Shire, sometimes goes to church and is the creature who dobbed me in to the Army when I was slow answering the call. If ever I send a shit sandwich to anyone ... But this is silly, wasting time and ire on Skunjher while the awful Collie lunches nearby, with cronies, at the Peeny Travellers. Burst in on him.   At last, Collie ... you tremble ... your face is ashen ... that's right, cronies—push your chairs back ... for those of you who are ignorant of what I'm doing I'm walking slowly towards your friend, Collie, emelcee ...

I then stand behind him, reach round, take his whiting, divide it into two portions and squeeze it into his ears, intoning   For what you are O family rotarian O hypocrite O manipulator of committees O harsh father ...

No, t'would be better to deal with his underling Skunjher first by filling in telegram forms with suggestive messages, soaking them in ink and stuffing them up his nose.

Skunjher looked up from the key, saw me and stared icily. Got to get out of this damned place. And so strong were my feelings I stepped backwards out of the post-office. I didn't intend it but once started there was no other way out. Skunjher came to the counter. Get your telegram from Sonia? he called. Before I passed from sight I bowed gravely. I hurried —in my normal manner—to the bench outside the Shire Hall. I was behaving ridiculously. I was pent-up. Aggravated. Astir. ANCESTRAL JUICES SURGED THEIR GIVEN WAYS. Had I been heard? Nobody paid any heed. Ancestral juices ... what next?

The midday hooter sounded and commerce took its rest. People walked, cycled. Citizens walked, cycled and drove to their homes. Relaxed and cheerful. Collie soon to greet his luncheon guests. Meals for the sake of the electorate. What an

248

existence! Sonia's evident bias towards him. I saw Skunjher ride from the post-office yard. What an interesting name he has. Scandinavian, Asian or Anglo-Saxon? Not such a bad man really. Has his job to do. A typical Peenyite with the standard objections to Uppersassians. Perhaps justified. And his inborn objections reinforced by my behaviour at the Rodeo Ball . . .

. . . Where my conduct had been inexcusable. Irma. In some ways so like Emma. Irma, Skunjher's second cousin's wife, rented a house in Peeny while awaiting her husband's return from a tour of duty in New Guinea. A patrol officer of some note, he was in the highlands under a cloud and she, Irma, his good wife, not wanting to go round all the time under an umbrella to save her from the muck flung at him, came to this peaceful town. And I met her at the Rodeo Ball. Tawny hair, eyes ever so green, slim (I heard her called skinny), and big arsed; odd, an odd big arse, because it wasn't like a pear, no, it was held high, and her breasts hung low, and they were like pears. She was a most contrary woman for this splendid arse of hers she bound in a sort of arse-to-armpit corset which pushed down the arse and pushed up her breasts so that she looked short in the leg and neck. We danced Erins, Barns, Schottisches and others to make up the fifty to go with the fifty moderns. We drank beer, oysters, custard and runny pavlova. The Skunjher and several of his loathsome kin did what they could to stop us dancing, and formed a roster of partners for her.

I went outside for a breather. Although the Rodeo Committee had fixed it with the cops so that the ball had beer, outside there were many men unable to adjust to this situation, who skulked drinking from hidden bottles. There were the usual snatches of abuse, a few drunks squatting or lying around, occasional retchings. I yarned with a few I knew then went along the side for a leak. Someone tapped my shoulder. I turned round and wet Skunjher's shoes. His punch missed me and I darted past him towards the street and lights. I looked behind, and when I turned I looked into the tight, expressionless face over a black tie and tuxedo of another Skunjher. He hit me in the face, I fell to my knees (thinking, Mustn't get the new suit dirty), I rose, and he punched me in the belly, I descended into agony and on the third wheeze spewed over his trousers. People hauled us apart, took me to a car and drove to the house of people called Brown, who put me to bed on the veranda, introduced me to the kelpie then put *him* into bed. I woke to the dog's growl. The air cold and still, the sky star-white. A hand on my shoulder and Ssshhh. Irma. I patted the dog. She'd come to see me, had heard what'd happened, they'd taken her home, she'd slipped away.   Come in here, Irma.   No.   No?   Well, I'm keeping my clothes on. I had to push the dog off and he didn't like it and crept about growling.   Let's go, Irma.   So we left the bed to the dog, and went to her place in stockings and socks to let the town sleep.   No funny business, Perce.   Lots of fearsome, funny and infallible New Guinea masks on the walls. I tried one on. Don't, she cried, You'll start a flood. She turned away. I tried another. She squeaked and bit her lip.   No— not that. Very edgy. In the lounge she poured me a brandy then went into the bedroom to change. I had to look after she hauled her corset off with a sound like a big rubber glove coming off. Her splendid arse and tits.   Eek—you beast—get out of here or get out. We had reviving brandies apiece. She on table, I on couch.   For god's sake, Irma.   I'd love to Perce, but my husband'll be here next month and he's a good man, I love him.   Show us your breasts, Irma.   That's all, mind.   Sweet jesus and look at your nipples.   That's enough. More, more, more Irma, Irma.   You act like a schoolboy, I'll send you home—I've heard all about you and Emma. All you think about.   Irma, you don't sound like a 21-year-old. What would you do if I pulled you onto the couch?   Kick you in the balls of course—stop that—put it away!   I'm not going to flash it—I'm all knotted—I don't think I can walk.   Her scornful disbelief. I stood up painfully, like a man commanded to walk after a miraculous cure. But no miracle! Knots. I felt myself. Ball-less! They have risen! Stuck amongst lungs. I fell back gasping. I could make you feel easier, she said coyly, but that's all, mind you.   No, let me sit quietly. I'm in an exaggerated condition.   You're lusty, that's all. You go into your room, Irma, I'll not bother you.   She went into her room, I stretched out on the sofa.

Lusty. Lust, that's my trouble.   What I lack is sublimation, I said.   What's that? she called.   I'm a one-tracker, Irma, and the end's over the horizon.   Go to sleep, Perce. Don't you want to talk, Irma?   For Christ's sake, Perce, fix yourself up and don't go on.   I must have dozed off. I had a horrible crick in my neck. My sexual organs, all stops out, sent a dreadful groan up through my throat. I sat up. AM I A SEXUAL MONSTER? I WANT TO CHANGE MY WAYS. Irma? Irma. Asleep. I lurched into her room.   Get out, Percy.   What followed is blurred in my memory. However. She allowed me certain comforts, but when I got between her legs she treated me with sudden severity. She stunned me with a wooden mask.

With dignity summoned from somewhere I tottered from the room, from the house, into the darkened town of Peeny. Along the crown of Main Street towards the house with the veranda with the bed with the kelpie. Pain! Opposite Grasper's Groceries I loosened my clothing and managed to ease my balls down, down, down, ahh, into their bag. What's this? Cords thick as a little finger! Oh gross testicular vessels! Should I ease? Never. Unease strengthens the willpower. Preparation for hard times. I straddled the bubbler and tried to cool myself. What was that? Hiss. On Main Street at 4.30 a.m., not a light anywhere, lights off at 12.30 because nobody should be abroad. Hiss. From a car I had passed thirty feet back. Peeping Tom? No, a passionate couple. Bad morality. On the street. I adjusted my clothing and went on, oblivious of discomfort, to

251

the bed, which the dog snarled over. Nice doggie. Remove pillow slip, use as garrotte. The dog whined, jumped off. I got into bed.

Woken by cockcrow at terrible hour. Grey dawn with sun soon to rise. Bright cock on fence. Rows and rows of broad beans. The house is situated in choice beanery. At dusk the cock rattles, expires, falls into beans and becomes them. Reborn at dawn.

I made my way to where I had left the Norton. As I walked out on the streets of Peeny, a cowman, a failed soldier, I knew I must try to find out what was wrong.

The concussions and repercussions of mating orgies. Contain them lest they shake me to pieces. But is the vessel strong enough? If it be the heart then skirts and coats continually rent. If in head, then headaches and blue-veined temples soft as cheese.

A whirring. It increases. The noise of disaster. Brain fills with it.   Good morning.   I stumble. Irma on bicycle. Want a ride?   Dare you, Irma? Early risers will see.   Hop on.   Agony of the saddle. So she sat and I pedalled.   No, Perce—to my place.   So we rode home, and into bed, and she kept me there all day. Damn the neighbours, I gasped. Please, she murmured.

Irma Rodeo. But I cannot dwell in the past because the roof leaks. Never met her husband. Nice man by all accounts, this particular Skunjher. May he remain Irma's fine plunger! Amongst other things. For sex is not all. Or, if it is, then it is. Either way I have a long way to go.

Thus my philosophical reminiscences concerning Irma.

ANYWAY. There I was this Friday in Peeny. And on my way to see Collie, emelcee, who was in Peeny this day to see his voters. He did not, of course, wish to see me, because I was not one of his voters and, even worse, I was after his disowned daughter. She had told him! Spasm and the evil (not Irma's) Skunjher had told him! Why she had to tell him I didn't know. Was she using me as a bullet? I did not care if she was. She had told her father in a telegram and every post-office person in Peeny knew. I was pleased that they knew, yet I regretted it, too.

I had half an hour to wait before Collie emelcee would be available during hours one to three. I would see him and remain calm. I would let him finish his whiting and beer in peace. However, if he knew about his daughter and me could he, possibly, be calm? Even though he had disowned her?

I went to the bakery, bought a pie and took it to the River Arms. On the way I conducted a conversation with the pie, but knew the answers before it replied.

In the pub I heard how Collie was hoping to get the Defence Department to acquire Uppersass and hundreds of square miles of hills and mountains. Why? Because the Army range at Singleton had been overused and ruin and erosion threatened it. Uppersass would be UTILIZED UNTIL SUCH TIME AS SINGLETON WAS RESTED AND RECOMMISSIONED.

His secretary was out. I went into his room. He resented my intrusion. He didn't know me. Wort? He excused himself and left the room. I saw him scanning the electoral roll on his secretary's desk so he could have names and data to use against me. To tell me he knew Uppersassians by their first names.

Sonia and I. I would tell him. But when he returned he led with: I have news of national importance for Uppersass. As you are well aware there are two schemes on the ministerial drawing board for the Uppersass region. There is talk of a third, which I will discuss later.

The First: that Uppersass becomes a national park.

The Second: that Uppersass become the catchment area for the Edinburgh Dam, a project dear to my heart. Think of the transformation of our region! Let me finish—irrigation, hydro-power. Dwellings, of course, cannot be allowed. Generous compensation will be awarded. Fish and water fowl will be lesser blessings.

Generous? I butted in. Generosity is against the principle of inundatory compensation. The spirit of Uppersass will die without Uppersassians-in-residence.

Nicely put, Mr Wort, you would make a fine debator. Have you any political affiliation?

I was once a member of your party, Mr Collie.

Once?

I have been a member of three parties.

Not the——

No.

You are only feeling your way. Uppersass is not strongly represented in my party, you know. We could do with a man of your ability.

Me! when you're planning to destroy the place? I refuse. You want more water to flush your shit away. Uppersass will block your arse and you'll wither with impaction.

You are rather horribly excremental, Mr Wort. Those electors who know of the existence of Uppersass loathe it. To use your language—there are many who would use a clyster on Uppersass. Whatismore, there is a third alternative for your hamlet. It has been decided that circumstances, economic conditions, spirit of the age, threat of conflagration, necessity for rationalization and the need to re-organize critical sectors of the economy make it imperative that Uppersassians and others be moved elsewhere. Agreements will be settled, drawn-up, cancelled, arbitrated, swallowed, digested and shot into intrays of various employers' organizations and government departments, all persons will be gainfully absorbed into the national economy. Uppersass is an area of reduced fertility, indeed it has never been much good. Therefore, it is best that the Army make use of it, and when it has served its purpose it will be restored.

You are doing what they do in Russia, I told him.

How dare you!

I don't mean fuck, you prickless old beetle, I mean liquidate us.

Red and gasping. His hands tight on the desk edge. Reached for the blotter. Nailed furrows of green.

Uppersass cannot remain aloof from national policy, he declared, We are not in the Eighteenth Century.

Why the Eighteenth?

Because of an interesting article in this morning's paper.

18th C. Press Gangs, mercenaries and duelling. Hat rack behind me. Darted to it, grabbed his stout stick. Fenced him. Parry. Thrust. He found his voice: Wha-what you're doing is—is dastardly. I mean I am a member of the government, your elected member!

Your member withered fifty years ago. I should squash you like a beetle, Collie, you detestable creature. Member of legislative coven. I'll hammer your gold pass up your arse. Up your arse, Darce. I danced round the desk, Douglas Fairbanksing. I changed to W. Lindrum, the champion billiardist, with the stick the cue to sink his gold pass in his fundamental pocket.

I'll have you committed!

To what? I politely asked.

To where, you mean—to Morisset or Callan Park. Or prison. The choice is our prerogative.

His proper colour came back. My evil was sucked into him. He would burst with his and mine. Poor Collie. I replaced the stick. He rose. With a terrible smile.

If you'll just wait a moment.

Mr Collie, your daughter and I hope to marry.

And that was that. He rattled, fell forward onto his desk and somehow did not slide onto the floor. I didn't rush to his aid. I could not move. Picture of late member. I then did a twitchy jig. I felt his heart pulse, pulled back his eyelids. Dead as a pinned beetle. His secretary arrived at her desk. I slipped out the other door. Killer of future father-in-law. Have progressed from personal disaster to another's disaster. Exit through the yard. Returned to the ute and huddled therein.

I saw Doctor Rood run to the hotel. Followed within moments by Cutler the chemist, Councillor Magnus and several others. Then came the Reverend Knott and Father Oats to vie.

Too late, brothers. The Collie barque has crossed the river, and moored at the jetty. What alerted you, brothers, was the sound of Collie taking wing for the regions of the damned and no leaping on your behalf will reach him.

The Peeny and District ambulance screamed up and driver and assistant, still fresh after their two hundred yard errand of mercy, dashed inside.

Had anyone seen me leave the hotel? There was nothing I could do but wait. The ambulance men reappeared and got their stretcher. Would I dare to watch as they brought out their sheeted burden?

Out they came. Collie was not sheeted! His hand lifted up! What post-mortem spasm was I witnessing! Father Oats took the hand and patted it. The other hand reached out and touched the Reverend Knott. Doctor Rood patted the Collie chest.

The alliance of doctor, chemist, clergy and barman had restored the emelcee.

I had conducted a pre-, not a post-mortem examination!

I would have had the man buried alive?

I had abandoned him, left him slumped across his desk. A craven, a coward. A creature insensitive to the pulse of life. Collie lives! Had my hatred of him been genuine surely I could have made sure he was dead by the simple act of smothering him?

[My brother, Thomas Wort, bro, Tom, jailer, the successful burgeoner, has now gone too far. He has overstepped things. In fact he has taken a running jump.

Two minutes ago he drove up the road in a HIRED LOUD-SPEAKER VAN. Casting his words before the swine. Percy—Perce—Percy Wort—come home home home home ome ome-omeome. Percy percy ercy ercy ercy Wort Wort wor wor wor rrrrr. No illillillillill feelings ings inggs ssss. Time to move on.]

I moved on. Into this.

I am encaverned. Literally in a hole, and see no way out at present. What a situation. Die here unless I escape. Some say holes are essential for human existence, that holes generate the need to escape, that if holes did not exist it would be necessary to invent them.   What is that you're making, Leonardo? It looks rather significant.   Yes, isn't it, I'm thinking of calling it Hole.   Indeed, Leonardo, may I ask why?   Yes, from holus-bolus, all together, at one gulp. You see I'm going to fill it with the heap of stuff behind you.   You mean this Jesus farewell-dinner canvas and sketches?   Yes, all together.

This hole I'm in. Get out of it. To what? Another, perhaps. But if there's to be another I'll have had the experience of this one, and the getting out of it. Which suggests I am a kind of predicament hunter. Anything forbid. Well, almost anything. Follow that predicament, Perce. And off I go, like a grey-hound, on two's or four's, after the blur ahead, closer, closer. It's likely to be a tin blur, but I can't stop. Snap, and my teeth are broken. Or, it's genuine fur I'm after and I get a kick in the face. Or it turns out to be a vixen, and my ribs are bared. Or if I close up quickly then it's a slow bull terrier bitch, and my ears are shredded. Or it's the hound of hell.

The greyhound is a false simile. I am not long and lean, nor am I fleet (unless Norton'd), nor greyhound colour. I am black haired. There are black dogs which must be the most formid-able of competitors: I mean, is it shadow or substance?

If only I had a musical instrument. To pass the time. Piano, even, and when I got out of this spot of bother I'd take the piano with me. Remove piddling wheels, fit pneumatics, rings for hauling ropes, or better still, three point linkage. Hauling along roads, assistants ahead and behind bearing signs Piano Coming, Piano Ahead. Could now and then stop and dash off a sonata. Hire out to farmers as alternative to milking music, so ending perfidious morning requests for Rocky Ned, Singing in the Corn and similar. Calm cows. Play in paddocks to make the grass grow. Introduce mimic birds to new realms of music. Farm pianists the rage. The coast a piano belt. Crows grow white feathers to match keys. Ab pea-pickers travel with pianos and discover five-year-old prodigies. Eventually, there's so much music, dehammering and unstringing viruses develop. Then piano music without pianos. Pianos on every hill, every skyline, in every paddock, mute testimony to the first piano period.

No. The transport would hinder. A mouthorgan better. Flute. I've always fancied the flute, off over the hills with birds and beasts following. I'd certainly draw rats. And my tune not wildly beguiling, but terrified and broken as the rats eat leather heels and start on flesh, and up the trousers. I'd flute them off, I'd break it on them, fur would choke holes, they'd grow in size as they ate their disabled fellows, a trail of bones behind me, and then they'd be on my shoulders and I'd go down and they'd have my heart out and fight in the breast, moving ribs as though I still breathed.

Perce, my friend, you should derail this train of thought. Such thoughts derange sleepers.

However, I am awake and aware. Which makes it a little less horrible. Correction, a lot less horrible for when I put them to paper I am calmed. A little. (I have just looked over my shoulder.)

When you are in a hole write yourself out of it. For example, think of all the long words beginning with A like Austral-ia, -asian, -orp, -oid, aluminium, arsenic, antimony, argon, alfalfa, artichoke, abacus, abecedarian, abutment, arithmetician, absolute and so on; into the Bs and right through the alphabet, and add and add and assemble at any, at all cost, always anchoring against an adjacent artifact allowing adequate adhesion as ants are actually addicted and are artful assimilators. Heap these words against the predicament and climb to safety.

Yes, literally in a hole. Point of entry eight feet above. Quite a small aperture and because it is alongside a fallen tree, well concealed though not enough as to have me in dark. This hole or cavern started out as a burrow or warren. Water found its way and in no time created what now contains me. The chamber is twelve feet long and ranges in width from three to eight feet. There is a drain hole at the lower end. The soil is light and mixed with stones, one of which shattered the case of the Remington. My sturdy 35-shot Remington, still usable though the ribbon is tatty.

Sonia, Emma, Irma . . . Mum, Dad, Fred . . . Tom. There's room for the lot of you down here.

If Claire Bloom appeared she would offer me a mild and flavourful cigarette. Albany no less! I must put up some shelves and carve a few niches in my walls for the supplies I'll get as soon as possible. Woods Great Peppermint Cure, The Family Remedy, because one should always keep a bottle in the home. Four gallons of Purr-Pull petrol with I.C.C. additive for the vehicle. Opposite the Albany and Claire Bloom would be Peter Jackson, the cigarette true to a great tradition. I would enjoy the protection of filtered smoking with my Gard crystal-filter cigarette holder. Enjoy Cream of Yeast life and banish headaches, nerve pains, neuralgia, depression, joint and muscular stiffness, coughs and colds, halitosis and coated tongue.

This cavity is indeed a fine home. Full of Cream of Yeast I lie back on my bag sofa, tune my wireless to Station 2BL and hear the current naturalization ceremony for New Australians in which they renounce their former allegiances and take the Oath of Allegiance to the Crown. Thus do I keep in touch

259

with the outside world. Though I have no wireless. You do not need one. The quizzes, talent quests, commentaries and advertisements go on. They have been heard so often they cannot be erased. What loads of messages we carry. I carry. I cannot speak for everyone. There are those who are able to let trivia pass out. I must have a fine-mesh mind.

This place is very snug. Bro would like it. One wouldn't be enough for him though, he would want more. He'd like a representative range of caves, holes and grottoes so as to be able to say I have a full range of caves, holes and grottoes and am able to satisfy anyone who seeks a cave, hole or grotto.

Such a hole as this has limitations. It can hardly be advertised as a dry dwelling because it owes its structure to rain water and with each fall of rain it increases in size until its very dimensions cause the earth above to fall in on it.

Still, it is very reasonable as it is. May the weather remain fine. If it does there will be drought. Grass will wither and milk production diminish. I do not think I care. I have had enough of rurality. I need the stench and clatter of city life. A job on the trams, for instance, or down in the woolsheds near St Peters by the canals—or is it canal? Jellied water scummed with oil, cats and bottles—the roar of planes—caryards—copra sheds swarming with grubs and beetles—bakelite extruders—disinfectant squirters—

I think I would rather remain here.

For ten minutes I brooded on remaining here. Brooding on remaining. It would be reasonable to remain here entombed. Going to the city to be racked is silly. Here it is pleasant. Basic. From earth to earth. Transformed into leaves—eaten! Ingested by worms—eaten! The trail into a myriadness! Snails. I do not fancy being taken into a snail. Ugh, or slug. I am going to gaze at the furthermost recess of my chamber, at the tree root two feet above the small spring-fed pool. Meditate. I cannot recall when last I meditated. I never found the companion who was so companionable as solitude. A wise

American wrote that. He elected to savour the bliss of isolation and silence.

It is now pitch dark. Night has fallen. *Tgiums scanoet. An mot lingru.* Rest.

I wake to dirt falling on my face and stare up at the hole through which I have plunged. I spring up, fearing an earth fall. Appetite has diminished considerably. Four dates, a handful of rolled oats and a pannikin of water from the pool.

I intend meditating until noon.   On the subject of verandas . . .

The verandas of Uppersass, Peeny, Dog Mountain, Dingo Crossing, Gum Brush, Jakara, Cedar Stand and other localities, have to endure all weathers and heavy traffic, generally human and canine though here and there piglets, calves and foals are nursed thereon and, in the cases of a couple of notorious families, any animal able to climb up is allowed to stay. Poultry, of course, are ubiquitous. The better quality veranda is tongue and groove. There is one somewhere with a tile surface. Tallowwood, flooded gum, paperbark, rosewood and plain gum are in evidence. No veranda roof, to this writer's knowledge, is lined. Rafters are therefore plain and unadorned unless fern baskets, meat safes, water coolers or party decorations dangle. The veranda is an accepted and un-commented-on aspect of life.

These past few days there has not been a veranda not occupied by someone LAMENTING OR CURSING ME, P. WORT. A veranda is a house's brim and I am running over with the observations and philosophies of veranda brimmers.

I allowed myself to be transported from my subterranean abode (or EDOBA, and why not? there is the precedent of EMOH RUO), moving stealthily about Uppersass and Peeny.

Before the crisis of my flight you will be interested to know that I was an occasional correspondent of the *Peeny Gazette*. Usually, Our Mountain Correspondent; occasionally, P.W.

I have concocted a competition for readers: THE UPPERSASS REPORTING PRIZE. For reporting the events of one morning. Entries are expected to vary greatly in quality and length. All, however, will be of interest.

The *Peeny Gazette* will have decided to terminate my services and will have secured another resident of the hills to act as Our Correspondent. We're sorry, Mr Wort but you don't spend enough time up there for you seem to spend most of your hours in or travelling to the city. No, Mr Wort, we do not need a Highway Correspondent nor do we have space for a Martin Place Esquire, Capt. Port Jackson or Circ. Quay. And may we remind you, Mr Wort, that the reason we drastically cut your last contribution which began as an ordinary account of the condition of pastures, Mr Tanks' two-headed radioactive calf and the state of the roads, was that you soon abandoned these laudable items and launched into what our printer Phil Laten denounced as gibberish. Why did you go on about an evangelist Jackson in Martin Place who turns the drinking water of a bubbler into port wine thereby creating a civil—uncivil really—disturbance in which the Cenotaph is desecrated by the presence of a man in white bird plumage who then flies up Martin Place, treads—the term used by bird fanciers, I believe—who treads a brazen secretary in a miraculously conceived nest (to your credit this coupling is hidden from the lascivious by leaves, twigs, bottle tops, bank-notes and leather scraps)—an act blessed (!) by the evangelist Jackson who then flees to Circular Quay where he joins a ship, the *Pearl*, loaded with camels, ferrets and film stars, which is about to cast-off on a film-making expedition about those intrepid desert explorers Burke and Wills, only the script has poor B & W in a sort of seagoing musical. *Why*? You didn't really expect us to run your piece, Mr Wort? We are not a circus act, you know. And your final line—We have been here before—carried a hint of the occult.

No, Mr Wort, we do not need a Theatre Correspondent, least of all in Uppersass where The Drama is unknown. Pardon?—you say that Uppersass is a stage and all the ratepayers merely players who have their exits and their entrances, and one man in his time plays many parts? That the performance is watched by Someone who weeps, claps, cheers and farts? Goodbye, Mr Wort. Goodbye.

Mr Peeny Gazette does not know. I tried to get him to come to a performance but he would not. If he happened to appear now he'd think himself just in time for the last act. But there's the rub—he'd enter in time for the penultimate scene of the first act.

Principal players are Mrs Tank, Mr Oats, Mrs Subbs, Sergeant Smogton, Mr Shrubb and Bro. They are here and there, between Uppersass and Peeny, round and about, sitting and standing still and pacing, sweet and bitter, morose and gay.

I present some entries in the competition. The first from A. Tank.

Tale from A Tank

The scene now, this Monday morning. Still, damp, dustless. Sergeant Smogton stands outside the Hall. His nostrils flare to catch the fumes generated almost thirty hours earlier, dawn Sunday, but his nostrils gauge his conceit because no one could possibly catch what had drifted away by noon Sunday. Had he arrived three hours afterwards instead of thirty I doubt he'd have sniffed the fumes. He sacrificed his sense of smell years ago to whisky and tobacco.

Still, he went through the motions of sniffing at the scene of the crime outside the Uppersass Community Hall, two hundred yards down the road from the sometimes-open one-time post-office-store which stands among three habitable houses. A hundred yards on to the remains of the butter factory, then, finally, scattered over a quarter of a mile the ruins—foundations, chimneys and odds and ends too awkward to plunder—of old Uppersass. Over this debris tower seven pines. Here and there the usual blackbutt and scrub gum, and, back a bit, waiting to move in, is the bush.

The Sergeant stares fixedly at the Hall. Then he notes the surroundings which I've already mentioned, and the two locals each of whom is there to see the other doesn't say too much. The Sergeant snorts, spins on his heel and strides to the sometime store where he hammers for attention, but Mrs Soaper slipped out the back when he started. The Sergeant calls on seven ratepayers. Then races to his Ford for a tyre-smoking return to Peeny.

I suppose it's enough to send any cop howling, especially one like him who's dead keen on promotion and getting away from—as he puts it—this crazy hick district where there's no respect for The Law.

In Peeny he reports: But they notify me the day after the day it happened! When they've had time to check and counter-check their alibis! And they answer me with, Gosh, Sarj, I was pretty full y'know, or, No Sergeant, I haven't a clue, I went home early. And to that I say, Early? *You* go home early from a party? And you know what these hillbillies answer? They answer, Well, Sergeant, we're dairy farmers/millmen/in the bush/with the Shire—we got to be up early.

The Sergeant has another whisky. Perhaps he thinks: Uppersass is unco-operative because of the state of the road. Just because the school bus goes over a bad bend they refuse to assist the works of law and order. There is at least one criminal up there and they're sheltering him. He used gelignite and gelignite is an offensive substance whether exploded or kept in a magazine; it is about the most offensive substance available and I don't care if it is sold next to the biscuits in the Peeny Co-op, I will never think otherwise. I have thought it an abominable substance since I read of a murderer wiring it to a starter in a car—all right, all right—I know nobody was hurt at Uppersass—there is a principle, however. I have seen grown men sniffing the stuff. Cold sweat. I have now seen what the Uppersassians do with it.

The only proper use for gelignite in this district would be the destruction of the Peeny-Uppersass road. Isolate them I say! Let them do what they will up there. Blast the road I say. He has yet another drink and opens yet another packet of cigarettes.

He's not far wrong about the road being a mess. Through Uppersass proper it's a sealed ridge road but the remainder of it is slashed and bitten from hillsides, unsealed. At the last Shire election the clique told us: Uppersass, an important part of our community, must be integrated with Peeny. How? by sealing not only every one of those straight, tortuous, uphill, downhill miles between Uppersass and Peeny, but also that part to the west of the village where lies a wealth of timber and dairy products. The election took place, the clique was returned, we were told: You rugged mountain people will wait a while, won't you—money is short—country roads grants have been reduced—and why? because of city-centred government. We regret, therefore, this city-bred delay to our sealing solution.

They then built the new Shire Hall in Peeny. And I hope this is not the reason we're hard to get on with, God I do.

With the Sergeant went the cloud, the thin morning cloud as though dispersed by his burning rubber. What sun there is now! The Hall will be sparkling with it, there'd be a million bits of sun trapped there, sparkling like a million sequins, a million staples holding the timbers together.

In Peeny they regard Uppersass as a contraction of Upper Sassafrass, which was the name of Peeny until they realized it was a bit silly seeing the place was on the flat; but to us Uppersassians the derivation is subtler—Uppersass from Uppersuss from Uppersussurus meaning higher-rustle from Russell who opened up the country and built the Hall among other things.

The Sergeant could have called in on his way back to Peeny and asked me: Mrs Tank, would you tell me what happened at the Uppersass Community Hall about dawn yesterday?

I'd have answered: I wasn't there, Sergeant Smogton, I'm not a dawn person, I don't go prancing on the dewy sward at dawn, I'm not that kind of person—nowadays—in my youth, yes, I could have been there prancing for I liked it, and I was regarded as very pranceable as a girl though nothing murky mind you, I was innocent through ignorance, and what is more, I did not live here as a girl, I dwelt in the city where I had to be content with prancing on the beach, in the park or on asphalt or concrete.

And another thing, Sergeant, there wasn't a dance at dawn unless you regard it as a dance of death though nobody died and there was no intention of killing anyone. It was not a dance unless the men at the bucks' party danced. I doubt this.

And Sergeant, I was here, at home, which is miles from the Hall. The noise wouldn't have reached here.

Sergeant: I know there was no dance, Mrs Tank. But just imagine for a moment that there was a dance. And there was this someone really crazy who didn't attend or perhaps wasn't even invited, and when the Hall is packed he lights the fuse. Bang. Okay, OK, I mean, Mrs Tank, Only so far as this supposition of mine's concerned—I do not agree with this sort of behaviour, you understand, in fact it is what a man of the cloth would call anathema to me. Bolshevistic. Anarchistic. That's what it is. But Mrs Tank—why should anyone want to gelignite the place at dawn when there's nobody present? Correction—not the place itself, but something nearby. Which when exploded would cause as much damage as one of those wartime blockbusters. Correction—as much damage as one of those wartime daisy-cutters.

Me: Sorry, Sergeant, but I've no suggestions.

He'd watch me for a few moments, his big red face hard-set and icy, his body rigid—like a tricky pointer almost—rigid with a kind of stymied zeal.

I suppose the Hall will have to be demolished. Probably not though, because bad things have happened before. Every restoration alters it. The roof has been iron since the cyclone took the shingles. The doors, cedar from Mullingar station in the first place—and stolen, unhinged five years ago by a holidaying city cabinet-maker and turned into bookcases for city socialites who paid him more than the parent tree would have brought—these doors are now of plywood. Then the end walls went, because of bodies drunk and bodies dancing, especially when jitterbugging started and people hurtled, these walls are now asbestos cement.

A hall erected sixty years ago. The size of a church hall. Named at first the Uppersass School of Arts because the settlers thought they were founding a town and wanted to have things right from the start. Later it was changed to Community Hall, because it was thought the old name would remind certain people of the late Russell. But for many years it was known simply as Russell's. It was he who had it put up. It was he—if you can believe any of the stories—who wanted it filled with books and papers and music. Russell V. Russell. Russell with his co-op saw-mills and cheese factory and farms where everyone, even in those days, worked thirty-nine hours a week. He crusaded along the tablelands and on the coast and in the city. Crying: People, people—for the people. Seek shorter hours for recreation and culture. Leave bigger wages for capitalists and would-be's.

Russell, short and thin, with quick bright eyes, red hair and a long spiky beard he refused to shorten. Even when they started shaking him by it.

He used to enter towns Fridays and Saturdays to hold meetings from a dray or a sulky. There are still bits of his posters in the Hall. The Coming Utopia. Marx, George and the Imminent Crisis. Is Marriage Desirable? Co-operative Communities and the Capitalists.

Shave off my beard? he said to old Osstich, Never—my chin's what is known as a weak chin and you know what people say about weak chins, don't you?

But when Harper, his assistant, had him certified and sent to the asylum he lost his beard. His enemies saw his tiny chin.

267

And they said—or shouted or screamed or whined or screeched or ranted—It's gone now, your beard! He wept, and tore at his face screaming: Delilas! They said: See? how mad he is. And he thinks he's surrounded by women. They leered and smirked. Would he know the difference? they sniggered.

The asylum was an old place with cells and bars and aspidistras in the hall. They made him librarian. He arranged it all himself. Superintendent Flair, Harper and a couple of others paid him a visit. Do we smell gas? Is that gas-hiss? Superintendent Flair's fatal weakness for cigars . . .

Today the Hall is battered and scarred. The end walls have gone again. The Gent's outhouse was cut-off at seat level and the pail holed, which is one way of getting it emptied, and the Ladies' rolled down the hill and the LAD- part of the sign hangs from the riddled guttering and raprapraps a dull funeral beat whenever caught by the wind. And the stuff that did the damage, the shrapnel, lies everywhere on the ground and in the timbers. It glitters in the sun. By night it moon-gleams.

Those damn fool Wort brothers. Grown men carrying on like desperados. I wonder how their father's taking it? Moping around, surly, hat pressed tight, shoulder blades out like wings. Their mother in a tense. The noise would have woken them. An alarm their clock could never give them. Put the cows off their milk. At least it would have made milking easier that morning.

Then, this morning, the two of them down at the bails and not a word between them, only the wireless: When the Bloom is on the Sage and Rocky Ned. Her, bustling around, bulging from her blue overalls and dairy boots, trying to ease him. And every now and then him stamping into the yard shouting: The Hall, why the Hall! And her racing to the house because her patience is limited. And him: The Hall's part of me. My son—my sons—which one?

Those Wort boys. Perce, shiftless and not a bit like brother Tom the townie. Perce always the same, always on the move.

In the city, round and about. Tom the smart one, the smartie one, the manager.

Though the explosion was yesterday the parents haven't said a thing. Everyone else has and the stories have built up. Soon it'll be legend. In twenty years' time people a hundred miles up the coast'll say: So you're from Uppersass eh, isn't that the terrorist town? They'll look at Uppersassians as though they're Arab or Jew or Balkan or Irish and shuffle back a few paces.

Perce and his father have a sort of stock dialogue. You're not going to the city again? Why not? When are you going to do something with your life? I am. Do you think your uncle likes your behaviour? Why shouldn't he? You've had a good schooling and secure jobs and you sit on your behind reading and dreaming or you work in a factory. So what? Your bloody motor bike, you could have started a herd for the price of it, you polish it, walk round it so much it's a wonder you don't fall giddy, and you know next to nothing about it, you treat it like a mystery which is not to be known. That's all right. And the junk you bring home— the material and the stuff in your head like rubbish about camels and ferrets and Russell, and the horrible hints you've dropped about making a monument. Dad, my interest in cows is limited. Tom, now, he knows a thing or two about money and improvements.

But it was Perce's idea to sell the bottles. He must have thought about them a long time and waited for the price to rise.

For years they'd been heaping, the bottles. Mullock. From the hundreds of turns at the Hall. Mullock from the dream mines. Most of them amber. One day Perce must have said to Tom: Want to be in on a quid? And he would have answered: Who doesn't? You know the Hall? said Perce. You kidding? said Tom.

For fifty years they'd been accumulating. Since Russell was taken away because he was an abstainer. The no-alcohol rule bent by a packed committee. Then the empties began to gather. From Release Russell meetings to Let the Poms Fight the Kaiser and We'll Stay At Home to card nights for money for the boys and Uppersass's war widow Agnes Banks to debates on Conscription and Billy Hughes to Welcome Home parties, union meetings, timber workers' and farmers' meetings and Country Party do's. More war meetings, Welcome Home celebrations, New State and Ban Margarine nights. The usual wedding receptions, farewell parties, cedar and dairy balls. And for about ten years when outsiders thought it smart to have dances here. The history of the Hall and the district on leaflets and posters on walls inside and out.

This unpainted Hall perched on stumps because of the slope. You climb three steps to enter the front door and if you leave by the back you go down fifteen or twenty. Five windows each side and the platform in the left corner as you step inside. Two water tanks on what turned out to be the safe side.

At most of the meetings the regular sound was that of bottles being opened and the glugging of beer or lemonade or stout or the unnameable home brew. The bottles dropped through two trapdoors. Slowly the heaps grew until the Hall sat on amber pyramids. When the floor tilted beneath dancers you'd hear screeching glass over the music. Sometimes when there was a rush for last drinks the pyramid beneath the bar would grind further into the dirt and the screech set teeth on edge. The most spectacular bar charge occurred when there was a gory debate about a one big union before the first war.

In the twenties, the Committee decided that the bottles had to be neatly stacked at least fifty feet from the Hall. So new heaps grew, but not as neat stacks. Pyramids again, as if, scattered throughout the district, there were Egyptian boozers. In 1942, with the Japs in New Guinea, the Volunteer Defence Corps estimated the bottles and Headquarters said they were mad and demanded a recount for operation Molotov Cocktail, and as this second census revealed another

20,000 the counters were declared idiotic and cirrhotic and posted elsewhere. Many people spoke of exploiting the bottles and a couple of loads went away but disaster went with them; there's one load in a gully, and the other lot washed into Peeny in a flood.

Perce said to Tom: we'll go fifty-fifty. Right, said Tom, Let's start crating them next Sunday after the party. OK, said Perce, But not the two far heaps. Why not? demanded Tom. I want to leave one heap, said Perce, And make something out of the other. No, you don't, said Tom. Oh yes I do, said Perce.

There was shouting and shoving. They're a link with the past, said Perce, And I want to make something for the future.

You'll have to buy them from me, said Tom. Eh? said Perce. Then: OK. Tom said he'd take a couple of days leave for the job.

On the Saturday night it was the buck's party for Robbie Stones. Near midnight Tom went up to Perce and told him he had decided all the bottles had to go. Perce was dumbfounded. Ten minutes later they spoke again. Tom king hit him and he was a long time out. Tom peed on him.

At dawn Sunday the heaps were gelignited, not the ones under the Hall, the others. Three plugs a heap is the estimate. Dawn was clear and bright with stars.

Tom rushed to the Hall and stood in the stinking air. Headlights lit the scene. Tom stood like a boxer who's just beaten the count, his fists wriggling. He slipped away from the crowd and went hunting with his spotlight.

The sunlight was bright when he returned and stood in the centre of the glass-blasted space. His breathing deep and savage as though he'd just finished a strenuous game. The sun on the glass glittered and sparkled. Necklaces shone round trees and posts and window sockets were diamantéd. LAD-rapped mournfully in the only breeze of the day, clapper against the cracked bell of the Hall and round and about in slivers and splinters the ı and ε and s.

My friend Agnes Banks has already sown the seed of another story. She says there's an amber and green mosaic of Perce in the weatherboards.

There's talk of the Hall being demolished or moved. They say we've got to destroy Peeny's notion of us being hillbillies. Those who want the Hall to remain are speaking of a red brick front with a pair of concrete pillars.

Tom has returned to Peeny. I suppose Perce has slipped back to the city. I hope he's well. He mightn't have much money but he certainly has his fun. Or whatever you call it.

Cultivated Oats

[Bernie Oats, fondly known to Uppersassians and others as Bibleman, did not attend the Saturday night function in the Uppersass Hall because he was preparing his vehicle for a holy journey to the consecration of the monastery of Our Father of Paspalum in the upper Hunter. He is the sole devout RC in the hills and takes his position extremely seriously. Only Mr and Mrs Oats are allowed to drive their car because the steering wheel is somehow blessed. Folk unaccustomed to the ways of automotive unction would be ill-prepared for the dashboard controls of the Oats' vehicle because the knobs and buttons are almost impossible to distinguish among the array of holy medallions, pictures and relics thereon.]

The Epistle of Bernard Oats, of Burnt Gum via Uppersass.

In the glare of the workshop lamp and the flickering candle I held the rocker box over the tappets the way the Bishop of Christ holds the crown over the man to be made King but instead of a tumult of bells I heard the rumble. Was this dawn to see the day of wrath? Has it, at last, come? Is this to be it? Whirlwind and firestorm? Pray let it not be. Is the dwelling of Our Father of Paspalum to be laid waste?

The bomb has fallen. Pyres hiss and rumble on every continent. How long will it be before survivors stream up to Uppersass and will they be welcomed or warned off? If we Uppersassians survive shall we set up camps on the outskirts of cities to succour them or will it be roadblocks and firearms to confine them?

The wife, busy preparing provisions for our pilgrimage, called from the house: Bernie, quick! I laid the grey rocker-box cover on its new cork gasket and ran to the house kneading cotton waste as far as the mulberry then losing it, telling myself I would get it later.

I comforted her. The windows had rattled. We prayed. The phone. Osstich, excited. Percy Wort had run amock. Our Father allow the demons in him but a limited tenancy. We did pray. And we did add our customary piece for our two fallen sons and the three children asleep.

Smogton Ringbarked

[Sergeant Smogton left his strong, unfanciful brick police station in Peeny. He looked over his broad shoulder at the flame tree planted two years ago. Already it was as high as the roof . . .]

Ah, the tree—will it push over the station? Will the roots heave up the foundations and weaken the cells of this solid brick structure? But the station cannot be solid brick because then there would be nothing inside unless you want to say that there is brick within brick. THERE WOULD NOT BE ROOM FOR CELLS. What use then the police station? Unless prisoners be made into bone-meal for mortar between bricks.

What a way to think. I am disturbed. When I think thus I am disturbed, I can always tell, it is a wonder I have advanced so far in the force. Perhaps I never think when making arrests? When I issue summons and warrants am I perhaps another? Then what is A. Nother doing with my pay? A. NOTHER

PLANTS TREES AND LAYS BRICKS. Give me a seed and I'll plant it, show me a brick and I'll make a wall. It would be interesting to build a replica of this police station somewhere up in the hills. A solid police station which would immure my other self. Mortar mixed with my sweat, trowelled with my badge. My solid brick edifice in red brick among a plantation of my trees. Far from the gadding crowd. Behind a high brick wall. I would then brick in the space between the wall and the solid brick police station and when the trees burst through, die.

That unspeakable Wort studded the trees round the Uppersass Community Hall with fragments of glass in an attempt to ringbark the tree of community. May he hang in a bark noose. That is a district of tree killers. I their vengeful summoner. Working on Sundays, drunk and disorderly, overloaded jinkers, illegal parking are my resorts. If I could but bring charges of silvicide I would have the population pickled and transported. My domestic fires are burnt offerings to the living green. A tree felled by age or natural calamity is my only source of wood. The felon-to-be Wort comes from a region of felons-to-be. His crime. I was not informed immediately. Not a true conspiracy of silence perhaps but a sort of one. They answered: We didn't think it was important, Sergeant. After all, nobody was hurt. There was no need to render assistance. A bit of damage, yes, but you know.

I hate them and their district. Not a scrap of proper respect for the law. If anything heinous happens that can't be hushed up, they let you know a couple of days or even weeks later.

When my good wife expressed interest in them I warned her off. Restrict your good works to your own community I told her. Create more good offerings in the new electric stove I so thoughtfully gave you for Mothers' Day, go on, scone yourself back to the earlier, happier days before you tried to force me into a transfer to the city so you could have a gas stove in which to lay your head. Grr the shame, ggrrr.

Oh I was tempted to transfer. Especially last Show Day when, suddenly, I was appalled by the layer of dust on my nickel badges and buttons. Let there be trouble this day, I prayed. Let these Peenyites suffer. Inflict on these joyous Uppersassians a ten-fold suffering. Strike these latter, O God, rend these mountain folk sparing not one no matter how seemingly innocent for the innocent are the worst. O God let there be an Incident: allow me to stop an Uppersassian for going through a Halt, and let him be unlicensed and driving an unregistered vehicle, and allow it, O God, to be in a dangerous condition; and permit him offensiveness, and let our struggle be protracted so that I have to draw on him; and let his family rush to me with bail; and, please, God, let their money be counterfeit so I can jam them into my two cells, let their number be many so they may experience what our poor lads experienced in Changi.   Grr.

The Keen Watcher

[Bert Keen can be seen any day on his veranda, scribbler and pencil in hand, neat tho' old brown striped suit over white open shirt over stout fifty-year-old body under grey felt hat . . .]

I have lodged two reports and am about to make it three and am prepared to go to ten if need be, each one in triplicate with one for me, one for the post-office contact and the original for headquarters, all for love of country without even postage allowance because I love a sunburnt country a land of sweeping plains of rugged mountain ranges which is where the trouble lies. Up there in the Uppersass hills and higher still, where it is indeed rugged mountain range, and if the current trouble at Uppersass is dreadful then what might be going on in the rugged mountain ranges I shudder to think, there is less oxygen, which affects the brain as in the Himalayas where strange beasts and Tibetans lurk. Thank Almighty God this happy land was spared an influx of Tibetans; Afghans were bad enough, we are a white people; thank the Almighty we held them back in Korea.

Percy Wort I know what you are up to with your gelig-
niting, motor biking and fornicating with the weak wives of
brave men serving their country. Your father William and
your brother Tom are almost as guilty because of their associa·
tion with you. I know what goes on up there in the hills because the road passes my twenty-five acres on the edge of
Peeny, land certain to appreciate when industry comes gliding
in on beautiful ball bearings. I am going to subdivide and
retire to my knoll on the lovely flat coast from where I'll be
able to see the gun flashes of the Army on its Uppersass range.
Yes, you'll be hunted down like a possum, Wort.

Soldiering On

[Colonel Eric Gambol (Rtd.) of Ruley Park, a delightful,
well-watered property running red polls, with white-painted
sawn-timber fences along the road, round the house and
gradually creeping all over the property because of prosperity.
He stands on his veranda scanning the hills through field
glasses; occasionally he scratches an old wound . . .]

There is a Wort up there, a wild weed, nothing more, and
why rumours should circulate concerning what is at most a
drunken act of no importance puzzles me. A bladder type
weed, an empty vessel making a loud noise. Met him at a
branch meeting. Seemed a reasonable sort of person, though he
could have tried to attend sober. He preceded Black of Dog
Mountain, I recall, and sat with a dog on his lap. Ho, ho, I
thought, here's an Uppersasser with delusions who's barking
up the wrong tree if he thinks he has an ally in Black of Dog
Mountain who is something of an extraordinary person. At
one time during the proceedings I thought of saying to this
Wort, You may have tricked the army doctor but to me your
heart murmurs Shirker, shirker, shirker. If only our hero,
Peeny man Harold Knox had been there! But Harold (Fox-
hole) Knox was fighting for his life, having upheld our demo-

276

cratic way of strife—I mean life. He returned to Peeny just last week, looking very well—in fact his limp somehow added to his air of well-being.

I could only spend half an hour at Knox's welcome-home. He drank too much and fell badly in the barn dance. I bent low over him and whispered an invitation to visit.

And he came this morning, as I stood on the veranda examining the hills for Wort and the boards for termites. I noticed a tawny frogmouth or Podargus something under the udder of an aged cow; what was the frogmouth, a night bird, doing in sunlight, I asked myself as Knox climbed on to the veranda with his photograph album under his arm. The snaps rekindled many recollections, for though our theatres were far apart the scenes were familiar, especially one, taken over squatting comrades, of a burning village in the hills near Pakchon. An enemy village where even the children served as ammunition porters. The rock formation was fascinating and the trees resembled those dwarf Jap things. Knox mentioned a woman. She was heated though nothing hot, he added. Perhaps, I replied, it was the quilted jacket worn by these creatures as they come surging over the hills in uncountable waves—to become a multitudinous sea incarnadine? We all had her, said Knox, then Ron kicked her head in. I say, I said, You want to keep that sort of memory to yourself. For five days, he snarled, We'd fought for this lousy village in poor country where the healthiest crop was moss on fuckin' great goolies or skinny dwarf sheep grazing on lichen . . .

It reminds me of Uppersass, I retorted. He laughed heartily.

The Bro . . .

You'll get little out of me, Perce, unless you want to include the bunch of fives I'm going to hang on you. If not more. I did intend to punish you severely but the fires have died down. After all, Perce, you did use gelignite and gelignite is not the sort of thing I expected from you, Perce. I know you didn't actually use it on me, but my pride tells me you used it against me.

Though informers, rumour-mongers and counter-informers alike tell me you have fled Uppersass, Perce, I know you're still around. So I'll wait. You're probably enjoying yourself out there in the bush and see yourself as one of those partisans, though the Remington you've got fires words not bullets. Why do you lug it along? I'm certainly not after it. Surely you don't expect to write brother-on-the-run memoirs?

You ought to come home. It's lonely out there and you spend too much time by yourself, either on the bike, or round about, or in the city, and you cannot keep it up for there is a limit to unnatural solitude, and I'm glad you've never taken up navel-watching Asian mysticism; though perhaps you have, and now I think about it you have expressed interest in that Russell nut who would have taken up fire-walking if he hadn't gone into the asylum. God knows Perce, I tried to get you to mix more. Scouts, debating, junior farmers, teams, the Party, and when the Army called you up I thought, well, it's not the best there is but at least he'll have to mix. And you got out of it, Perce, because of a heart murmur. A heart murmur, as though your tongue wasn't enough? What kind of conversation did you have with the doctor per stethoscope? Are you by any chance ventriloquial? If you threw your voice in order to avoid serving your country . . . I have heard voices, Perce, and seen nobody—was it you? Have you by any chance indulged in mesmerism? That Peeny woman you were on with —did you use your tricks on her? I'm ashamed of you. I hope you stay away.

It was me in the plane, Perce. I sought you from horseback and loudspeaker van. I'd bring in blacktrackers only there's a limit to the time I can spend away from work. The police won't be told everything if I can help it. I can't say the same for the Army because the government sees Uppersass as a possible range so if you hear tanks clanking don't hold it against me, will you.

278

Bye bye, Perce, I've got to supervise the loading of some bullocks. And you'll be interested to know, Perce, that the cedar I was after in the gorge behind Barrenbrush has been got out. A pity it was the last one. But at least I've got 66⅔rds of the last cedar, the remainder going to Clatter & his Cat men. Despite what you've done to me I'll give you a piece, you can have it made into a stool and if you behave yourself I'll now and then let you bring it into my office so you can sit in front of the 6 x 4 desk I'm going to have made. All this and several hundred quid from one tree. Percy, if you need a life-quest why not become a cedar-hunter? A rugged, heroic calling in the jags and gorges of the back country though I have to admit that if there's cedar up there it's because it can't be got out. However, Perce, you could at least try. Then I wouldn't ask you not to come to my wedding, which is going to be a full-dress CMF affair. You won't feel out of place amongst all the uniforms and bravery because I'll write a little card at my cedar desk explaining, tastefully and plainly, why you have not served. After the toasts you could, perhaps, rise to your feet and entertain us with heart murmurs.

Once again: bye bye Perce. Do come out soon and take your medicine.

MURMURING OFF

I cut hand- and foot-holes to make entry easier. Gladys Moncrieff the singer, a stout woman, descended, singing: I believe in President. I believe in every Australian cave owner owning Australia's finest refrigerator. That's why I believe in President, Percy.

If I had a President, Gladys, I'd be able to accommodate the two thousand North Koreans captured a few years ago by the boy bugler of the Fifth Regiment.

Percy, did you serve in Korea?   No, Gladys, I was too young for that particular conflagration.   Percy, did you serve in Malaya? No, Gladys, the problems of tin and rubber were handled by others more accustomed to finance, insurrection, communism and industrial management than I.

Percy, have you served? Gladys, a cardiac murmur exempted me from national service. I resisted the doctor's conclusions because at the time I thought Army service would entitle me to certain rehabilitation benefits. That is so, Percy, they would have given you a battery and wired your heart, and had you achieved promotion you would have been fitted with an amplifier for a musical instrument. Gladys, may you sell many President refrigerators!

A large man joined us. Where had I seen him? In advertisements for greater public morale. The pipe-smoking Ford salesman, H. Hastings Deering! Life moves along at a vibratory speed, he declared. *Colgate dental cream removes enzymes that cause bad breath and tooth decay.*

I did not say that! shouted H. Hastings Deering. Nor I, sang Gladys Moncrieff, the sweetheart of song. Nor I, said a short general. True to a great tradition am I, Peter Jackson. The talent for command has itself been moulded by tradition —the tradition of regiments whose exploits have shaped history. Peter Jackson cigarettes command respect and satisfaction. Let us go to the aid of the French in Indo-China. Smoke out the Vietmink!

H. Hastings Deering thoughtfully removed his pipe from his large hand and placed it in his determined mouth: We met, Sir, at Palm Beach, at one of the season's many gay parties, and our friend, Percy, here, came as a cardiac murmur, oh so many times, until, I'm sorry to say, he overdid it. Did I sing there? enquired Gladys Moncrieff, I have sung at so many functions.

The hilarious adventures of the Hardy family, presented each week direct from Hollywood, are firmly established listening favourites: Mickey Rooney, Lewis Stone, Fay Holden!

I, Percy Wort, bade my visitors farewell. They ascended. I

resumed my contemplation of the earth around me. A band of moonlight intruded so I shut my eyes. My heart murmured to me. In the stony stillness I wait for change. The beard on my face like dry moss.

For a short time after death hair continues to grow. Deathly hair. Catches dust and soil. Gritted air. Such as the determined cheerfulness of: There are 24 Hours of Sunshine, every Day when you're in Love. Grit'd get me out of here but for heavy smell of . . . ? Dead love. But I did try it before it died.

Resuscitation is possible. Subterranean resuscitation is, however, quite hopeless. Therefore, my ascension from this cavity is essential if I am to put my idea to the test. Leave everything behind. Rise naked. Remove clothes from Tank's scarecrow in spent and weedy melon patch and leave straw-padded wooden cross as my temporary memorial.

A naked man was *not* seen running from burrow to scarecrow, though he did indeed run, and was, for the duration of this jaunt, a mild man of the bush. I am tempted to powder pigment and mud from the walls of the edoba, mix it into paste and daub myself for this scamper to Tank's scarecrow; and in my hair fix leaves of tree and herb, and round waist hang girdle of grasses, and round ankles and round wrists, and round neck plaited ropes of dried grasses and berries, and leave them as offerings to the birds.

I do not think I'll do this.

I will get out though, because I am beginning to feel unsettled here.

My heart has just completed an inchoate monologue. In reply I told it I was leaving and that if it did not act politely I would leave here pigmented.

It chatters still. To show who's master I intend going daubed and naked after all.

I am. I wish I had a mirror. Red and brownish hands. Feet blackened with charcoal and silt. As yet I am without garlands, for these must come from the surface. Quite pleased with myself. I can go now, in daylight, or wait until late when there's moonlight.

After a quick survey, I have re-descended. It was marvellous up there. A visit to a new world, and like all discoveries, not without pain. Thistles. Damned heart twittering like a bat. Wants to stay down here. I am master. I intend going naked and daubed to collect suit.

And Percy Wort did this. But he failed to reach Tank's scarecrow. His heart stopped murmuring and uttered a final shout. Three days later I saw the crows. And found Percy. Found him, sat on haunches, pondered awhile, then gathered wood. Burned what the crows had left. Old fashioned, quite illegal, but final.

I stayed till what was left was cool. In quirk, I paper-bagged a handful. Recently sent you an ink-bottled token. Thus we avoided the scandal of a painted man. That is, poofter, madman even. Years later I found his hole and his belongings. I did tell two people, but was not believed. I saw him in a newsreel, said one. I had an unsigned postcard, said the other. You knew him too well, said the one, You are in danger of emulating him. There were always similarities, said the other, And I think *you*'re at risk. Beware his conceit and selfishness.

I am beyond risk, and I have gone my own way, Thomas. I have used culverts as tunnels, have crossed double lines, seen red as green but never been involved in a thrall. Have disposed of the estate, sunk the boat, loaded up animals and pissed into the wind.

We move on. MATTERS